MEN AND MALICE

MEN AND MALICE

AN ANTHOLOGY OF MYSTERY AND SUSPENSE
BY WEST COAST AUTHORS

Edited by DEAN DICKENSHEET

Published for the
ELLERY QUEEN MYSTERY CLUB
by Walter J. Black, Inc.
ROSLYN, NEW YORK

All of the characters in this book are fictitious, and any resemblance to actual persons, living or dead, is purely coincidental.

ACKNOWLEDGMENTS:

Up a Tree, by Jessamyn West, copyright © 1970 by Jessamyn West. Reprinted from her volume *Crimson Ramblers of the World, Farewell* by permission of Harcourt Brace Jovanovich, Inc.

Down the Long Night, by William F. Nolan, copyright © 1957 by Arnold Magazines, Inc., and first published as *Laugh Till You Die* by Frank Anmar. Reprinted by permission of the author.

The Savage, by William Arden, copyright © 1969 by Popular Publications, Inc. Reprinted by permission of the author.

The Sleeper, by Sheila Lynds, copyright © 1967 by Leo Margulies Corporation, and first published in *The Man From U.N.C.L.E. Magazine*. Reprinted by permission of the author.

ISBN: 0-385-02779-6
LIBRARY OF CONGRESS CATALOG CARD NUMBER 72–89303
COPYRIGHT © 1973 BY DEAN DICKENSHEET
ALL RIGHTS RESERVED
PRINTED IN THE UNITED STATES OF AMERICA

THIS BOOK IS DEDICATED TO
THE MEMORY OF MY FATHER,
AND OF ANTHONY BOUCHER;
BOTH OF WHOM I SINCERELY HOPE
WOULD HAVE ENJOYED IT

CONTENTS

Introduction	DEAN W. DICKENSHEET	ix
Up a Tree	JESSAMYN WEST	1
The O'Bannon Blarney File	JOE GORES	26
The Goddess of the Cats	THOMAS N. SCORTIA	39
Beggarman, Thief	MIRIAM ALLEN DE FORD	52
Down the Long Night	WILLIAM F. NOLAN	60
Amphora	AVRAM DAVIDSON	77
"Silence!"	DANA LYON	90
Bunco Game	RICHARD DEMING	99
Killer Out of Work	JACK LEAVITT	115
The Ghosts at Iron River	CHELSEA QUINN YARBRO	126
Quoth the Raven	RAY RUSSELL	148
The Savage	WILLIAM ARDEN	156
An Inside Straight	SUZANNE BLANC	168
A Stretch of the Imagination	RANDALL GARRETT	174
A Matter of Taste	MICHAEL KURLAND	189
The Sleeper	SHEILA LYNDS	196
The Maltese Falcon Commission	FRANK MC AULIFFE	210

INTRODUCTION

Probably the earliest major crime writer on the West Coast of the United States of America was John Rollin Ridge. Although he wrote but one book of note, and that a slim ninety-page yellowback, it was published in 1854—only thirteen years after Poe's "Murders in the Rue Morgue," eleven years before Mark Twain's "The Celebrated Jumping Frog of Calaveras County" and fifteen before Bret Harte's "The Outcasts of Poker Flat." Yet this pre-eminence has gone almost unnoted. Ridge is scarcely known outside a small circle of historians, while the subject of his book, nominally an actual person but almost entirely a fictional creation of Ridge, is world famous. For Ridge's book, written under the name "Yellow Bird," was *The Life and Adventures of Joaquin Murieta, The Celebrated California Bandit.*

There is, curiously enough, far more factual information available about Ridge than about "Murieta." Ridge was born in New England in 1827, son of a New England girl and John Ridge, eldest son of Major Ridge, Georgia planter and Cherokee Indian leader ("Yellow Bird" may have been, indeed, Ridge's tribal name). He saw his father die at the hands of Indian hotbloods during the infamous Cherokee Migration, and, after his own New England education, found himself charged, probably falsely, with murder. Fleeing first to Missouri, where he tried valiantly but unsuccessfully to raise funds for a fair trial (he was, of course, considered a mere Indian), he headed, in 1850, for the gold fields of California.

Gold, however, evaded him, and by 1853 he was, in his words, "Deputy Clerk, Auditor, and Recorder, in the county of Yuba, California, at $135 a month." But he was also a journalist, contributing to the San Francisco magazine *The Pioneer*. Then there appeared the "Joaquins."

There is definite evidence from the press that there were bandits in the gold country in 1852-53; some of them were Mexican; those who were all named, seemingly, "Joaquin." (Somewhat reminiscent of most eighteenth-century English highwaymen apparently being named "Jack.") Some last names were mentioned, including Carrillo, Bottilier, Valenzuela, Ocomorena . . . and Murieta.

Thus, there *may* have been a bandit named Murieta, whose first name *may* have been Joaquin, but no one was ever to know. For the California Legislature authorized an ex-Texas Ranger remarkably named Captain Harry Love to capture the band led by "the five Joaquins" with a $1,000 reward for the capture of any one of them, dead or alive.

On July 25, 1853, Love's party came upon a group of Mexicans near Panoche Pass. In the ensuing battle two men were captured alive (one drowned on the way to jail, the other was lynched) and two were killed. Of these, one was readily identified by a mutilated hand as one Manuel "Three-Fingered Jack" (!) Garcia; the other was said to have been the group's leader, but had never identified himself. As evidence for the reward, the hand of Garcia, and the head of the other man, were severed and preserved in spirits. This summarizes what little is known of the owner of the head. The proprietors of the Stockton, California, hotel which was "privileged" to display it were the first to identify the head as that of "Joaquin Muriatta" (sic).

On this slim basis, Ridge formed his story of the heroic, wronged, California Robin Hood. The original volume (San Francisco, W. B. Cooke, 1854) exists in but a single copy. But the centenary reprint (Norman, University of Oklahoma Press, 1955), with a voluminous introduction by the late Joseph Henry Jackson, though prized by collectors, is still accessible. Much of the romantic narrative resembles the life of the "heroic, wronged" John Rollin Ridge; one incident, the undeserved beating of the hero, seems to have been lifted bodily from an earlier work, *The Shirley Letters*. But there can be no argument that, with a single work, Ridge laid claim to having written the first true-crime book on the Pacific Coast, the first (or one of the first) authentically grounded Western romances . . . and the first volume of West Coast suspense fiction.

There is one more notable element to Ridge's career. Although his book gave rise to scores of piracies, rewrites, and adaptations, which in turn built Murieta into a looming mythic figure, Ridge, at the time of his premature death in 1871, had not received a single cent for any of them. Even worse, his original publisher apparently absconded, depriving him of any profit whatsoever from the book.

From such an origin, it is only logical that the suspense fiction of the West Coast should turn to action and realism rather than cerebral theorizing. Twain's frog-toting con-man and Harte's society-victimized outcasts were a beginning. The Pacific Coast with its combined roles as New Golconda and New Botany Bay produced a blend of cynicism and humanism, of perception and introspection which gave rise to Sam Spade and Philip Marlowe, to Lew Archer and Fergus O'Breen, to Todd McKinnon and Luis Mendoza.

* * *

In selecting the stories for this anthology, I have attempted to reflect the nature of this West Coast style, while presenting as wide a range as possible of plot and concept. Somewhere along the way, there arose the secondary idea which is reflected in the title; that crime is seldom a one-to-one event, that one or both sides are usually multiple—if not always obviously so. Finally, I felt it essential that the stories be, insofar as possible, new or unfamiliar to the reader. Thirteen have never been published; of the others, two were published in small-circulation, no-longer-published mystery magazines, the remaining two in non-mystery sources.

These points aside, the stories range widely, from an oddly familiar 1920s San Francisco to an odd 1970s London. Three involve Indians, three involve "birds," at least six are set on the West Coast; more than half involve murder, less than half involve theft; six are by women writers, and three concern series characters. All, however, in the West Coast tradition, concern human relationships and, I sincerely hope, all will be enjoyable to the reader.

DEAN W. DICKENSHEET
San Francisco, 1972

You have a gift, sir, (thank your education,)
Will never let you want, while there are men,
And malice to breed causes.

—Ben Jonson
Volpone
Act V, scene i

MEN AND MALICE

For all practical purposes, only one thing needs to be said about Jessamyn West: Jessamyn West. Almost every American reader, and most others, are familiar with the gentle, perceptive, persuasive style of such books as *Cress Delahanty, Except For Me and Thee* and, of course, *The Friendly Persuasion.* Admirers of her novels may be less familiar, however, with her short fiction, including her single superb mystery.

"Mystery? Jessamyn West?" Yes, a mystery, originally published in her collection *Crimson Ramblers of the World, Farewell.* A mystery, a murder mystery, or at least a death mystery. And yet the Calloways, Eugene, Inez and Eugenia, are as memorable as any of the characters in Miss West's novels. Perhaps a bit more so; but more of that later.

Up a Tree
JESSAMYN WEST

I called Harold Fosdick, the attorney, at about four o'clock. I thought of him because he was the one my mother had gone to see when I was fourteen or fifteen. I was afraid that attorneys, like bankers, might quit work early and that Mr. Fosdick would already have gone home.

"This is Eugenia Calloway," I said when his secretary answered. "I'd like to speak to Mr. Fosdick if he's in."

"Oh, Miss Calloway," his secretary said, with that special something in her voice I was beginning to be accustomed to hearing. "He's with a client just now, but I'll have him call back in a short time."

He called back at once. "Eugenia," he said.

He didn't really know me well enough to be calling me Eugenia. I'm almost nineteen years old, and so far as I know he's never seen me except for that one visit to his office. But I was glad to hear my first name. I'd been "Miss Calloway" all day, and I was glad to have someone speak to me as though I were a friend or a relation.

"What can I do for you, Eugenia?"

"Nothing, maybe," I said. "I'm just calling to ask you about my legal rights."

Mr. Fosdick was silent for a second or two. Then he said, "Ted Hughes is your father's lawyer, you know."

Of course I knew that. "I don't know Mr. Hughes personally," I said.

"You don't know me."

"I was with mother that time when she came to see you. You were very nice to her."

Under different circumstances he might have said, "I'm always nice to the ladies." But the circumstances weren't different. "Your mother was an unusual woman, Eugenia." No one was going to contradict that. God knows I always thought so myself, and still do, though in a different way.

"All I want is some information. It might not even have to be from a lawyer."

"If I give it, it'll have to be from a lawyer, I'm afraid."

"Okay. What I want to know is, do I have to see all these reporters? Have they any legal right to question me? Have they any . . ."

Mr. Fosdick broke in, as if I were in court and testifying, "Legal right? They haven't even any *human* right."

"Then I'm not required to answer. . . ."

"Required to answer? Eugenia, you're not a child. You surely know a reporter is nothing but a man hunting news. He has no more right to ask you . . . about your mother's death . . . than he has to ask you . . . Well, he has no right. Spit in his eye."

"There's too many of them. I don't have that much spit. How can I keep them from pounding on the door?"

"Move away from there for the time being. I'd think you'd want to anyway."

I didn't want to move away from there. "Where would I go?"

"Don't you have any relatives?"

"You know who mother's relatives are. Out in Riverside County."

"Well, you wouldn't feel at home there. Where are your father's people?"

"Back east. If he has any. He never mentioned them."

"Move into town to a hotel. A hotel could protect you from intruders."

"I want to stay here. And I want the reporters to stay away."

Mr. Fosdick was quiet for another few seconds. Then he said, "There's a lane runs into your place from the main road, isn't there? The house is at the back of the ranch?"

"You weren't ever out here, were you?"

"Not since you've lived there. But that ranch is a lot older than you are. How old do you think those eucalyptus trees are?"

I didn't want to talk about the eucalyptus trees, so I didn't say anything.

"There should be a barricade, at the entrance to the lane. 'Private

Property, Entrance Forbidden.' That would take care of the reporters."

"I don't know how to build a barricade."

"Isn't there anyone there with you?"

"Not unless you count the reporters."

"Well, they're not going to build you a barricade. That's a cinch."

"They're not here now. They've gone back to town to file their stories. Or to get something to eat. Anyway, I'm alone, now."

"I'll send my yardman right out. He'll build you a barricade and put up a sign. That should take care of the reporters. Have you already talked with a lot of them?"

"I've really only *talked* with one."

"Smith? The young fellow from the *Star?*"

"How did you know?"

"He's sympathetic. And nice looking. He's the one a girl *would* talk to. What did you say?"

"I don't remember, exactly. But quite a lot, I'm afraid."

Afraid? I *knew* I had talked to him a lot. I had been dying, it seemed, to talk to someone. Especially Smith, once I got started. Three days had gone by, and except for Mr. Hughes and the reporters there had been no one. Three days and all that wondering and remembering. Trying to put two and two together. And trying even harder not to put two and two together.

I read somewhere recently that a person at twelve has all the intelligence he is ever going to have. I believe it. I could have dealt with this at twelve just as well as I can now. Perhaps better. At twelve I knew exactly what was right and what was wrong. Or thought I did. Now I'm not so sure. Also I now know that it is easier to love the dead than the living. That confuses me. And I know that pity can bind you closer than love. You feel that you owe more to pity than you do to love. Love gives you joy; pity, pain. And isn't what pain says more to be trusted than what joy says? Pain says you have cancer. Joy says he loves you madly. You're prejudiced in favor of joy, aren't you?

Mr. Fosdick said, "Eugenia. Eugenia. Are you all right?"

"I'm okay. I was thinking."

"You've got plenty to think about. I grant you that. Look here, I'm coming out in the pickup with Tony. While he's putting up the barricade, I'd like to talk to you."

I was tired. "I've been talking all day, Mr. Fosdick."

"That's one of the reasons I want to see you. I'm a friend of Ted Hughes."

"I didn't say anything to hurt Mr. Hughes. Or Father."

"You said you didn't know *what* you had said."

"I don't *know* anything that could hurt Father. So it doesn't matter what I say."

"Have you seen your father?"

"Since he's in jail, you mean?"

"That's what I mean."

"No."

"Why not?"

"He said he'd rather not just yet."

"That's strange. Well, I'll be out in an hour. I've a man here I have to finish with. Then I'll pick up Tony and be right out."

"Okay."

"I'm not coming as a lawyer, you understand. I'm coming as a friend. As someone who knew your mother."

"Okay, I'll be here."

"Meanwhile, don't talk to any more reporters. Not even Smith. And don't let them clamber around that platform."

"You don't have to worry about that. The police are taking care of that. Mr. Fosdick?"

"Yes?"

"Do they have a right to keep me away from it?"

"Yes, they do."

"It's on our property. It's practically a part of my home."

"Well, it's a peculiar part now. I wouldn't think you'd want to go up there now. I'd think wild horses couldn't drag you. Now you stay put where you are, and I'll see you in an hour."

It was two hours. I knew it would be. The client would take more time than Mr. Fosdick had expected. It's fifteen miles between here and Santa Ana, where his office is, and when he got home he wouldn't be able to locate Tony at once. After that he'd have to buy lumber for the barricade. So I could just relax.

I had told myself and told myself to stop looking at Mother's picture. Stop peering over it with a magnifying glass like some mad old Sherlock Holmes. I had to use a magnifying glass because the picture was a snapshot, and though good of Mother, it wasn't very clear. It was good of Mother because it wasn't taken by Father. When he took a picture of her, she was self-conscious. She knew he didn't like her looks, and she was too proud to bridle and smile for him and try to look attractive and appealing. (What she was, I now see, was downright starkly beautiful.) This snapshot was probably taken by her brother, Uncle Eloy. I think the strand of leaves hanging over her head was part of the bougainvillea vine which covered the tank house at the Souza place. She knew Eloy liked her, so she was relaxed and smiling. Facing Father was like facing a firing squad for her.

The beautiful woman in the picture was a woman I had never seen before. When she was alive, she was like a painting, so close to me that all I could see were blobs of paint and brush strokes. Death had moved her far enough away so that I could see her true outline. She had a strong face, with high cheekbones, heavy brows, and a nose that was large, but neither sharp nor long. In the snapshot there is a shadowy smile at the corners of her mouth. Her face is manly but beautiful, like a tender Indian chief's, or a great resolute Egyptian queen's. Her hair, clipped together at the back, is hanging down like the switch tail of a black racing mare. She was thirty-eight when she died. Three days ago. I don't know how old she was when this picture was taken. Twenty-eight, perhaps. If Katharine Hepburn had a stronger face and was madrone-colored instead of pink and white, she'd look a lot like Mother.

I had been shoving the picture, after I looked at it, to the very back of the drawer of the library table, promising myself not to look at it ever again. I hadn't appreciated her when she was alive. What was I doing now, gazing and gazing? Pretty soon I would be kissing her picture and crying, "Never leave me, dear Mama. Forgive me, dear Mama." Now I put the picture and the glass on the top of the table. Okay. So I hadn't appreciated her when she was alive. Never thought of her as an Indian chief or an Egyptian queen in my life before. Thought of her instead as someone Father and I had to put up with. If death taught me better, well, better late than never. Such thoughts wouldn't do Mother any harm now. And they might do me some good.

"Good-by, Mother," I said. "I'll be back before dark."

This was as crazy as staring at her picture through a magnifying glass. Crazier. When Mother was alive I never told her anything. Father and I were in cahoots together. Talking to her seemed disloyal to him. And Mother never asked me any questions. Sometimes I resented this. Other mothers wanted to know what time their daughters got in and who they were out with and when was their last period. I wanted to be worried over a little. Maybe I was. But Mother never said so, and I wouldn't ask. So we were both lonely, I guess; though I had Father to talk to and she didn't.

It was a little after five when I went outside. In mid-October with daylight saving, the light is still strong, but beginning to slant, at that hour. It was unnaturally quiet and clear; Santa Ana weather, the hush before the strong dry wind blows up the canyon from the east. Our ranch is at the very edge of the Santa Ana canyon, beyond what used to be the town of Olive. Olive was just beyond Orange. But everything has run into everything else now in Southern California, and beginnings and endings are all mixed up.

Our ranch is still a ranch because Father, being a doctor, hasn't had to subdivide. He doesn't have to make money ranching. In fact, he can lose money ranching, and it helps his tax bracket. Though that isn't the reason he has kept the ranch.

The place began fifty years ago as an olive ranch. Most of the olive trees have been replaced by avocados now. The olive trees that are left are gnarled and scaley. But they bear good crops still, and Mother cured her own olives in big stone jars of brine.

It seemed lighter outside than it really was because our house was so dark. It was built about the time the olives were planted and has never been remodeled, except for the bathrooms and kitchen. It's old-style California with a screened porch on all four sides. That's one reason for the darkness, though it would have been dark anyway because of the redwood paneling inside. Old-time Californians liked it that way. That was the point, they thought, in coming indoors: get away from that hot glare. Being Easterners (not Mother, of course), their eyes weren't adjusted to so much sunshine. Around the house are all the trees the old-timers planted for shade and coolness, peculiar kinds that didn't grow back east. Pepper trees, with trunks gnarled as the olives. Peppers have tiny little dry red berries. When the wind blows, a clump of pepper trees sounds like a tangle of rattlesnakes practicing buzzing. There are palms of every variety, of course. When a Santa Ana blows, the palm fronds clash against each other with the sound of scraping timbers.

At the east end of the ranch, next to what's left of the old grove, is a big double row of eucalyptus trees, planted fifty years ago as a windbreak. Everybody planted eucalyptus windbreaks in those days. Mostly they've been dug up or cut down now. They get in the way of subdivisions. People say they are dirty because they drop their limbs sometimes in storms. The few ranchers who are left don't like them because eucalyptus saps water from the soil. Father didn't have to worry about any of these things. So our windbreak still stands and is a landmark for miles around. It can even be seen from out at sea. Mother loved it. So do I. No other tree as large as the eucalyptus gives itself so easily to wind; or is so open to the sun. When the sun shines and a Santa Ana blows, a big eucalyptus shimmers and glitters like a bonfire of green-white diamonds.

I walked down toward the windbreak, slowly, breathing in the sharp aromatic eucalyptus smell. In the old days people with lung disease were advised to live near a eucalyptus grove. Doctors thought the smell was healing. The Indians still pound up leaves to make a kind of poultice to use for chest colds. The trees don't smell medicinal to me: they smell fresh and free, like the old days Mother talked about and the open country she knew.

The platform was toward the south end of the row of trees. There were two policemen there. They sat on upended orange boxes, with a third box crosswise between, which they used as a card table. They had put their cards away when I came down that morning. I don't know whether it's against the rules for policemen to play cards when on duty or whether they were afraid I'd think they weren't paying proper respect for the dead.

I looked up at the trees at that end of the windbreak and at the platform. I didn't intend to go near the policemen again. They couldn't do me any good, and all I did was to make them uneasy. They sat at the foot of the ladder that leads up to the platform. The platform is built between two trees, seedlings, I suppose, which grow a few feet away from the double line of the real windbreak trees. Mother had it built six or seven years ago. I don't know who the Police Department thinks would want to go up there. I do, but they wouldn't expect me to want to. And I can get up there without using the ladder. I can shinny up to the platform between the two trees, and the police would never know I was there.

Police brutality? I don't suppose the most aggressive men are chosen to sit in olive groves to watch bird-watching platforms. These two men would look okay in checkered aprons baking cookies. They have their revolvers on the orange-box card table like old-time TV gamblers. I don't know what they would do if I started climbing the ladder. They're too portly to climb after me. Would they shoot me in the leg? That would be brutal but maybe they would consider it in the line of duty. Enjoy it, maybe; I don't know.

While I was watching them, one of the men stood, then picked up his pistol. "You're not allowed down here, fellow," he called. He put his pistol in his holster, but he had showed that he was armed and meant business.

"I'm not coming down there. I was looking for Miss Calloway."
"She's right here in front of you."
"I can see her now."

I recognized the voice. It was Smith, the man I'd talked too much to. I turned and walked back toward him.

"Hi, Smith," I said.
"I've got another name," he said.
"I know. Don or Ron or Jess or Steve. I don't want to know it."
"What makes you so mean to men?"
"I'm not mean to men."
"Just me?"
"You're a reporter, aren't you?"

But he was right. Brush them off at once, then you can console yourself by thinking, Well, what did you expect from someone you treated like that? No one's going to fall for a mean-mouth like you.

"Do you hate all reporters?"
"Of course not. I don't know all of them. But I talked too much to you."
"That's why I came out. To show you what I wrote."
"I don't want to see it."
"This isn't anything about the case. In this, it's what you told me about buzzards."
"Buzzards are in the case."
"I suppose they are. This is a special piece, though, just on them. It doesn't mention the case. I wanted to check some of the facts. I tried to quote you exactly."
"I'm in the case. How do you think you can be writing about me, and about buzzards, and make people think that's all you're talking about?"
"I don't suppose I can. I don't care, actually. I want it to be a good piece of writing about buzzards and about you."
"The *Star* is a lousy paper. If your piece is good, they won't use it."
"It can be good about buzzards. Buzzards aren't political. They're human interest."
"Human or inhuman?"
"I saw a piece of yours in the *Yucca*. It's not much good either."
"You're frank, anyway."
"I didn't mean what you wrote. I mean the *Yucca*."
"What do you expect? It doesn't pay. And it's conscientious. Somebody there reads every word I send them."
"Where else have you been published?"
"Nowhere. But twice in the *Yucca*. What do you read it for if it's no good?"
"I read everything. Would you like to hear the buzzard piece?"

"No."

"I'll read it to you, and if you don't like what you hear, you can walk off. It's nothing but what you told me."

He began reading before I could say a word.

"'Buzzards live the year round in the eucalyptus windbreak at the east end of the Calloway property. They don't nest there. Their nests are in the rocky hills still farther east. But the eucalyptus windbreak is their home. They soar in at dusk after their days of hunting food are over. In October, for some reason naturalists don't understand, hundreds of buzzards congregate in one spot for a fly-in.'"

"I didn't say 'fly-in.'"

"I know you didn't."

"I would never say that. It sounds too cute."

"I'll take it out. 'The windbreak on the Calloway ranch is one of these congregating spots. The buzzards don't get together to mate or to hunt. They do nothing but fly in crisscrossing patterns, so tight you'd expect twenty collisions a minute. They miss by a feather's breath.'"

"I didn't say that."

"I know you didn't."

"It's okay, though. It's the truth."

"'It's a beautiful sight. They aren't flying to get anywhere. Or to kill anything. Just for joy. Just for pure joy. They don't even fly; they soar. In perfectly still afternoons, with no wind to support them, they find updrafts which send them, without their moving a wing, skyward. They fill the air with black scissors. All they cut in two is sky. All they snip off is joy.'"

"That's pretty fancy for the *Star*."

"You said it."

"Okay. What else did I say?"

"You said, 'A couple of hundred birds will decide at the same time to light. All of them at once will slide into and among the eucalyptus leaves and limbs where there isn't any opening to be seen. The trees seem to open up for them, the leaves to lift for them to enter, and the limbs to stiffen to hold them once they've landed.'"

"'Leaves lift and limbs stiffen.' Sounds like Swinburne."

"You said it. There's only one more sentence. 'And all this without a sound.'"

I didn't intend to cry.

Smith said, "I didn't intend to make you cry."

"It's okay. I've wanted to and couldn't."

"Couldn't?"

"I didn't have the right. You don't have any right to cry for someone who's gone when you've wished a thousand times he was gone. *She* was gone. If you've wished she was gone, you should rejoice when she is gone."

"But you don't?"

"No. Of course not."

Smith gave me his handkerchief. "Why did the buzzards make you cry?"

They were floating homeward at that minute, sliding down the sky from the south to the trees.

"I never saw a buzzard until my mother spoke of them. I didn't hate them the way some people do; they just didn't exist for me. Mother would stand about where we are at twilight to watch them come home. I don't know how old I was when I first went out to stand beside her. She said they were beautiful. I told her they ate dead meat."

"So do we," she said.

"They eat rotten meat," I told her.

"They don't kill it."

"Neither do we."

"Somebody does for us."

"Somebody does for the buzzards."

"The buzzards don't pay them to do it. Nobody dies because of a buzzard."

"Is that why you like them?"

"That's one reason. Another is, they're beautiful."

"Beautiful?"

"Watch them fly."

I did and I saw that they were beautiful.

"And they're so quiet."

"Is that better than singing?"

"There's screaming and squawking, too. No one wants to be quiet but a buzzard."

"If you could be an animal, would you choose to be a buzzard?"

"I am an animal. We're all animals. The buzzards are good animals."

"May I put this in my piece?" Smith asked.

"No. You can't put anything else I say in the paper either. Otherwise I'm going in the house."

"I promise you. She sounds like a wonderful woman."

"She was."

"But you didn't like her?"

"No. I was ashamed of her."

"Because she was half Indian?"

"Partly. Most people thought she was Mexican. She didn't look Indian. Not like the Sobobas anyway. Have you ever seen a Soboba?"

"No. Not and know it, anyway."

"Well, look at me. Pudding shape, pudding face, pudding nose, pudding mouth. That's a Soboba."

Smith didn't contradict me. How could he? He said, "I never heard of a Soboba with red hair."

"No, I've got Calloway coloring and Soboba shape. It was just the other way with Mother. Soboba coloring and a face like her father's. It made her a beauty. But I didn't know it when she was alive. They called her a greaser at school. When you're ten years old, you hate having a greaser for a mother. She did queer things, too. She didn't like a lawn. She liked a yard she could sweep. So we don't have any grass. She didn't like to work inside. So she shelled peas and things like that sitting out in the yard. She washed out in the yard. Herself, I mean. She went fishing and brought fish home in a gunny sack."

"Where could she find any fish around here?"

"Down at Newport. She would sit all day on the pier along with kids and old men and Negroes."

"And your father didn't like this?"

"*I* didn't like it. I don't think it made any big difference to him."

"There must've been something that rubbed him the wrong way."

"I think he didn't like so much devotion."

"That's a queer thing not to like."

"Maybe you've never had too much."

"That's right. But I can't imagine not liking it."

"Polishing your shoes?"

"Okay with me."

"Waxing your car?"

"No complaints."

"Calling you to the phone when other women call?"

"Ideal."

"Well, doctors are different. They like something to fight. They wouldn't be doctors if they didn't. They want to fight and win. Mother was already *won*. She wasn't a challenge any more. She accepted Father completely no matter what he did. He was her husband, and what her husband did was right. I never heard her complain about anything."

"Even the women?"

"She was his *wife*. They weren't."

"What do you think?"

"I thought that Father and I were putting something over on Mother. 'Us Calloways.' That's the way I thought of Father and me. Us Calloways against the redskins. Mother was an outsider, and Father and I put up with her. I was trained that way. It began when I was too young to know what was going on. But I can remember when I was six, going along with Father to call on ladies. I had a nap or played with the puppies while he doctored the lady. That's what I thought he did."

"In a manner of speaking," Smith said, "I guess he did."

"What makes doctors so irresistible?"

"They aren't."

"Father was."

"He'd have been irresistible as a grocery clerk. If you look like a professional football player, you don't have to be a doctor."

"How do you know what he looks like?"

"There've been plenty of pictures of him in the papers. Besides, he took out my tonsils. *And* my appendix."

"You must've been a sickly kid."

"No. Doctors pushed such things when I was a kid. And my folks had the money."

"Father's way past stuff like that now."

"I know. Open-heart surgery and so forth. Why did he marry your mother if her devotion got on his nerves?"

"Me. I was on the way. *That* kind of devotion didn't get on his nerves, ever. He didn't know she had the other kind yet. He was a poor nobody and she was a beautiful Indian maiden. I don't *know* that. Maybe it was a shotgun wedding. Maybe her relatives out on the reservation threatened to bury him in an anthill. There would've been other women no matter who he married. Only, another wife would have divorced him. Mother wouldn't. She loved him. He was a fine man and her husband, and she was proud of him and proud to be his wife. And a woman expected a man to be manly."

"'Being manly.' Is that what your mother called cheating?"

"She didn't *call* it anything. That's how I think she felt about it. He was her husband, and it was for life."

"So your father had to . . ."

"'Had to.' I didn't say a word about had to. I don't intend to talk about my father."

"You talk about your mother."

"She isn't in trouble. He is. Besides, she wouldn't want me to talk about him."

Smith said, "Maybe you *are* a Soboba."

"I told you I was the exact shape of a Soboba."
"Okay. Yes. You did. Okay. What about the buzzard piece?"
"What 'What about it'?"
"Is it okay with you?"
"Don't quote me."
"If I don't quote you, I don't have anything."
"You say what you want to say about buzzards, and I'll say what I want to say."
"A lot more people read the *Star* than will ever read the *Yucca*."
"You know what a lot of people want to read. I don't. You give it to them. But not Mother's buzzards. They're too good for a lot of people."

Mean-mouth again. But not to put Smith down. That's what I truly felt. The sun had set. To the west the sky was red and gold, and buzzards were silently sliding home to the trees. In the east the sky was pink, and against it Old Saddleback was grape-bloom blue, but as solid looking as the big mountains, Baldy and Wilson. Smith was watching the buzzards, too.

"I'll give you a can of beer if you come up to the house." It was about the first invitation I'd ever given to a male since I was sixteen. I expected Smith to have a date in town. Instead, he said, "Okay, that would taste good."

We were halfway to the house when Mr. Fosdick turned into our lane, stopped to let Tony out and to put down the lumber for the barricade.

"There comes a man who told me not to talk to you," I said.
"I'd better be on my way then."
"You show me your buzzard piece, and I'll show you mine. If I ever write it," I said.
"It's a deal," Smith said. He started his car, but waited for Mr. Fosdick to drive in before he drove out.

I took Mr. Fosdick into the living room. I showed him to our best chair, the fumed-oak Morris with the brown corduroy cushions. It was old, but in a way it was modern because it had an adjustable four-position tilt-back. Mr. Fosdick didn't sit. He turned a full circle, like a man in a museum trying to make up his mind what to look at first. Then he took off his specs. When he did that, I remembered who he had reminded me of when Mother and I called on him. He hadn't changed a bit and he still looked like the same man: Woodrow Wilson. I had been studying American history then and had spent a whole week seeing Wilson's picture in the chapter on World

War I. The horn-rimmed spectacles were wrong, of course, and with them off he looked more like the President.

"My God, my God," Mr. Fosdick said.

Mr. Fosdick used the name of God, Christ, Jesus, Heaven, Hell, the Devil, and damnation very often. I wouldn't exactly call it cursing. It was more as if he felt himself the resident of a universe where there were more powers and personalities than were visible, and that this was his courteous way of letting them know that he was aware of them and was trying to include them in his life. He certainly included them in his conversation. In some ways it was embarrassing. I felt like an eavesdropper to someone praying. This shows how different it was from real profanity, which would have made me mad. I wouldn't care to be cursed. And there is no obscenity that disgusts me.

Mr. Fosdick patted his chair all over as if it were a horse before he sat down. "Jesus, sweet Jesus," he said. "I never expected to see a room like this again. I didn't know there was one like it left in California."

"What's so queer about it?"

"Mission furniture. Redwood paneling. Leaded-glass doors to the bookcases. Grass rug. Eucalyptus portieres between dining and living room. Clock held up by lions' heads. Why, hell, Eugenia, you must know all this. It surely hasn't been changed since the day Gene bought it."

"It hasn't."

"Why didn't he modernize it?"

"He didn't care. He wasn't here half the time. And Mother thought it was wonderful."

"After the reservation, I suppose it was. Why didn't you change it?"

"I didn't have the say around the house."

"Who did?"

"Around the house . . . Mother."

"Eugenia, I didn't come out here to talk about the furniture. How are you? How're you feeling?"

"I don't know. I'm changing. I don't feel the same as I did at first."

"Do you remember the day you came to my office with your mother?"

"Yes. That's why I called you."

"I've never forgotten your mother. I never will. And not just because of that damned idea she had."

"It wasn't such a damned idea. And she had her way, finally."

"Not exactly, I wouldn't say."

"She got there. That was what she wanted. A book influenced her. Did she tell you that?"

"A lot of people told me that."

"Mother's whole life was changed by that book, about how Californians were buried."

"It was Americans, not just Californians."

"Americans. Mother didn't think it was fair that undertakers should make the rules about how persons were buried."

"Well, my God, who said anything about fair? But Christ Almighty, her ideas were a lot worse. Who could put up with thirty-foot platforms all over the country with dead bodies stretched out on them?"

"The Indians could."

"Not *her* Indians. The Sobobas never went in for anything like that."

"She was a half-breed. She didn't have to be tied down by what any one tribe did. All Indians were being discriminated against, she thought."

"Nobody's going to dispute that. If your poor mother were alive today, she could have people organized and burning down mortuaries so that Indians could have platform burial again. My God, they're tearing down whole universities now for less. Soul food and Swahili! Jesus, how do *they* stack up alongside something important like how your ancestors were buried?"

"Mother would never have done anything like that. Organized or torn down or burned down. She wouldn't even protest. She was shy. She was born to endure. She was afraid to go to your office that day without me."

"What good could you do her? You were nothing but a kid."

"I was Father's daughter. And I was white. And she thought I was smart. I know now that's what she thought. She saved every one of my report cards and every composition I ever wrote."

"You probably were smart. Probably *are*. You're Gene's daughter."

"I'm Mother's, too."

"She was plenty smart in her way. Except for that idea of hers that a lawyer would be able to fix it up so she could be on a platform and be eaten by buzzards instead of worms when she died."

"I would prefer it myself. Wouldn't you?"

"After I'm dead, I don't care what eats me."

"She cared."

"What did your father think of all this?"

"He didn't say. Nothing, I suspect. He lived his life and she could live hers."

"Up a tree was okay with him?"
"I never heard him say it wasn't."
"What did he say when she had that platform built?"
"Nothing. It was for bird watching."
"Buzzard watching."
"They're birds. She watched them. So did I."
"Did your father ever climb up to that platform?"
"Not that I know of."
"He must've once."
"You believe that?"
"It's nothing I want to believe."

Mr. Fosdick put his glasses back on, began to cry, and had to take them off. "I don't want to believe it. Gene was my friend. I'd a thousand times rather be where your mother is than where Gene is."

I watched Mr. Fosdick polish his glasses.

"Eugenia," he said, "you are one-hundred-per-cent Indian. Here your mother's dead, your father's in jail accused of her murder, and I'm the one doing the crying."

"I never was encouraged much to cry when I was young. Mother didn't believe in it, and Father was never around to notice. I'm sorry Mother's dead. But being in jail doesn't mean you're guilty."

"You don't get there without damned strong evidence that you belong there."

"They haven't much evidence against Father."

"Mrs. Crowther swears that Gene said on his way back to town that he'd see that his wife didn't cause them any more trouble."

"She never caused Father trouble."

"She wouldn't divorce him. That's trouble if you want to marry someone else."

"He didn't want to marry anyone else."

"Mrs. Crowther came out here with your father, and he told your mother . . . Well, you heard it all. You were here."

"When they started quarreling, I left."

"Your mother and your father?"

"Mother never quarreled with Father. Father and Mrs. Crowther."

"What were they quarreling about?"

"I don't know. I tried not to hear."

"Did your father threaten your mother?"

"No. But Mrs. Crowther did. Maybe Mrs. Crowther killed Mother."

"Mrs. Crowther has an alibi from the minute she got back into town. Your father hasn't."

"Maybe I killed her."

"Don't be blasphemous."

"There were times when I wished she was dead."

"Fortunately, you didn't tell anyone that. And fortunately, she wasn't found dead after you said it. Where did you go when you left the house?"

"I took my bedroll and went out to spend the night in the hills."

"Alone?"

"Sure, alone. I'm no hippie."

"Did anyone see you?"

"I don't know. I didn't see anyone."

"When did you get home?"

"Next day. About noon."

"Was your mother here?"

"No."

"Weren't you alarmed?"

"No. I didn't ask her when I wanted to go someplace, and she didn't ask me."

"Where did you think she was?"

"Uncle Eloy's. Out by San Jacinto. That's where she goes when she leaves for a while. That was Sunday night. I phoned Uncle Eloy on Tuesday. He hadn't seen her."

"Then you called the police?"

"Yes."

"Why didn't you call your father?"

"I didn't know where to find him."

"Did you try his office?"

"They didn't know where to find him."

"And the police couldn't find her when they came?"

"No."

"But you did?"

"Later, yes."

"How did you know where to look?"

"I didn't. I went up there by chance."

"You didn't see your father carry her up there?"

"I wasn't here. I told you that. She was a big woman. How could he carry her up there kicking and screaming?"

"She didn't have to be kicking and screaming when he carried her up. Though he was a strong enough man to have done that if necessary."

"How did he kill her?"

"Who knows? What can you tell from bones that have been stripped bare? He knew that. And he knew that I'd come forward with evidence that some years ago she'd seen me about being buried on a platform."

"Buried on, not killed on."

"Okay. Buried. There must have been a lot of buzzards up around that platform for a couple of days. It's a wonder you didn't notice them."

"This is the time of year buzzards from all over come to these trees."

"To the trees, maybe, but not just to that platform. But you didn't see them?"

"I don't spend my entire time watching buzzards."

Mr. Fosdick took off his glasses again. I don't know why he wore them. When he seemed to want to see something particularly closely, he took them off. He leaned forward and looked at me as if I were a strange animal. Or a page of print in some language of which he knew only a few words. I was standing in front of him. I had never sat down since he came in. I felt more alert standing up. He had stopped swearing. I remembered that when Mother and I had gone to his office there had been no swearing. Perhaps he saved swearing for his social life, but when it came to business, he was all business.

"Did Ted Hughes send you here?" I asked. "Or maybe Mrs. Crowther?"

"You called *me*, remember?"

"I haven't said anything to hurt Father."

"You certainly haven't. I'll tell Ted that. Why don't you go up to see your father?"

"I told you that, don't you remember? He doesn't want to see me. He said he wouldn't talk to me if I came."

"You'd think he'd *want* to see you."

"He's probably ashamed of being in jail. How can they keep a man in jail just because of what some woman says? Probably she was trying to get even with some other woman when she said it."

"They couldn't keep him in jail. Except that the wife's dead, and he said she'd cause them no more trouble. And there's no other explanation. Is there?"

"Maybe not. But don't you feel sorry for him? His wife dead. And the woman he was going to marry, according to you, accusing him of murder. Don't you pity him?"

"My God, yes. He was my good friend. I've shed tears for him. That's more than I've seen you do."

"Well, he wasn't a very good father. Let's face it. He kept me from loving my mother."

"Eugenia, come home with me. This is no place for a girl to be staying alone after what's happened here."

"Nothing's happened here."

"You weren't here. Remember? So how do you know? Come home with me. My wife would be glad to have you. Clarice will be home from Pomona. She must be about your age."

"She's my age exactly. No, I don't like to be in town. This is home."

"Okay then. If you need me, phone, and I'll be right out. Tony's barricade should be up by now, and you shouldn't have any more trouble with reporters."

An hour or so after Mr. Fosdick left, I went down the back way to the south end of the windbreak. The Santa Ana that had been threatening was already beginning to blow a little. There was a small moon, short of full quarter by a night or so. I could've made the trip in pitch dark, but the pale moonshine plus the stars of a clear night made the way plain—besides making me feel more tranquil and peaceful than I had for days.

I could have climbed right up the ladder. One policeman was nowhere to be seen. The other, stretched out on his sleeping bag, was dozing. I was barefooted. Though I did not like to be called the daughter of a greaser, I liked to play at being a hundred-per-cent old-time Indian, who could move noiselessly through a forest never slipping on a twig; and able to make an owl's soft hoot, absolutely owl-like, but recognizable as a signal, too. I gave the hoot then, to try out the cops, but the one I could see never so much as twitched.

So though I could have climbed the ladder, I wanted to go up the hard way, and out of sight, for practice. I wanted to see if I could still do it. People never expect me to be agile because I'm so stubby. They are mistaken. I am agile. I can put my head to the floor and look at you upside down and backward from between my legs, the way a baby can. A baby is not tall and thin either.

The way up to the platform, on the back side, without using the ladder and out of sight of the police, was by a mountain-climbing maneuver. You go between the two trees that hold the platform, back against one tree, feet against the other. The trees are exactly the right distance apart for inching up that way. It's no trick to reach the platform, but it's a little tricky getting onto it. For a second you hang by your arms thirty feet in the air.

The platform is about six by six. You can stretch full length on it, either direction. I lay down flat on it facing Saddleback Mountain. There was enough of a Santa Ana blowing to rock the platform gently. Above were the dark forms of the buzzards roosting. They look so much smaller roosting than they do flying. They are mostly wingspread and feathers. I have never held a live buzzard, but I think they would weigh less than a young chicken. Without feathers they would be almost nothing.

The last time I had been up to the platform I had used the ladder. There had been the first tiny thread of a new moon, which is shaped like a eucalyptus leaf. Mother believed, and so did I, that you will have bad luck if you don't see the new moon the first night it is in the sky. It is also discourteous not to give your attention to something that is making a start. I looked at the new moon that night, because I knew Mother would want me to; but I could not see much luck in it. I said to it, "Prosper, prosper, new moon," though I had never done that before and was disgusted when I had heard Mother, a grown woman, talk to the moon as if it were alive and had ears. It was a part of her queerness; and when you're young, the last thing you want is a queer mother, a mother who talks to the moon and puts fish in a gunny sack.

Somehow I had believed that the buzzards would be ceremonious when they stripped the flesh from bones set out for their feasting. Mother had talked that way, as if they were as dignified and professional as undertakers; only not hirelings. But they had scrambled her bones, pushed them every which way. In my mind I truly believe I thought they would arrange them as neatly as a corpse in a silk-lined casket. I expected to be able to lie down beside Mother, she on one side of the platform, I on the other, and together we would rest there and remember and decide what to do. She was not even all there. Some of her bones had been pushed to the ground. I went down and brought them all up. That was what she had wanted, to be in the sky, not on the ground. But there was no use trying to arrange them as they had been when they were covered with flesh. She wouldn't care about that, and, besides, I didn't know how to do it. The thin thread of a moon had left the sky by the time I got back on the platform. It was warm, and I stayed there all night, sometimes sleeping. I was asleep at first light, and it was the buzzards, creaking a little as they levered themselves upward, that awakened me. I lay perfectly still, wondering if they could tell that I was alive. They swooped low across the platform but never stopped. My flesh was alive and Mother's was gone. I went back to the house, and after a day had passed I phoned the police to tell them what I had discovered.

This was a different night. Mother's bones had gone to where she had never wanted them to go, to an undertaker's. But first she had been where she wanted to be. Father wouldn't let me talk to him, but I understood that, too. I didn't really want to talk to him or see him. I didn't care if the silence was between us forever. Except for him, I think I might have loved Mother *before* she died. Maybe not. Anyway, he had fixed it so the love I had once had for him had changed to pity.

I lay on the platform, the wind rising, the platform swaying rock-aby, and the cop who had been dozing snoring now, full out, tired of silly tree watching and of pretending that he *was* tree watching.

Out of habit, not thinking, I felt around to the back of the far eucalyptus where a limb had dropped off leaving a hole as deep as two hands and as wide as one. When I was learning to smoke, I had kept cigarettes there. Mother kept binoculars there, a pencil, a pad of paper. She wasn't just a buzzard lover. She wanted to remember what they did, how many were in the sky at once, and so forth, like Thoreau. I let my hand lie in there touching Mother's things that had meant nothing to me when she was alive. "Mother's bird-watching junk." And I could have been up there with her learning with her when she was alive. And I would have been, too, I think, except for Father, who made me *his* child and not hers. But above everything that she loved, birds, the new moon, me (I now believe), she loved Father.

I went back up to the platform very early the next morning. The cops were both there, not even pretending to watch. Sleeping like hounds, twitching and grumbling with dreams. I stayed quiet until sunup. Then I called down to them.

They hopped out of their sleeping bags with only their shorts and undershirts on. Before they grabbed for their pants, they grabbed for their holsters.

"Put on your pants and don't shoot," I said. "I'm Eugenia Calloway. I've found some of Mother's things up here I'd like to have."

"There is nothing up there," the first one who finished said. "That platform has been gone over with a fine-tooth comb."

"They're not on the platform."

"What are you doing up there?" the tall Sherlock Holmes-looking one said.

"I am being where Mother was."

"How did you get up there?"

"Climbed," I said.

They'd been sleeping like skunks, so what could they say? They had to say something.

"It's forbidden."

"Why?"

"That's none of our business. Or yours."

"I'm not trying to break the law. That's why I told you what I'd found. I could've sneaked it out."

"What did you find?"

"I didn't take the stuff out. What I can feel is Mother's binoculars."

"Out? What's it in?"

"A hole in the tree."

"You come on down," the boss cop said. I came down the ladder as if I'd gone up that way. Carefully, too, like a clumsy young lady. The plump cop, agile like me, did the climbing.

"I don't see anything," he called down.

"Feel around in back of the big tree," I told him.

He began to bring out objects—binoculars, pencil, notebook, a package of Life Savers, some Kleenex, and the big plastic bottle with just a few red capsules rattling around in the bottom.

Down on the ground, the two cops looked at their treasure trove, especially the plastic bottle.

"Is this medicine your mother took?"

"She didn't take any medicine that I know of."

"Seconal," said the tall man. "Sleeping pills. Did you ever see this before?"

"You don't have to answer," the plump cop assured me. "Anything you say can be used against you."

"We oughtn't to be saying anything ourselves."

"Nothing being said is official. This isn't a big city. We're all neighbors here, so to speak. This girl's father relieved me of a kidney stone once."

"I've seen the bottle before. It was in the medicine cabinet. Father took a sleeping pill sometimes when he'd been working too hard and was too strung up to sleep."

"Was it full or empty when you last saw it?"

"Almost full. Father was no drug addict. I don't think he took a pill once a month. You can ask him," I said.

The scholarly-looking cop, now that he had his pants and jacket on, was leafing through Mother's notebook. It was a plain flappy-backed twenty-five-cent book. The binoculars were expensive, but the notebook was small and cheap, big enough to hold buzzard facts, but small enough to fit snugly into the hole.

"Your mother was quite a buzzard authority," he said.

"Yes, she was."

He came to the last page that had been written on, about two-thirds of the way through the book. He stood staring at the page he had come to. The plump cop and I stepped closer to have a look. The page was blank except for two words. Three, if you count "good-by" as two. It looked like mother's handwriting—and it didn't; her writing, if she was writing in the dark. Or was sick. The words were, "Good-by. Hello."

"Everything else is buzzard stuff," the tall man said wonderingly, as if he had been reading a cookbook that suddenly started to print obituaries.

"I think we'd better get this in to town," said the Dr. Watson of the two.

One should have stayed, I thought, to guard the platform, if that was what they'd been doing. Maybe they thought the platform wasn't so important any more. Whatever they thought, they got on their motorcycles, leaving me, their sleeping bags, and the buzzards stirred up by the noise of their cycles and circling wildly, alone in the clear early-morning air.

The funeral was three days later at ten in the morning. Mr. Olmstead came over at nine with a big spice cake his wife had made and four combs of honey. He kept bees and he always brought Mother honey because he said that without her trees his hives would be empty. Eucalyptus honey is a little strong, deep amber-colored, but very good if you don't use too much. Mr. Olmstead looked like a Pilgrim Father, tall, wrinkled, and worn to the bone. He was a rancher trying to make a living ranching. He and Mrs. Olmstead and Mother liked each other. The Olmsteads were bee fanciers the way Mother was a buzzard fancier, and they made jokes when they got together, saying that they were going to talk about the "birds and the bees"; which of course they really did.

I suppose I showed my amazement at the amount of honey he'd brought. And the size of the spice cake.

"We thought you'd need it for the folks who'll come in for lunch after the funeral."

I hadn't planned to have folks in for lunch. "It don't need to be a sit-down affair," Mr. Olmstead said. "But your mother's relatives will be here, and they'd like to have a cup of coffee and talk, I expect."

And Mother would like them to. "It's better the way things have turned out," Mr. Olmstead said. "Not good. Nobody could say it's good to die at thirty-eight, but it's better this way. I'm glad for your sake."

"It's the way Mother wanted it," I said.

The funeral was just a graveside ceremony. Mother had been born a Catholic; I don't know how much she'd lived a Catholic—more than I knew, perhaps. Perhaps her sticking to Father had been as much a part of her Catholicism as anything else. Anyway, no matter what she was born or how she had lived, she was being buried a Catholic. And if you have to be taken down from the birds and the trees, that is a good way. The ceremony seemed bird-old; and the priests were black as buzzards and red-nosed in the chilly morning air.

The burial ground is an old one on the hillside beside the first adobe church in these parts. It's not much used any more. The tombstones bear the old Spanish and Mexican names Yorba, Sanchez, Ortega, Sepulveda, Novano. Now there would be a new name: Inez Souza Calloway.

There were twenty-seven people there. Half of them, almost, were Uncle Eloy's family. I stood with them. Uncle Eloy had got the whole Soboba works: squat body, round face, small steady eyes, dark skin. I stood as close to him as I could. He was a good man, a school-bus driver, and my mother had loved him dearly. When he took her picture, her love for him showed. The Olmsteads were there, of course. Smith was there. Mr. and Mrs. Fosdick. Father's lawyer.

Father never once looked at me. I looked straight at him. I wanted to catch his eye. I don't know what I would have said with my eyes had I had the chance. But I didn't get it. He kept his head bowed and his eyes on that box of bones. He knew why he was there instead of in jail; and he knew why she was there. Knowing these things, I suppose he couldn't look at me.

It didn't make me sad to have Mother's bones buried. Her flesh had gone where she wanted it to go. And I think she might even have been glad to have those old words said above her bones. After the casket was in the ground and the earth placed on top of it and the words about dust and earth and ashes had been said, I did what Mr. Olmstead had suggested; I asked people to the house—the Olmsteads; Uncle Eloy's family; Mr. and Mrs. Fosdick. I didn't ask Smith, but he marched right along with Uncle Eloy's kids as if all that talk about buzzards had made him one of the tribe.

I didn't ask Father either. After everything was over, he did look at me. And I knew, from that one look, that he would never again set foot in that house. He walked away from the graveyard fast, so fast that his lawyer, Ted Hughes, who is shorter than he is, had to trot to keep up with him.

I looked one last time at the grave. After a Santa Ana has blown itself out in the fall, it often clouds up to rain. It was doing that now.

The first fall rains in California are a benediction. Everyone loves them. "Rain, rain," I said, like Mother talking to the new moon.

My cousin Gertrude Souza was waiting for me. She is fourteen years old and about six inches taller than I am already. She wears mini-skirts.

"I never saw anyone buried before," she said.

"Neither did I, Gertrude."

We walked toward the cars together, and she said, "We are first cousins."

"From now on," I promised her.

AFTERWORD

Miss West is convinced that "Up a Tree" is almost too straightforward a murder story to be a proper mystery. She writes: " . . . the story is told in first person by one of the people involved—so you can't bank on a word she says." And also: " . . . readers should guess that papa did in mama."

But can the reader bank on *that*?

When this story was being considered for this book, it was read by five seasoned mystery enthusiasts who came to five different conclusions concerning the facts. Just perhaps Miss West is a better mystery writer than she is aware.

We suggest that the reader reread the story and consider whether the crime is suicide or murder; if murder, by whom; if there has been concealment of evidence, and if so what, how, why, by whom and when. Attention should be paid to the changing relationships of Eugenia to her father and to her mother, both before and after the Death; to the *two* trips up the tree; and to the unusual conversation which ends the story. Perhaps you will become as confounded, and as enchanted, as this editor and his friends.

Probably the most misrepresented character in modern literature is the private investigator. Despite the large number of current stories to the contrary (many of them excellent entertainment; some of them excellent literature), the private eye does not spend his days waiting with a pitcher of martinis for a statuesque blonde bearing a major felony. But neither does he merely—in the words of the late Stuart Palmer, describing his own semi-pro career as an investigator—"contract pneumonia and arthritis while waiting in an alley for a co-respondent to come out a back door."

Joe Gores, like Hammett and Chandler, has had a good look at the job—as an operative for an agency specializing in skip-tracing and in repossessing property (mostly vehicles) for creditors (mostly banks). If this sounds tame and clerkish, then one has no idea of the length to which Californians will go to defend the shiny symbols of their status, pride—and manhood. It is a job for the tough-minded, if not the tough-hearted, but it is not devoid of humor. Certain of us gleefully recall Joe Gores assisting the San Francisco police to remove a trailer-truck from the slopes of Telegraph Hill—by picking the locks of a dozen illegally parked cars.

Then there is Patrick Michael O'Bannon of the Kearny Agency. There are three cardinal insults to a San Francisco Irishman: calling him English, refusing him a drink, and sending him out of the City on the greatest Day of the year. Dan Kearny was too intelligent to forget the first two; and too busy to remember the third. But the mantle of the good Patrick was wide enough for even The Ballard and The Kearny.

The O'Bannon Blarney File
JOE GORES

"*March seventeenth!*" Dan Kearny fell back weakly in his chair, cold gray eyes fixed in disbelief on his desk calendar. "My God, Giselle, it's—"

"—St. Paddy's Day," she said hollowly. Giselle Marc was a tall, slender, wickedly curved blonde who was much too intelligent to be so attractive. "To O'B, it's Christmas and New Year's and the Fourth of July and Happy Hanukkah and his Saint's Day all rolled into one."

"And *you* send him off to Sacramento! Out of town, on St. Paddy's Day, with one of the new men . . ."

"Larry Ballard isn't exactly *new*, Dan. He's been a field investigator with DKA going on two years."

They were in Kearny's soundproofed cubbyhole in the basement of the old narrow Victorian ex-bawdy house which served as head offices for Daniel Kearny Associates. Kearny scowled, hunched ex-prizefighter shoulders, stuck out his ice-breaker jaw. He was a stocky, thick-chested, compact man with thinning curly hair.

"Too new to ride with O'B on St. Paddy's Day. Remember last year? O'Bannon came off the freeway, loaded, at seventy miles an hour and broadsided a new Polara with a cop standing on the corner—"

"He talked the cop out of the ticket, Dan," said Giselle meekly.

"An *Irish* cop. And by some miracle the other guy was driving on a suspended license." He shook his heavy graying head bitterly. "How could you *do* this to me, Giselle?"

* * *

It must be admitted: O'Bannon Had Been Drinking. But, as he pointed out to Larry Ballard, Kearny was to blame. Expecting O'B to work on St. Paddy's Day! And worse, in *Sacramento* instead of San Francisco! As well Dismal Seepage, Arkansas.

"It isn't *Dan's* fault that our Sacramento man let that guy slam a car hood on his back," Ballard pointed out.

"I'm not so sure," said O'B darkly, leading the younger man into yet another bar's cool shadowy interior. It seemed to Ballard that they had spent the day playing liar's dice for drinks in a succession of undistinguished bistros; yet they had somehow closed out a disconcerting number of open cases.

"Sacrilege!" exclaimed O'Bannon.

Ballard, who admitted to no ethnic affiliations, stared about in bewilderment. "What do you mean?"

The Rathskeller, as its name implied, was a German-style *Bierhaus* of darkly varnished woodwork, a back bar lined with heavy steins, and imported beer on tap. Now, however, the place was wildly decorated with giant shamrocks, cardboard Leprecauns, and twisted streamers of green crepe paper. Behind the stick was an apparently Teutonic gentleman with thick hairy forearms and the pale butch-cut hair of a Hitler Youth. He was just raising a mug to his lips; festive green food coloring had been added to the beer therein.

"Sacrilege," repeated O'Bannon brokenly.

The bartender lowered his tankard, did a slow take around his establishment, then took in the Irishman's shamrock green tie, flaming red hair, and lean freckled drinker's face. Finally he nodded.

"I'll lay you a double shot of Bushmill's that I'm more Irish than you are, Red."

An unholy light came into O'Bannon's eyes; he began shamelessly gargling his r's. "Holy Mither presairve us." He rubbed his hands briskly together, then laid his driver's license on the bar beside the three doubles the bartender was pouring. "Faith, and 'tis Patrick Michael O'Bannon I be, begorra—as confirmed by the Department of Motor Vehicles of this gr-r-reat state."

"Man, you're a Mick, all right. But . . ."

The bartender almost regretfully produced his own license and laid it next to O'Bannon's. Their heads drew close over it. After a long moment, O'B heaved a bitter shuddering sigh, and very slowly laid a ten-dollar bill on the stick next to the three double Bushmill's.

The publican's name was Seamus Sean Irish.

* * *

"We should have phoned in *hours* ago," Ballard said weakly.

O'B, in the outdoor phone booth next to The Rathskeller, was having a little trouble finding the slot with his dime. He paused to pontificate. "The trouble with you, Ballard me lad, is that you're too cautious. *Strike* . . ." his gesture would have carried him outside the booth if the metal flex from the receiver hadn't stopped him. His dime popped from between his fingers and catapulted into the slot. ". . . while the iron is hot. Observe people, Ballard me lad. Study them. Every man has his weakness . . ."

"What's my weaknesh . . . ah, weakness, O'B?"

"Sad-eyed women who either kill themselves or put something in your coffee." He paused to give the long-distance operator the collect call. "Mine is never taking *a* drink. Dan Kearny's is a deplorable lack of faith in my ability to . . . what? Hello?"

Ballard could hear Giselle, clearly speaking with her mouth pressed close to the phone. "The Great White Father is on the warpath, O'B! He wants—"

"O'BANNON, WHY IN HELL HAVEN'T YOU PHONED IN? WHERE ARE YOU?"

O'B held the blaring phone from his ear, wincing, then answered in a tour-guide's singsong. "Sacramento, the historic capital of California, is center of the 'forty-nine gold rush—"

"DON'T GET CUTE WITH ME, O'BANNON! I sent you up there to work cases, not get Ballard drunk in some cheap gin mill. What about that Drake Plymouth? We've been chasing that guy for three months—"

"Plymouth's in the barn, Dan. It was laying on the residence address with two flat tires and cobwebs on the steering wheel." He tipped a wink at Ballard; they actually had spent two hours digging the guy out of the woodwork by convincing a relief mail carrier that they were telephone repairmen.

"Oh." Kearny sounded almost crestfallen. "The client thinks the MacDonald woman who embezzled those negotiable bonds skipped—"

"Her new address is 6316 North Rosebury, St. Louis, Missouri."

"I . . . see." Then Kearny's voice became triumphant. "What about the Wellman Toronado, huh? The client's really *screaming*—"

"Toronado's on the tow-bar, Dan. I'm looking at it right now."

Ten minutes later, slouched in the rider's side of O'Bannon's Chev Caprice with a headache, Larry Ballard wondered why O'B was the only person he'd ever met who could leave Dan Kearny speechless. Hell, here was Ballard, twenty-five years old, half an inch under six feet and weighing 184 pounds; but when Kearny cut loose, he just hung on grimly, like a barnacle on a rock. There was O'B, forty-two years old, just touching five-eight, 155 pounds, whose only admitted sports were bar whiskey at night and steam baths in the morning. But *he* calmly ignored Kearny's outbursts as an umpire ignores heckling from the stands.

Was it because O'B had heard all of the world's sad tales at least twice, and had never believed any of them? While Ballard believed almost all of them?

"I thought you were going to tell me what files we have to work on the way home," said O'Bannon from behind the wheel.

Ballard studied the cases as the linked Caprice and Toronado sped southwest through the Sacramento River flatlands. There were two of them. First was a 1972 Cougar registered to a Dorothy Soderberg, last known address of 458 West D Street, Dixon. Client was Fairfield First National Bank.

"Where the hell is Dixon, O'B?"

"Little burg twenty miles down the road."

Orders were REPOSSESS ON SIGHT, which meant they didn't have to talk to anyone, just grab. If, of course, they could spot the car. Fairfield, home of their client bank on the Cougar, was a somewhat larger town another twenty miles beyond Dixon. Fairfield was also where the second case was located.

But first, *la* Soderberg and her 1972 Cougar; one case at a time was all his aching head could encompass. Then he realized that O'B, who had taken the Dixon overpass, was pulling off on the shoulder.

"What's the matter?"

"Let's drop the Toronado off the tow-bar here by the overpass. We can pick it up again on our way back out after we work the Cougar."

Dixon reminded Ballard of his own home town. The same grid of north-south streets intersecting similar east-west streets; the same drive-in where the teen-agers would congregate; the movie house, volunteer fire department, drugstore, bars, churches, supermarket; trees arching over frame-housed residential streets.

The address on West D was the O-Kay Kleaners. Closed.

"Let's try the volunteer firemen," said Ballard.

On duty was a teen-age boy watching television. "That'd be the Soderbergs," he said. "Two blocks past the stop sign, right-hand side of the street. They just seeded the front lawn . . ."

They drove past the Soderberg house, circled the block, went down the alley. No Cougar. Dusk had fallen, lights were winking on; through the front window they could see a middle-aged man watching TV. He wore old-fashioned arm garters. A fresh-faced girl of high school age opened the door.

"Dorothy Soderberg?" Ballard asked.

The girl's dark eyes slid away. "I . . . she isn't . . ." She turned toward the front-room TV-watcher. "Pops . . ."

The man asked them in as a gray-haired stocky woman came from the kitchen to appraise them with shrewd faded eyes.

"Dorothy owe you, too?" she demanded harshly.

Ballard hesitated, but O'Bannon said immediately, "That she does, ma'am, that she does. For the Cougar."

"She's our daughter-in-law," said Soderberg. "She's a *good* girl, but our son was killed in Vietnam, and Dot . . . well, she . . ."

Sorrow and scorn had been battling in the woman's face; sorrow lost. "Six weeks, and already she's dating other boys!"

"Now, Mother, these men aren't interested in—"

"Well, I don't care. She got that government insurance money, and she just went crazy spending. Big fancy car, running up to Tahoe weekends to ski . . ." Her shrewd eyes pried at the investigators. "If we tell where she is, do you intend to take that car away from her?"

Again Ballard hesitated; again O'Bannon spoke immediately. "Yes, ma'am, that's what we're here for."

She looked defiantly at her sad-eyed husband.

"She's moved back in with her pa out west of town—three miles beyond the freeway overpass. Tudor, his name is. Can't probably read the mailboxes in the dark, but being it's a chicken ranch . . ."

It was dark out. As they drove back out past their parked Toronado, Ballard opened his window. Through it came clean fresh country air, the scent of new grass, the rich smell of damp earth, the . . .

"Whew!" exclaimed O'B. "That's *got* to be our chicken ranch."

From the road they could see lights; O'B played his spotlight across the barnyard, the coops, the open-ended machinery shed. No

Cougar. They stumbled across a rutted yard; faint light through the screen door showed that a long and skinny man wearing bib overalls was sitting on the top step in the dark.

"Mr. Tudor?" asked O'Bannon.

"Yep." He uncoiled his length until he was an easy six-and-a-half feet tall, slat-thin. He thrust a thumb through his overalls bib. "Pointa fac', *Royal* Tudor. *De*scended of the Tudors of England. Lookin' fer Dot, ain'tcher? Men come, nights, it's gen'ally fer her. T'other one's too little yit—least, hope she is. Dot's in town . . ."

The screen door creaked open, then slammed three diminishing times. A girl about fourteen paused where the light from inside would clearly outline her shape through her thin cotton dress.

"Bet she's drivin' 'round after a *boy*." She turned to silhouette her precocious bustline. "Taldy *Ben*son. *He* works at the garage, an' *he's* got a new Corvette Stingray auto*mo*bile."

They returned to the scattered lights of Dixon, where O'B parked across from the drive-in and changed places with Ballard. "I've just got a feeling this is going to call for a finesse from the Old Maestro." He chuckled. "How did you like the little sister? Tobacco Rhoda. Makes you feel that old lady Soderberg probably had a point about Dot. She must wear those widow's weeds pretty lightly."

Ballard stiffened. "There she is."

A new Corvette had passed, tail-gated by a screaming red Cougar with a laughing blonde behind the wheel. She had good facial bones and wide-set reckless eyes. Beside her was a round-faced brunette.

"Next time around, join the parade."

Within a few minutes, Taldy Benson had pulled into the drive-in. As O'B had expected, Dorothy kept going.

"The Old Maestro is about to strike. Pull alongside."

Ballard gunned up even with the red car. The girl looked over, then slammed on her brakes and called through her open window.

"Why are you following us? We'll tell the police!"

"*Dorothy baby!*" yipped O'Bannon.

"Who . . . are you?" But her wide, go-to-hell mouth was already quirking at O'B's lean, freckled, equally go-to-hell features.

"This is *Red!* Don't you remember? Tahoe . . ."

"Were . . . you the man who helped us with the tire chains . . ."

"That's right!" cried O'B. He muttered, "follow us," to Ballard, and slid from the Chev. He opened Dorothy's door, in a moment was behind the wheel with the girls emitting shrill squeals of laughter beside him. Ballard heard, "Your Old Man said . . . in town . . . my car conked out . . . the overpass . . ."

But it wasn't until the tail lights of the red Cougar, a quarter-mile ahead, brightened just behind the parked black Toronado that Ballard understood. He cut his lights, drifted closer in the dark. They were clearly visible by the glare of the Cougar's headlights. It was pulled up close behind the parked Toronado, and the brunette was out on the shoulder to check the match of the bumpers. That left Dot . . .

Ballard went slowly by, tires crunching gravel. O'B was gesturing. "Dot . . . check on this side, will you?"

Ballard pounded his steering wheel gleefully. The Old Maestro indeed! She had slid obediently out, was standing in the road to watch the bumpers come gently together.

"Don't scratch . . . car . . ."

She was out of earshot by then, but Ballard could see in the rearview mirror that the cars were nose-to-tail. Then the red Cougar moved. It shot *backwards*, away from the car that the open-mouthed girls had thought O'B was going to push. He paused momentarily before whipping a U-ie to speed safely away.

"Lady," he declared solemnly, "you've just been repossessed!"

* * *

"Gailani Funeral Home." Ballard was reading aloud from the file. He stifled a satisfied belch; his headache was gone. "Client is California-Citizens Bank, San Mateo Branch. Hmmm . . . Short $76.85 on the January payment, down $193.75 each for February and March . . ."

"And we're after a 1969 Oldsmobile hearse," mused O'B.

They had rendezvoused at a pizza joint in Fairfield. Ballard had driven the Caprice, with the recovered Toronado dragging behind on the tow-bar. In the unencumbered Soderberg Cougar, O'B had been half a pizza and a whole pitcher of beer ahead when Ballard finally had arrived.

"What are the instructions?"

"*Contact subject, collect all delinquent funds or store unit. No exceptions.* O'B, why in hell wouldn't a funeral home pay for its hearse?"

O'Bannon shrugged. "Maybe the guy's got expensive tastes. Let's hit the residence address first; he's probably home this time of night."

It was just after midnight when they pulled up across from the rambling ranch-style house. Ballard parked his linked vehicles behind the Cougar, joined O'B on the walk. A dog thundered inside. O'B punched the bell, to be rewarded with a female voice asking who it was.

"Sorry to bother you so late, Mrs. Gailani, but it's important that we speak with your husband."

The dog growled softly. The woman said, through the closed door, "He's down at the shop, finishing up some work."

"The *shop?*" muttered O'B as they returned to the cars.

Gailani's Funeral Home was a fine new box of aluminum, glass, and Permastone, set off Massachusetts Street between a hospital and a branch bank. It looked like a liquor store with pretensions. Ballard made a loop through the hospital drive to end up behind the red Cougar. He grinned as he noted the name of the bank next door. Fairfield First National. Talk about coincidences! In the mortuary's blacktop lot gleamed a row of three hearses. O'B jerked a thumb at them.

"I'll check if it's one of those—you go talk to the man like the instructions say. Remember, cash only."

"Hell, O'B, he won't have cash tonight."

O'B winked. "I've always wanted to repo a hearse."

The night bell brought forth a fortyish man in white shirt, no tie, and black trousers. His shoes and his eyes gleamed blackly, his hair was too black to be convincing. Ballard was assailed by the rolling chords of an organ and warm air cloyed with too many flowers.

"Mr. Gailani?"

"Yes." His voice was a well-oiled baritone.

"I represent the San Mateo Branch of California-Citizens Bank." The subject maintained his oily beam, so Ballard said in a harder tone, "About the Oldsmobile hearse."

A frown marred Gailani's hitherto tranquil brow. "Ah. Of course. Come in."

A coffin was laid out in the same chapel as the organ; flowers and ornate candlesticks bearing dull orange tapers flanked it. The upper half was open to display a stern waxy profile, but it was the organ which made Ballard's hackles rise.

No one was playing it.

"Runs off a tape," beamed Gailani. "I've just been . . . ah . . . clearing up a few odds and ends . . ."

Which one was the corpse, Ballard wondered. An odd or an end?

"Ah . . . there was something?"

"There was—is—$464.35 in cash, Mr. Gailani, plus my charges. Or I'll be forced to store the vehicle."

"The Olds hearse? Oh dear. You didn't receive word I'd paid?"

"Do you have proof of payment, Mr. Gailani?"

"I spoke with Mr. Verdugo on the phone at four-thirty today." Ballard surreptitiously checked the case sheet; Verdugo was indeed the bank zone man who had assigned it. "I asked if my check for the payment had arrived, and he said it had." Gailani frowned. "He said investigators from a . . . Kenny Associates? Kearny? That was it, Daniel Kearny Associates, were on the case, but that he would call them and tell them to close their file."

Ballard sighed inwardly. O'Bannon had called in *before* 4:30, so they had not gotten the cancellation. No hearse-repossession for O'B that night. Gailani was shoving an open check book under his nose.

"See? There's the check stub, dated yesterday, made out—"

"I believe you, I believe you," said Ballard.

"I'm *most* relieved. You've no idea how I feel about my hearses." His mouth pursed erotically. "That Olds is a . . . mighty . . . fine . . . *piece* . . . OF . . . *IRON!* And business has been so *brisk* that I need it! Tomorrow the departed in the next room makes his final journey; there's a delivery to San Francisco early in the morning . . ."

Ballard paused outside to breathe air not cloyed with death's cosmetics. After 1 A.M., fifty miles to the city towing that damned Toronado. He pulled open the door of the red Cougar.

"O'B, the guy already paid—"

He stopped. O'Bannon was not within. Ballard swiveled to look at the three hearses in the parking lot, feeling distinctly unwell as he did.

Only two hearses were left. The Old Maestro had struck again.

*   *   *

O'B would wait for him—but where? Fairfield was too small; the subject might see his repossessed hearse parked outside a bar and just take it back again. A bar it would be, of course. But . . . Yeah. A bar in the next big town south toward San Francisco. Near the freeway.

Ballard drove at the even 50 m.p.h. the law allowed vehicles with a tow, took Vallejo's Magazine Street off-ramp, pulled into a slanting blacktop lot beside a bar, from which he could swing the linked autos easily back onto the freeway. His hunch had been right. Behind the building, out of sight, was the hearse.

Inside, on a stool, was O'Bannon. "You have the makings of a detective after all, Ballard me boy." He clapped a dice box on the bar. "I'll fight you for last call."

Ballard sat down, shook his dice box idly until the bartender had departed for their beers. He said: "O'B, the guy paid."

O'Bannon's freckled face paled. Repossessing a vehicle on which the payments were current could lead to lawsuits; lawsuits led banks to quit using the investigation firm which got them sued.

"What proof did he have? Certified check carbon? Stamped payment book? Canceled check?"

"Just a check stub. But . . ." Ballard outlined the facts, concluding, ". . . and he obviously *had* talked with Dick Verdugo at San Mateo. Do we try to sneaky-pete the hearse back to his lot—"

"No way. I reported the repo to the Fairfield police; they'll have an official record of it." He brightened. "After all, Larry, check stubs aren't *proof* of payment. If we take it back to DKA, in the morning get to Verdugo before the subject does—"

"That isn't all, O'B." Ballard stared glumly into the mirror. "I moved the Soderberg Cougar to the mortuary lot, but—"

"So? Hell, one of us can pick it up tomorrow . . ."

"The bank? Next door? That's our client on that car."

Watching O'B take the news was like watching one of the Roadrunner TV ads, where the coyote ran into a wall and then cracked apart and fell into several separate pieces. Finally O'Bannon sighed deeply.

"So if our client happens to look out the window tomorrow and recognizes that red Cougar—which isn't exactly inconspicuous—he'll wonder why it isn't safely in the DKA storage garage in San Francisco where it's supposed to be, and . . ."

Ballard nodded. "Scratch one client."

"So I've blown both of them. And on St. Paddy's Day, yet." Then O'B shrugged and stood up. "Well, let's get the hearse down to the city. We can make out the condition report right here—there's plenty of light in the lot."

They circled the hearse, noting dents, scratches, general mechanical condition, the amount of usable tread left on the tires. They checked mileage; extras such as power steering, brakes, seats, windows; the condition of the interior upholstery. That left the itemization of all personal property found in the vehicle.

"I'll check the back end," grunted O'B.

But when he drew aside the curtains behind the seat, there was one of the long pauses of the sort Victorian novels delighted in characterizing as pregnant.

A casket reposed in the curtained hearse.

Ballard began, in a hushed voice, "You don't suppose . . ."

O'Bannon lifted the display half of the coffin's top. He shone his flashlight within. They craned forward, then pivoted to look at each other. O'B lowered the lid reverently.

"Now *that's* what I call personal property," he breathed. Then he snapped his fingers, began rummaging through the glove box. "Just a second, I thought . . . yeah." He read aloud. "*George: con-*

sign to Eternal Rest." He looked up at Ballard. "Gailani said they had one to deliver to San Francisco, didn't he? There's an SF directory in the Caprice . . ."

Larry Ballard returned riffling the Yellow Pages. "Here it is! Eternal Rest Funeral Home, Geary Boulevard at Twelfth Avenue. But we can't just—"

"We sure as hell can't store it in the personal property lockers at the office." O'Bannon rummaged again, came up with a chauffeur's cap. He touched the visor with a diffident finger. "Call me George."

* * *

Eternal Rest was to be found in a narrow rose-colored building flanked by a florist's shop and a bank parking lot. An alley slanted up between the florist and the mortuary to a small concrete loading platform with double doors. Ballard was beside O'Bannon in the hearse; the Chev and Toronado were parked a block away. At 3:30 A.M. the boulevard was deserted and dark.

"Now, as the Great White Father says, we shall play it by ear."

O'Bannon backed the hearse's long shining shape up the alley. Cap in place, he mounted to the double doors and tapped on the glass with his ring. Finally the single caged light bulb over the platform went on, a bolt snicked, handles clanked, and the doors opened outward. A short dumpy man appeared, egg-bald and wearing a rumpled morning face armored with bad breath.

"You guys are early enough." He shivered, clicked porcelain teeth together. "Which one's this?"

"From Fairfield," said O'Bannon with a picturesque yawn.

"That'd be Anna Osborne—died all over the cake at her daughter's wedding reception. Chapel B. Lemme get my shoes on, this cement's cold."

When he returned, Ballard and O'B had the rear doors open and the casket slid out on its oiled telescope runners. The three men wrestled it on to a wheeled dolly. Then the two detectives stole quickly away.

"Like falling off a log," chortled O'B as they drove away. He sobered. "After we dump this and the Toronado at the storage lot, let's find an all-night Turkish bath. We have to be on Verdugo's phone when he comes into the office at eight-thirty."

Four hours later, at 8:20, they arrived at the DKA basement rumpled but refreshed. Along the left wall were the field agent cubicles; along the right, banks of screened personal property lockers into which Anna Osborne would not possibly have fit. As they entered, the sliding glass door of Kearny's office at the far end of the basement opened to let his massive jaw emerge. It was followed by Kearny. Kearny was beaming, like a spitting cobra about to spit.

"You lads are up bright and early," he said toothily.

"You know us, Dan. Company Time is Company Money."

"I'll bet you fellows repossessed a Cougar from a little girl named Dorothy Soderberg up in Dixon last night, didn't you?"

O'B and Ballard exchanged glances. O'B cleared his throat. Dan Kearny beamed invincibly.

"And you know what? Fairfield First National Bank has been on the horn. Our clients. Miss Soderberg came into their Auto Contracts at eight o'clock—beat on the doors until they opened them up. And she *paid off that car!* In cash. And *now*—she wants her car. *Right now* she wants it. AND I SUPPOSE YOU HAVE THE CAR DOWN HERE—"

It was O'Bannon at his finest. He cut in airily, "Tell them to look out the window."

"DOWN HERE AND . . . What?"

"Tell our client to look out of his side window and he'll see the Cougar parked in the lot that's . . . ah . . . next to the bank."

"But . . . how did you . . ."

O'B spread deprecatory hands. "I *knew* she'd pay it off this morning, so I left it there. We had a long chat with her before the repo—right, Larry?"

Ballard had trouble with some obstruction in his throat, but finally nodded. "Right," he got out.

Kearny looked from one to the other, rapidly, like a tennis spectator. Dammit, O'Bannon had done *some* unorthodox thing that . . .

The intercom buzzed. He snatched up the closest phone, listened to Giselle from the clerical offices above. He nodded, eying O'B and Ballard malevolently. When he spoke, there was honey in his voice.

"Tell Mr. Verdugo that we have the field agents on that Gailani repossession right here. Yes. Assure him that any charge-backs will come right from their salaries . . ." He said crisply to O'Bannon, "Take extension three."

O'B picked up the phone as if it were booby-trapped, but his voice bubbled with carefree *bonhomie*. "Dicky Verdugo! How's tricks, reverend?"

He listened, nodded, then finally spoke with virtuous horror. "A *corpse?* In the hearse *we* repossessed? Dicky, I can *personally* assure you that there's no corpse in that vehicle. And . . ."

Kearny jerked his own phone back to his ear. Dammit, O'Bannon *couldn't* be getting away with it after all! If . . . He heard Verdugo speaking.

" . . . real *relief*, O'B. A stray stiff would make some real *waves*." Admiration filled his voice. "What I can't figure out is how the hell you *knew* that guy's check was rubber, and repossessed the hearse anyway. I mean, he conned me *plenty* on the phone yesterday. It was only when our Vallejo branch called this morning that I found out he's been sailing kites all over Solano County . . ."

Kearny had no stomach for further listening. He tossed the receiver in the general direction of the phone and stalked majestically back into his cubbyhole, slamming the door behind him hard enough to rattle it on its padded runners. Once safely alone, he plucked a cigarette from his pack with outraged fingers, then flopped in the chair behind his big blondewood desk.

By God, how in *hell* did O'Bannon do it? Pull all sorts of cute crap, ignore proper procedure, give a younger man like Ballard every sort of bad example—and come out rosewater. St. Paddy's Day, that had to be it. What had Giselle called it? O'Bannon's Saint's Day?

He puffed furiously at his cigarette, stubbed it out, lit another. And there would be more to come, he knew. The redheaded Irishman would try to ram an eye-popping expense account from the Sacramento foray down his throat. And expect him, Dan Kearny, to swallow it.

Yes, and even *that* wasn't the worst of it. Hell no.

The *worst* of it was that Dan Kearny would.

There is a legend that Queen Victoria, having greatly enjoyed Lewis Carroll's *Alice in Wonderland*, asked for more works by this author, and was presented with a stack of incredibly abstruse works on mathematics. To some extent this same pit may await new readers of Thomas Scortia.

Besides being the author of some 150 short stories and three novels, written both before and after his departure from the aerospace industry (a departure nearly prematurely precipitated by his iconoclastic 1960 novel about the field, *What Mad Oracle?*), he has also authored and co-authored such beguiling works as *Solid Propellant Characterization and Selection for Space Missions* and "Oxidation-Reduction Potentials of the System: Selenourea-Formamidine Diselenide." He is currently working on a novel, *Artery of Fire*, and an anthology, neither of which will, hopefully, require an advanced degree or a security clearance to read.

His story here is that of Jesús Miguel de Sanchez, *muralista*, who journeyed to northern California to give life to the designs of Nefia; he is a man of great artistic integrity, and with a most singular sense of justice.

The Goddess of the Cats
THOMAS N. SCORTIA

In the nude darkness of the early morning, she cried "Oh." Miguel tightened his hard muscles and thrust his young body forward as she sighed, "Ah!" Then she sobbed a deep, wracking sob and he let her fade from him into the anonymous no-light and rose from the bed. He toweled his now flaccid loins. Ignoring the red coal of the cigarette somewhere in the rumpled white sheets, he walked from the room, through the studio and out of the apartment into the chill morning air of the passageway. He descended the steel and plaster stairs to his basement apartment, made his quick worshipful sign to the image of the Old One in the corner and fell into a fatigued sleep on the pallet in the corner of the bedroom.

The sound of trucks, collecting the week's rubbish, wakened him at 8:30 and he lay for long moments, feeling the after-lethargy of making sex before he rose, dressed and left the basement apartment without breakfasting. The shoes felt uncomfortable on his feet and he longed for the open freedom of sandals or bare feet, but he knew the *gringo* looked upon his kind with contempt when they wore these. When he entered the court of the Mermaid, however, he shed his shoes and squatted, bare feet caressing the pebbled roughness of the concrete as he mixed the mortar.

Only during the mornings when he worked upon the Mermaid did Jesús Miguel de Sanchez forget for a moment the cold barrenness of this godless land. The cold sun flowed bleakly across the northern California sky and fused the soft brown of his fingers with the deeper ochre of its shadows. For those few hours his body and his soul were one with the fingers that shaped the ceramic bits into alien forms upon the wall. Under his touch that made love to flesh and stone and enameled clay alike, the submarine beauty of Nefia's mercreature flushed with life. His heart filled with the surge of pride at his artisan skill, knowing that he had come from a ragged barefoot boy out of the Guaymí to this place of honor as the best *muralista* in the northern provinces. Why else would they have brought him north to this bleak land of metal and strange gibberish to breathe the Nefian designs into the lifeless chaos of stone and tile and dank plaster.

Under his fingers the form of the Mermaid grew on the ground and then magically reappeared, transposed to the three-story wall. She was not the mermaid of trivial western legend with dull fish tail and accentuated breasts. Rather, her lower body was thick with a mothering beauty that spoke of a sea-born fecundity. She was a creature of the harsh Atlantic coasts. She had lain at the bottom of the bay in sight of the gods of Popacatapetl and cried in the night at the long boats opening the waters of Vera Cruz in a wound that had bled unstanched for four centuries. Her tail multiplied not into pitiful fins but into the multitudinous tendrils of the hydra that tore a man's flesh with flagellae, bringing death in a bright ecstasy of pain. Above the imperceptible merging of flesh and scale, her full body grew breasts sensual and filled with the earth flavor of blue-haired women of his childhood mountains. She gestured distantly with alien hands and it was moments before one realized that the fingers were long and possessed each an extra joint. Above this the head was crowned by sea-matted hair sparkling with glints of light caught from some vagrant ocean current. Around her spread small sea things . . . stars, sea urchins, drifting strands of algae, all of which filled the bottom of the mural and merged into the fountain basin, ending at the upthrusting rusty steel of reinforcing rods in the unfinished pool.

She was a thing of strange and compelling beauty to Miguel. (For reasons that were awkward he never thought of himself as Jesús. Better not to anger the new gods, especially when you bore the name of one of them.) In the darkness of the apartment in the basement where he lived, she would come often, floating in on the gossamer pathways the moon traced through the wisteria trees that tongued his window with their fronds. (He knew she was a part of the cactus world when he ate the god-flesh called teo-nanacatyl by his people but she had a greater reality than most of the visions.) Beautiful but without a heart—still forever beckoning to love promised but not consumated. It was a small thing, this flaw in his creation, but he knew that one day he would repair it and she would be complete with the secret niche in her breast filled with richness.

The afternoon sun was growing hot and the mortar was not setting properly. He gathered the pieces of ceramic he had removed from the mosaic, placed them in the acid bath to soak free of the doughy mortar and wiped the white stuff from his hands. He gathered together his tools and walked slowly along the cantilevered gangway, by the apartment manager's office and paused for a moment to admire the view.

The apartment complex, three stories and a basement of open stucco, steel and tile, had been only halfway completed when he came north to do the murals the first owner had commissioned from Nefia. He had finished the mountain lions poised in the midst of sunbaked hills on the outer wall in the spring followed by the grape-harvesting scene with bronzed men and women smiling amid purple fecundity in the early summer. In the meantime, Señor Warburg who had built the austere beauty of the complex with its artificial stream, banked by moss and watercress winding amid transplanted ancient cypress and new wisteria, had become, as they said, bankrupt and the Gray Giant from the north place they called Canada had bought the complex.

Miguel did not like the Gray Giant whose name was Duchotte because his eyes were ice when he looked at the hot southern murals of Nefia and spoke contemptuously of "prettying up the place." When he had spread chicken manure over the fertile grounds, Miguel had worked for a month in the thick cloud of flies born from the maggots that had come with the manure. The people who occupied the finished units complained and left. The Gray Giant shrugged and left for two weeks to return with concrete benches whose standards were cast *fleur de lis* and several truck loads of polished gray Vermont marble which he had bought somewhere at a scrap sale. Miguel shuddered at the thought of marble on the bright walls and tried to think only of the joy of his work and the beauty of the whole that even the Gray Giant couldn't destroy.

The apartment was poised in dynamic balance against the side of the mountain and below the town patterned itself in stark shades of light and dark in the afternoon sun. The *gringo* still called it Los Gatos and thought that there had been mountain lions in the hills when the Spaniards were there. *Dos gatos montes*, the two mountain lions . . . inferior concrete sculptures . . . marked the entrance to their college on the freeway above the town but who in this heathen land would have known the fierce masculine ecstasy of communicating with those beasts?

They too he knew in the silence of his room when the day was done and he could do the thing with the buttons that returned him to the earth and the living flesh of his hill people. He trembled at the thought, at the wonderful terror of . . .

"Wear your shoes," the woman said from the doorway of the apartment that adjoined the office.

"I am sorry. I forget," he said, coloring and feeling the killing anger rise in him that she could accept his body in the night and treat him with such scorn in the daylight.

"This morning you promised to sit for me," she said.

"Oh," he said, "Señora Martin, I did not promise for today." She stood in the door impossibly red, her hair drifting like blood light about her head. Her hands were clawed and her ragged nails still held the stain of the clay she worked with. "Of course you did," she said. "I'm still working over the preliminary model." Then in a softer voice, she said, "I thought you might like a glass of wine."

"I think perhaps . . ." he began.

"Come in, come in," she said and in the half reverie of his preoccupation he found himself drawn through the office into the apartment without awareness of movement or purpose. It was often like this with him and he did not find it surprising when he seated himself in a large wicker chair and found in his hand a glass of warm red wine from the Christian Brothers whose vineyards covered the mountainside just above them. It was good wine with a warm earthy feel on the palate and he sipped appreciatively.

The room, intended as a living room, had the cluttered look of a junkshop. The strong north light from the glass wall leading to the ground level patio threw harsh outlines on the half-completed bits of clay and ceramic. One item dominated the room: a half-rounded stone of perhaps a meter in height, shaped very much like the ancient altars he had seen in the museum at the university. (The one in what they called Mexico City showed the fading ancient brown stains of great and happy souls whose blood had steamed in the nostrils of the ancient gods, perfuming the senses of Huitzilpotl and the Nameless Ones. It had been so long since he had spoken the secret names in the Guaymí hills with his friends, fearful of the priests that everyone said knew all.)

"Sit here in the light," Señora Martin commanded.

"I am not finished with my wine," he said petulantly.

"Do as I say," she said. "You can carry the wine with you."

He sat in the wicker chair she indicated so that the light from the courtyard fell on his high-cheekboned features. She cast aside Spanish shawl and the wet cloth that draped her work and began again to mold new clay into the gray of his image. He shuddered, remembering what the old women of the mountain did with such images. In another time and another place, he would have destroyed the thing in very fear of his life and soul.

"Oh, sit still," the Señora Martin said.

"I am sorry," he said. "It is that it is uncomfortable."

"You can be very exasperating," she said. "All young men are exasperating at times."

"You did not think so last night," he said.

"The day is another matter," she said, frowning at the clay smearing her hands. "Don't forget that," she said.

"I will not," he said wearily and rose from the seat.

"Where are you going?" she demanded.

"I have work to do," he said, and left before she could answer. Outside in the bright sun he fought down the anger that boiled up within him. In his mountains he would know how to deal with her. Women were for grinding corn and washing the sweat-stained clothing of their men and not for this acting like a man with papers and typewriters and writing of checks. A good heavy stick would teach her some respect. Only you did not do that with women in this land and they walked as if they wore boots and carried seed between their legs. He spat on the ground.

As he passed through the garage area to the unloading dock, he came upon the Gray Giant who said, "Here you, give a hand here."

The Gray Giant and another man were unloading wooden crates, each of which contained a gray marble slab approximately two feet square and two inches thick. The Gray Giant lifted one with a great puffing and set it down on the loading dock. Miguel ignored the man and continued walking.

He did not hear the man leap from the truck bed and come up behind him until the massive hand grabbed his shoulder and spun him around.

"When I speak, you listen," Duchotte said angrily.

Miguel shook the hand from his shoulder and looked up at the Gray Giant. "I am not a *peón*," he said darkly. "I am *muralista*."

"You work for me," the Gray Giant said angrily and "you do what I say." His speech was thick with French accent of his native tongue and Miguel could barely understand him.

"I came to do the murals," Miguel said. "I did not come to dig or to carry or to do the things you have workers for."

"Damn you, heathen," Duchotte roared, "you will help or I will break your head."

Miguel looked at the man, feeling the deadly hate. It was only with difficulty that he controlled himself. Finally he spat on the ground and walked away. The Gray Giant stood shaking with rage.

He spent the afternoon in his room, dreaming of the hills where at night the old women came out and sat, shredding the god-flesh into the food that the men would eat as they communicated with the gods . . . the Jesus that the foreigners had brought centuries before and the still older ones who roamed the hills and moaned in the cold winds.

He must have dozed for when he was next aware of the room it was dark and his stomach was empty and paining him. In the stove oven he found a pot of *frijoles* left from the day before. As he warmed them, he busied himself, clearing away the sketches and the small cards of notes which strewed the floor from the day's work. He paused for a moment to marvel at Nefia's design for the Mermaid before he returned the masses of color-keyed paper to the bulging portfolio. Finally, he sat and nibbled on the beans, wondering if he felt hungry enough to prepare something more satisfying.

It was nearly eight o'clock, he saw with some annoyance. She would expect him tonight again with her heavy scented body thick with lust. It was an impossible thing, this business with a *gringo* woman who accepted his body because it was smooth and young and rejected him because of his darker skin and black eyes and flat Indian features. During the day she would never be seen with him and at night she made love in the dark so that she did not have to look upon him.

He lighted a cigarette, puffed nervously and then snuffed it out. He longed for home and the thin mountain air with its chillness and the dark women with their bare feet and heavy breasts, their hard feet that scraped an erotic path over the back of his thighs while they held him and made love sounds.

At eight-thirty he rose from the floor where he had been sitting, pulled on a shell jacket he had bought in one of the Los Gatos stores and left his basement apartment. It was just as well to let her wait a bit, he thought. She was too sure of herself and her power. Outside he lighted another cigarette, leaned against the wall and smoked it leisurely and finally sent the hot butt spiraling into the flowing stream below the walkway.

It was almost nine when he knocked at her door and waited. When there was no answer, he knocked again and finally heard the rustling sound of bare feet on carpet from inside. The door opened slowly on the night latch and she said,

"What do you want?"

"It is Miguel," he said softly.

"I know who it is," she said irritably.

"Let me in."

"No," she said. "Go away."

"If that is the way you want it," he said.

"Go away," she said and slammed the door.

He stood for a moment, listening to the movements within the room and then walked down the courtyard. He paused beside the unfinished fountain for a moment, his fingers testing the jagged sharpness of the steel rods jutting from the uncast rim. In the soft moonlight his Mermaid was a creature of dreams, her seaborne hair softly glistening as though it floated out from the hard mosaic surface and wafted into the dark air.

He knew why he was waiting but he would not admit it to himself. When he heard the rattle of the night chain, he moved back into the shadows. Finally the fingernail of light appeared at the edge of the door to be extinguished in the next second and the door opened. He saw the giant form silhouetted against dim radiance from within and the faint grunt of satisfaction as the Gray Giant turned and held her roughly for a moment before closing the door.

The heavy form moved clumsily along the walk, weaving a bit as though he had too much to drink. At one point a huge philodendron leaf brushed against the man and he thrust it away violently, breaking the stem. Miguel stood silently, fearing to move. He had waited too long, he realized.

Duchotte paused perhaps twenty feet from his hiding spot and said, "Who's that?"

He said nothing.

"There's somebody there," the man insisted. "I know you're there."

Miguel remained silent, easing his body slowly around the niche where he hid. He reached down and carefully, silently removed his sandals.

"I know who you are, damn you," the Gray Giant shouted. He weaved unsteadily forward and Miguel slid silently past the fountain, his bare feet making the faintest wisp of sound on the concrete's exposed aggregate. He heard the man blunder forward as he fled.

He ran down the steps and entered his apartment, bolting the door. Finally, he sat, feeling his heart surge in fear and anger.

He knew that this was not the time for the god-flesh, that only tranquillity and the full peace of the soul gave the honor the god needed, but he could not avoid the need. He ate and sat, feeling the air coagulate about him as the moonlight became a solid viscous substance that entrapped his body and squeezed the breath from his lungs. Outside he heard the distant sound of *dos gatos montes* and he went to the glass wall facing the patio. Down along the stream in the full moonlight he saw them, their great thews in sharp relief in the harsh light. They paced the stream and paused every so often to shriek their challenge into the night. He slid aside the glass panel and called to them but they would not answer. They knew he had profaned the god-flesh by bringing his passions to it and they would not come.

He sighed and returned to his darkened room. There he sat as the air filled with the small terrors of darkness and his body steamed with fear. There were things on the floor and they slithered and coiled around his feet and ran their rough tongues along his bare legs while colors of purple and dull red and nauseous green filled the dark. He smelled the scent of rot and putrification and he shivered in the delirium. When he finally fell asleep, his body was dripping with perspiration and his clothing was matted damply against his body.

The first light of dawn pierced his eyelids as though they did not exist. He awoke, feeling chilled and fatigued. After he had showered and breakfasted, he felt better. He gathered together the designs he would need that day and left the apartment. As he was working on one of the mosaic starfish, the Señora Martin appeared, her red hair carefully brushed and two rather obvious spots of color on her cheeks.

"Good morning," she said.

"It is a good morning," he said, trying to keep the anger from his voice.

"Mr. Duchotte wants you to help later today."

"I have told him I will not do this," Miguel said.

"He has some hand-pressed brick coming. He wants you to supervise the men who unload it."

"He can do this better than I," Miguel said. Then, "Brick? Why does he want brick?"

"He has some ideas on using brick and marble to accent the hallways."

Miguel shuddered. "It is a beautiful building. It does not need ornamentation."

"It's his building," Señora Martin said with a dainty shrug. "Besides, he has some very good ideas."

"It would seem that this is true," Miguel said.

"That's none of your business," she said coloring.

"That is true," he said.

"You forget who you are," she said and turned to walk angrily away.

Miguel sighed. After all, he thought, what did it really matter? He was rather glad to be freed of his task of servicing the woman. He had not really understood how the *gringo* women would absorb a man until he had rather casually started the affair. Still, it irritated him to be replaced by the Gray Giant who was old and ugly. There was the thought that the Señora Martin depended her livelihood on him . . . and he did have money which made great impressions on the *gringo* women.

At noon the Gray Giant sent one of the workmen to tell Miguel that he wanted to see him. Miguel ignored the summons and went to his apartment. He was eating when Duchotte appeared in the open doorway.

"Damned you," the Gray Giant said. "When I send for you, you come." His voice in anger was thick with the French accent.

"I am eating," Miguel said simply.

"Well, you will listen and listen well to me."

"I am eating," Miguel said simply, holding the sandwich carefully to avoid spattering himself with the dressing. Duchotte strode into the room and with one swift movement of his massive hand, knocked the food from Miguel's hands.

"This is just enough," he said. "You will pack and be gone by the end of the week."

"I have a contract to do the murals," Miguel said.

"The hell with your curse'd contract," Duchotte shouted. "You will be gone by the end of the week."

He paused at the door, "And you will stay away from the Madame Martin."

"So, she has you captive now," Miguel smiled.

"Swine of an outlander," Duchotte said. "Stay away and me, I will break every bone in your body."

"That is not too easy," Miguel said and smiled lovingly at the sharp knife on the breadboard. He picked it up and looked questioningly at Duchotte. The man said nothing, but reddened visibly. Finally he said:

"By the end of the week," and turned and stalked away. When he appeared that afternoon for his modeling session, the Señora Martin said, "I don't think I want to continue with this. It isn't turning out right."

"No," Miguel said, "it is not turning out right."

"You understand," she said . . . somewhat sadly, he thought.

"I understand," he said.

He found that he could not work. Several times he had to remove bits of tile which were going on roughly. The mortar was too thick and the Mermaid reproached him for the bad job he was doing. Finally he quit for the day and started for his quarters.

In one of the passageways he came upon Duchotte and a workman who was mortaring one of the marble slabs into place. The effect of polished marble, rough mortar and hand-pressed brick in itself might have been attractive but against the austere earth colors of the building it was offensive and degraded the pure beauty of the building to something out of a circus.

"Sanchez," Duchotte said. "You can stop work on the murals."

"I was brought up here to do Nefia's designs," Miguel said.

"That's all over with," Duchotte said. "I'll see that you get your money but I don't want any heathen images on my building."

"They are beautiful," Miguel said.

"This is something I decide," Duchotte said contemptuously and turned his back on Miguel.

Miguel slept the afternoon and in the early chill of dusk he returned to the courtyard and talked silently with his creation. She told him of what she had seen and the far things in the future which would greet her great passionate eyes. Once he was aware of Duchotte passing but the man did not see him as he knocked lightly on the Señora Martin's door and was admitted.

Finally Miguel returned to his apartment and in due course She came to him and talked of many things more and the great cats prowled outside on his patio and screamed their cries of brotherhood. The night was filled with light and passion and he scarcely cared for the small physical lusts that were expended somewhere upstairs in the dark apartment.

The next morning he had just completed mixing the mortar when the Gray Giant appeared and said:

"I told you to stop work."

"The Mermaid is not finished," Miguel said. He was scarcely aware of Señora Martin coming from the office and walking toward them.

"I do not want it completed," Duchotte said.

"What's the matter?" Señora Martin asked.

"I gave this heathen his notice," Duchotte said. "How do you make the fool understand?"

"You are the fool with your chicken dung and your ugly marble and brick," Miguel said hotly.

"By God, I do what I wish with my property," Duchotte said.

"Let him finish the mural," Señora Martin said.

"Do I have to contend with you too?" the Gray Giant snapped. "Just because he warmed your bed for a while is no reason to take up with him."

"She is a woman a pig like you should not have," Miguel said.

"Oh, shut up," Señora Martin said. "You are the fool when you don't know when to keep silent."

"Get out," Duchotte said. "Get your dirty rags out of my building by the end of the week."

"The Mermaid . . ." Miguel began and the Gray Giant hit him. The blow sent him sprawling across the rough concrete aggregate.

"Stand up and I'll knock you down again," the Gray Giant said.

"I will kill you for that," Miguel said.

"You're not in your own country now," Señora Martin said angrily. "I tried to help you and you ruined it. Now do what he says."

Miguel picked himself up and stood, rubbing his face where the Gray Giant had hit him. All at once both of them, the man and the woman, were featureless red masses burning with his rage. He turned without a word and went back to his quarters where he placed a cool cloth on his swollen jaw.

Just before noon he looked out the bedroom window and saw Duchotte and two of his workmen carrying two slabs of marble up into the courtyard. A short time later the workmen passed his window, carrying each a hod of bricks. It was not until after dinner that he suddenly realized what this meant. He rushed from his quarters and up the stairs to the courtyard. There was no one in sight but the first slab of marble had already been mortared over his mural. Above him the Mermaid's sea eyes looked down in horror at her approaching fate.

He clawed at the brick and the marble slab, but the concrete had already set sufficiently so that he could not move them. He ran back to his quarters and found the steel mallet he used in his work. He returned and began to smash at the brick and marble. The slab cracked and splintered and the brick powdered under his onslaught. In seconds he had broken away the offending masses, leaving only the stain of concrete on the bright tiles. Finally, exhausted, he threw the mallet on the ground and stumbled back to his quarters.

He sat and thought of the Gray Giant and the woman who, even in this small thing, had betrayed him. He found the last shreds of the cactus in its moist bag and the god-flesh was sweet on his lips. Then he sat, feeling the warm sun flow around him. The great cats came up from the valley, the first time they had dared to approach during the day and the room was filled with the musty scent of their pelts. They crouched silently as She came floating into the room, her eyes misty with the sea spray, and the dank smell of seaweed was in his nostrils.

When Duchotte burst into the room, his eyes wide with rage, Miguel ignored his shouting and smiled kindly at him. The man grabbed him and he casually brushed aside the great hand, knowing what was to come. The great cats roused themselves and moved forward, their voices piercing the gelatinous air of the room. Duchotte screamed once as they attacked and bore his crumpled form to the floor. He scarcely bled from the great lacerations of their claws.

For this and the many favors of the god-made flesh, Miguel knew he owed a special debt and now was the time to pay. Huitzilpotl and the Nameless Ones were whispering in his ear and telling him the way that would bring favor, talking silently of the special scent that was good to their nostrils. He left his quarters and walked up the stairs in a dream, the office was empty, but he heard her through the connecting door in her own apartment.

He entered the apartment and when she resisted him, he struck her, knocking her back across the couch. Then he took her, tearing her clothes aside. The ripping sound was like the taste of the god-food on his lips and in his excitement he hurt her still more.

"Miguel, Miguel," she moaned.

He said nothing and worked his fury upon her.

"Strong . . . beautiful . . ." she moaned. ". . . like this always . . ."

He lifted her and carried her to the stone in the corner of the room, bending her back as he spent his seed in her. She shuddered in the final explosion of his lust and did not notice what he did until the great pain exploded in her chest. If she cried out, he did not hear but he knew what to do. All the old ways were clear and her eyes filled with the wonder of her fortune. Before they glazed in death, he held out her still pulsing heart for her to look upon.

Then he wrapped the treasure in the Spanish shawl draped across the clay figure and walked into the sunlight. He could hear voices all about him and after a moment the sound of a woman screaming. He walked into the courtyard and looked up with love-filled eyes at his Mermaid. He found the mortar bucket and climbed the scaffold up and up, holding the treasure in his hand as footsteps sounded on the stairs far below. Once he looked down and saw blue-uniformed men gesturing in his direction but he was too intent upon this final task.

In the last moments he threw the shawl away and placed the bright red heart in the niche in her breast, the secret spot he had created long ago. He ignored the shouts of the blue men at the foot of the scaffold as he mortared the last bits of tile in place, admiring the richer red that infused the white mortar.

He turned then and looked out over the sun-dappled mountains as the blue men drew revolvers and fired at him. Pain laced his senses. He spread his arms in ecstasy.

"*¡Yo puedo volar!*" he cried once . . . "I can fly; I can fly," and leaped into the thick air. As he poised for an instant in the incredible beauty of his flight, he saw the ragged rods protruding far below from the unfinished basin.

They waited for him.

It is becoming surprisingly difficult for an editor to say anything original about Miriam Allen deFord. The numerous introductions to her astonishingly large output, in a vast variety of fields, have managed to touch on almost all of her talents: author, journalist, encyclopaedist, historian, critic, anthologist, penologist, to name something less than half.

One thing I doubt has been mentioned is that Miss deFord is one of the few women mystery writers who have been, in the larger sense at least, private investigators. At one time, Miss deFord was the first and only female insurance claims adjuster in America. It is rumored that her superior (an early male chauvinist) was uneasy about the situation and sought to discourage her with a succession of his most difficult and taxing cases. Anyone who knows Miriam will realize how diametrically wrong this approach would have been; probably he gave up at last, and Miriam resigned when the work *ceased* to provide an adequate challenge.

Her story is the account of an incident in the career of Max Spandau, self-esteemed successor to William ("Willie the Actor") Sutton, and of Pete Farrin, the worst choice of partners a man could make. Or . . . maybe the second worst.

Beggarman, Thief
MIRIAM ALLEN DE FORD

I'm back here in Big Stony again because Pete Farrin is a lunkhead. I guess I'm a lunkhead too; I'd celled with Pete, and I ought to've known that he'll take orders and follow directions but if you let him plan anything for himself he'll make a mess of it. Which he did.

But I had this perfectly foolproof scheme (or I thought it was foolproof), and Pete had this decent car his old lady had been nursing along while he was inside, and I needed a car and a crackerjack driver, which I knew he was. Besides, I was on parole and he was out free, three months before I hit the street, and he could do errands for me I didn't want connected with me. I would be taking enough risk accounting for time off from the service station job I was paroled to and conning my parole officer.

I suppose what I ought to've done was just give Pete his simple directions and not explain. But he began right away making objections and I had to calm him down. That's another thing; Pete's too excitable to make a good bank robber. Heck, he'd just finished doing a three-year stretch for fouling up a simple hold-up in a liquor store.

He believes everything he hears. Here he was, with nothing but a toy gun, but he'd got the guy scared paralyzed and cleaned out the cash register, and then the clerk looks past him and says, "O.K., officer, grab him." And what does Pete do? He turns right around to look, and the clerk comes out of his paralysis and gets an arm around his neck and pins him to the counter with one arm—Pete's not much on size or muscle—while he dials the phone with his other hand. Actually, he hasn't brains enough to be anything but a square.

When I looked him up after I got out—all very hush-hush, of course, because being on parole I wasn't allowed to associate with ex-cons—and asked him if he'd be interested in going into a caper with me for a quarter of the profits, he jumped at the chance. That's what put me off my guard; he kind of disarmed me. "Sure, Max," he said right away. "Whatever it is. I guess I'm not much good on my own, but I can trust you, and I'd be proud to work with you."

"All right," I told him. "I want you for two things. First I want you to go to one of those places that sell trusses and rubber stockings and all that, and rent a wheelchair."

"Rent it?" he says. "What for? I can break in just as easy and wheel one out—"

"Yeah, and get caught again, and ruin the whole thing. I'll give you the dough, and I want a receipt. Rent it with your real name and your real address so it'll be all on the up-and-up; tell them you've got an invalid brother or something coming to visit you, and you want it for while he's here."

That's where I made my first mistake; I gave him an idea, and Pete Farrin isn't safe with ideas.

So of course he wanted to know what I wanted the wheelchair for, and, mistake No. 2, I told him.

"Oh, you can't do that!" he says. "The first fuzz comes along will haul you in for panhandling."

Mistake No. 3. "Look, Pete," I answered him. "Don't you ever read the papers? You had three months' jump on me, but I knew more the day I came out than you know now. Haven't you heard about this big show-off they've got here now for chief of police, and his cute little campaign to prove the policeman is everybody's friend and wouldn't hurt a fly? Haven't you seen where he ordered the cops to go easy on 'minor borderline offenders' like beggars and drunks and jaywalkers, and Boy Scout old ladies across the street, and help tourists find out where they're going, and all like that? Haven't you noticed how often you're panhandled these days every time you walk around downtown? It won't last, of course, but while it's on I'm taking advantage of it."

Oh-oh. Pete's little mind began dreaming right away.

So then of course he asks the $64 question: How did I expect to get away with holding up a bank where everybody had been familiar with my face for a week or more.

That was just too much. I looked at him coldly, and said, "Have you forgotten the bald man with the limp?"

See, for four years here at Big Stony I'd been the lead or next to the lead in the Drama Group. We put on a show every year and guests came from outside and from the newspapers, and I want to tell you I was *good*. I'd had notices that singled me out and one of them called me 'a born actor who could go far on the professional stage.' Not me—acting's fun, but I've chosen my profession and I'm not changing it. But at that I guess I was pretty proud of all the praise I'd got—and that was a dumb question for him to ask, as if he'd never seen me act.

What had happened was that Pete and I were cellmates the time we put on *Men in an Iron Cage,* and of course he'd seen the first performance, just for our own boys. So the next evening he says to me, "Max, I can't figure out which one was the bald man with the limp. I didn't recognize him at all."

What did he think I did with the Drama Group—raise and lower the curtain?

"From the day I get that wheelchair you or anybody else won't 'recognize me at all,'" I told him. "White hair and white whiskers and greasepaint in the right places, including a scar down my cheek from the accident when my legs were amputated—I'm having to tell you now so you'll know who I am when you come to pick me up, after."

He stared at me in admiration with his stupid mouth open, and I gave him the final instructions.

"Pay no attention till the first rainy day. It's got to be raining in the late morning; the bank opens at ten and I'll wait till the first rush is over and there are only a few customers around. Then you cruise around the block, keep passing the bank, and when you see me in my wheelchair up against the window next to the door, that's your signal. Get that heap of yours parked in front fast, with the motor running, and when I come out and get into it, start going. No rush, no panic; there won't be time yet for the alarm to be sounded. We'll just drive quietly to your place. Your old lady will be away at work, so we'll be alone."

That was one reason I'd picked Pete—his wife away all day, in charge of a department store ladies' room, and no kids.

"I'll get out of the disguise there and you can get rid of the wig and clothes and stuff; drive out to the dump that night, or put them in garbage pails in different parts of the city. Nobody's seen us together since we were up at the pen, and nobody's going to connect us."

"And the loot?"

"I've got a safe place to stash that. We'll meet in a few days and I'll give you your divvy. Me, I'll go back to my job and lay low till the heat's over. I'll report in to the parole officer as per usual. The story will be, with him and at the service station, that I've been down with the flu and just got over it. I mean to keep on working and keep my nose clean for the two years I still have to do. Then I'll blow town, and from then on Max Spandau will have disappeared for good. Maybe, if this works out all right, I'll try the same caper a few other places. I'm not getting any younger, and some day I want to retire on my earnings. It all depends on how much I get from this operation."

"What about the wheelchair? You can't turn up at your rooming-house all of a sudden like that, can you?" He saw me frown, and added hastily, "Oh, sure, you won't even be looking like yourself. How'll you manage?"

What do they say—pride goeth before a fall? I guess I'd gone overboard congratulating myself on how smart I was and showing off even to a lunkhead like Pete.

"Don't worry," I said, and I could hear my own lofty tone. "I'll move out where I am as soon as you get the wheelchair for me, and rent a first-floor room as a poor crippled old guy, under another name. I've got it all figured out."

Pete still had another objection to make, or two of them. One was, where and how would he get the chair to me. The other was, what if he couldn't get space to park in front of the bank in the split second I had to have him there and ready? For the first, I told him all he had to do was to have the chair delivered to his house and I'd come after dark and take it away. With a tarpaulin over it, I could leave it in a corner of the service station, behind some junked cars the boss had bought cheap to cannibalize for parts. A lot of the time the boss was in the office and I was alone on the outside with no car driving in. When I moved out of my room I could collect it, after I'd changed into my disguise in the men's, and then go out looking for a room for a cripple. I'd come in that morning coughing and feeling rotten. I'd tell the boss I was afraid I was getting the flu but I'd stick it out as long as I could. I'd attend to my getaway my first chance after he went to lunch—there were only the two of us except on weekends—and after he got back I'd phone and tell him

I hated to leave the place alone but I'd got so much worse I had to beat it, that I was at the doctor's and he said I must go home and go to bed and stay there. Another call to the parole officer, and that would be that. Everything had to fit together like a jigsaw puzzle, but I knew I could handle it.

As for being able to park, that was Pete's part of the affair and what he'd be paid for. It was absolutely vital and it was up to him to take care of it. "Use your brains, Pete, that's what they're for. I know I can depend on you," I said, buttering him up.

Oh, brother! That's where I goofed. It looked simple to me; if I'd been in his place, I'd just have been in and out of the no-parking space over and over again, if necessary, so fast nobody would notice me. Pete was a super-driver, and I thought I could leave that much to him. Instead, the balloon-head got ideas.

Well, everything went like a computer intake, just the way I'd planned it. I got the wheelchair O.K., got everything fixed up with the boss and the parole officer, moved out and in, in a different neighborhood, and on the next Monday morning before nine o'clock I was sitting in my wheelchair against the front wall of the bank, a poor shriveled up old guy with a blanket covering where his legs used to be, and a battered felt hat upside down on my lap with a few pencils stuck in it.

This big "be kind to the public" racket was still going strong, as I knew it would be. Several times every day either a prowl car passed by or a harness bull on foot would walk past me, but whatever they wanted to do they had their orders and none of them bothered me or told me to move on. Once, believe it or not, one of the fuzz threw a quarter in my hat!

When I was a kid, I thought bank employees actually worked ten to three, banking hours. Maybe that's why I first got interested in banks as a source of supply. Of course I'd learned better by now. The clerks and tellers and all the rest had to be on the job by nine, just like any other white-collar squares. I wanted them to get used to seeing me there, and I wanted to get to know them all by their looks and make up my mind which of the tellers would scare the easiest. After a day or so, several of them began donating a dime or a quarter as they passed. Just one guy had the nerve to extract a pencil, and I made a note to remember him and avoid him when the big moment came.

The person I took most pains with was the guard. He was easy. He must have had an old dad or somebody he was fond of. He started smiling at me and handed me something every morning, and I smiled back. We got quite chummy—"Good morning," "Good night," and "How's it going?" and all. I stuck it out till the last one was out of the bank, by 5:30 or so, and then wheeled myself home before the night guard and the cleaning women came on duty.

I watched the weather reports as if I was going to take a civil service examination. Out here we have a dry season and a rainy season, and the rainy season had begun, but that doesn't mean, naturally, that it rains every day. We were having a spell of nice weather, but I was all prepared for news of a storm on the way.

It didn't rain for one solid week. I had to call my boss and the parole officer to say I was better but couldn't get back for a while yet. All the weekend I had to stay holed up in my new room. But by Sunday it was clouding over, and when I got down to the bank around 8:45 Monday morning I knew I was all set to go.

Everything now depended on Pete. But he'd been over two or three times to my room, and he was all agog and wasn't going to slip up. I knew he was watching the weather too, and that any day, like this, when rain was on the way he'd be driving to X-marks-the-spot.

I waited till the rain really got good and hard, and I was wet and shivering. Then, timid and appealing like, I wheeled myself right through the automated door (if they'd had one of those old-fashioned revolving doors I'd have picked myself another bank from the beginning) and slowly crawled up to the guard, wheeling the chair with my arms, my sleeves dripping, and asked him, "Would you mind if I sit in a corner here out of the way till the rain lets up a little?"

He glanced around cautiously—maybe he was looking for the tough officer or whoever he was who had snitched a pencil from me—and then he said, "O.K., Dad, I don't see why not. Just keep out from under the customers' feet."

I planted myself where I had a good view inside and outside. Sure enough, in a few minutes here comes Pete in his car. He hesitated a second as he passed, but I'd been careful to stay where he couldn't see me, so he went on driving down the block. The streets were all one-way and he could make it indefinitely in the traffic till I gave him the signal. There were too many people milling around at the moment, and there was too long a line at the window of the teller I'd picked for my big surprise.

It was about eleven—everybody's coffee break over and only two or three customers at the windows and nobody at all at the window I'd chosen—when I got ready to act. As soon as I saw Pete approaching again, I wheeled over to the front window. He saw me and stopped and I wheeled myself rapidly into the main part of the bank, on the checking tellers' side. The guard was standing at one of the counters down the middle, looking away toward the savings side, which was another thing I'd been waiting for.

So fast it made even me dizzy, I dashed to the window I'd chosen, reached under the blanket for the bag and my gun, and jumped out of the chair on two very good legs. (Boy, the way I'd had to exercise them every night, so they wouldn't get flabby from sitting in that thing all day!)

"Quick," I said, real low, to the scary teller. "Let the alarm alone and hand out everything fast, from tens up, and you won't get hurt."

That was the moment, of course, when the guard should have realized what was happening and winged me. It's the moment in every hold-up when you're as near death as you'll ever get till it arrives. But these bank guards for the most part are older men, usually ex-fuzz and sometimes even retired fuzz. I was pretty sure by this time that this was one whose mind didn't work too fast. The guy behind the window was the color of a yellow candle and his hands were shaking, but he was obeying orders. He shoveled the notes out and into my bag, and nobody else seemed to cotton to a thing. I know the big boys used to break in with three or four others and have helpers holding everybody at bay while they went around and cleaned up one teller's window after another. But I figure I get almost as much from one window, and keep it, as if I had to cut up ten times as much half a dozen ways. Anyway, that's old stuff, from the mob days; hardly anybody handles it like that any more.

The whole thing took less time than it's taken to tell about it. Three minutes from when I'd signaled Pete at the window I was on my way out, running with a comfortably heavy bag, leaving the wheelchair behind me, and if I ever did any praying I'd have been praying that Pete would be in front with the engine running and the door open.

And he was. In half a minute more I was in, I'd slammed the door, and he began to drive away slowly as I'd told him to do.

And before we'd gone half a block a prowl car came behind us and crowded us to the curb.

I didn't get a chance to talk to Pete till we were both in jail waiting for trial, neither of us with enough money to meet the bail they'd put on us. He kept evading me but finally I cornered him.

"Well," I said, "what happened?"

He looked down at the floor of the recreation area and gulped. He was ashamed to meet my eye.

"Max," he brought out at last, "I did just what you told me. I was there, wasn't I? And the car was ready for you to hop right into."

"Sure," I answered, kind of sarcastic. "And that prowl car must have been stopped right behind us, or we'd have got off safely."

I wasn't as sore then as I am right now, for it did seem just bad luck. But then Pete, the great brain, spilled his bright little idea.

"You know yourself," he said, "you briefed me on all this cops-be-mothers'-helpers stunt, didn't you?"

"So what?"

"So when I saw you at the window I drove up and stopped the car. And right away this prowl car comes along and one of the fuzz leans out and says, 'Sorry, but no parking there.' So I thought fast"—*he* thought!—"and I said right back, 'But officer, I'm calling for an old gentleman in a wheelchair, a cripple. I have to carry him in and then tie the chair on the hood. It won't take a minute, and he'll be right out.'

"So the other fuzz, the driver, says, 'Well, O.K., if you make it snappy.' I thought they'd drive off then, but I guess they were remembering their orders and decided to stick around to see if I needed help with the poor cripple.

"And just that second, here you came, running, with the bag, so I guess it looked funny to them and they took after us.

"I'm sorry, Max," he wailed miserably, "I guess I just forgot you wouldn't be in the wheelchair any more."

He forgot.

I gave him one look and turned my back. And that's the last conversation I've had with Pete Farrin. You can bet we're not cellmates this time.

I've got one consolation, though. The poor idiot doesn't understand yet that even if he hadn't pulled that dumb trick and I'd got away safe as I should have done, *he'd* have been caught before he'd even had time to wonder how soon I was going to pay him a quarter of my take.

I left that wheelchair spang in the middle of the bank, didn't I? And how long would it have taken them to find out where it came from, and who had rented it?

Sure, even if he didn't squeal on me they'd know we'd been pals up here, and even a mush-headed detective would have done some investigating and decided things pointed very much my way. But I'd worked it out on purpose to provide for my own protection.

By the time they got around to me I'd have been long gone. And I'm a born actor, and I could disguise myself so that Sherlock Holmes or J. Edgar Hoover themselves would never have spotted me.

Well, the Drama Group's still functioning. They're tickled to death to get me back—for ten whole years this time.

And after all, it's what they call an occupational risk, in any profession.

Occasionally, a story may be lost to its audience through being published in the wrong place. This story by William F. Nolan was originally printed, with a suitably lurid title and illustration, in a magazine devoted to "horror" fiction. Since the horror implicit in the story is not exactly of the basic-grue variety, we take pleasure in reintroducing it here, especially recommending the fine manipulation of the reader accomplished by the use of viewpoint.

William F. Nolan's accomplishments run from co-authoring an excellent science-fiction work on population control, *Logan's Run*, to compiling the award-winning *Dashiell Hammett: A Casebook*. He has even combined the two *genre* in his spoof of the Private Eye in the Future: *Space for Hire*.

Down the Long Night
WILLIAM F. NOLAN

The ocean fog closed in, suddenly, like a big gray fist, and Alan Cole stopped remembering. Swearing under his breath, he jabbed the wiper button on the Lincoln's dash, and brought the big car down from fifty to thirty-five. Still dangerous. You couldn't see more than a few yards ahead in this soup. But he said the hell with it and kept the Lincoln at thirty-five because he wanted this mess over in a hurry, because he wanted to hold Jessica in his arms again before the night was done.

Above the damp Santa Monica pavements, looped tubes of neon glowed coldly, like colored seaweed; but there were no other cars. Cole shot through a blinking amber eye.

Actually, he thought, I should have turned him down flat. I should have said, Look, Paul, last week you ripped it. Period. So I don't give a good god damn *what* kind of trouble you're in.

But then he heard Paul Bowers' anxious voice again, hard and metallic: "*I've got to see you, Alan.*" And he knew that, despite everything—even the way the guy had been acting since Jess had given him the shoulder—he did care. Why?

Nearing Ocean Pier, he thought about the telephone call, attempted to form an attitude. What would he say? For Godsake, how do you talk to a man you've called a loser and a phony and a coddled neurotic?

It had come just after lunch. Cecile couldn't say why she'd put it through against his instructions, except to remark that it sounded important. Of course it had to be Paul. After that screwball telegram from San Francisco, which didn't even start to make sense, Alan had been expecting the call. A big play to get in as a 'friend of the family', no doubt. A well thought out pitch on how sorry he was that he'd blown his stack and, needless to say, he wished them both the best of luck, and would they please forgive him—maybe even invite him to the wedding?

Except it didn't turn out that way . . .

Cole punched loose a cigarette, lit it, and went over the conversation for the umpteenth time, searching for clues.

"*I've got to see you, Alan.*"

"*No go. They're shooting this scene tomorrow, and I can't—*"

"*Alan, listen—I'm in trouble. I need your help.*"

"*Like hell. You don't need anybody's help—unquote.*"

"*Wait—Look, I know I said a lot of stupid things last week. But if our friendship ever meant anything to you, for the love of God listen!*"

"*Paul, I said I'm busy. I meant it. Let me give you a ring tomorrow.*"

"*Tomorrow is too late.*" The pleading voice had seemed to crawl from the receiver. A pause. Then: "*The police are after me.*"

"*You're kidding.*"

"*I swear it! Meet me at the pier when you get off work. Crazyville, the funhouse—you know. And don't laugh. It's the only safe place. I'll be waiting for you, Alan. Don't fail me. It may mean my life . . .*"

And then the sharp click as Paul had hung up. Damn him, and damn the day they ever met!

Still, Cole thought, unaware that the Lincoln was wavering on the wrong side of the double white lines, still—it was through Paul that he'd met Jessica. They were engaged then. At least, that's what Paul thought; the poor guy couldn't see how bad he was for the girl. She had been impressed with him, at first. Then, like everyone else, she became disenchanted. And, like everyone else, she had a hell of a time pulling loose.

Was it *my* fault, Cole demanded of himself, that the two of us hit it off so well? I didn't take Jess away from Paul. He'd lost her a long time ago . . .

He spotted a parking place and nosed the car in, cut the engine, sat a moment, quietly, then opened the door.

Chill air went into his throat; it tasted of brine and heavy salt and fathoms. As he locked the automobile, turned and started to walk down the deserted street, Cole remembered how he had always hated this cold, which had nothing of winter in it; and how Bowers had always loved it. As usual, they disagreed. Over the years their likes and dislikes had seldom coincided. Bowers the social lion, the studied Bohemian—to all outward appearances sophisticated and intellectual; and Cole the recluse, the quiet one, the guy over there in the corner. How, Alan wondered, could two such people ever have formed a strong friendship? And was it really that?

Up ahead, the pier stretched, fog-draped and empty. Only the frozen spokes of the ferris wheel and the rotting wooden lacework of the Hi-Boy rose above the pressing blanket of gray.

Alan moved down Marine Street toward the pier, watching his image ripple and flow past streaked shop windows.

What was it with Paul, anyway? What the devil had he done? Robbed someone—no, that was hard to take, not Bowers' long suit. Or—

He passed a window filled with photographs of wild-eyed matted men in silk trunks. Lord Perkins; The Boston Bull; The Strangler.

—murder?

No.

Another window promised salvation to the penitent, damnation to the wicked.

Hotels, shops, missions—all empty and silent. As they had been a million winters ago, when he and Bowers and Jess had walked this street the last time.

Where are the people? he had wondered then. He wondered it now.

Maybe there aren't any people. You never see them moving behind glass. Maybe—

Alan shook his head. Ease off. You're just nervous. Paul's in trouble of some kind, so you're nervous. This place is nothing more than an amusement park, shut down, closed for the season; and that's all. So knock it off, Cole. You're a big boy now.

Yet, Alan felt a slow fear building in him—an uneasiness. With every step, years were peeling away, stripping off in layers. A few moments ago he was Alan Cole, thirty years old, a moderately successful screen writer and not anxious to be anything else. Now . . .

Marine Street flowed into the wide concrete length of Promenade. Alan hurried across, listening to the thin cries of circling gulls and to the lonely night beach.

Taking a final drag on his cigarette, he ground it underheel and turned into the amusement park.

Again the sense of something amiss. Partly Paul and also, this place. As if only a moment before, every stand had been open, every ride spinning and whirling and rolling in colored movements, the walk itself alive with people. And as if magic fingers had been snapped, causing all the people and the movement to vanish instantly.

Passing the roller coaster, Alan could almost hear the chant of the bored, slick-haired ticket seller:

"The Hi-Boy! The Hi-Boy! Don't miss it, folks! It's safe! It's exciting! The Thrill of a Life-Time!"

He glanced at the sheeted train of wooden cars, waiting in coiled silence on their tracks, and hurried past.

His stomach felt light. Dizziness had returned with memories. ("Jess, I'd like you to meet an old buddy of mine, Alan Cole. Alan, this is my gal, Jessica Randall. Isn't she a doll?") He quickened his step past the closed concessions, endless rows of shabby canvas curtains; past the rifle range and the Whirlagig and the Caterpillar; past the arcade where you can watch a thirty year old strip-show and then leave, wondering how the dames look today.

A hundred yards ahead, on the tip of the pier, he could see the fog-buried angles of Crazyville.

Paul would be waiting there. And it would all be over soon.

He'd see to that, by God.

The ticket booth was a gigantic smiling head. Within its mouth between the plaster teeth, a sign read: CLOSED.

Alan paused at the wicket gate and glanced back along the walkway. It was empty.

He vaulted the gate and peered across the yard. A tiny, twisting path marked LOONEY STREET horseshoed around mad wooden building fronts.

Gravity seemed missing here; it was a force that belonged entirely to the outside world. The houses convoluted above the cobbled walk, gables and roofs and walls leaning at impossible angles, one upon the other.

Alan cupped his hands about his mouth. Softly, he called: "Paul."

No answer.

He swore. He hadn't changed; not a bit. This idiot place was supposed to make you dizzy, so—he was dizzy.

And where the hell was Paul?

He moved toward the bat-wing doors which opened to the black maze of damp tunnels. Beyond this point lay a man-made night so intense and so impenetrable that, once inside, you could no longer imagine day.

"Paul?"

He hesitated, glanced up. A ragged, toothless crone sagged drunkenly from a second-story window. Her throat had been carefully sawcut; her eyes protruded in dumb disbelief.

Bloodied faces peeped from every window, each with a name and a history. Paul had once claimed that they were his only friends, these plaster nightmares, the only ones who truly understood him.

Standing in the silent yard, Alan felt the familiar horror of the Funhouse engulfing him again. The death-figures seemed to writhe just beyond the perimeter of his vision: he could almost *hear* their frozen cries.

He drew a deep breath, pushed open the doors, and hesitated there, divided squarely between the interior shadows and the solid reality of the outside.

"Paul—you in here?"

Like a huge sounding-box, the wooden tunnels bounced the words along, echoing, finally lost.

Then: "Alan?"

"Yeah!" He wiped perspiration from his palms. "Come on out."

A pause. "I can't." The voice was faint.

"What do you mean, you can't?"

"Too dangerous. I might be seen."

"There's nobody around for miles."

"I—can't afford to take the chance."

"All right, all right. God! Where are you?"

"Just follow the tunnel. First room."

"All right, but—this better be *good*."

Alan stepped into the long night of the tunnels; into a colored blackness that danced before his eyes in a million tiny specks of light. The walls, damp and slippery beneath his groping hands, smelled of the sea; the odor of soaked and rotting wood seeped up from the floor. Far below hidden waters sloshed against tired pilings.

The walls began to narrow as he moved forward. The ceiling lowered gradually. He was forced to crouch, turn sideways.

The walls ended.

Alan extended cautious hands, encountered nothingness.

"Okay, so I'm out of the first tunnel. What now?"

"You're fine." The voice was much closer. "Keep coming."

"I can't see a damn thing."

Alan remembered his lighter, got it out, thumbed the wheel. It sparked feebly, failed to ignite. Another spin. A tiny guttering flame this time.

He shielded it with his left hand and peered ahead. A cleated platform led upward. He slid his feet over the cleats and reached a wide opening.

"In here, Alan."

The light flickered. "Well, turn on a flashlight or something, will you! I'm going to fall flat on my ass."

Of course, he realized, Paul must know this place as a blind man knows his own bedroom. Always running out here to "think." Or to bang quail. Or—what?

Alan advanced carefully, tapping. A heavy object brushed his shoulder; he hissed, leaping back. The lighter clattered to the plank flooring and winked out.

Total darkness.

"Paul?"

"Over here."

"Over *where?* What am I, a goddamn cat or something?" There was a scrabbling, a fast padding, "Look, buddy, this routine is getting old at a rapid clip. In fact, the hell with the whole thing. I'm getting out of here."

He patted his handkerchief pocket, removed a matchfolder. He struck one.

The object that had brushed against him was, he saw, a body—swinging from a thick rope.

No—not a body. By adjusting his eyes to the feeble glow, Alan saw that it was a scarecrow. One of many. The room seemed filled with hanging straw corpses, all revolving in submarine slowness on their corded lengths of hemp. Scarecrows . . . papier mache trees . . . Now he remembered the room. Horse Thief Hall, or something like that.

The flame bit into his finger.

Blackness.

He lit another match, dropped it, tore the last one out savagely. "Okay, kid, you wanted to talk—here I am."

Silence.

He swung the match in a slow arc above his head, knowing, suddenly, that it was useless, knowing that Paul Bowers' entire phone conversation had been another fake. The sincerity and the pleading and the desperation: all fake. Part of a final, elaborate practical joke. Paul didn't need help; what he needed was a long overdue kick in the teeth!

"Fun's over, Cole catches on!" he called.

Silence.

The third match burned out. Alan turned to retrace his steps, thinking about Jessica's probable reaction to a stunt like this. Maybe he oughtn't to tell her. The less said about Paul in her presence, the better.

It takes a certain talent, he thought bitterly; a certain definite talent to be a perpetual fall-guy. Drop the hook, I'll bite!

He'd almost reached the doorway when four naked green bulbs, one in each corner of the room, bloomed into silent life.

Alan blinked, the pale glow burning into his eyes. He scrubbed at them, realizing, vaguely, that Paul had found the central control box and activated a switch.

The swinging scarecrows came into focus. Alan's fist knotted. His head jerked about the room. "Listen!" he shouted, "I'm going to walk back out of here, Paul. Don't try anything cute. Because if you do I swear I'll break your damn neck. Is that clear?"

He started for the opening. Another scarecrow bumped against his shoulder. He wheeled, buried his fingers in the mouldered straw, and pulled, furiously. The figure tore loose at the neck, collapsed to the floor with a wet, pulpy sound.

Soft laughter from the tunnels.

He was about to push his way through the hanging figures when he paused.

Everything inside him paused.

Sensation became thought: *Scarecrows are made of straw.* And the object that had just touched him was *solid!*

Alan turned, and jammed a fist against his mouth.

Hanging there, swaying amid the rotting scarecrows, was Jessica Randall.

For a long moment, Alan could not move. His body was incapable of movement; every muscle locked tight.

His mind tried to reject what his eyes saw.

She was naked. And cold. Her flesh, once warm and vibrant, carried now an icy chill; and her eyes, though unseeing, were open.

Her sheer silk stockings had been knotted about her throat and about a ceiling beam, and supported her slight weight easily.

"Jess!"

Alan put a trembling hand to the girl's breast, and then he knew she was dead.

Jess was dead. And Paul had killed her. He knew that, too. Because she had fallen in love with someone else. Paul had done this, just as he'd promised in that crazy speech he'd delivered to them. They hadn't believed him, or taken him seriously, because Paul Bowers had always been a lot of talk, a thin red-faced clown full of empty promises and emptier threats. And they'd been wrong.

Alan saw Jess's clothes, her red blouse and white skirt, her undergarments, her black leather ballet-shoes—all folded and placed neatly in a corner on the floor. And he knew a hate and a fear, then, that he had never dreamed of.

Run! he thought. Try to stay calm and get out of this place. He wants you to panic. Don't panic. Just get out, quickly—then wait and get him.

He pulled a shutter in his mind that closed off the reality of Jess and what had happened to her. Out, the same way, he thought; but it wasn't so easy. He'd turned so many times that he had lost all sense of direction. Three separate doorways opened on the room of scarecrows and only one of them led back to the first tunnel: the others were phony. And he couldn't be sure which was which.

He'd taken a single step forward, aware now that the laughter was mechanical, not human, issuing from the cracked lips of a plaster fat man, when the ceiling lights blacked out again. Paul was still at the switch and that meant he had little time. Hurriedly, he knelt on the plank flooring and groped for the fallen lighter. Without luck.

Okay, so you move in the dark—but by God you move!

He touched one wall of the room. He moved along, tapping the rough wood: he would have to try one of the doorways and hope it was the right one.

He thought of Bowers, at home in the darkness, gliding through the looping maze of passageways like a swift fish in green waters, perfectly at ease, perfectly in command.

The funhouse was Paul's world.

Abruptly the wall ended, but not in emptiness. He'd fumbled himself into a corner. A corner—Without knowing exactly why, he reached up and touched a light bulb. It was still warm. He unscrewed it in quick short motions and dropped it into his pocket. Then he followed the next wall and reached one of the doors.

Careful to walk slowly, he entered the tunnel. And walked head-on into a pocket. Wood on all three sides.

Alan groaned softly, his throat went dry. He tried to swallow and couldn't.

All right, you missed. Now turn around and go back to the next one. Move, damn you, move!

He re-entered the still black room and groped numbly along to the second doorway. At least this one would lead somewhere. Alan stepped out onto the cleated platform.

This must be it! It seemed to possess the same dank odor, the same narrow twistings ...

He pressed forward.

A buzzing, a whirr of turning machinery, and the blackness blazed into light. Far off, the laughter again. Within a niche in the wall directly to Alan's right, a huge gorilla raised its fists, swiveled its savage head back and forth, snarling.

"You son of a bitch, Bowers! I'll kill you."

The apparition faded behind him. He was running now, knowing that this tunnel led deeper into the funhouse. Toward Paul's voice?

Six explosions, deafening, somewhere in the dark. Gunshots. Paul had a gun. But why waste bullets?

To let you know he's armed. To let you know he's waiting ...

Alan ran on, constantly aware that in order to get Bowers, he would have to get into the open, into *his* world. He stumbled, barking his knuckles on trick partitions, pushed himself forward, his face sweatsoaked, legs weak and trembling.

A dragon sprang into colored life. It lay on painted rocks, a fat reptilean creature, its green-scaled head nodding, forked tongues licking in and out.

Sudden shrill gusts of wind hissed up from the floor.

And the infernal laughter, mocking him, following him wherever he went—

He ran on, crouching, sometimes on hands and knees, blundering forward, knowing, even as he ran, that he was close to death. A bullet or a knife would meet him in the darkness; and he wouldn't have a chance.

Then he saw light—faint, but only moments away. Only a few more steps!

The floor dropped away beneath him. Alan felt himself plunging downward; he thrashed his arms, clutched at shadows and blackness.

The trap-door closed.

The room was full of people. Frightened, angry, staring people, all seated at the bottom of a long slide.

A memory clicked into place for Alan Cole. The Mirror Room— where you spend an hour, alone, trying to find your way out.

He licked his dry lips and wiped the perspiration from his hands.

He listened. Footsteps.

You're unarmed. Move!

Jerkily, he thrust himself into the corridors of glass. He saw his image reflected in a thousand bright distortions as he slammed through the maze, bumping, cursing, moving, moving.

He reached another glass tunnel. A tall, freckled, crewcut man faced him.

Himself. He caught his breath. Everywhere, mirrors. A small skylight above for ventilation. But no exit that he knew of.

"Alan?"

He narrowed his eyes, located the voice, found that he was staring down a dark corridor that could not have existed.

A figure stood there, motionless. Something glinted in the figure's hand.

"Writers should never run," the voice from the darkness said. "It makes their faces turn red. Take a good look at yourself in one of these mirrors, Alan. You've no idea how ridiculous you look!"

"You lousy bastard!"

Alan's perspective had melted; now, suddenly, it reformed. Until this moment he had not been entirely able to connect the man who had murdered Jess with an ineffectual guy he'd bummed around with. Sure, Paul Bowers had been a whiner and a loser and a neurotic; but, God, not a killer. Killers were what he wrote cheap movies about. Yet—

Alan recalled a book he'd once read for research. A study of criminology. It postulated that every human being on Earth was a potential murderer, needing only the right set of circumstances, the right personal motivation, to turn killer. A world full of dynamite sticks, waiting to be sparked. His engagement to Jess had sparked it for Paul, had set the fuse burning. And it had been burning for a week.

Kid-gloves, boy. He's nuts now. You read books on psychology, okay, be psychological. Or, brother, you're dead, too.

"Paul, listen—can't we talk or something?"

The figure did not move. "Clear the air, you mean? Get it all tied up in a neat package?" A small chuckle, like a tapped siphon.

Alan recognized the words, the same words he had used when he gave Paul the straight goods that night. "I didn't mean everything I said. Honest. Is that it?"

"Part of it, Alan."

The blackness stirred. A shape took slow form.

Paul Bowers stepped out of the tunnel, smiling. He was, as always, impeccably dressed. His charcoal gray suit tailored to make him look heavier than his 175 pounds; his shoetips gleaming; his pale, bony face clean-shaven and smelling of lotions. Across his high forehead, the fine blond hair was neatly, perfectly combed. "By the way," he said, "don't try anything dramatic. You're much too clumsy."

He looked white and businesslike and totally unlike a killer, except for his hands. They were powerful and bright red, ending in thick fingers; the hands of a longshoreman or a mechanic—or a strangler. In one of them, held firmly, was a twelve-inch blue-steel hunting knife.

Alan looked at it.

"Ugly monster," Bowers said. "But a hunting knife seemed appropriate for the occasion. Borrowed this one from you quite a while ago, if you'll remember. And I thought, 'Now *there*, by God, would be a touch!' And so it is. At least give me that."

Alan's blood grew hot. "Why did you kill Jess?" he blurted, before he could stop the words.

"The old story, pal. You know: 'If I can't have her, then by the Holies, no one—' Etc. Besides, I wanted to see if I had the nerve. Sort of practice, you might say. For you."

"Paul, listen."

"Of course."

"What do you want me to do? Do you want me to beg for my life, is that it?"

"That would be kind of fun, I must admit. But to tell you the honest to God truth, I'm getting a little tired of the game." Bowers stepped closer, smiling. His eyes were misted over. And the laughter still echoed down the halls.

"You're sick. You know that, I suppose."

"Oh, yes. Mad as a March hare." It was the Party Paul, the bored intellectual who built his words and rolled them out on oiled casters. "I would describe my illness as Acute Reaction to Prolonged Injustice. The prognosis is fair, however; fortunately, I know the cure. Jess was part. You, Brother Rat, will complete the treatment."

Alan's throat moved convulsively. In all his films, a man with a knife was a pushover. You kicked it out of his hand, or rushed him before he could use his arm, or bluffed him. But that was the movies. In real life, it worked out differently. A man with a knife was a man with a formidable weapon. If he knew how to use it—and Paul knew —you might as well be in front of a .45 or a cannon.

"Paul, you'll be caught. The police will investigate sure as hell, find we were all friends and track you down wherever you go."

"You really think so?" Bowers lowered the blade, as if bemused by the thought, and Alan stepped forward; but then the knife was up again, and Bowers was laughing. "Alan, you don't give me any credit. You never did, of course." His voice rose in pitch. The smile had become fixed and deadly. "Exactly how long did you think you could go on kicking me before I kicked back, anyway?"

An auto horn bleated out beyond the pier. A strange sound, part of a different world.

Alan remembered the skylight, was very careful not to look up. Was it possible that he could reach it? No. Too high, too small . . .

"I gave you friendship, Alan, and what did I get in return? Betrayal. Oh, I didn't expect you to break your neck trying to give me a little help, but I thought at least you'd appreciate what I'd done enough to stand by me. Not say, 'Thanks, Paul'—no, not that—but maybe show a little loyalty." He was trembling. The hunting knife jumped in short darting flashes in his hand. "Always take, take, take, and never give. Never a helping hand. No; it's good-bye, Paulie, I'm a big man now. Lots of money. Lots of fame. Too busy to help a two-bit loser like Paul Bowers—after I pushed you to the top with my bare hands. Do you deny it?"

"I—"

"Do you deny that it was I who got you in at the studio, introduced you to Kay, almost forced him to hire you? And who was it that stayed up till four every morning helping you to make that lousy script acceptable?"

"I don't argue that you helped me, Paul. I'm grateful for it."

"Grateful!" The thin man drew his lips back. He breathed heavily. "I guess that's what accounts for your aceing me out, playing along with the rumors about, 'Poor old Bowers, all washed up!' And I guess it was the final expression of your gratitude to turn Jess against me?"

"That's a lie, Paul. I—damn it, Jess just fell in love with me. I couldn't help that."

Bowers' jaw muscles twitched. "I believed that for a while, Alan. Felt that maybe I really *was* the oddball you said I was. But then I started checking around. And I found out a few things. For instance, who it was that talked Kahn into giving me the sack. And who it was that got me blackballed right afterwards." He stepped forward. "I know you pretty well, Alan, enough to know you probably still think of yourself as a noble guy in an embarrassing situation. Those shutters in your mind. They won't let you remember the filthy things you've done."

"It's not true."

"The convenient little shutters won't let you face the fact that you've been scared of me ever since we met. Scared spitless. You know I'd got you in solid at Galactic, so your ego forced you to get rid of me. And it was easy, because I trusted you. I trusted you with Jess, too. All the time you were filling her mind with dirty lies about me, *I trusted you!* And I didn't wake up for a long time. When I did, it was too late. But not too late for me to spoil your little play—"

Bowers raised the knife.

At that instant, Alan grabbed the light-bulb in his pocket and hurled it to the floor with all his strength.

The explosion whipped Bowers' head around. In that split second, Alan leapt for the skylight. His fingers closed over the heavy beam; held. Hidden sacs seemed to burst and flood strength through him. A single surge pulled his body up and over the edge. He could feel hands clutching at his legs, slipping, gathering the cloth of his trousers. He kicked, viciously, at the hands, and swung his ankles against the wood. Bowers' hold loosened. He kicked again. The weight fell away.

Alan drew his legs up swiftly, pivoted, and stood up on the slate roof.

Cold bit into his skin; the fog, a wash of wet mist, billowed and pressed in upon his eyes. He balanced there on the slippery roof a brief moment, breathing.

Take it easy, he thought. Try to run and you'll end up cartwheeling off the edge headfirst.

The roof was an iced pond, impossible to run across. Alan squinted. If he could only see! How far down was the pavement, anyway? Where was the edge? He was on a slat island, surrounded by moving gray tides.

And now Paul Bowers' hands were closing over the beam.

Alan crouched above the opening, braced himself and lashed out with his foot. The blow tipped Paul back, forced one hand off. Alan lifted his right foot, prepared to send it heel-down on the strained white fingers.

Something grabbed his ankle, jerked.

He caught a glimpse of Paul's face, grinning, blazing red, as though every blood vessel had ruptured and tendriled out.

Then Alan fell.

With a grunt, Bowers heaved through the skylight, landed nimbly, and took the knife from its belt position.

Alan struggled up, his eyes on the long blue sweep of steel in Paul's hand.

"Shutters open, Alan? Or do you still think you're a hero?"

Now!

The blow caught the side of Paul's head, sent him reeling back. Alan felt his muscles go cold: bright color fireworked in his mind. He struck out again, blindly, throwing his entire weight into the blow. Soft inner nose cartilege crunched beneath his hand.

He had not fought for a long time, but now hate activated him, put strength into his arms, goaded him. But even as he swung, he knew that he could never win out against Paul and the knife. Perhaps the blade had already entered his body—they say you don't feel a knife thrust right at first—and his life was, even now, ebbing away.

"Go ahead, Alan, fight! You're doing fine!"

He aimed his fist, drove for that grinning red face. Bone and flesh yielded. But the fury of the lunge pulled him forward. He stumbled, slid, his head striking a ledge of plaster at the roof's edge.

More fireworks. He tried desperately to shake them away. He tried to shake away Paul's burning words, the image of Jess . . . *Was it true?*

Paul Bowers glided toward him, smiling, calm, the knife poised high.

All over now. Done. Finished. He closed his eyes. *In a second now. Another second.* He waited, his breath in a bottle and the bottle sealed. He could smell the honed steel and the rough leather handle; he could taste the metal in his throat.

A strange sound, then. Like the last drops of water draining from a sink—a short bubbling indrawn scream.

Alan opened his eyes.

Paul had slumped to his knees, teetering, making thin dry noises and staring, staring.

Then he toppled, spilled sideway to the roof, and lay there. His fingers spasmed on the wet slats like the overturned legs of two giant spiders.

Then he was quiet.

In his chest was imbedded the long steel of the hunting knife.

Alan rose, shakily. The roof listed, heaved, settled. A sharp wind from the ocean had cleared some of the fog. Without trying to understand, he located the roof edge again and the pavement below. Less than ten feet.

He jumped. The ground was made of needles and electricity. It buckled his knees. He fell against the rusting ribs of an ancient trolley, and leaned there, trying to swallow.

He began to walk. He listened to the sound of the sea washing in on the beach, and the gulls cloaked high in night, and his footsteps.

Is it true? That was all he could think. He knew that Jess was dead and that Paul was dead and this was no nightmare, no bad dream, but something real; yet, he could only think: Is it true? Did I do those things to Paul, actually, turn Jess against him, actually—

The sky revolved: Alan felt that it had suddenly shaken loose. The peppermint striped shroud covering the Caterpillar began to shimmer and twist darkly; the towering wooden immensity of the Hi-Boy swayed and separated into bright pieces and showered soundlessly down upon him.

He staggered on, out of the amusement park, down a street, to an all-night cafe.

He lifted the receiver off its hook. "Give me the police," he said, in a soft, tired voice.

It was 10 A.M. when they knocked on the door. He'd fallen into a pit of black exhaustion, not bothering to wash or change clothes and getting out of the pit was difficult. When he awoke, he didn't question that the night had been real: his hand ached and his head throbbed and he still felt the numbness.

"Just a minute." His mouth was sour. He could barely remember talking to the police, waiting while they checked his story, staggering out of the squad car.

Alan Cole opened the door. A large man in a brown double-breasted suit stood there. He was flanked by two cops in uniform.

"Yes, what is it?"

The large man stepped inside the room. "A good yarn you told us, Cole," he said. "Mighty good yarn. We swallowed it."

Alan shook his head. This was the man he'd spoken to last night. Captain Boylen, Homicide. But now he looked different.

"What do you mean?"

"Cole," the man said, "you can make it easy, or you can make it tough. It doesn't matter much."

"I—" Alan sat down on the bed; his senses began to swim. "I don't know what you're talking about."

"Then I'll tell you," the man said. "Your story washes out. Point one: We found six bullet holes and a 32.20 at the funhouse. Pistol registered under Paul Bowers' name. We examined the knife. It's yours—"

"I know. I admitted that, didn't I?"

"Then I suppose you know that rough leather won't take prints."

"So what?"

The policeman removed a cigar, skinned off its cellophane wrapping, lit it. "Guy was pretty well armed, wouldn't you say? Gun *and* a knife."

Alan sat quietly, trying to understand.

"Point two," Boylen went on. "We got a report from the medical examiner. It's his opinion Bowers didn't commit suicide. Man decides to kill himself with a knife, Cole, he stabs within an area of a couple inches, like this—" The policeman made stabbing motions against his chest. "There were *four* wounds in Bowers. One here, in the ribs; and here—and here—and finally the one that got him. All spread out. Suicides don't do that, Mister. Care to say anything?"

Alan remembered Paul's telling him of the criminal medicine course he'd taken in Zurich—a course for student lawyers and insurance investigators, the purpose to show the difference between a murder victim and a suicide . . .

"Keep talking, Captain."

"Point three." The policeman removed an envelope from his breast pocket and tossed it over to Alan. "It's been photostated," he said. "Read it."

Alan removed the letter. Flawlessly typewritten, with thick margins. From Paul, addressed to the police.

"Mailed sometime yesterday afternoon, late," Boylen said. "Downtown got it. Sent it over to me early this morning. Go on, read it."

But even before he began, Alan knew. Everything fell instantly into place. The screwy telegram from San Francisco, (*"Sorry it turned out this way. The best man lost. Paul."*); the shots in the dark and the pistol (to make it appear that they had struggled); the borrowed hunting knife.

He forced himself to read, knowing what the letter would say, knowing fully.

> Homicide Div.
> LA Police Department
> Los Angeles, California
>
> To Whom It May Concern:
>
> I hope that this letter will end up in your crank files and that I'll wake up tomorrow feeling pretty ridiculous about the whole thing. But record—just in case.
>
> I have reason to believe that Alan Cole, an employee of Galactic Pictures, Galactic City, Calif., is preparing to do harm to my fiancee, Jessica Randall. Cole and I have been friends for years, and I know him well. He was engaged to Miss Randall up until two weeks ago, at which time Miss Randall confessed that it was I whom she loved and wished to marry. Cole pretended to take it well. But this morning

he called Jessica, asking her to have one last drink with him at a little bar they used to frequent, across from Ocean Pier, Santa Monica—Bisco's. I tried to dissuade her from going, but she likes Alan and doesn't feel there's anything to it.

Maybe there isn't. But, as I say, I know Cole. Somewhere inside him, there is definitely a strange and vicious streak. He is a man capable of almost anything.

It's likely nothing will happen. In that case, I'll phone tomorrow. If not, and if this fear of mine turns out to have any justification—contact Alan Cole. But make sure you're armed.

Sincerely,
Paul A. Bowers

Alan folded the letter and put it back in the envelope and handed it to the large man.

"You want to tell us about it, Mister Cole?"

Alan thought of Paul's words, of shutters that would not close inside his mind; of Jess and the clever lies he had told her, unconsciously. The lies he had told everyone, including Alan Cole . . .

Hell of a script, he told himself. Who's the hero? Who's the villain?

"Sure," he said, thinking this was *one* job he wasn't going to ruin for Paul. "I'll tell you about it."

Then he started laughing, and it sounded like the mechanical man at the funhouse. Only he couldn't turn it off.

Practically the only thing that Avram Davidson has not written is a series, and he is working on that. His science fiction has ranged from golems to dragons to multiple universes; his mysteries from an execution famed in English verse, to the investigations of the High Sheriff of New York City, to the peregrinations of a revolver in an urban ghetto. Obviously, the man is incapable of using the same concept twice; only the vast, near cosmic scope of his projected series will allow him such self-imposed limitation.

Here we meet Thomas Jefferson Nothrup, oilman and amateur of archeology; Luigi di Benedictus, engineer and inventor; Gladys and Eddy, a badly misplaced young couple; and a native architect of great patience.

Amphora
AVRAM DAVIDSON

The octopus who hunted in the shallows off Capo Tortuga sped after the crab, and would have caught it, too. But the huge shadow from overhead distracted it for a second, and the crab scuttled away. Even so, the octopus might still have caught it, sunk its horny beak through the shell into the soft flesh, and made its meal, but it did not care to leave—as close pursuit would require—the area which was its own peculiar territory. Bound by something having the force of instinct, it never went very far from its den, which it had barricaded against intruders. The great shadow passed on—whatever creature cast it evidently posed no immediate danger. The octopus continued its prowl.

The man bent to the oars was young, sun-dark and sinewy. The woman was merely sunburned, and not so young. A smear of white salve or ointment had been laid upon her nose, but it was melting, and revealed the angry red skin beneath. "I still don't know why you need me," she said, tilting her enormous straw hat farther over her face.

"Well, gee, Gladys, you do so know," the man said. Sweat and oil beaded his skin, ran in rivulets between the banks of muscles on his chest and back.

"You could find it without me if you really wanted to," she muttered. The gaunt escarpment of Capo Tortuga loomed to their left. To their right was Africa, stretching huge and dry and hot all the way from Spanish Sahara to the Red Sea. Ahead was the yacht which had been chartered in Villa Cisneros, an ancient wooden hulk powered by a primeval diesel engine.

"That's not the only reason."

She affected not to hear him. "My stomach is acting up again," she said. "And my head feels like it's going to split wide open. And no sugar and almost no coffee left. Boy—"

He started to look over his shoulder, gave it up. "Is it far?" he asked.

She glared at him. Then her look softened. "No," she said. "No, Eddy, it's not far at all."

The oars creaked, the water burbled around their blades, the sun beat down. "Gee," Eddy said, "some fresh meat would sure taste good."

Conversation between T. J. Nothrup of Sweetwater, Oklahoma, and Luigi di Benedictus of Lugano, Switzerland, had not gone very smoothly at first. Not that there was any element of hostility between them, far from it. But Mr. Nothrup wanted to talk only of his archaeological theories ("Facts, I call them. Not theories, but facts!"), and Sr. di Benedictus wanted to talk only of his amphibious housecar ("A new innovating principle in self-cooling, self-lubricating engines—revolutionary!")

"They'll tell you that no white man ever came this way by sea until the Portuguese," declared Mr. Nothrup.

"How foolish to believe that because of aeronautical progress no new systems of surface transportation are needed," Sr. di Benedictus argued.

"They'll tell you that the Greeks never got past Spain. Haw!"

"Is one to maintain that no market can exist for such an improved mechanism? Absurd!"

Sr. di Benedictus was engaged in proving the practicality of his car and engine by circumambulating Africa in it. He was a plump, pale little man with thick eyeglasses. Disturbed political conditions did not disturb him, he bore the passport of a neutral nation. Hazardous geographical conditions—from swamps to deserts, mountains to rivers—he merely welcomed as tests of his equipment. He had constructed his vehicle in his spare time as inspector for a sewing-machine company, from which job he had taken a year's absence to make his grand tour.

Mr. Nothrup listened to him, finally, in patient silence, not especially paying attention to anything the Swiss man said. As soon as the machinist finished, Nothrup said, "Well, it certainly is a lucky thing for you that you came along in your tin lizzie right at this minute, because you're going to be on hand for what I mean the biggest breakthrough in archaeology in just years, my friend, just years."

"Ah, you are an archaeologist. I thought from the accounts of you given me in Villa Cisneros that you were a petroleum explorer. Need I point out to you how exceedingly useful, mightn't I say indispensable, my house-car and engine should be to the pursuit of either activity."

They stood out in the burning sun in the middle of Nothrup's camp on the shore of the bay formed by Capo Tortuga, and neither one paid any attention to the heat, the sand, or the barren wastes and blinding sea. The captain of the chartered boat sat in the shade of the cooktent drinking hot bottled beer, watching his one-man crew (who also acted as cook) play dominoes with the local headman. As the cook-mate made up his own rules and the headman simply cheated, the game was not without interest. Of the three natives who had shown up for work today—sometimes none appeared, sometimes the whole tribe—one sat cross-legged looking at the pictures in a tattered and greasy Spanish comic book, and the others took turns searching one another's hair for lice.

"You are absolutely right and I will buy up a whole fleet of them soon's you get the bugs ironed out, as they say, and after I am finished on this project here," Mr. Nothrup said. "By profession, yes, I am an oilman, I have what they call wildcatted all over the world, and also worked on a contract basis, not that I'm so engaged here, because the Spaniard gover'ment wouldn't give me a license, not that I particularly wanted one, just thought I'd keep my eye open for likely oil terrain whiles I'm here, and in fact I believe that so-called captain you see setting on his duff over there and poisoning his system is a spy to make sure I don't prospect or more likely to see if I do, *where* I do. But I'll sure surprise them when I come back with proof, with *proof*, I tell you, Professor Benedict, that the ancient Greeks came exploring and trafficking in this whole area before the time of Alexander the Great.

"And I'm the man who can do it, too . . ."

The operative word for Thomas Jefferson Nothrup was *thin*. He was thin in frame, had a thin and leathery face, wore spectacles with thin gold rims, and spoke in a thin voice like the creaking of a locust on a hot Oklahoma night.

Had Professor Benedict ever heard of Henry Sleeman? inquired Mr. Nothrup. The Swiss man explained that he was *ingierno*, not *professore*, and what, please, was the name of—Ah, ahah, yes, the gentleman who discovered Troy, assuredly, Heinrich Schliemann. Well, Mr. Nothrup was what you might call a modern-day equivalent of that same fellow. That same fellow made his own pile in wholesale groceries, but his heart, his heart was in archaeology. They claimed that Troy was a fairy story, didn't they? You just bet they did! Wouldn't give old Hank Sleeman the time of day, let alone a single penny to finance his expeditions with. But he showed them. He showed them *good.* Went off and found Troy on his own, just full-up with golden treasures and everything. And they laughed on the other side of their faces then.

You just bet they did!

It all began quite some years back, when T. J. Nothrup was prospecting in the jungles of Nicaragua, just himself and his wife and a native crew. Gladys came with him wherever he went, sharing his hard times as well as the good: he believed in that, believed that a wife's place was at her husband's side, and so did she. It was at that time, observing all those Aztec ruins in Nicaragua, and comparing them with his own historical readings that T. J. Nothrup made the important discovery that the clue to the whole business was right there—Atlantis, the Phoenicians, the Incas, Etruscans, and the Lost Tribes of Israel.

"That's where the bug bit me," Mr. Nothrup said, with a thin smile. "Up 'til that time, alls I'd really thought about seriously was oil and money. History and archaeology and the mystery of human origins, they were just mere diversions, pastimes. But—no more! After what I found out there, I couldn't eat, I couldn't sleep, 'til I'd demonstrated my numerous theories and proved them beyond shadow of a doubt."

Engineer di Benedictus blinked a bit, cast a reassuring glance on his house-car, a structure the size of an American school bus, but mounted on wheels so huge, and slung so low, that the rims reached almost to the roof. He turned his look back to his host. "And you have proved them?" he asked.

"Why, certainly, I have," Nothrup said, surprised. "Don't you fellows there in Switzerland consult your own university libraries? I published three books, illustrated with numerous photographs and maps, had them printed up for me in Tulsa, and sent copies to learned societies and universities throughout the world, as well as prominent independent thinkers in many different countries. What a correspondence that started! I more or less have devoted meself to the subject ever since, and that's what brought me here all the way to Spanish Sahara and Capo Tortuga, just a mere hop, skip, and a jump from the Mauretanian border . . .

"That," he said, "and the amphora . . ."

"This isn't my idea of the way you ought to conduct a scientific expedition," Eddy said, grunting, as he helped Gladys Nothrup up from the rowboat to the wallowing old yacht. "When T.J. sold me that bill of goods I thought it would be like in the movies, with native boys to do all the hard work. Native boys! Why, those natives, you know that, honey, half of 'um are *grand*fathers, for gosh sakes! And they ain't even black, like I thought they'd be, and they never wash—not that I'm any better, 'salt-water soap'—old T.J. and his damn salt-water soap!"

Gladys looked distastefully around the littered, peeling deck.

"Where could it be?" she murmured. "Where could it be?"

"How about a kiss?" Eddy asked, taking her in his arms and hugging her, pulling her off her feet till his lean and muscular back arched.

"Ohmigod, Eddy, my *sun*burn!" She pulled away from him. "Not until you find it," she said coyly.

The young man scowled. "How come if I'm assistant leader of this expedition that I got to do all the dirty work?" he demanded. "Sifting all that sand dirt, like we were going to make mudpies or something? He never told me I'd have to do stuff like that. And what did we find, after all that dirty work, a wonder I didn't get killed by sunstroke? A half-a-dozen old brass cartridges, and a camel bell and a broken teakettle, that's what, and that's all."

The woman bent over, grimacing, and tugging at her blouse where it bit into her sunburned neck, and rummaged in a heap of clothing. She had started shaking each item out and poking into pockets when a roach-like insect the size of a mouse hit the dirty deck with a plop and went scuttling rapidly away. Gladys screamed, dropped the clothing, and jumped backward.

"You can't tell me that the ancient Greeks used cartridges," Eddy said, stepping indifferently on the bug with a noise that fetched another scream from Gladys. He scraped off his shoe. "The ancient Greeks didn't use teakettles, and they didn't go riding around on any camels, either. I know *that* much." He put out his chin and gazed defiantly at the shore, addressing his absent employer. "As for the Lost Continent of Atlantis, that all those ancient Greeks were supposed to have been trading with along here in the olden days, well, Mr. Tom J. Nothrup and all your old sweet talk that sucked me into coming along on this trip. I think your Lost Continent of Atlantis was a fake. Just like you are a fake."

Gladys, who had been staging a little war dance on the heap of clothes designed to drive out any further lurking giant water bugs, said, as she picked up a shirt and prodded around in it, "He wasn't any fake when he used to be just a plain old oilman. He could smell oil a mile under the ground. He made plenty of money, too, let me tell you, Eddy. All over the U.S.A. All over Central America. Why the Hell else do you think I let him drag me around with him? I had malaria, I had two miscarriages, my insides are ruined forever, it'll be a miracle if I don't really have cancer of the skin from all the terrible beating my skin's taken from the sun all these years, like that Spic doctor I sneaked away to see in Villa Whatever-it-is hinted in no uncertain terms. Would he let me stay at home even once back in Sweetwater? Would he consent to a decent divorce and maintenance like a gentleman should? Ha, ha, ha, I'm laughing, that lousy old son of a bitch. Where *is* it? It *has* to be here, I looked all over back at the camp, and in his clothes when he was sleeping; so it just has to be *here*. I stuck with him because he made *money*, honey, and I figured that sooner or later he would either drop dead or retire. Eddy, please, help me look, dear."

Eddy felt rapidly through the clothes, kicked them aside. "Maybe in the cabin," he said. "Let's go look in the cabin. I still don't know what we really need it for, I could break the rack open. It wouldn't be hard." He flexed his muscles.

She looked at him, admiringly, then, taking hold of the upper part of one arm, walked toward the cabin with him. "Yes, but honey, I know you could, that's not the point. Suppose he came back, suppose, I don't know what I'm saying, this heat, this sun and all these years . . . and notices the rack is busted? No, dear, my idea is the best." It was at first a little cooler in the cabin, but the hot and close air soon asserted itself. Boxes and cases and valises and loose items of gear and clothing lay all around. "He made plenty of money, Eddy. Before he got this bee in his bonnet. Expeditions and printing books, which he gives away by the thousands, and chartering boats . . . It's going, Eddy. It's going, going, going, and it's not coming in. The ancient Greeks aren't going to bring in any money."

Eddy tried a wooden locker, pulled it open with a jerk that splintered the rotten wood. A khaki bush jacket hung on the hook, and he rummaged around in it. "How much you say is left, about?" he asked.

Gladys settled down on the grimy bunk. She looked old and ill. "Oh, I don't have to say, 'about,' " she said. "I know exactly, and only too well. There's sixteen thousand dollars left, is all. And this old tub is eating up its own value, just about, every day he keeps it here, so he can go scooting up and down the coast looking for ruins with his binoculars. He can eat up that sixteen thousand dollars real soon, and then what? And then what, Eddy? Hmmm? Tell me."

He replaced the bush jacket. From the pocket of his shorts he took a pack of cigarettes and a lighter. After a moment, and a puff of smoke, he said, "Well, I can tell you this much. The boat's got to go back to port in a couple of days for fuel. And unless the great Mr. T. J. Nothrup has found buried Greek treasure by then, well, I ain't going to stick around. Bye, bye birdie, and I guess I never will get my picture in the *National Geographic.*"

A frightened look came over her face, gave way almost at once to one of determination. She got up, wincing. "Let's be systematic. I'll go through the cabin, you go through the hold. But look *carefully*. He won't be gone forever with that crazy Swede or Eyetalian or whatever he is, with the funny wagon . . . Eddy. Eddy? I couldn't stand it, all by myself, with him again, Eddy . . ."

After directing his wife and assistant to "kind of keep an eye on things," Mr. Nothrup had climbed into Sr. di Benedictus's vehicle to go for a ride. He considered that it was for the purpose of giving the inventor a chance to look at some promising ruins near the border; the inventor considered that it was for the purpose of demonstrating the functions of the machine itself: both men were content.

Quite far from that were the two Americans left in camp. The Spaniards had lapsed into a siesta, the tribesmen were making motions with a pick, pickax, and a shovel. Partly visible in the side of a hill were stone fragments which might have been a wall or a foundation; Nothrup had informed them to stop work when they had cleared down to within a foot of the remains. At their present rate of progress he might have remained away a week without reaching it.

"Well," said Gladys.

"Well, what?"

"You know what."

Eddy shrugged. Then he said, "I guess some fresh meat would taste good, at that, huh?"

"*I* am certainly tired of rice and beans and that canned camel or whatever is in those dirty old cans he paid a king's ransom for. Give Ali a rifle and let him go shoot a gazelle or a deer, like he said he could."

The young man got up with determination, then looked around, helplessly. "He ain't even here," he observed.

"He's here. He'll come out if we call him, from where he's been hiding, now that T.J.'s gone. He doesn't want T.J. to see him. His feelings are hurt. What did T.J. want to go and hit him for, just because he kept begging him to let him borrow the rifle and go shoot game?"

Eddy scowled. "It's a good thing he never hit *me*. Couple times

I thought he was going to, but he thought better of it. I might just as easily hit *him*, old's he is, if he talks that ugly way to me any more."

She shook her head, urgent and anxious. "No, Eddy. Absolutely not. We'll just do what you said to do yesterday, when we were talking about it. We'll give Ali the rifle to let him shoot game."

And he nodded his head. Their eyes met and dropped. Their understanding was perfect. Ali was the best marksman, the best hunter, in the tribe, but he had—somehow—lost his gun, could not afford to buy another. He was proud, sullen, keen, smouldering, eager; he was in these last few days above all and quite obviously revengeful. The border of Mauretania, a nation which had no particular reason to be zealous on behalf of Spanish justice, lay not very far away; on the other side dwelt the other moiety of the tribe: friends and brothers, refuge.

Eddy and Gladys knew that whatever game Ali might bring down, his first shot would not be for gazelle.

The windows of the house-car were of tinted glass, as its inventor pointed out. "Observe, also, how smooth the ride—eh? Because of unusually broad tires, adapted from aeroplane tires. Excellent for the sand, equally so for the mud and marsh."

"Tell you what brought me here," said the other. "I was heading for Guinea, the French had pulled out, bag and baggage, and I said to myself, 'Why should the Russians get to take over everything there? Now, an experienced and independent oilman, a geologist and engineer even if largely self-trained at both, a man like yourself, T.J., with no ax to grind, now why shouldn't you come to some sort of agreement with the Guinea gover'ment about doing some oil scouting and development for them?' So I took off, but the air transport situation was in some bit of confusion and I wound up in Liberia, and that was as far as I could get at and for the moment. Since there was nothing doing just then via air, figured I'd make my way by land, either cut through the bush to Guinea directly from Liberia, or head all the way along the coast by way of Sierra Leone. I come to a place called Robertstown and lo and behold, what did I see but this woman carrying a load of water on her head. Now, Mr. Benedict, you may question what was so odd or unusual about that, don't they carry things like that all the time? Correct, they do. But whereas the other women were using old gasoline cans for the purpose, this little old gal was using an amphora."

His host spun the wheel to avoid a depression, turned proudly to mark the reaction to the ease which the large vehicle took the wheel;

perceived that something had been said which required comment, found that he had none to make, said, "Pardon?"

"An amphora, Mr. Benedict! An . . . ancient . . . Greek . . . amphora! One of those classical-type pottery jugs with a taper to the sides and two handles and a wide mouth. Well, wide, I say 'wide,' matter of comparison some are wider than others. You could of knocked me over with a feather!"

"Oh, so. Very interesting. In Sierra Leone, I will pass, of course, through—"

Robertstown was not in Sierra Leone at all, not for one minute; it was in Liberia. "Now, maybe Hanno the Carthaginian has passed that way, was my first thought. Or—*maybe the ancient Greeks their very selves!* Seeking the Garden of the Hesperides, for after all what were the so-called Golden Apples but your citrus fruits, or maybe even trading with the Lost Continent of Atlantis. Proof! Proof positive! I like to of snatched that jug off the poor woman's head. Where'd she get it, I wanted to know. Where'd she get it? Well, at first she only giggled and tried to give me that Boss-no-no-savvy business, but I got me out a silver dollar and she savvy'd soon enough, let *me* tell you!"

The woman's story was that the amphora had come from the Spanish island of Fernando Póo, in the Bight of Biafra, where many Liberians had used to go to work on the cocoa plantations. The woman was a morganatic wife of a local man, a Mr. Tolliver, and with the latter's assistance they were able to establish the very spot of origin of the amphora on Fernando Póo, the garden of Mrs. Widow Colonel Alvarez.

"Took me a while before I could get passage for Fernando Póo, it cost me plenty, too, but that widow lady was as friendly and helpful as she could be—touched with the tar brush, my personal opinion, but be that as it may . . ."

Colonel Alvarez's widow recalled the urn quite well, but could say of its past only that her late husband had had it with him when he was transferred from the mainland colony then known as Rio de Oro, but now called Spanish Sahara.

So Mr. Nothrup saw there was nothing to it but head for the Spanish Sahara, or, at first, more particularly its capital of Villa Cisneros. No one there had ever seen or heard of any amphora; no one recognized the photographs he had made of it. Colonel Alvarez was remembered as Major Alvarez, and it was further recollected that he had often visited in the line of duty the district near the former French and present Mauretanian border.

"Oh, yes . . . Now, the hydraulic principle which—"

"So here we are!" T. J. Nothrup sailed triumphantly, unheedingly, over the hydraulic principle. "I'm going to stay here and excavate if it costs me every penny I've got, and before I'm through, the name of T. J. Nothrup will go down in history along with that of Bayard and Sleeman and St. Vincent and Rawlinson and Ignatius Donnelly. If I could find just one amphora, Dr. Benedict! Just a single one! Tell you what, let's stop here, or we'll be across the border before you know it, let's stop here and I'll get out my old binoculars and we'll scout around for those ruins. Too bad my work near the shore has prevented giving more attention—but, who knows, the shore may of shifted since those days."

The bare and lifeless sands stretched all around.

Eddy emerged from the hold dirty, annoyed, and sweatier than ever. He wiped his face on his forearm, smearing both, and looked at the waters of the Bayo Tortuga. "Swim would sure be nice, right now," he said. A noise from the cabin distracted him, and he turned, scowling. There was a confused sound, and then Gladys came running out.

"I found it!" she screamed, her burned face almost scarlet in excitement. "Look! Look! The key to the gun rack!" She waved her hand in front of her as she ran forward to meet him, and something glittered and sparkled in it . . . something which glittered and sparkled in the air, arching from her impetuous fingers over the side of the boat as she watched, her mouth open, her expression almost ludicrous in its shock. Without hesitating and almost before the key hit the water, Eddy had leaped to the railing, poised, and dived after it.

The key glittered and turned all the way down, fish of many colors regarded his slim, intruding form with mouths as round as Gladys's had been; he was almost quick enough to have caught it as deftly as the diving boys of many ports catch coins flung into the water for that purpose by tourists.

But not quite quick enough.

Still, he marked the descent of the key, saw it vanish into an opening on the floor of the bay. Sea fronds waved, and a school of tiny fish fled in tiny terror. Eddy reached for the hole into which the key had vanished, missed it, touched something, something which moved at his touch, and the hole moved with it. The weedy surface, encrusted with shells, rocked a bit, exposing an undersurface as pink as old brick. It was a jar, a vase; he recognized the shape, to his mild surprise—a recognition which barely penetrated his mind—it was an amphora. He would bring it up with him, fish out the key. He tugged, the amphora rocked again, but, wedged as it was between rock and rock, it could not be pulled loose.

He felt the first familiar press of air surging for release, thrust his hand in, groping for the key. The amphora was full of small stones, or so it felt, but finally his fingers closed on the key, and he pulled out his hand. But not all the way out. The stones had settled around his wrist, pulled up with it, fitting between it and the mouth of the urn, narrower by far than the body of the urn. Was he to be caught like the monkey with a fistful of nuts, in the story? Not damned likely. He released the key. He tugged again. And again.

The house-car came careening down the slope toward shore, sand spurting from beneath its great wheels. Inside there reigned a degree of excitement which had penetrated the single-track mind of even the usually calm Swiss engineer.

"I'll make it worth your while!" Mr. Nothrup said, for the tenth or eleventh time. "I'll charter you and your big old tank, I'll give you a thousand dollars a week, agreed?"

"Agreed, agreed," said di Benedictus. "And very probably I am able to raise some Swiss capital to match the American capital you speak of, as you suggest. But I must ask you—" And he asked him for the tenth time: "Are you sure? Are you quite sure?"

"Of course I'm sure! Hot diggetty! Won't Gladys and the young fellow be tickled when they hear! I haven't done right by that girl, Professor, and I admit it—dragging her all over Hell and Creation; she lost two little babies, did you know that, sir? I figured we'd make our pile and settle down and have more, safe at home, but—I'll buy her—no! I'll build her—the biggest damned house in Sweetwater, Oklahoma. As for that young fellow, he isn't so bright he'll ever set the world on fire, but I kind of taken a liking to him, and I'll give him a cut of this, my word is my bond, I'll make him rich before I'm through, if I've talked rough to him on occasion, why, it was only for his own good, and—"

"But the Mauretanians. Will they agree?"

"Will they *agree*? Will a bear scratch in the woods? You bet your belt buckle they'll agree! Why shouldn't they? Look what they save —the whole costs, enormous, of a search—look what they get: infinite riches! Make their own deal! A new nation, starting from nothing, why *shouldn't* they agree? I won't ask for much, just five percent; Gulbenkian asked for just five percent and the King of Persia made him a lord and he died worth scores of millions, sir! scores of millions! Where are they? Where's Gladys? Where's the young fellow? Hey, look there, Doctor, out at the yacht, the rowboat's tied up at it. I see Gladys. Wonder what they went out there for? Don't matter. I'll send up a smoke signal or something, bring them ashore."

A pale, faint blush suffused the full cheeks of the Swiss inventor. He smiled, a slow, proud smile. "It is not necessary to devise a smoke signal to bring them ashore. You have forgotten that the di Benedictus improved hydraulic house-car is also amphibious. *Hollo!* Watch. Watch, watch—"

The ponderous vehicle moved with deliberate speed down the crest to the beach. Its master pulled switches, gears, levers. The car rolled down to the water, entered the water, breasted the water, rode upon the water. "*We* go to *them!*" cried the Swiss.

"I'll be darned," said Mr. Nothrup. "I'll be damned."

His new associate giggled. "So," he observed, "you think no more of ancient Greeks and Grecian urns . . . eh?"

Mr. Nothrup's mouth opened, first to surprise, then to laughter. "No," he said, "no, I don't . . . didn't . . . don't . . . I tell you, Doc, the moment I spied that absolutely gi-gan-tic dome in my binoculars, I thought no more about that whole history business than I did about a grain of sand! Why, I wouldn't trade my chances of five percent of what's under it for every single Greek amphora that ever was! Don't expect there ever were any around here, anyway. But I know what there is!"

"But are you *sure?*"

The boat grew nearer, grew larger. Gladys sat on the deck. "*Of course* I'm sure, how many times do I—look: in order to find oil, you got to find sandstone or limestone, because the oil has accumulated under it and *remained* under it. Now, when I spotted that gigantic surface structure over across the border, when I saw that perfectly enormous surface structure indicating that underneath there just has to be what we call a ground rising or a doming, elevation for elevation as near as I could see and feature for feature i-dent-i-cal with the same thing I spotted that time in Tishomingo, Texas, the one that had the whole Sam Houston Pool underneath it, and not only that but it was practically a recapitulation of what I checked out over the Balboa Pool which I personally discovered myself in Central America, to say nothing of Montana and California and—but, Lordy, I've been running on and on and I don't want to bore you—"

"No, no," the Swiss said earnestly. "You do not bore me. Go on. Go on. Go on."

Sunlight glittered off the water, and off of Mr. Nothrup's spectacles. "Won't Gladys be surprised?" he cried. "Won't she just probably go out of her *mind?*"

Once again a shadow passed overhead, a huge shadow, larger than before, though not so huge as the great shadow, seaward, itself. As always, the shadow passed on. No danger. The octopus, which had darted away at its approach, returned to what it had been doing. It had been investigating something untoward, at its lair. Uncertain, disquieted, it darted back and forth, coming nearer each time. It had taken pains, in its own way, to make the lair safe from intruders, bringing small rocks in its arms and settling and arranging them inside so as to leave room for itself, but nothing else. Now an intruder had come, was still there, completely blocking the entrance. Its eyes stared at the octopus, its mouth was open. Gradually, the octopus approached, touched, assured itself that there was no danger. The entrance had to be reopened. But not immediately. Satisfied, the octopus lifted its horny beak and began to feed.

One of the frightening by-products of militant liberation movements is the difficulty of distinguishing between the demonstrative "overt action" and mere enthusiastic vandalism. This is, of course, most readily noticeable on the college campus, but with the proliferations of "Lib" movements, reaching even into the family circle, one can not be certain that events such as those described by Dana Lyon have not already begun to occur.

Miss Lyon, until recently known for her novels, exhibits an equal competence for the psychological suspense short story. The puffs of icy wind they produce at the neck-nape properly qualify them as "ghostless ghost stories."

"Silence!"
DANA LYON

1

The room in which the club gathered was dark except for the moonlight that flowed in through the unglassed windows, falling brightly on the floor which was so new that it still gave off the fragrance of freshly cut lumber. Bare wires dangled from the ceiling, and a workman's ladder leaned against the unpainted walls.

A group of small people sat cross-legged on the floor at one end of the uncompleted room, where the moonlight fell brightly upon them, and at the other end in only faint light was an upended orange crate on which was perched a taller, older person. He was eighteen. Beside him, on a smaller box, sat a young boy with a composition book on his lap. The light was dim, but strong enough from the moon so that he could read his own handwriting in the book which was partly prompted by memory; he had read the minutes over a number of times behind the locked door of his bedroom as soon as he had checked the date of this meeting with his superior, for they must wait for a full moon since they could not use lights, and the weather must be clement.

The tall boy, sitting beside and above him, now said, "Read the minutes, Scurvy."

2

It started out in such a small way.

The young Mrs. Wayne, happily busy about her home as she

readied it for the small party this evening, had happened to glance out the kitchen window toward her service yard, and at the precious lace tablecloth (bequeathed by Grandma Pritchard) which she had so carefully laundered and hung on the line that morning. Something about it caught her eye and she stood still in her tracks; something, but what? A lack of symmetry, one corner hanging down farther than the others when she knew she had hung it straight, so that it would dry that way?

She hurried out, and went to the line and examined the delicate lace of the cloth. It was torn at one corner and hanging down almost to the ground in a hopeless mass of old and beautiful linen tracery; it was not torn at the seams or cut across the lace itself but had been pulled apart in such a manner that there was no hope of restoring its beauty. Mrs. Wayne held the torn bits of cloth against her as if they had been a wounded child, and the tears welled in her eyes and she thought, "My grandma's, the only truly *good* thing I have," and then she grew angry, and then frightened. She knew that the cloth was intact when she had hung it up, there was a high fence around the yard, there was no sign of any trespasser nearby, and there were no pets in the family. She had hung it up this morning and then she had taken out the station wagon and driven to the shopping center for her supplies for tonight and then she had come home and busied herself in the house and when she had looked out the window, there was this terrible sign of destruction. All the neighborhood children, as well as her own, were in school, but even if they hadn't been, who would do such a thing? She hurried in the house again, too enraged now, too frightened now, for further grief, and went through it carefully; but nothing else was touched. Just the ragged, destroyed tablecloth, still hanging on the line . . .

Some seven blocks away, and a few days later, Philip Tressler backed his car out of the garage, on his way to work, and immediately had two blow-outs. On investigation he discovered a number of large, flat-headed tacks on his driveway. He swore, changed the tires, blasted his children that night since he could conceive of no other culprit, and went to bed with a guilty conscience for having disrupted the serenity of the dinner hour, his usually good relations with his wife and the knowledge that he, who had always prided himself on his fairness though he doubted that his two sons appreciated this, had condemned his defenseless family for no reason other than his own frustration.

Mr. Tressler was unknown to Mrs. Wayne.

Not far distant, in the middle of the day, Mrs. Iris McLaine was reclining in bed, indisposed by means of a bottle and a half of sherry, when a delivery man arrived with a large package. Sign here, please. Groggily she signed. Groggily she opened the package and its layers of fresh tissue and ribbon inside. She screamed and backed away and stumbled back to her sherry and bed. The package contained a dead cat, mangled and bloody.

She was slightly known to Mrs. Wayne but not at all to Mr. Tressler.

All of these families, and a number of others who had suffered similar experiences, therefore did not connect the horrifying details of another occurrence which could hardly be called a crime but which was far more than a petty annoyance, with their own misfortunes when these details appeared in the local paper. The occurrence, since no crime on the books actually took place, was completely confusing to both the police and the public who read about it, though all names, for obvious reasons, had been omitted. What had happened was that a young girl, of good family whose names had never appeared in the papers aside from the society columns, had been, one early evening, pulled into the bushes of a park by two people in slacks with stockings pulled over their faces, and had then been deprived of her clothes—all of them—and turned loose without a scratch or any kind of molestation whatever. It had been done in silence, so there was no chance of the voices being identified, the night was balmy and therefore she was in no danger from exposure; the only danger was that done to the emotional make-up of a young girl, barely twelve, who had been taught modesty from an early age, who was already a little embarrassed by her suddenly flowering breasts and pubis and who, turned loose on the street of an early evening with nothing whatever to cover her, had cowered under the bushes alongside the park until a kindly man, passing by, had heard her sobs, had covered her with his coat, called a cab and driven her home, and had then been denounced by the girl's hysterical mother until the child was able to explain what had happened. "I wish," said the man who had been on his dutiful way home to wife and four children, "to God I had left your daughter where she was for the rest of the night; and perhaps she would have been rescued by some hoodlums who would really have harmed her. Good-day, madam."

The child was hysterical; she remained hysterical for some time to come, and ended up at boarding school where her unfortunate experience could remain undisclosed. But a tiny bit of her innocence had been chipped away. For good.

The police were busy trying to find the two creatures (who might have been girls, boys, men or women for all they knew) without any clues whatever, least of all motive.

There was no question of these events being put together and analyzed, discussed, probed and investigated by either the victims or the law-enforcement agencies, for these people either knew each other slightly or not at all. To each of them, the onslaught of persecution was a personal matter, perpetrated by people with a lewd sense of humor or someone psychotic or with a fantastic grudge to pay off . . . With few of them was the persecution a one-deal matter: Mrs. Wayne, the soul of modesty, propriety, and obeisance to household gods to the exclusion of everything else, including her family, received an occasional obscene phone call, which she relayed to the police who did their best which amounted to nothing since the calls did not come regularly, were spaced far apart and appeared to come from different people. She heard words that she did not even know existed.

Then there was the matter of Mrs. McLaine, who began missing things around the house: first, a few not valuable ornaments, then change from her purse, then some fairly large bills hidden in her dresser drawer against the day when her husband would kick her out without a cent and which information she did not, of course, dare relay to the police. Instead, she flew at her two teen-agers, grounded them for a month, told her husband they were growing continually more disobedient and she knew of no other way to get them back in shape, a matter which he, as manager of the local bank, shrugged off as being her responsibility, not his. A few days after this disciplinary measure had gone into effect, her few good jewels turned up missing. The children were in school, and she herself had been out at a bridge party, as usual turning down the offer of a before-lunch glass of sherry, smiling with a shake of her head though hardly able to wait until she could get home to her own private bottle, and on her return she found the jewel case on her dressing table, empty of all but trifles. She called the police. No forced entry; nothing else in the house touched. Which left her only Annie, the twice-a-week cleaning woman who had been doing chores for the last seven years for the McLaines and for several of Mrs. McLaine's friends, whose services were now terminated. The jewels were not found, in either Annie's home or in any pawnshop, but Annie remained out of work until she moved to another town.

There were other incidents, none connected, few reported to the police; no culprits were ever found.

3

The boy called Scurvy read: "The last meeting was held on May 21st in the unfinished house at the end of Nora Lane, with votes taken on whether to admit a new member, name of Toby Hansen, who cited many indignities from father since mother deceased last year. Members voted on eligibility; no blackballs . . . Reports on activities for last month: all missions accomplished. Checked almanac for next full moon and whether present house would be completed by then. Answer affirmative but probably not occupied, any change in meeting place would be passed along. No further business. Meeting adjourned."

The tall thin boy on the upended orange crate glanced at the assembled company with old, bitter eyes. His face was in darkness, as he wished it to be, but the group before him, almost cowering, were as clearly depicted by the moon as if a piercing searchlight had been turned directly on them. The periphery of light fell faintly on the secretary who was ready, pencil poised, to take down the current minutes.

"Now to get on with the new business," said the leader. "As you know, we voted in a new member, Toby Hansen, at our last meeting, who has plenty of legitimate complaints about his father and feels that this is the only means he has to defend his rights. Christ knows," the thin boy went on, a bit of fervor beginning to amplify his voice, "it's the only means any of us have. Toby Hansen, stand up!"

A boy of twelve, scuffling a bit, stood up, and the leader said sharply, "Quiet. That is one of the first rules of this order: quiet; and, above all, obedience. You understand that we have certain rules that must be obeyed if we are to continue our activities?"

"Yes," said Toby. "Sir."

"Very well. Now you understand what the purpose of this group is or you wouldn't be here. We are all victims of perpetual persecution by our parents, who have power that no dictator on this earth has ever possessed. From the time we are born until we reach our majority—a whole generation—we must obey them or suffer the consequences. They expect us to be grateful for having been born, but sometime you just ask yourself why. By now, you all know how you happened to come into this world, but do you suppose for a minute that while your parents were having a good time in bed they were thinking about some baby that wasn't even born yet and what a favor it would be to bring it to life? No. We are all the result of our parents' lust and most of us weren't even wanted *after* we were born. So our parents get back at us by making us subjects of their kingdoms for the most important years of our lives. There is no comeback. We do what they say, or else. Moreover, no matter how unjust their edicts are, there is no court that can reverse their decisions. Power is what they want and power is what they've got.

"This club's sole purpose," he went on, his voice, deeper than a boy's should be, growing grim and hard, "is to thwart that power in every way possible. It takes time, but sooner or later they'll catch on. They can't pin anything we do on their own kids, because it's always some other kid that does the dirty work. You get something on your old man, like cheating at golf or his income tax, and he gets a blackmail letter, but he can't figure out how the blackmailer ever found out. Same with everything. Money gets stolen, an expensive tablecloth gets destroyed, but oh no, *their* little kids are safely in school.

"We've got three hundred and fifteen dollars in the treasury. Where did it come from? From parents' purses and pockets. Where is it going? Not into any members' hot little hands, you can bet. It is to be used only in order to employ other methods of bringing the parents into line, in the event there is some expense involved.

"The rest of you all know these things," the thin boy went on in a more controlled voice, "but our new member has got to be briefed thoroughly on what we are and what our purpose is. We don't take in anyone with just one beef, that's something anyone can have. Our members are composed of those of you who are treated like serfs on a day-to-day basis and have no possible comeback. Except here. That is the purpose of our club. Now," he said, moving from the general to the specific in his attention to the new member, "do you have any questions?"

"Yes, sir," said the new member. "I understand why you've got this thing going, and I understand why I asked to join up. But supposing I—supposing somebody doesn't want to belong any more or gets sore at the other members and decides to blab—"

"Nobody blabs," said the leader grimly. "Not any more, they don't. Get this through your head, Toby Hansen, this isn't any kid stuff. We're in it for keeps, and we play rough when the occasion demands. You know why I'm here in the first place? *My* precious parents left me in a railway station when I was three days old. Then I ended up in an orphanage until I was six and *then* I was adopted by some doting parents who'd just lost their son and wanted another the same age, and after that every time I'd get out of line, they'd sob and say, 'Oh, our own little Junior would never have done anything like that', so now I'm a real good guy when I'm home but a lot of things have happened to them that they can't explain and never will. Like the old man in jail on a hit-run charge when he was safely home in bed, and a fire in the house when the insurance lapsed, because guess who copped the letter with the premium check in it and then set the fire?"

His voice was shaking; he stopped talking for an instant during which no one dared break the silence; then he cleared his throat, once more turned his attention to the new boy and continued.

"So you want to know what happens if you change your mind about belonging to this club. It is simply this: you can never drop out. You can omit meetings, you can sidle up to your parents again if you've got something to gain by it, you can skip any further complaints or any further activities, *but you may never, as long as you live, become a non-member!* Is that clear?"

"Yes, sir."

"You may well be thinking," said the other, "that what's to stop you if you want to drop out and tell the authorities everything you know. Well, I'll tell you what's to stop you. Things happen. Not to you, so there's no use telling yourself that you're brave enough to go through with what could only be called heresy in the event you report our operations to anyone whatever. Not to you, but to your family, and there is little we don't know about them now. You may recall, not long ago, reading in the paper about the girl who had all her clothes stripped from her in the park and was found naked by a man who took her home? Believe me, it didn't do her any good. This happened to the sister of one of our members who decided that he didn't want to be one of us any longer and squealed to his father, who never found one iota of evidence, but this meant no more activities, no more meetings and a bunch of scared kids for a while. It was demoralizing. Since then, we have had another member who decided he'd tell, until he was convinced otherwise by the things that could happen to his family. Particularly his baby sister.

"So let me repeat, Toby Hansen, not only to you but to the entire group here assembled, that the reprisals will become worse for each person who rats on this group. The next reprisal will be as follows: someone in your family will disappear. That person will not reappear. That person will be a brother or sister of the member who rats, and if there is no brother or sister, it could well be a parent. We do not make idle threats—I think we have proved that. *The one unbreakable law of this organization is permanent silence!*"

He paused, and the boy Toby stood still, thinking. "You mean I can't ever tell anything about this club, without something happening?"

"That is correct," said the other. "Up until now the reprisals have been insignificant; from now on no one will dare to breathe the workings of this group to another living soul, not even to each other. When you leave this room your minds are as blank as to what has happened here . . ."

"But what if we can't get away from home to come here?" the new member inquired.

"You'll manage," said the other grimly. "Like this: A says he is going to B's house to do his homework, and B says he is going to A's. If a parent checks up, then both of them claim they went over to C's house. If you can't get out, even so, then you'd better have a damn good excuse at the next meeting . . . Parents have too much power." His voice was shaking. "Hitler was stamped out, Mussolini was stamped out; parents can't be stamped out but they can turn their power over to us, and we are in the process of forging the first links that will bring this about. That is the reason why none of you must speak about this group to any adult or anyone else. One weak link destroys the chain."

He glanced at the new boy again, puzzled by a strangeness—a lack, rather—in his expression. The other kids had all looked scared when they first became members. This one merely looked thoughtful. Suddenly the leader himself was frightened, and enraged because of this fact; it was the *others* who should be frightened, not himself.

"Remember what I told you," he said, his voice quiet but toneless. "There will come a time when you may not hate your parents the way you do now, when you will want to protect them instead of bringing them into line. When you will want to be sure that nothing happens to them or to the rest of your family. The only way you can protect them is to keep silence *forever*. Is that clear?"

There was a murmur from the group huddled in the corner of the room, a nod of the head from the boy Toby. "All right," said the slim lad on the orange crate. "Meeting adjourned."

4

Toby Hansen lived alone with his father. There were no siblings and his mother had died the year before from what his father claimed was a fall downstairs though Toby knew better—he had been an unseen witness to that last terrible quarrel.

Toby's father was a big, overbearing, successful salesman with a mind concentrated on sales, liquor and the floozies he'd been bringing to the house ever since his wife died. He made promises to Toby that he never kept. ("Sure you can have a bike if you bring home a decent report card"; "Yeah, you can go away to military school next fall"; "Your allowance gets raised, son, as soon as I recover from April 15th. Ha ha.") The only promises he ever kept were those relating to punishment which invariably was inflicted when promised, whether deserved or not depending on the old man's state of mind and whether or not he had a hangover or had had a bad week in the sales department.

The day after his first meeting at the club, Toby approached his father who was on his third martini in the rumpus room reading the evening paper.

"Pop?" he said.

"Yeah, what is it?"

"Something I want to talk to you about."

"Like the birds and the bees, huh?" and the man went off into a roar of laughter.

Toby bided his time. He waited for the roar to subside.

"No, Pop," he said. "I'm serious."

"So? Some littler guy beat you up at school today?"

The gorge rose in the boy's throat and forever relieved him of any qualms concerning what he was about to do. *Nothing ever happens to the members, only to their families.* "Pop," he said, "there's this club I think you ought to know about . . ."

Richard Deming is so talented and prolific in the mystery field that it would be easy to think that his writing has been limited to it. This is far from the case; his recent books have included a biography of pitcher Vida Blue, a series on the workings of the American legal system, and a Junior Literary Guild Selection titled *Sleep, Our Unknown Life*. Of course, his mystery writing has been equally diverse, including not only short stories but novels and novelizations of television series, including *Dragnet* and *Mod Squad*. His short stories have been frequently anthologized.

The Mystery Writers of America, founded in 1945 with the slogan "Crime Does Not Pay . . . Enough," is accurately depicted in Mr. Deming's story, save, perhaps, for the gullibility of its members. It must be admitted that, at one stage of its existence, the headquarters of the organization was the victim of a series of burglaries, centering principally on the not insignificant liquor supply.

There is more to be said about the MWA and Mr. Deming's story, but that must wait as an afterword.

Bunco Game
RICHARD DEMING

The springboard for the gimmick was a casual meeting with a mystery writer in a New York bar, but it was some months before Handsome Harry Gannon developed all the details. At the time it merely struck him that if R. L. Stevens was typical of all professional writers, the breed would make excellent marks. He had no definite plan at all when he began to ingratiate himself with the writer. He was merely indulging his con-man habit of never bypassing a potential mark.

Gannon had just arrived in town from Cleveland that day with five thousand dollars in his pocket, the life savings of a gullible widow who had been under the impression she was intrusting the money to her future husband. It was the largest score he had ever made, and he celebrated by checking in at the Belmont Plaza Hotel instead of some second-rate motel, as was his usual custom.

After a leisurely dinner he had a taxi drop him at Times Square and wandered along 42nd Street. He entered a bar just off the square.

The stool to the left of the one he took was vacant. To his right sat a squarely built, pleasant-looking man in his thirties. Accustomed to evaluating strangers' financial statuses at a glance, Gannon noted that the man's suit was of excellent cut and that he wore an expensive wristwatch.

With a five-thousand-dollar stake, Gannon wasn't on the lookout for marks, but from force of habit he asked the man for a light. He met many of his marks in bars. Usually they were women, but he was no specialist. He had no objection to fleecing men when the opportunity arose.

As usual the borrowed light was enough to get a conversation going. After a few exchanges about the presidential campaign, the Jets and the latest raise in subway rates, Gannon offered to buy a drink. When the stranger accepted, Gannon introduced himself, though not by his own name.

"I'm Harry Garner," he said, holding out his hand.

The man grasped it cordially. "Glad to know you, Harry. My name is Stevens. R. L. Stevens. Friends generally call me Steve."

The name struck a familiar note, but Gannon couldn't quite place it. He said, "R. L. Stevens. That rings a bell. Where have I heard of you?"

"Maybe you've read some of my stuff," Stevens said with a modest smile.

Gannon placed him then. "The mystery writer," he said. "I've often seen your stories in *Ellery Queen's Mystery Magazine.*"

Stevens looked pleased. "Not many readers remember the names of magazine story authors, unless they're famous ones such as Ellery Queen or Rex Stout."

"I know," Gannon said ruefully. "And nobody at all ever notices who wrote a non-fiction magazine piece."

The comment had been instinctive. Handsome Harry Gannon was so used to playing parts, it was quite natural to step into the role of a writer now.

"You're a writer too?" Stevens asked with interest.

"Uh-huh," Gannon said, improvising as he went along. "Mainly travel stuff. I free lance for *Holiday, National Geographic* and a few lesser magazines. Currently I'm doing a travel book on South America."

It seemed a safe bet that Stevens wouldn't be familiar with the names of all professional article writers. What Gannon had said about people not noticing the bylines of magazine non-fiction writers was true, and there was no reason a mystery writer would be any more observant than the general reader.

The man's reaction was predictable. Out of courtesy he didn't want to admit he had never heard of a fellow professional writer.

"Harry Garner," he said reflectively. "You write under that name?"

"Harry's a nickname. I use Harold Garner."

"Oh, of course," Stevens said. "I think I've seen your stuff in *Holiday*."

Gannon was amused by the pretense.

They had another drink together, this time Stevens insisting on buying. By then they were old enough friends to exchange information about their backgrounds.

Stevens said he lived in Rochester and was in town to talk to the publisher of the annual *Mystery Writers of America Anthology*. He explained that this was a book to which MWA members contributed stories free, and all royalties went to the organization. Each year a different member of MWA acted as editor, and this year it was his turn.

He was staying with fellow mystery writer Albert Avellano while in town, Stevens said, but tonight Avellano had another engagement, which had rather left Stevens at loose ends. Usually he brought his wife Pat with him to New York City when he had to visit it, he commented, but this time she had been unable to come. He hated being alone in New York City. Tentatively he inquired if Gannon would be interested in joining him for a night on the town.

Gannon made some vague reply that committed him to nothing, without being an outright rejection of the invitation. He preferred to see what developed in the way of possible financial advantage to himself before he committed himself to a whole evening with the man.

He did volunteer an equivalent amount of information about himself, though, all of it fictional except his statement that he was unmarried. He said he lived in Los Angeles and was in New York to work out the terms of a contract with a publisher for the travel book he was writing. In the event that something developed that would make it unwise for Stevens to be able to locate him, he said he was staying at the Plaza.

When it came time for a third drink, Gannon decided to test to see if a small bunco game would work. He had paid for the previous drink with the change from a five-dollar bill he had laid on the bar when he had his first drink alone. There wasn't enough change left for another round, as highballs were a dollar ten each.

Gannon picked some change from the bar and excused himself to get a pack of cigarettes. Glancing over his shoulder as he fed coins into the machine, he saw that the mystery writer wasn't looking his way. Quickly he removed the bills from his wallet and slipped them into a side pocket.

When he returned to the bar, he said to the bartender, "Give us another drink."

As the man started to mix drinks, Gannon took out his wallet, glanced at its emptiness and looked startled. Replacing it, he felt in his side trouser pocket, then looked at the mystery writer with rueful embarrassment.

"I must have left my money clip in my other pants when I changed to go out," he said.

"Need some money?" Stevens asked quickly.

Gannon was a little startled. At worst he had expected Stevens to pay for the drink he had just ordered, at best to have the man volunteer to treat him for the whole evening. The immediate offer of money made him proceed cautiously, so as not to make the mistake of settling for less than all he could get.

"You don't even know me," he said.

"You're a fellow writer," Stevens said reasonably. "In this lonely business, that's recommendation enough. You never gave me a definite answer about hitting a few spots when we leave here. Want to make an evening of it?"

"I did, but I'll have to run back to the hotel to pick up my money clip. We could take a cab over there together, then go on from there."

"The Plaza is too far. Why waste cab fare? The place I planned to show you first is only in the next block." He took out his wallet and separated two twenties and a ten from a sheaf of bills in it. "Here. You can pay me back tomorrow."

The bartender had delivered the drinks and was patiently waiting to be paid. With a show of reluctance Gannon accepted the money and handed the bartender the ten.

"Where will I see you tomorrow to pay you back?" he asked the mystery writer.

"You free for lunch?"

"I have a morning appointment with my publisher, but I should be free long before noon."

"Then how about meeting me at Tony's on Madison Avenue? Know where it is?"

Gannon shook his head.

Stevens explained in detail how to get to the place. When Gannon indicated he could find it, Stevens said, "MWA is just up the street from Tony's. After lunch I'll take you over and introduce you to some of the members."

"MWA? Oh, you mean the Mystery Writers of America that you're doing the anthology for."

"Uh-huh. We have a little place for meetings at the Hotel Seville, at 29th and Madison. We're looking for a new place, because we're in the heart of a high crime area."

"I should think that would be appropriate for mystery writers," Gannon said with a grin. "The atmosphere should be good for plot material. Sure, I'd be glad to meet some of your colleagues."

He had already decided to repay the fifty dollars the next day. If the mere mention that he was a fellow writer was enough to make R. L. Stevens open his wallet, perhaps other professional writers felt the same close bond with members of the writing fraternity. There was no percentage in settling for a mere fifty when there was an opportunity to meet a whole group of potential marks.

They hit four separate night spots and saw three different floor shows before the closing time of 3 A.M. Although Gannon drank drink-for-drink with his newfound friend, he had a much larger tolerance for alcohol than the mystery writer. Stevens was in a pretty carefree frame of mind when they finally separated to take cabs in different directions.

Gannon arrived at Tony's promptly at noon. Stevens was already waiting in a booth, nursing a hangover. He gave Gannon a reproachful look as the handsome con-man seated himself opposite him.

"You've no right to look so healthy," Stevens complained. "It took me a pint of tomato juice loaded with Worcestershire sauce and pepper before I could even face coffee."

Gannon grinned. "It must be old age creeping up. We young fellows never have hangovers. I was eating bacon and eggs at eight this morning."

Stevens shuddered.

Gannon handed him fifty dollars and thanked him for the loan.

"Don't mention it," the mystery writer said, preoccupiedly pocketing the money as he studied the menu. "As a matter of fact, don't mention anything about last night. I think I'll just have tomato soup, but you order what you want."

After lunch, which Stevens insisted on buying, they walked the short distance to MWA headquarters. The Seville was an old, genteely shabby place with a lobby full of worn furniture. They climbed stairs to the hotel's second floor and walked along a narrow corridor to the two-room suite rented by MWA.

There were several members present. Gannon met Brett Halliday, Ed McBain, Richard Marvin and his wife Susan Marvin, who was also a writer. Later two more mystery writers named Susan came in—Susan Richard and Susan Marino—and Stanley Hamilton and William Jeffrey also dropped by.

Everyone accepted at face value his introduction by Stevens as a fellow writer, and he sensed immediate rapport with all simply because he was assumed to be a member of the select fraternity of professional writers.

The pose was a perfect in with this group, he decided. Just being a professional writer seemed enough to create an instant bond with other writers, even when they were total strangers.

A little later Stevens took him into the other room, which contained the business office. There was a stenographer-clerk named Mary Baker working there. She was a cute little blonde of about twenty, and Gannon turned on all of his charm for her.

Within minutes of meeting her, he had made a date to take her to dinner that evening.

As they left the office, Stevens gave him a look of indulgent admiration. "You certainly work fast," he said. "Most of our bachelor members have been trying to date Mary for the whole six weeks she's been here, I'm told, but nobody's scored yet."

When Gannon picked up Mary Baker that evening, he as yet hadn't devised even a tentative plan for relieving any of the mystery writers he had met of their money. When, during the course of the evening, he learned from Mary that Mystery Writers of America had 585 members spread all over the country, he decided not to attempt any sort of dodge immediately. With a sucker list of that size, it would be wiser to wait until he could dream up some plan to take a lot of them simultaneously.

The immediate problem was to get a copy of the sucker list.

This wasn't very difficult for a con-man of Handsome Harry Gannon's practiced charm. He talked Mary into typing him up a list of the members' names and addresses by telling her he traveled so much, it would be nice to be able to get in touch with fellow writers when he found himself alone in a strange town. She agreed to prepare the list and told him he could pick it up the following noon.

During the rest of his two-week stay in Manhattan, Gannon took Mary out several times. Meantime Stevens had gone back to Rochester, but other MWA members had invited him to drop by headquarters any time he wished.

When he finally decided to move on to the west coast, his leave takings from everyone he had met were cordial. While he had exercised all his charm on Mary, he had carefully refrained from committing himself romantically. Her final good-by was wistful, but she made no attempt to pin him down about writing her.

He still had no definite plan for using his new sucker list when he left New York. As a matter of fact it was in Los Angeles some months later, after repeated visits to Hollywood Park racetrack had reduced his stake to less than five hundred dollars, before he seriously began to think about it. Then he locked himself in his hotel room for a whole afternoon and stared at the ceiling.

When a plan finally began to take shape, he got out his sucker list and examined it. There were fifty-one members of MWA within a radius of a hundred miles of Los Angeles. On the principle that names familiar to him were probably the most financially successful on the list, he placed a check mark before each of these. When he finished, there were twenty checks.

The next morning he was at the Los Angeles Public Library when it opened at ten. In the mystery fiction section he checked for authors who were not on the Mystery Writers of America membership list. He rejected all those who were widely known on the grounds that they might be personally acquainted with some of his potential marks, even though they didn't belong to the organization. He also rejected all those who had recently published books, even if they weren't particularly famous.

He finally came to a row of six books by a writer named Max Franklin. He recognized the name, because he had read all six of the books in his teens. He even recalled that the protagonist in each book had been the same private eye, a heavy-drinking, blonde-chasing tough guy named Al Cooney. He didn't recall having seen a new book by Franklin in years.

Taking them down one at a time, he checked publication dates. The first had been published in 1944, the last in 1950. The book jacket blurbs had been pasted on the insides of the covers, and he read each one carefully. There was no biographical data about the author included in any of the blurbs.

Perhaps Max Franklin was a pseudonym, Gannon thought. Checking the copyright notices, he found that all six books had been copyrighted in the name of Max Franklin. He was familiar enough with publishing practices to know that if the name was a pseudonym, the copyright would be in the name of the publisher.

Just to make sure, he went to the library's alphabetical card catalog and looked up the six cards filed under the author's name. Standard library practice is to list the real name of an author on the file card in parenthesis when the published name is a pseudonym. Max Franklin was the only name appearing.

It is also standard library practice to list the birth and death dates of authors behind their names. These cards all read Franklin, Max (1911–). That meant he either was still alive, or his obituary had escaped the notice of the watchdogs at the Congressional

Library who checked out such data and passed it along to public libraries.

He hadn't published his first book until he was thirty-three, Gannon noted, and would now be sixty-one if still alive.

If he were alive, why had he stopped publishing? But perhaps he hadn't. Perhaps, after publishing six hard-cover books, he had merely switched over to writing nothing but paperback originals, which public libraries didn't stock. With the plethora of books on the newsstands, it would have been easy for Gannon to miss his name.

There was a simple way to check that. Going to the reference room, he consulted the *Consolidated Index of Book Titles in the English Language*, an enormous compendium of many volumes that listed in alphabetical order all books published in English since 1900. It also listed book authors alphabetically, with the titles of their books, publishing houses and years of publication behind their names.

The individual volumes of the permanently bound set covered ten years each, and were about the size of an unabridged dictionary. In the volume for the period 1950 to 1960, *Franklin, Max* had only the last book that appeared on the library shelf listed behind his name, with the publication date 1950, indicating that during the next ten years at least he had published nothing. He was not listed at all in the volume for 1960 to January 1, 1970.

There were thinner books covering the individual years of 1970 and 1971. On the shelf to their right were even thinner, paperbound volumes listing publications for each month of 1972 so far.

Gannon checked clear up to the present month. Max Franklin had published nothing since 1950.

Despite the catalog file cards, he must be dead, Gannon thought. It really didn't matter for the gimmick he had in mind, so long as his death wasn't general knowledge. The important thing was that his name had once been well known, but he had published nothing in years.

Although it really wasn't necessary for Gannon to know anything else about the man, he liked to be thorough. When he got back to the hotel, he phoned long-distance to Mystery Writers of America headquarters in New York. It was 1 P.M. when he made the call, which made it 4 P.M. in New York, so Mary Baker was still at the office. She sounded delighted to hear from him.

After her gush of pleasure subsided, he said, "I'm calling for a favor, Mary. Do your membership files go as far back as the forties?"

"To 1945. That's when the organization was born."

"Good. I'm trying to find out something about a mystery writer named Max Franklin. He wouldn't have been a member of MWA during the past fifteen years, if he ever was. Could you check to see if he ever belonged?"

"Sure," she said. "We have a card file of past members in alphabetical order. That's Franklin like in Ben?"

"Uh-huh. Max Franklin."

"Hold the line."

About two minutes passed. When she returned, she said apologetically, "Sorry, but he was never a member of MWA, Harry."

"Well, thanks anyway," he said.

"Are you ever planning to come back to New York?" she asked quickly.

"Maybe in a few months," he said in a noncommittal tone. "I'll give you a ring when I do."

When he hung up, he decided the call had been worthwhile. If the man had been a member of MWA and was dead, undoubtedly his death would have been reported in MWA's monthly bulletin. Even though the announcement were years old, there would be a chance that some present member of the organization would recall it.

His next move, after having some lunch, was to call at a small, dingy photography studio in downtown Los Angeles. The proprietor was a grimy little man in his sixties with a stubble of gray beard.

"I need a California driver's license, Pops," Gannon said. "How much?"

"Half a hundred," the little man said dourly. "Cash."

Gannon counted out fifty dollars.

After taking his photograph, the little man got out a driver's license application form and silently handed it to Gannon. Gannon filled it out under the name of Max Franklin, but entered his own vital statistics. He put down a San Francisco address.

When the little man checked the form to make sure it had been properly completed, he asked no questions. He merely said, "Noon tomorrow."

From the photography shop Gannon went to a theatrical supply house, where he purchased a gray wig, an eyepatch, and a small make-up kit. Then he went to a secondhand clothing store and bought a fairly well fitting but worn suit.

He really didn't contemplate having to use this disguise. It was merely another example of his thorough planning. On the unlikely chance that one of his marks decided to deliver money personally instead of wiring it, he wanted to be prepared.

The fake driver's license he did intend to use, though. He needed it to identify himself as Max Franklin when he went to pick up his money orders at Western Union.

The following noon he picked up the fake license, checked out of his hotel and drove to Ontario, California, about thirty miles east of Los Angeles. He had picked it as his base of operations because none of his potential marks lived there. The closest was at Colton, twenty miles to the east, the farthest at Ojai, a hundred and twenty miles north.

He rented a motel room in which to stash his disguise, but he made his phone calls from a public booth at the bus station. Deciding he would start with the mark farthest away and gradually work closer, he told the operator he wanted to make a collect call to Richard Xavier at Ojai.

Giving her the address, he said, "I don't have the phone number. You'll have to get it from information. Tell Mr. Xavier Max Franklin is calling."

The operator obtained the phone number from Ojai information, announced it to Gannon, then rang the number. Gannon heard a male voice answer, then the operator said, "A collect call from Mr. Max Franklin for Richard Xavier. Will you accept the charge?"

"From who?" the male voice said. "I don't know any Max Franklin."

That was the first hurdle passed. If Franklin had been known to the mark and the call had been immediately accepted, Gannon would simply have hung up. He had no desire to converse with any old friends of Max Franklin.

Breaking in, he said, "Operator, tell him it's Max Franklin the mystery writer, and that it's important. I'm sorry I have to call collect, but I'm in a phone booth and all I have is a dime."

There was a pause, then, "Oh, that Max Franklin. Where's he calling from, operator?"

"Ontario, California, sir."

"Well, that can't be a very heavy charge. Put him on."

"Go ahead, sir," the operator said.

Gannon said, "Mr. Xavier?"

"Yes."

"I'm sorry to impose on you like this, but I'm in a rather desperate situation and don't know where else to turn. I remembered from the blurb on one of your books that you live in Ojai, and just took a chance that you would talk to me."

"Uh-huh. What's your problem?"

"Are you familiar with my work, Mr. Xavier?"

"Well, somewhat. Don't you do the Al Cooney series?"

"Did, Mr. Xavier, not do. I've been blind since 1950."

After a pause, Xavier said, "I'm sorry."

"Oh, I'm not completely blind any more. About six months ago the Lions Club back home arranged a cornea transplant for me. I now have about fifty percent vision in one eye, not enough to get my driver's license back, but quite enough to work a typewriter. But after twenty-two years without turning out a single book, I'm pretty well destitute. An old friend of mine here in Ontario offered to board me and my wife free while I knock out a book and get back on my feet. He sent us transportation money to get out here. We arrived yesterday, only to discover he'd died while we were en route. His only relative is a cousin in Canada, who inherits everything, but doesn't plan even to come to the funeral. Naturally the police won't even let us in my friend's house."

"You are in a jam," Xavier said.

"You haven't heard it all. We arrived here dead broke. I'm sixty-one and still half blind, so I can't even get a job as a dishwasher. We've been to public welfare, but they can't help us because we're non-residents. The Salvation Army offered us a meal, but our real problem is transportation back home. We haven't any permanent place to stay there, but at least we have friends who would put us up until we can get on public welfare. I know this is a terrible imposition, but I'm absolutely desperate, and all I could think to turn to was a fellow mystery writer. I'm not asking for a handout, but if you could find it in your heart to make me a transportation loan, I'll guarantee to pay it back. It'll probably be six months, because I have to write a book first, but I have a publisher's offer of a three thousand advance as soon as I finish the book."

"Where's your home?" Xavier asked.

"Chautauqua, New York."

"Hmm. What's the fare?"

"Seventy-three fifty each by bus. That's a hundred and forty-seven dollars."

Gannon didn't add that food would be required during the several-day trip. He figured it was better psychology to let this occur to the mark spontaneously. Once a mark was hooked with this type of gimmick, Gannon had learned from experience, it was more profitable to bank on his natural generosity than to try to squeeze a few extra dollars out of him.

There was a period of silence while Richard Xavier thought things over. Finally he said, "I can hardly leave a fellow mystery writer in the jam you're in. I'll take a chance. Do you have any money at all?"

"Just the dime I used to call you. The operator gave it back. I can't even get up there to get the money."

"You have any place to stay there tonight?"

"No. We slept sitting up in the bus station last night."

"I'll wire you a money order," Xavier said. "Take my address down so you can return it when you get back on your feet. Do you have a pencil?"

"A pen. Go ahead."

When Richard Xavier had given his address, which naturally Gannon didn't bother to write down, the writer said, "That must be a several-day trip by bus. You'll need food en route, plus a few bucks to tide you over when you get there. Suppose I wire you two fifty?"

"I'd certainly appreciate it," Gannon said. "As I say, it'll probably be six months before I can pay you back, but you'll hear from me the minute I get my advance."

"I'm sure I will," Xavier said. "I always liked the Al Cooney stories, and wondered what had happened to you. I'm glad you're on the road back. I'll get a money order off right away. I think there's only one Western Union office in Ontario, so you can pick it up there. Good luck to you."

"And God bless you," Gannon said. "I'll never forget you, Mr. Xavier."

That was easy, he thought when he hung up. He decided that after he had finished calling the names he had checked, he would try his luck with the less familiar names on the list.

On two of his twenty calls women answered and said their husbands were out of town. On one there was no answer at all. With the rest no one refused to accept charges and his hard-luck story worked every time. By noon he had been promised sixteen money orders varying from two hundred to two hundred and fifty dollars each.

He had lunch before calling the last name on the list, which was in Colton.

The man in Colton was named Stephen Dentinger. When the operator asked if he would accept a collect call from Max Franklin, the writer said in a tone of surprise, "Max Franklin, the mystery writer?"

The words suggested that Dentinger might be personally acquainted with Franklin, but it was possible the man was merely familiar with his work. Deciding he could always hang up if Dentinger was a personal friend of Franklin's, Gannon proceeded to find out.

"That's right," he broke in.

"Well, well," Dentinger said. "Put him on, operator."

"Go ahead, sir," the operator said.

It was sounding more and more as though Dentinger were personally acquainted with the man Gannon was pretending to be, but there was no danger in making sure. He said, "Mr. Dentinger?"

"Uh-huh. What can I do for you, Mr. Franklin?"

At least Dentinger and Franklin weren't close enough to be on a first-name basis, Gannon thought. But he would still have to hang up if it developed that they were even remotely personally acquainted. He said, "I don't believe we've ever personally met, have we?"

He was relieved when the man said, "Not that I know of."

Gannon said, "I asked because my name seemed so familiar to you. I know yours just as well, of course, but yours has been considerably more in evidence than mine in recent years. I haven't published a book since 1950."

"Yes, I know."

"I'm sorry to impose on you, Mr. Dentinger, but I'm in a rather desperate situation and don't know where else to turn."

"What's your problem?"

For the seventeenth time Gannon repeated his tale of woe, and for the seventeenth time it went over just as smoothly. The only variation was that when it came time to discuss how Dentinger would get the money to the fake Max Franklin, the writer decided on personal delivery.

"I have to drive into L.A. this afternoon anyway," he said. "You say you're at the bus station?"

"That's right, Mr. Dentinger."

"I'll have to stop by the bank to get the money, so I'll probably be about an hour. How will I know you?"

"It won't be difficult. I wear a patch over one eye."

"Okay," Dentinger said. "See you in about an hour."

That was a nuisance, Gannon thought when he hung up. But it was worth donning the disguise for two hundred to two hundred and fifty dollars. Of course he was supposed to have a wife with him, but he had already worked out an excuse for her not to be present. His wife, who was a devout Catholic, had gone to afternoon Mass. Dentinger would hardly want to wait around to meet her, since he would be en route to Los Angeles.

Since he had a full hour, and by now there had been time for all the wires to arrive, he decided to stop by Western Union for his money orders before donning his disguise. The manager there was obviously curious about so many money orders from different localities for the same person, but he asked no questions other than those designed to make sure Gannon was the correct recipient. Gannon had to tell him from whom he was expecting each money order and the expected amount, then had to show his fake California driver's license to identify himself as Max Franklin.

He walked out with sixteen money orders totaling thirty-six hundred dollars.

He took pains with his disguise. In the past he had adopted many roles and he was an expert with make-up. He didn't make the mistake of applying greasepaint wrinkles to age his appearance, because greasepaint would show in daylight. He merely applied a coating to his face and hands which he mixed himself and which muddied his complexion to the rough texture of a sixty-one-year-old man in good condition.

After putting on the gray wig, the secondhand suit of clothes and the eyepatch, he examined himself in the full-length mirror on the bathroom door. He was completely satisfied with what he saw. No one, he was sure, would suspect his disguise even in strong sunlight, let alone under the ordinary lighting of the bus station.

He was back at the bus station fifteen minutes before the hour was up. There were two men in the waiting room who hadn't been there previously, but when neither paid him any attention, he decided neither could be Stephen Dentinger. They were seated side-by-side on a bench, although they gave no indication of being together.

He had been waiting about ten minutes when a portly man of somewhere around sixty entered the waiting room. The man glanced around, his gaze first resting on the two men seated side-by-side, then moving on to Gannon. With a smile of recognition, he came over to where Gannon was seated.

"You Max Franklin?" he asked.

"That's right," Gannon said, rising. "You're Stephen Dentinger?"

"Uh-huh. Where's your wife?"

"She was so relieved when I told her you were going to help us, she went off to Mass to pray for you. She's a devout Catholic."

"I see," Dentinger said. He drew out a thick roll of bills. "I brought you two fifty, figuring you would need some food money on the way home. That okay?"

"It's more than generous, Mr. Dentinger," Gannon said devoutly as he accepted the money. "I'll never forget you."

"I'll bet you won't," a voice said behind him.

Gannon threw a startled glance over his shoulder. The two men who had been seated side-by-side were right behind him. One grasped him by either arm, forced his wrists back and handcuffs clicked into place.

The money cascaded to the floor and Stephen Dentinger began to scurry around picking it up.

"What is this?" Gannon demanded indignantly.

Both police officers ignored the question. One held out his hand to the portly writer. "We'll have to have that as evidence, Mr. Dentinger. You'll get it back eventually, of course."

The other officer was giving Gannon a thorough shakedown. He drew the sixteen money orders from his inside breast pocket. Skimming through them, he let out a low whistle.

"Boy, you've been making a real kill, haven't you?" he said.

Gannon said sullenly, "You guys have nothing on me. Those were sent to me voluntarily."

"It's still fraud," the man who had searched him said cheerfully. "You accepted money under misrepresented circumstances."

Gannon looked at the portly Stephen Dentinger, who was examining him with a mixture of curiosity and amusement.

"You picked the wrong sucker," the writer said. "I phoned the sheriff's office."

Gannon examined him in return. "What tipped you off?"

"Elementary, my dear fellow. Max Franklin didn't quit writing because he went blind. He quit because he got tired of Al Cooney and wanted to try his hand at books with a little more substance. I thought I had buried Max back in 1950."

Gannon stared at him. "You mean you were Max Franklin? But that's impossible. It wasn't a pseudonym."

"There's more than one way to skin a cat," the writer said with a smile. "When I decided I no longer wanted my name associated with that idiot, Al Cooney, I realized the most effective way to disassociate it was to legally change my name to something else. So in 1950 Max Franklin legally ceased to exist and Stephen Dentinger was legally born."

AFTERWORD

Mr. Deming has added to his story an inside joke for mystery writers and enthusiasts. Dealing as it does with pseudonyms, the story is filled with them; all the names except Handsome Harry Gannon and Mary

Baker are ones which have appeared as bylines on fiction, and all are pseudonyms.

As Mr. Deming writes: "The writer Handsome Harry meets in the New York bar and the writer who undoes him in the end are two pseudonyms of the same real life author. Four of the writers Handsome Harry meets at MWA headquarters are pseudonyms for one writer who uses them all.

"Max Franklin happens to be an old, no-longer-used pseudonym of mine, although I never wrote about a series character named Al Cooney."

Knowing Dick Deming, however, he may, he may!

As most mystery enthusiasts know, Melville Davidson Post (1871–1930) was a practicing attorney who, some years before he wrote his renowned *Uncle Abner: Master of Mysteries*, startled and outraged the legal establishment with books about Randolph Mason, a lawyer who used the defects in the law to defeat it. Pointing out the failings in the legal structure, Post contended, could do only good.

Jack Leavitt, a California attorney turned editor (of law books) and writer (of mystery stories) seems to feel the same way. In this story, written, Jack wishes to state, with the assistance of Phil Richards, he introduces us to Allan Shortridge, a rising young lawyer whose "Masonic" training is more Randolph than Perry; and who, by using the correct decision, makes the wrong one.

Killer Out of Work
JACK LEAVITT

Six stories high and bureaucratically gray, the State Building filled an entire block in San Francisco's Civic Center. As attorney Allan Shortridge dodged in cadence with the civil service personnel who jostled each other on the wide-stepped McAllister Street entranceway, he weighed and reweighed, considered and reconsidered the unemployment insurance case that could save Charlie Baron from the gas chamber.

"Or send him there direct," Allan reminded himself. Regardless of quirks in the law, the public admission of a gangland killing was a rough go for an old-time mobster.

Nothing in Allan's appearance indicated the urgency of his thoughts. Five-foot ten inches tall, he had curly black hair, soft greenish eyes and a respectful smile toward the world at large. His worn briefcase seemed perfect for carrying picnic lunches and vintage wines.

"*Escamilla v. Superior Court*, 271 Cal. App. 2d 730," Allan registered the precedent on which he was betting Baron's life. "The perfect cure for a killer out of work." A precise technician, he had even memorized the dissenting judge's disgust: "In my opinion, this is an example of an inexcusable attempt to secure an 'immunity bath' by a person previously informed against for a major crime." But the dissent, by definition, had failed. The immunity bath had worked once—and should work again! Or should it?

Slightly chilled—"How safe am *I* if we fail?"—Allan strayed to the blind concessionaire's counter in the lobby. The sightless old man, presiding over racks of chewing gum and cigarettes, cocked his head at Allan, listening for the sounds of merchandise being slipped into a customer's pocket.

"Glycerine cough drops." Allan slid a fifty-cent piece on the counter and waited for Ralph Brewer, Baron's liaison man and security chief.

The old man hefted the coin and let it drop in a straight fall. Satisfied with its authentic ring, he made change while Allan unwrapped the tablets.

"Throat dry, counsellor?" Brewer eased over to the refreshment stand. Dressed conservatively, he spoke quietly and had never been penalized for any crime more serious than overtime parking.

Together, Allan and Brewer walked down the corridor toward the Golden Gate Avenue side of the building. At their left was a Highway Patrol office with the door invitingly open. The duty officer was busily gesturing at a city map to a bewildered civilian. "If the referee boxes me in, you'd better begin figuring out how many *cruzeiros* your dollars will buy. Night life in Rio comes high."

"I like it here, counsellor."

"So do I, Ralph. So do I. The law's a noble profession."

A hall clock caught their eyes. 9:38. Allan checked his wrist watch, with its calendar band, and asked, "Has it been a full month since Harvey Winters was shot?"

"Was he shot?" Brewer looked blank. "I wasn't there."

"I'm on good terms with my newsboy, Ralph." Allan traced an imaginary headline with his forefinger. "GANG LEADER SLAIN, Bodyguards Wounded." With a hard snap he bit the cough drop in two. "I understand there was a getaway car waiting."

Brewer flicked at a hangnail. "I ride taxis myself."

"So far"—Allan retreated into the morning's business—"I don't know who's opposing me. I'm not listed as attorney of record, and the insurance company has so many house counsel I may draw someone who'll co-operate with me."

"You mean the schedule might go faster than we figured? Our friend'll be right out?" Brewer broke stride and waited for an answer.

Shaking his head, Allan pivoted northward before they reached the Highway Patrol office a second time. "Co-operation would destroy us."

"You're the one who talked everyone into this performance."

Allan paled, the first outward sign of his knife-edge tension. "Look, Ralph, let's go through it again. If I knew, really *knew*, someone was going to kill Harvey Winters, I couldn't ethically have mentioned the busboy job. Whatever I said, I said carefully. Every client has the right to know what his lawyer knows about the law."

"You're an ignorant man, counsellor," Brewer agreed. "I like your style. You draw fine lines."

Side by side, sure-footed professionals, they walked along the corridor, occasionally overtaken by the wandering public. "No sense arriving too early," Allan decided. "I'll pick-up the hearing room assignment in a minute."

"Tension getting to you?" Brewer's inquisitive smile reflected the yellowish overhead lights.

"Well, damn it! What pushed our friend to give Winters his personal attention? Wasn't there anyone"—Allan stared tenaciously at Brewer—"who was better trained to handle a dusting job?"

Brewer's eyes turned predatory. "Whenever you give advice, counsellor, you walk on eggs. 'Don't tell me *that*,' you say, 'or I'll have to report it. Just act like you've got an idea for a television show.'"

"I never sell out a client, Ralph, and I never push him too far. That way he's safe and I sleep easily."

They approached a bank of elevators. Signaling for them to hurry, a mail carrier used a Fragile-stamped package to hold back a thrusting elevator door. Allan waved gratefully but shook his head. The elevator door slid closed and the mechanism hissed upward.

"Counsellor, our friend didn't have a choice. You know better than anyone what the statute of limitations is for Penal Code 187." Brewer's tone was icily precise.

"There's *no* limitation on murder prosecutions." Allan visualized the bright red volume of California's criminal statutes. "Our friend would have to worry about doorbells for the rest of his life."

"Where I live we have a night clerk to announce visitors. Our friend does, too, but he's still strung out with worry. He's sure somebody close wouldn't mind if the police leaned on him."

"Then why settle Winters in the first place?" Allan looked perplexed.

"Didn't you know, counsellor? Our friend was desperate. The word back East was that he couldn't hack it any more. West Coast spiritual leader was too much for him."

Allan mused about the organization. "Anyone our friend tapped to settle Winters"—Brewer grinned agreement at the emerging thought—"could easily have been tapped to settle him instead." Brewer's grin became overwhelming.

One flight up stood the highly glossed, natural wood finish of the door to Room 2004. UNEMPLOYMENT INSURANCE APPEALS. ENTER.

Allan patted his briefcase and hurried up the stairs. Brewer remained in the north end of the corridor. As Allan reached the door, he glanced back and saw Brewer run a forefinger along his nose in a studiously casual gesture. A light-suited, light-haired man became suddenly visible as he stepped away from the wall, nodded in Brewer's direction and headed for Golden Gate Avenue. The limousine he wanted was undoubtedly circling the block, obeying the speed limit and honoring every stop sign on the way.

"The river rises." Allan stepped into the administrative office. At a deserted high counter next to a sign-in sheet, a Xeroxed list gave the calendar assignments for the day's litigants. "Claude Charles Berchowsky, Petitioner v. Wendover's Restaurant, Inc., Respondent, 1UE—67743—SF." To be heard by Referee Matthew Simmons at 10 A.M. in Room 2236. Opposing counsel had signed-in earlier but his illegible handwriting left him anonymous.

"Finicky Matt." Allan visualized the rap sheet on the hearing officer he had yet to meet. "Still bitter he was made only a referee instead of a judge." Drumming on the countertop, Allan sketched out the courtroom strategy that would best annoy and then intimidate the referee. "Unless he's annoyed more than he's intimidated."

In the second-floor corridor, Allan passed a patiently waiting Brewer. The security man, as usual, seemed hardly aware of the passing scene. Without breaking stride, the attorney quietly said, "Room 2236" and bore to his right, down a narrower hallway that led to the hearing room.

Set-up like an economy-sized courtroom, with little space and no frills, the windowless hearing room provided two-dozen chairs for the general public. Only one seat was occupied. "That's Wendover's day manager." Allan knew. "A cousin of Baron's accountant." Toward the front of the room, in the area reserved for counsel, a heavy-breathing attorney had already mobilized his files on the green table. Allan sorted through his memorized data. "Either George Quincy or B. E. Christopher."

"Ready to kill 'em, counsel?" Allan snapped. "I'm Shortridge."

"The name's Christopher. Bunker Hill's claim department. That stupid guy deserved to be fired."

Condescending to an irritating inferior, Allan privately sized-up his opponent. "Bernard Eugene Christopher . . . former insurance adjuster . . . graduated last year from Thomas Jefferson Night Law School." With an apparently surprised "What's this?" Allan reached down and grabbed a pad of Christopher's handwritten notes.

"Hey!" the defense attorney tugged the pad as Allan pulled at the uppermost page. "What the hell . . ." The top sheet ripped in half. "You damned guy!"

"Oh, come off it." Allan seemed peeved. "A lawsuit isn't a sporting contest. Didn't they teach you anything in night school?" To himself, he cheered, "Stay angry, Mr. Christopher. Stay angry."

From the hearing room's public entranceway appeared the light-suited man Allan had seen slip away at Brewer's signal. Instinctively, Allan ran a forefinger along his nose. The man edged backwards toward the door and slowly opened it. Into the room stalked Charlie Baron.

Like the busboy he briefly was, Baron fidgeted at the courtroom's strangeness. Its off-yellow walls could too readily be changed to steel bars. Dressed in dark brown slacks and a blue windbreaker, bargain store acquisitions of the previous month, he wore a heavy new mustache and a newly purchased, slicked-back toupee. His elevator shoes added inches to his usual short stature, and shell-rimmed glasses neutralized his truculent eyes. A trickle of sweat past his sideburns defied his attempts to remain outwardly calm.

Allan pointed to a chair at the attorney's table. "Be comfortable, Mr. Berchowsky. You'll soon be on the stand."

"I warn you," Baron hissed. His saliva dampened the air.

"All in good time, sir. I know I'm not your regular attorney. But we've got a nasty opponent practicing law he learned in the dead of night. He's probably eavesdropping on every word."

Christopher fumed. "Damn you, mister."

Appearing smug, Allan clicked to attention when the court reporter, a slim blonde, walked into the hearing room from the restricted area, two steps in front of the business-suited referee. Matthew Simmons appeared indignant that no bailiff called the session to order.

"Yes, yes," Simmons mumbled while he seated himself on the low platform that set him apart from his constituency. His station was at an ordinary desk between the national and state flags, rather than at the high bench judges use. "Who's on?" He waved a single page assignment list.

"May it please the court," Allan spoke respectfully, then grew bewildered. "That is, you're not really a *court*, are you, sir? Meaning no offense, that is, about your rank."

"Get on with it, counsel!" Simmons was livid.

"Well, referee, my name is Allan Shortridge, substituting for counsel of record. We claim the petitioner's entitled to unemployment compensation benefits because he was wrongfully fired by Wendover's Restaurant."

Attorney Christopher cut in. "Waste of time, Your Honor. He stranded my client during the lunch rush hour . . ."

Referee Simmons rapped on the desk with his fist, regretting the absence of a gavel. "Come to order, both of you. Will this take long?"

"I really don't know, Mr. Referee." Allan sounded unprepared. "Maybe I should have had more time for preparation."

On his feet and shuffling papers, Christopher shouted, "Too late now. He can't get a continuance! Every minute is costing us money."

The court reporter tapped each angry syllable on her Stenotype tape. To prevent herself from becoming interested in the people whose words she was recording, and then forgetting to immortalize their remarks, she stared hazily at a distant thread of dust. "In that machine," Allan watched her work, "rides the big gamble."

"All right, counsel. I don't encourage opening statements. Put on your case." Simmons settled back in his padded, high-backed swivel chair. The janitorial service's housekeeping deficiencies engrossed him as much as they did the reporter.

"Petitioner Claude Charles Berchowsky to the stand." Allan signaled Charlie Baron to move forward and be sworn-in by the reporter. Allan's forced calm and Baron's barely repressed fury were their only means of camouflaging the fear they both felt. One thoughtless look would strip off the disguise.

Seated in a wooden armchair which leveled an unplugged microphone attachment at his chin, Baron stiffened as Allan stood buoyantly for the direct examination. From the mobster's damp cheeks the sweat dripped down to his tight collar and, in a final fall, dotted his windbreaker. After the eventual congratulations stopped coming in and the empty magnums of champagne were carted away, Allan would have to prepare himself for the inexcusable blunder of seeing Baron so terrified. Win or lose, he faced spiked hurdles.

"Is Claude Charles Berchowsky your true name?" Allan stood behind the counsel table with his fingertips pressed against the rim, and steeled his thoughts away from future dangers.

"That's what's on my birth certificate."

"Were you working for Wendover's Restaurant, a California corporation, on August 23rd of this year?"

Baron nodded.

"No, no." Allan raised his hands, palms outward. "The reporter can't take down headshakes. Please answer yes or no."

Baron glowered. "Yes."

"What was your job?" Allan once again pushed his fingers against the table rim, this time to keep them from trembling.

"Busboy," Baron rasped. The temperature on the witness stand appeared 20° warmer than in the rest of the courtroom.

Allan's next question came promptly and clearly. "Were you at your station during the lunch hour that day?" Offhandedly asked, the question triggered an elusive vision in the attorney's mind. With menacing unreality, he saw before him the acid-filled bucket into which the State would drop two cyanide tablets to carry out the penalty for first degree murder. Inside the gas chamber an agonized face kept dissolving from Baron's features to Allan's. The mourners, suddenly gathered, were all from Allan's family.

"No, I wasn't." The mobster's actual voice wavered as he forced himself to end his answer without volunteering anything.

"Were you"—Allan projected surprise—"doing something else?"

Baron became virtually inaudible. Several rows away, seat-shifting by his light-suited underling nearly drowned out the response. "A personal matter."

Allan stared in apparent bewilderment, knowing he could never ethically lie to the court but gratified that Referee Simmons had free reign to mislead himself. "Mr. Referee"—Allan emphasized the subordinate rank—"I said earlier that someone else was the attorney of record here. At this stage, perhaps the best thing to do, would be for me to, well, if you granted, say, a week's continuance, or ten days, and I would talk to that other lawyer . . ." Allan's request trailed off raggedly.

"Objection, Your Honor!" stormed attorney Christopher.

"Sustained!" shot out Referee Simmons's answering barb. "Apparently, Mr. Shortridge, you didn't think the facts mattered very much in my jurisdiction. Next time, get properly briefed."

"Yes, sir," Allan sounded despondent. "At the present time, under the circumstances, I have no further questions." He seated himself with pained deliberation.

Bobbing up like a spring-loaded toy, attorney Christopher announced, "Cross-examination, Your Honor. All right, sir, what was this personal matter you were doing?"

Baron wiped the back of his neck. ("Self-control, damn it," Allan silently pleaded. "Stop looking so guilty!") After a time, Baron stared down at his knuckles. "Something for myself and for the good of the whole community."

"Spell it out!"

"I want it private."

"But you also want your unemployment benefits, don't you?" Christopher rattled his pad at the witness.

"It's coming to me."

"Then tell us exactly what you did on the August 23rd lunch hour."

"Don't say anything, Mr. Berchowsky." Allan pushed himself to his feet, an outclassed fighter refusing to accept defeat. He glanced at Baron, who was supporting himself with the microphone stand, and groped for an argument. "Mr. Referee, that's a question I have to object to."

"But your objection's bad, Mr. Shortridge. You know that. If your client was fired for cause, nobody has to pay him anything. Let the witness answer."

"What I was doing . . ." Baron haltingly began.

Allan broke in hurriedly, the drowning man clutching at a constitutional straw. "Oh, wait. I mean"—he drew inspiration from the flag standing at the referee's elbow—"it may tend to incriminate him." Allan clapped his hands together, as though convincing himself he had finally hit on a valid point.

"Ha!" blurted the defense counsel.

"Look." Referee Simmons took command. "Your client said he wanted his benefits. Don't raise frivolous objections. I'm ordering him to answer, on pain of contempt."

"You mean you're just ignoring my objection? But it's based on the constitution," Allan whined.

"Your objection, counsel, is noted for the record . . . for whatever it's worth."

Christopher tore into Baron. "What was the business that took you away from the restaurant?"

Slumping back into the witness chair, eyes averted, Baron announced in a soft, irregularly pitched voice, "Harvey Winters was a crook and a dope peddler. We're all better off without him. I left my job, where I was trying to learn the business, and shot Winters. He deserved it."

"Did you get that down?" Referee Simmons gasped at the court reporter.

Without interrupting her fingerwork, she called back, "Yes." She stared at her printed hieroglyphics in disbelief. Open-mouthed, attorney Christopher looked stunned and delighted. He had saved his company $42 a week. Allan forced back a sigh.

"I'm putting you under arrest." The referee jabbed a finger at Baron.

"Please, Your Honor," Allan gradually regained his apparently vanished poise. "You don't have general powers of arrest. And my client's certainly not in contempt for obeying you."

"He admitted the killing right here. What nonsense is this, counsel?"

Allan stood before the referee, speaking judiciously, while his small audience strained to hear him. "Your Honor, respect for the law means that we're obliged to obey even the laws and precedents with which we disagree. Perhaps I didn't know enough facts in this case to satisfy you, but I do know my constitutional law. That's solid. Unimpeachable." Baron jerked his head in frightened agreement. "Will you trust my memory or, better yet, get Volume 271 of the California Appellate Reports, Second Series?"

"Get it? Why should I?"

"Because it'll prove, by a decision this court is bound to obey, that you have to free Mr. Berchowsky."

"Don't be an idiot, counsel. He's publicly confessed."

"That's why." Allan yielded to the omnipotence of the absent higher tribunal.

The referee excused himself for three minutes. When he returned to the anxious hearing room—where everyone had waited in an immobile, silent tableau—he carried a light tan copy of the official reports. Two armed highway patrolmen paraded at his side. "Get on with it, Mr. Shortridge," he ordered.

The pistol-wearing officers terrified Baron, who crouched back exhausted in the witness chair. Never before had he been so few breaths from the gas chamber—and solely because of his own words. Allan impassively watched Baron's eyes broadcasting only fear.

With what had imperceptibly become a fully respectful manner, Allan addressed Referee Simmons. "Our case is *Escamilla v. Superior Court*, 271 Cal. App. 2d, somewhere around page 700. Its holding is simple. In a hearing for unemployment compensation benefits, if a witness is compelled to answer questions, even if the answers 'added nothing' to the unemployment case, the witness *cannot* be prosecuted for the matters about which he testified. He can't. It's an all-fours decision."

The referee began riffling pages. "It sounds like a trick."

"That's what the dissenting judge argued, sir. He lost."

"You know a lot about this," interrupted Christopher. When the light-suited underling leaned forward in his seat, ready for action, Allan caught the threat and inconspicuously waved him back.

"I know *Escamilla* because I spend my nights reading cases for emergencies. Would you like to match citations for $5 a throw? To charity," Allan added.

In disbelieving surprise, the referee announced, "He's right." As if seeking immediate protection from himself, he waved for a highway patrolman to march closer and examine the printed decision. "Incredible!" While the officer glanced past his shoulder, Referee Simmons read aloud:

> "Any person may knowingly and intelligently waive his constitutional rights, but no court or referee can force him to waive them without a compensating protection which, here, was the right not to be prosecuted or subjected to any penalty or forfeiture from any matter about which petitioner was compelled to testify."

Allan's briefcase rested in his hands. "If Your Honor please, all things considered, I'm ready to postpone the remainder of the hearing. We've had a strenuous morning."

"Wait a minute!" A khaki-clad officer pushed Baron back into the witness chair.

"Wait yourself!" Allan thumped the table. "All you can do is impound the reporter's Stenotape. The only evidence against my client is the evidence that keeps you from trying him. You wanted it! You forced it! You got it!"

Flustered, out of his depth, unsure of whether he could be sued for ordering Baron's arrest, Referee Simmons stammered, "I don't . . . you *lied* to me."

"Not once, Your Honor. Check the record. And now, by your leave." Alan took Baron's elbow and nudged him toward the rear of the hearing room. The light-suited spectator sped ahead to open the door. Like discredited intruders, the police stood by awkwardly, certain they lacked probable cause to make an arrest. Baron's underling slipped protectively through the door, followed by the still-agitated mobster. Last in line, Allan reached the corridor as Brewer, the poised security chief, was shaking Baron's hand.

"McAllister Street exit, Charlie," Brewer whispered. "Northwest corner."

Baron turned a sodden face to Allan, furious at the last hour's strain. "I'll see you later," he spit past the attorney onto the door of Room 2236. Wiping the back of his neck once more, the mobster strutted down the corridor with exaggerated arrogance.

Allan marked time for an instant and slowly began to follow Baron downstairs. Brewer touched him on the shoulder. "Only a minute, counsellor."

"No longer suitable company for an innocent man?" Allan shrugged.

"You always knew he had a short memory, didn't you?" Brewer remarked. "That's why I like your style. You'd help him again."

"I told you, I'm in a noble profession. I'd do this for anyone."

Crumppp! At the McAllister Street end of the corridor, the window glass fragmented and smashed to the floor. Down the hallway a dull, explosive boom volleyed back and forth. A fire extinguisher jerked from its restraining bracket and clattered down. Allan dropped forward, hands and briefcase protecting his face. Brewer, oddly calm, remained erect.

"*Down*, Ralph. What was that? A bomb?"

Brewer looked thoughtful. "For all I know, everyone's going to blame Harvey Winters's boys for blowing-up our friend. They're probably right." Slowly, he rubbed his nose.

"Did that explosion kill . . ."

"Counsellor," Brewer interrupted, "it might have been a gas main. But if someone we know did get wasted, I wouldn't mind having a good lawyer of my own." With a relaxed fist he tapped his billfold pocket.

From his crouching position, Allan helped himself up. "I promise you, though"—he hefted his briefcase—"it'll cost."

The Royal Canadian Mounted Police are one of the most famous law-enforcement agencies in the world, and have suffered lamentably as a result. Most people not in immediate contact with the force tend to hold an image which is an amalgam of Nelson Eddy, Sergeant Preston of the Yukon, and Dudley Do-Right; the true competence and heroism of the RCMP has been lost in a fog of red coats, pistol-lanyards, and "always get their man" jokes. The North American Indian ("Amerind," if you please) has fared even worse—what the dime novel began, the movies have magnified, and the occasional film *apologia* seems to have had little useful effect.

Captain Liam Grey may, then, come as a bit of a surprise: a thoughtful, competent policeman who still retains the true dedication to the Force. So may the Iron River Indians, from anthropologist and ex-la crosse star James Raven Feathers and lawyer Charlie Moon through elders William Wilson and Aaron Jackson to the Red Militants, Henry Running Bear and John Yellow Sky. They form an unusually vivid portrait of the varying adaptations made by the Indian to modern society, while retaining his individual view of tribal ethics.

Chelsea Quinn Yarbro is the fascinating name of a fascinating young woman, who is enamored of mystery and science fiction, playwriting, gastronomy, opera and her husband, who is himself a phenomenon in art and invention. Having retired as secretary of The Science Fiction Writers of America, she is devoting herself to writing, among other things, a mystery novel featuring attorney Charlie Moon.

The Ghosts at Iron River
CHELSEA QUINN YARBRO

"Damn it, Nicholson, not over there!" James Raven Feathers yelled at the soccer players as the ball rolled between the staked mounds. "That's sacred ground! Cut it out!"

"Sorry, chief," came the call as Ian Nicholson retrieved the ball.

"Yeah. Just make sure you keep it away from here. Understand?"

The young man waved good-naturedly, jogging away across the dry grass. Nine other students in soccer togs followed him as James turned back to the RCMP Captain who stood with him in the staked enclosure at the end of the wide meadow.

"Aren't you being a little hard on them?" Captain Grey asked with a wink. "Should have thought you'd be out there yourself."

James Raven Feathers shook his head. "Not for me. Doctor's orders. And this is more important." He nodded toward the burial mounds.

"Right. I assume you've got it all cleared with the chief? There isn't going to be any nastiness over this." From the way he said it, Captain Grey was doing more than hoping. He straightened his rangy six feet and pulled on his gloves. "We got to stay around while you get the bodies moved, but after that, if you want to do anything special over them . . ." He left his thought open.

"Thank you," James said quickly. His dark, intense eyes were out of place in his young face. He scowled at the mounds. "First we'll have to open them. My grandfather will oversee that. Then we'll have to make sure all the skeletons are complete. They were buried wrapped in leather, but once that rots, there might be some drift. It's very important, a complete skeleton. My students are all set for that. When we're through, your men can come in and take care of the hauling."

"A lot of trouble for a . . ."

"A bunch of dead Indians?" demanded James fiercely. "You bet it is. But no one will move from here unless those dead Indians go with the live ones. And if we don't go, you don't get your hydroelectric dam."

Captain Grey shrugged. He liked young Wilson (Raven Feathers, he reminded himself) and trusted him to make the Iron River Indians move as uncomplicated as possible. He knew that the younger men were touchy about being Indians, and he tried to go easy around them. But the habits of thirty years died hard and occasionally he blundered.

"We *do* value our dead," James said forcefully.

Grey sensed more irritation than usual in the Indian. "Has Chief Jackson tried to interfere?"

"No. It's not that. There was an article in the *Globe & Mail*. Davidson was kind enough to mail me a copy. One of their reporters had talked with Yngvessen."

"Oh? Who?"

"That muck-peddler Choffe." James fairly spat the name.

"What did he have to say?" Grey kicked a rock out of the path as he asked.

"The usual garbage. That we're a child-like, simple people, lacking culture and civilization, and that it's the responsibility of intelligent, progressive Teutons to look after the poor, incompetent Red Man." He snorted. "Predigested to words of two syllables."

"As bad as all that?"

"Yes, and we have to take it. Sometimes I wish Berenet had lived long enough to publish that bloody book of his. At least he had a different point of view. As it is we're saddled with that *dreck* of Yngvessen's."

"I see," Grey said, involuntarily looking at the bleak setting of the Iron River village.

James followed his glance. "Grandfather wants to talk to you. Today, before you leave. He told me to tell you."

Grey nodded. "Good. I'll go now. Always like seeing William. He's been a lot of help over the years. He sure knows how to handle people." The praise was genuine and it won him a wintery smile from the sullen young man at his side.

"Yes, grandfather has always been a peaceful Indian. A real model of failing culture." There was just enough resentment in his voice to make Liam Grey say sharply: "Now, you look here, James, being peaceful kept your people together more than once. Back in the '20s the tribe almost got broken up and William fixed it. Even when Berenet disappeared, your grandfather kept everyone here out of hot water, in spite of Yngvessen. You've got no call to speak of him that way." He had begun walking back through the mounds toward the few, plain houses that were the homes of the Iron River Indians.

"Grey, he's my grandfather. I know what keeping us all together has cost him. Lots." The straight dark brows drew down over his eyes. "And we're still getting moved."

"The tribe voted to move," Grey reminded him.

"With half the province looking over their shoulders. And with the experts in Regina and Calgary quoting that damned book of Yngvessen's. A lot of choice we had."

Although Grey secretly agreed with the young man, he had had enough. "You stop being a professional Indian, James. If you want to do that to your students at McGill, fine, but don't try it around me. I'm trying every bit as hard as you to keep this tribe together." Abruptly he stopped talking.

"I'll take you to my grandfather," James said stiffly. "Follow me." Without looking at the Captain he moved ahead of him. At the door of the largest house he stopped. "He's inside. He hasn't been well. It's his eyes."

"I won't be long." Grey smiled with what he hoped was warm assurance, and went into the house.

The room was a fugitive from sunshine. The curtains had been marshaled against the windows, the colors vague and dim. Even the big-bellied stove showed only a faint ruddiness at the grille.

In the corner between the stove and the bookcase was an old leather chair, made so comfortable with use that it was nearly shapeless. At the moment William Wilson sat in it, his near-blind eyes trained on Grey.

"Good afternoon, Liam," he said.

"Good afternoon to you, William," Grey answered.

"My grandson been giving you a piece of his mind?"

"No more than usual."

The old man chuckled. With his white hair braided neatly down his back and his high-necked robe he looked more like a venerable Korean scholar than the medicine man of the Iron River Indians. "He has even lectured me. Wants me to change my name to Raven Feathers. That was his father's name, of course. Mine is Hand-of-Water." He pointed to a chair. "Sit down, Liam."

"They're ready to start digging out there tomorrow, William," Grey said gently.

Wilson simply nodded. He pulled the blanket on his knees higher up his chest. "Watch out for John Yellow Sky. He wants to turn this into an incident." He shook his head. "An Indian informing against an Indian. A thing James deplores."

Grey tugged at his gloves. "What kind of incident?"

Wilson shook his head again, this time with disgust. "Yellow Sky wants headlines, and with Maxwell Choffe, he'll get them. Aaron Jackson almost called a tribal council over it."

"But he didn't." Grey wondered how much pressure had been put on the chief from both sides to bring things this far.

"No. I stopped him. He's left the running of the tribe to me for the last fifteen years, anyway. He knew he couldn't handle it. Well, I can. I suggested James have a little chat with Yellow Sky." He reached out to the stove and the pot of coffee. "Don't think James understands Yellow Sky. John wants the blood." He poured himself a cup, returning the pot to the stove with the handle toward Grey. "James wants justice. John wants vengeance."

Grey rose and poured himself a cup of coffee. He had learned that this was the simplest form of hospitality, and that if he had been offered the drink, then the endless ritual of repaying would begin.

"Better be on the alert, Liam."

Grey sipped the coffee. "Who else is in with Yellow Sky?"

"Eddie Two Foxes. Both of the Harris boys . . . calling themselves Hare-in-the-Snow these days. David Lynx. Henry Running Bear was with them, but shied off a while back."

"As far as you know?"

"As far as I know," he admitted. "Talked to Aaron about it. I hoped he'd take a hand for once, but he's sitting on this. I think he wants it to go away."

Captain Grey did not like Chief Jackson the way he liked William. To him, the old chief was evading the issues, letting the tribe grow dangerously polarized. He said: "Is he planning to be here for the disinterring?"

"Don't think so. Told me he thought it would be better if we all kept away. Let the university people handle it."

After a moment Grey said cautiously, "He's asking for trouble."

William nodded. "Yes," he said.

James was waiting for him when Grey left the old man. His Indian calm had returned and he looked at Grey with remote severity. "My students are waiting for you. We want to discuss the arrangements for tomorrow."

Grey considered his answer. "Good," he said at last.

"They're waiting at the trailers."

"Right." Grey started toward the four small house trailers that hid behind the wooden buildings as if ashamed of their shiny aluminum bodies. "Coming?"

James did not answer but fell into step beside the Captain.

The students were gathered around the ashes of a campfire in the circle of the trailers. They had changed from their soccer togs into more practical camping clothes, and now they were getting ready for the long northern twilight of summer. Grey thought them all very young, especially the tawny giant who was laying the fire.

"A little early for that, isn't it?" James asked sharply.

"The sun's down," said the short stocky one. James introduced him as Sandenny.

"And that's Nicholson, Adams, Kepple, Feyette, Alyoisu, Stuart, McCloud, Whiting, and over there is Bates."

Grey nodded to each and hoped he could keep them straight. Nicholson was easy, the blond giant; Adams, wiry; Kepple, lean and lantern-jawed; Feyette, unremarkable; Alyoisu, absurdly handsome; Stuart, carrot hair, no freckles; McCloud, nothing noticeable; Whiting, big-chested and sturdy; Bates, retiring and unfriendly. So long as he could keep Feyette and McCloud straight he would be fine.

"Go ahead, Captain," James said.

He stepped forward. "About your project tomorrow: we'll be here to help you, and to keep publicity at a minimum. You aren't old enough to remember the trouble when Berenet turned up missing fifteen, sixteen years ago. Yngvesson took advantage of that incident in his book, as you probably know. We're going to try to keep that from happening again. Now, some of the young men of the tribe might try to force our hand here. If that happens, you're to stay well out of it. Let the RCMP handle it." Grey hated this kind of talk and knew he did it badly. Doggedly he continued: "For the rest you take order from Professor Raven Feathers—he's in charge of the whole operation, even the police. We rely on his judgment. Are there any questions?" He hoped for a response just to show that they'd been listening.

"Captain Grey?" Stuart, red hair. "What should we do about reporters? Chief Jackson said we might have some around."

"Do as Dr. Raven Feathers tells you. He'll know best what the press should cover and what is private to Iron River. Any more questions? Mr. Kepple?" This last was in response to Richard Kepple's hand tentatively in the air.

"Suppose the press is pushy? And we can't manage them? Should we call you?" He was obviously referring to Choffe.

"If a reporter won't be referred to Dr. Raven Feathers, and is not respecting the barriers you've set up, all you have to do is ask for our help."

Ian Nicholson put his huge paw into the air. "What if John Yellow Sky and his bunch try to make trouble? They've said they would. What are you prepared to do to stop them?"

This was a question Grey had dreaded. He thought about his answer very carefully. "I know what John Yellow Sky has been saying about the moving of the tribe. I've read his statements about the obligations of the white man to Indians and the restitution he feels are due. I will not debate that question now or later. But I know that he wants to create some particular reaction here for the moving of the burial grounds. The whole project is supposed to take a week, and his group could cause trouble at any time throughout the week. We know that he will certainly be present most of the time. But until he has actually done something, leave well enough alone. My men have handled John and his"—he almost said boys—"bunch before. We can do it again. If we have to, keep out of the way."

"Any more questions for the Captain?" James asked briskly. When none were forthcoming, he turned to Grey. "That does it. But just one more thing: a couple of Yngvessen's students might show up with Choffe. What are you going to do about them?"

Grey shrugged. "What can I do? Lock them up? Toss them in the river? They've got a right to be here if Chief Jackson gives them permission. If they don't have his permission, then they get sent out. That's all I can do. Sorry, James."

"Aaron Jackson will let them in," James said with certainty.

"Yngvessen scared him gutless with that book." He frowned. "All right. Thank you for speaking with my students." On cue there was a ragged bit of applause. "We start tomorrow, and work for a week."

"Yes," said Grey. "I'm glad you're in charge, Jamie. You're a good man."

Reeling mentally between the insult of his childhood nickname and the compliment of being called a good man by someone who had known him most of his life, James Raven Feathers found himself stammering for the first time in years. "I . . . I'll . . . walk you back to your car," he said lamely.

"I'll be glad of your company." He turned to the group around the fire. "Tomorrow morning, then. Thank you for your co-operation."

The young men at the campfire waved before they turned back to their projects.

As they walked away from the trailers, Grey said to James, "We do know that there will be reporters from Calgary and Regina here to cover the moving, not just Choffe. And a sports writer is coming from Winnipeg to get a story on you for his magazine."

"Shit!" James said through clenched teeth.

"Wants a story on what a famous la crosse player does in his spare time," Grey added apologetically.

"I'm not even playing any more. What makes them think that the only thing I do is play la crosse?" he demanded of the air.

"You were doing pretty well until that accident. You're still headline material in sports."

James was about to speak and then thought better of it. Finally he said, "Well, it paid for my Ph.D. even if I got a chunk of steel in my arm that tells when it's going to rain." He glanced shyly at Grey. "It felt good, all that fame. For the first year I thought I was king of the world."

They walked on in silence, letting the understanding slip away. Then, "Was it hard to give up, James?"

The young man laughed abruptly. "Yes. I thought that they'd fix me up like new. *Really* like new." He pushed out with his hands before jamming them into his pockets. "Well, they didn't. They couldn't."

With a sympathetic smile Grey said, "I know how I felt when I read about the accident. Dreadful."

"Another poor Red Boy proved he couldn't take care of himself, huh?" James asked bitterly.

He had not understood. Grey looked at him with a certain shock on his weathered face. "No. I thought that William's grandson was pretty bad hurt."

Unable to express either shame or contrition, James took refuge in petulance. "And hoped there wouldn't be a fuss. How did we get on this, anyhow?" he went on in a different voice. "This is too depressing."

They had reached the Land-Rover that Grey drove in the rugged country of Iron River. It was equipped with every extra that was available. The Captain had once used the winch to pull four stranded cows out of a mudbank. Grey put his hand on the door but made no move to open it. "About tomorrow," he began awkwardly. "We might be in for more trouble than we counted on."

The dark eyes that looked into his blue ones were flinty. "Yes?"

"I can have guards if you think it necessary. Now, don't fly off the handle, James," he added quickly. "I know that gets your back up. But there's going to be reporters and everything here tomorrow. You know that John Yellow Sky isn't going to let an opportunity like this slip by. And some of Yngvessen's people are bound to be here with Choffe. He's trouble all by himself. So think it over. I'll do what you think best." He opened the door. "Don't make me any speeches, just think it over. I want you to be sure." He stepped into the car, fumbling for the keys as he moved.

"What if I don't want any guards, after all?" This was a challenge.

"It's your decision, James. If you think it's better without guards, all right. That's the way we'll do it."

"What about stand-by?" James shifted uneasily as he looked beyond the Captain to the burial mounds.

"Certainly. As many men as you want. I'll check with you first thing in the morning." He slammed the door before James could say anything more. He started the motor, gave it a minute to warm up, then drove off down the rutted dirt road of the Iron River reservation.

James watched him go, then walked thoughtfully back toward the circle of trailers.

The signs were all over, the next morning. Written in clumsy block letters, terse, simple, they framed the burial mounds.

THIS IS THE WHITE MAN'S LEGACY . . . THE ONLY GOOD INDIAN IS A DEAD INDIAN . . . WE HAVE A RIGHT TO OUR WAY OF LIFE . . . ELECTRICITY IS MORE IMPORTANT THAN RED DIGNITY . . . SINGING LOON BETRAYS US and cryptically, JACKSON'S FOLLY.

James Raven Feathers stood looking at the signs for a few minutes, his eyes hooded. "Yellow Sky, damn him." That was said softly. The next was not. "Sandenny! Nicholson! Whiting! Get out here!" He started purposefully toward the trailers.

"Something wrong?" Bert Adams bounced out of the trailer first, an eager smile on his face. "Are we late?"

"Go look," James said stonily as he walked to the trailers and began to pound on the doors.

The first grumblings and stirrings were heard inside the trailers as Bert Adams ran back from the mounds. "That's going to have to come down, sir, isn't it? They're in awful deep."

"Yes. It's going to have to come down. Feyette, get out here!" he bellowed as Bates, McCloud, and Stuart stumbled into the morning.

"What's the matter?" asked a sleepy Richard Kepple as he opened his door.

"Yellow Sky is playing games," James said violently. His hands clenched at his side. "That bloody fool. He's going to turn this into a grandstand play if it kills him." He took three deep breaths, saying more calmly: "I want one of you to get my grandfather. We need him here."

"Right," one of the young men said.

"And I'll want to talk to Henry Running Bear. He ought to know about this, and he's cowed. He'll tell us what Yellow Sky is up to."

"I'll do it," McCloud volunteered.

"Good. Thank you." He nodded. McCloud took this for an authorization and trotted off toward the houses. "The rest of you, get some hatchets and come with me. We've got to get those signs down before Captain Grey gets back here with the observers." He stood while the others went for their tools, muttering, "Damn Yellow Sky. He makes Yngvessen look right."

"I've got the hatchets. And Dave's bringing the shovels," Nicholson said as he came up to James. "Where do we start?"

"Come along," James said coolly, taking a hatchet from Ian and heading back toward the mounds.

"Is there going to be trouble?" Ian asked amiably as he trotted beside James. "I'll do my bit, if you want, Dr. Raven Feathers."

James stopped in his tracks. "Ian, don't. You try anything and you'll be playing right into John's hands. And Choffe's. He wants headlines, dirt, savages. He thrives on ugliness." He looked up into the wide blond face. "Don't let this get out of hand."

"Okay. I just thought you wanted Yellow Sky's head on a pole."

It was a terrible admission for James to make. Here was a Nordic giant beside him asking about a fellow Indian. Inside, James allowed that Nicholson was right, but he could not say so. "We've got work to do," he said and resumed walking toward the burial grounds.

McCloud was waiting for them. "Your grandfather will be along shortly. He wasn't up yet. He sent Charlie to find Running Bear for you. Looks terrible, doesn't it?"

"Yes." James glanced back toward the trailers and saw that his students were following him. He waited for them to catch up, then he said, "We've got about forty-five minutes to get all that crap down. Chop 'em down or dig 'em out, I don't give a damn which. Just don't disturb any of the mounds. The ones close to the mounds, use hatchets on them. Anything beyond the stakes, those you can dig out, if you're careful."

"We'll be careful," Michael Whiting assured him as he started toward the signs. "Boy, they really set those things up." He grabbed one of the poles and shook it. "That's in deep," he said and started to dig.

The others selected poles and began either to dig or chop while James anxiously watched in case the burial mounds should be disturbed. The first of the signs had come down when William Wilson joined his grandson by the signs.

"I am not surprised," he said when he had had the signs read to him. "John Yellow Sky wants to make trouble here. He is just getting started. Watch. This is so."

James shook his head at his grandfather. "This is a grandstand play. If we handle it right, he'll leave us alone."

The old man wagged his finger at James. "He is a dangerous man, Jamie. You will not contain him so easily."

"I've sent for Running Bear. Between us we should get some sense out of Henry." There was a stubborn set to his mouth, so William did not press him further.

"There is not much time," he said.

Then, "Doctor . . ." Mark Alyoisu said from where he was digging. His eyes were frightened in his handsome face. "There's something down here. I thought this was safe. I didn't know that there were other mounds . . ."

"What is it?" James went to him, puzzled. "You're outside the area . . ."

"But I've hit some . . . one . . ." He was quite pale now, white around the mouth. "There's a body down there. I didn't mean to do anything. Honest. I thought it was safe."

James pushed him aside and looked into the small hole Alyoisu had dug. He knelt, and scooped the dirt away with his hands. Then he stopped. "You're right." He said it quietly, but they all heard it.

Old William stumbled toward James. His fading eyes tried vainly to see what was in the hole. "This is not the sacred ground. It is too far to the north. This is not right."

James rose. "There is someone down there, grandfather. I had my hands on the ribs."

"Yellow Sky!" William said in a terrible rage. "He has desecrated the graves of his ancestors. For his futile posturing he has done this! I am ashamed." The leathery old man stopped shouting quite suddenly. He turned to his grandson. "Call Liam. Tell him what has happened. See if he can stop the visitors until we can find out how far his sacrilege has gone."

"Yes, Grandfather."

"And call Aaron. No. I will call him. I want him to know what his vacillation has done to us." And feeling his way he stalked off to his house.

The rest stood, looking into the hole.

Finally Edgar Bates asked, "Should we go on digging?"

"Better not," James said slowly. "Not with this." He looked over the burial mounds. "But you'd better clear away around that one. Make sure you don't disturb the skeleton. Keep it intact if you can. I'll have to talk to Grey and see what he wants done. We might just need those guards after all."

As he walked off the young men began, reluctantly, to dig.

Twenty minutes later Grey came barreling down to the houses. His face was set and his shoulders were tense.

"And I thought Berenet used to take chances on this road," James greeted him as he slammed out of the Land-Rover. "We don't need another accident on our hands."

"What's this all about?" Grey demanded without preamble.

James hesitated. "It's pretty awkward." Then, as Grey strode angrily toward him: "We found an extra body. The boys are digging it up now."

"What do you mean, an extra body?"

"Just that. It was beyond the mounds, oh, about ten feet. We thought it was safe."

Grey clamped his hands to his hips. "What the hell were you doing digging, anyway? That wasn't supposed to start until we all got here."

Realization dawned on James's face. "That's right. You don't know about the signs, do you?"

"What bloody signs?" So as they walked toward the mounds and the extra skeleton, James explained about the morning. "And now we have this extra body to deal with. I don't even know who it was. I was hoping that grandfather might tell us."

"Yellow Sky," Grey said as James finished. They were next to the staked mounds and James's students were taking down the last of the signs with their hatchets.

"I've told them not to dig any more out. There might be more."

"You haven't brought this one up yet?" Grey cocked his head toward the hole. He did not want to get too close to the stakes.

"No. I don't want to disturb more than I have to."

"Good. What about Yellow Sky? Seen him about this morning?" Grey pulled out a small notebook and began to sketch the sign and the hole. "Go on; I'm listening."

"Well, I've sent for Henry Running Bear. Probably won't do any good, but I hope he might be able to fill us in on what John is planning to do next. This may only be a warm-up," he said grimly.

Grey snorted in agreement. "How is William taking it?" He toed the sign that lay in the dirt at his feet. "He sounded very upset on the phone."

"He is. He thinks that John opened the mounds or moved the staking so that the graves could be desecrated." James paused as he thought it over. "Does that make any sense to you, Grey?"

It was Grey's turn to think about it. "No," he said at last. "Not John Yellow Sky. This isn't his style. He wanted this for publicity, for a soapbox, not to shut the place down. This isn't flamboyant enough for him, not this way. Unless he's got something more in mind, other than a skeleton." He looked around again, squinting against the sun. "This is going to be real trouble if Choffe gets ahold of it."

James said nothing. He sighed unhappily. "But it would have worked," he said wistfully.

"I know."

Then James shook off his mood. "Do you want that body brought out of the ground?" he asked briskly. "I've told them to start, but this might be in your sphere, not mine."

"No, not yet. There are some other questions to take care of first. I'm going to talk to William now. Keep Henry around wherever you are. I don't want him wandering off until we have a little chat. Who's picking him up?"

"Charlie Moon." James gave a half-smile at the mention of his lawyer cousin. "Ogilvie, Tallant, and Moon decided they could spare him, so he flew in last night. He said he had a feeling we might need a good attorney. We turned Henry over to him. Charlie will take care of him."

Flipping his notebook closed Grey said, "I don't doubt it." He started walking toward William's house. He went slowly, reluctant to disturb his old friend again. He turned over all the questions that faced him in his mind. He was fully aware of the trouble this would bring to the tribe. With one Indian agent disappearing, followed so closely by that ruinous book of Yngvessen's, this might well be the final disaster for the Iron River Tribe. More than either James or William, he knew the ambivalence most people had for Indians. A thing like this, well, it was a great excuse to scatter the tribe. Even Yngvessen had suggested it; it would be a way for them to upgrade their culture. He was deeply afraid that this would be the end. His heels bit more deeply into the pathway. He did not know how to influence the reporters who were coming to cover the disinterring, especially Choffe, who was armed with Yngvessen's opinions. He hoped that they could all be held back, if only for a few hours. Otherwise it would be difficult.

"Come in," said the old voice in response to the knock. Grey pulled the door open.

"Come in, come in," William ordered. "Want to talk to you. Don't want those foolish heads outside to hear us." He grunted impatiently as Grey secured the door.

"Now then," he continued as Grey walked forward, "we have got a proper mess now. There's a body out there in the wrong place. John Yellow Sky put it there . . ."

"I'm not sure he did," Grey said quietly. He was silent, waiting for William to go on.

"What do you mean?" The old man rose and came toward Grey. He was a head shorter than the Captain, but he seemed taller. "What do you mean, Liam? What is that body there for? Who put it there?"

Grey shook his head. "I don't know. I don't think Yellow Sky did it. There's no point to it. I think that either the stakes were moved or the old mound was flattened in the '43 flood. You remember? You said some of the old graves were lost."

"That was thirty years ago. Even before Berenet came. It could be." The old man shuffled back to his leather chair. "What if Yellow Sky found out about the body and planned this?"

Grey shook his head reluctantly. "It doesn't fit the pattern, William. What publicity would he gain?"

"You're as bad as Berenet with that endless history of the tribe he was writing." William paused, then reached for his coffee mug. "I don't know. That's puzzled me, too. Yellow Sky is usually direct."

When the coffee pot was returned to the stove Grey helped himself. "Can you get Aaron to keep the reservation closed for a few more hours?"

"I will try." He drank half the coffee in silence, then went into the other room where the tribe's one telephone was kept. Chief Jackson lived in town, visiting the reservation only when necessary.

Grey waited while the call was made, meditatively sipping his coffee. He could hear William's voice raised in anger, but could not make out the words. He refilled his mug and sat down.

"The old fool," William was muttering as he came back into the room. "He told me to shut the thing up. Choffe is flying in from Saskatoon in two hours, and I'm supposed to shut it up. How do you shut up a body? Told me to have them bury it again and leave it. And he's an Indian." The scorn in his voice almost choked him.

"May I make a suggestion, William?" Grey asked, as soon as the old man had stopped talking.

"Go ahead. Won't hurt anything more. He's keeping the other reporters at the gatehouse for an hour so that George Snake Killer can give them a lecture on the history of the tribe. Without Yngvessen's theories. That's all he's willing to do. More than that would look suspicious, he says."

Mentally Grey damned Chief Jackson for a fool, but he said, "Let's take the body out. Remove it to the hall, get it out of the way. Then we can dig up the others, and claim that the sign poles were part of the preparation for the disinterment. We can tell them that only Indians were allowed to attend that ceremony."

For a moment William was silent. Then he chuckled, "We do this for us Indians?" He grinned at his friend. "All right. It is not what I would want to do, but there is no time for that. I will order the body to be removed from the area and placed in the meeting hall so that I can set to work finding out who it was." He hesitated for a bit, folding his hands across his chest. "There is no need for you to support us. That was your decision. I am proud to have you my friend." Which was as close as he could come to saying thanks.

"There is still going to be the devil to pay. I just brought you a suggestion. All we've got is very little time." Grey said this hastily as he rose from his chair, determination back in his manner. "I'll get the boys on it. Guess James will go along with us?"

With a steely smile, William said, "Oh, yes."

The students were standing uncertainly outside of the staked area when Liam Grey returned to them. "All right," he told them, "it's back on. Dig him out. Put him in the hall when you've got him out. You've got about half an hour." He looked around as he heard his name called, and saw Charlie Moon coming toward him, a wolfish grin on his pointed face.

"I've got a surprise package for you, Grey. He's waiting in the trailer. A nice little teddy bear." He waved offhandedly to the students. "James is keeping him company, but I think you'd better come along. James can be pretty rough on toys."

Promising the students that he'd be back shortly, Grey strode off with Charlie Moon to the trailers.

"What has he said?" he asked the young attorney at his side.

"Denies all knowledge of the skeleton. He said that they only put the signs up to annoy James. I get the feeling that John is saving the main event for later."

They turned into the circle of trailers. "Any idea what?"

"No," Charlie said as he opened the door of the second trailer.

James was seated backward in a chair, his arms folded across the back, chin resting on his arms. In front of him was a sturdy young man trying very hard not to look frightened. He was saying ". . . and all your talk about reconciliation with the White Man. Look what it's got us. We have to move and . . ." His voice trailed off.

"Hello, Grey," James said without turning. "Glad you could make it. Henry here was telling me about how you've abused us. Do you think you've abused us, Grey? Do you think Berenet abused us?"

Quickly Grey took over. He feared that otherwise it would degenerate into a name-calling contest. "Hello, Henry. You know about our find out there?"

"I don't know anything," was the fast sullen answer.

"Not even about the signs," Grey assumed incredulity. "I thought you were in on that."

"Well, on that . . ."

"And I thought you might know if John Yellow Sky had any clever ideas about planting skeletons? No?"

"I don't know what you're . . ."

"Forgetting for the moment that you broke the law when you put up those signs . . ."

"I didn't . . ."

"Yes, you did, Henry. Unless I say otherwise, you did. Now, where are John Yellow Sky and the Harris brothers?" He waited. "Well?"

"I don't know."

"Make a guess," said Charlie Moon gently.

"You can't make me . . ."

"I can't," Grey agreed cordially. "But James and Charlie might want to." He let that sink in. "I don't have time for any more nonsense, Henry. We've got a hell of a mess on our hands right now. If you're going to play Martyred Indian, then off you go to jail until I find out what's happened."

"You're trying to bully me," Henry Running Bear lurched to his feet. "You stinking, genocidal White Man!"

"That's enough!" James's voice cut like a whip. "Let us talk to him, Liam. We can find out."

"Give him a chance," Charlie smiled. "He's read Yngvessen's book. He knows we're not civilized. He knows that our hard lives have made us brutal, stupid and violent. Right, Henry?"

"Hey, Captain, they can't do this." Henry looked beseechingly at Grey. "Can they?"

"If I know about it, they can't. But I told you, I don't have much time. If you haven't given us an answer I'll have to leave you with them." He managed to sound sorry.

"But that's not fair. You lousy cop!" He took two steps toward Grey. "It's not. They don't understand. They've already talked to John and he told them he . . ." Henry looked around uncertainly. "He told them how he felt about the move," he ended defiantly.

"Do you think he'd tell me?" Grey asked. "I haven't got much time, Henry. Remember that."

"I don't know. I don't," he said desperately. "He went back into the woods last night, after we put up the signs. I don't know where he is. I don't know if he'd talk to you."

"But he is planning more . . . entertainment?" Charlie suggested.

"He didn't tell me. Really." He was certainly scared now. "I asked him what he was going to do. He just said he had a real surprise for them. But it wasn't for today. It wasn't." He looked from one man to the next, pleading with his eyes. "I didn't think he'd do a thing like . . . that . . ."

"Right," Grey said firmly. "Tell us where he is."

"In the woods. That's all I know. Back in the woods on the North Fork. He and Lynx and Two Foxes are up there. The others are off in Calgary. They left last night. They're going to get supplies. So you see, they can't do anything until they get back." He spoke in a rush.

"Anything more?" James asked.

"I don't know any more!" Henry yelled. "I don't! At least . . ." He glanced uneasily at Charlie Moon. "You're a lawyer, Charlie. You got to protect me."

"Oh, I will," he said pleasantly as a grin split his face.

"No, Charlie. Really. You got to help me . . ." He stopped for a moment. "John might show up sometime while the press is here. But that's all I know. Honest, it is. Tell him, Charlie."

"All right, Henry. We believe you," Grey smiled down at him, taking full advantage of his height. "But let's suppose we get it all on paper, just on the chance you're wrong?" He pulled out his notebook and pen.

There was a knock on the door and Jerry Feyette stuck his head in the door.

"It's McCloud, James," Liam Grey said.

"Feyette, sir," he corrected. Then: "Sorry to bother you, Doctor, but there's something you should see before we move the body." He was uncomfortable, rubbing his hands on his overall as he spoke.

"Is it urgent? Can't it wait?"

"No, sir, I don't think so." He pulled his earlobe. "There's something you'd better see."

James shrugged. "Oh, all right, if it's important." He rose from the chair and turned to the other two men. "Keep Henry company until I get back." With that, he slung his jacket over his shoulder and went out the door.

"What did you find?" he asked Feyette as they walked back toward the mounds.

"There's something strange about the skeleton. I figured you might know . . ."

"Well, what is it?" he demanded.

But Feyette shook his head. "Better wait until we get there." He did not speak again until they had reached the gathering around the pile of bones on the ground.

"Now what is it?" James demanded as he came up to them.

Michael Whiting stepped aside for him as he pointed to the skeleton. "Take a look. The right arm, just above the elbow." James twinged, but knelt next to the skeleton.

"There. Right there," Lincoln McCloud said, touching the bone with the toe of his boot. "Look at it."

Puzzled, James picked up the humerus and turned it over in his hands. There, imbedded in the bone, slightly above the elbow, holding an old fracture together was a pin of stainless steel.

"One of you go get Grey," he said softly. "Tell him it's urgent." Gingerly he moved around the rest of the skeleton. When he got to the skull he stopped.

"That's the other thing we wanted you to see, Doctor," Leon Sandenny said cautiously. "That sure got bashed, didn't it?"

James picked up the ruined skull, trying to keep the fragments together. "This isn't anyone I know," he murmured.

"Did that happen after he was buried?" Bert Adams asked, a little frightened.

"I don't know. The break is in the back. I don't think so . . . I doubt it," James said dubiously. Somehow all the objectivity he had felt in Peru vanished now that his own tribe was involved. He put the skull down carefully. "Don't disturb that, all right?" he said to his students. "I want Grey to see it this way." He fingered the head of the pin in the bone. "No Indian I know has one of these. Except me." He studied the bone around the pin. "That was one hell of a fracture."

"What caused it?" asked Leon Sandenny as he squatted next to James.

James shook his head. "Some kind of accident. It put his arm out of commission for months, by the look . . ." Suddenly he remembered back. When he was ten? eleven? Berenet had had an accident while driving at his usual murderous speeds on an icy road. He had worn his arm in a cast for quite a while . . .

"What is it *now*?" Grey demanded from above him.

James snapped out of his reverie. "You'd better take a look at this skeleton." He rose and stepped back. "Take a good look."

With a grunt and a perfunctory obscenity Grey dropped to his knees. "Pretty tall, wasn't he?" he asked of no one in particular.

"The skull and the right arm," James prompted.

"Right." He picked up the skull, handling it with great care. "He really got his, didn't he?"

"With metal."

"The proverbial blunt instrument," Grey said drily. He looked up at James. "You're the anthropologist. You should be able to tell me what did this."

James knelt again, taking the skull from Grey. He turned it over slowly, checking the splintering of the bone. "I don't know, but I'd put my money on a hammer from the side. You see how this angle here . . ." He touched the edge of the hole in the skull. "I think it's a hammer."

"And the arm." Grey had picked up the bone and touched it with some worry. "This . . ."

But James tugged at his arm. "Yes. I want to talk to you about that, but not just here." He stood and drew Grey aside. "Do you remember the way Berenet drove? Didn't he have a bad accident about fifteen years ago, say a couple of years before he turned up missing?"

"His arm was in a cast. The right one," he said reflectively. "You think that's Berenet?" he asked suddenly.

"It's not an Indian."

Grey sighed. "I'll check it out. I'll have to phone out. It might make it worse, if this isn't Berenet and Choffe or Yngvessen gets wind of it." He looked evenly at James.

The look was returned. "We've got to do this, no matter what. The body's got to be identified. There's a little time yet."

"Right." He stood, his weight slung into his hip, thinking. "You've got tools for sifting?"

"Sure. We were going to use them to be certain we got all of the effects in the mounds. Taken out with the bones and reburied in the new site—that's what we planned."

"So you're going to refute Yngvessen?"

"Not a chance," James said bitterly. "He's like Moby Dick. I'm not up to him."

"Gadfly?" Grey asked with a twinkle. "You can use those sieves now, to find out if there was anything else in the hole with that poor bastard."

"We'll get on it right away." He paused. "Can Grandfather buy us any more time?"

"I don't think so."

"Well," said James. "We can try. About half an hour, you'd say?"

"About that. Maybe William can hold them at the houses for a little while, but half an hour is the best I can guarantee." He shook hands with James and went off to the houses.

Twenty minutes later he had his answer, all the way from Regina. Yes, Agent Claud Berenet had had a bad accident; yes, it had resulted in a multiple fracture of the right humerus; yes, it had required surgery. Yes, a pin had been used. Grey fingered his notebook, lost in thought. If the skeleton were Berenet, then who killed him? Why did the whole tribe deny knowledge of it? Grey thought that he knew William well enough that he could trust the old man to leak information like that to him. True, this case was fifteen years old, but he hoped that William had been sure of him even then . . .

He left the house, walking slowly back toward the mounds. Nicholson and Alyoisu were waiting for him, triumph in their eyes. "What have you found?" he asked.

Nicholson held out his hand. On his palm lay a tarnished silver crucifix and a St. Christopher's medal. "The chain was almost completely corroded. We found this under the head."

Grey touched the crucifix. "I see. Catholic." He stood still for a moment. "Where is Dr. Raven Feathers?"

Alyoisu cocked his head in the direction of the trailers. "He and Leon are processing a couple more things we found. It's all lab work for them."

"What things?" Grey asked, frowning deeply at the hole and then at his watch. There was very little time left.

"We found a few items that might have been caught in his clothes. Of course, they might be his, but they might be his murderer's too. Dr. Raven Feathers is waiting for you." Nicholson smiled benignly at him. "Should we fill the hole in, Captain?"

"Hum. Oh, certainly. Go ahead. The press should be along any minute now. Which trailer is Dr. Raven Feathers in?"

"The green one. You'd better knock before you go in. They're using some ruddy awful chemicals in there," Nicholson said happily. "Tell Dr. Raven Feathers we'll finish this up out here. And Mike Whiting will pitch them some guff about anthropology until he's free to talk."

"Good idea. Thanks for thinking of it." He kicked at the moist earth with his boot. "Make it neat, will you?" Before they could answer he had moved on toward the trailers.

Whatever chemicals James was using, they stank. Grey paused in the doorway as his lungs objected, then he went into the trailer, closing the door behind him.

James and Leon Sandenny were bent over the sink, each working with jeweler's pliers and small shards of metal. "Hi, Grey. I think we've found something."

"Yes?" He peered over their shoulders. "What is it?"

"Part of it," James said enthusiastically. "The rest is on the table over there. Be very careful with it."

Grey maneuvered to the table and saw there, on a strip of muslin, four or five tiny bits of metal like an incomplete jigsaw puzzle. "What is it? It looks like it had a chain."

"Right on the first try. It had a chain. It was under the left hand."

"Could it have been *in* the hand?" Grey held his breath as he bent over the table.

"Yes, it could have. There's a magnifying glass on the seat there. Have a look at that bottom line." James had not taken his eyes from the bits of metal in the sink.

As he picked up the glass, Grey asked, "What's on it. What am I looking for?"

"Look at it."

Curiously Grey moved the muslin into clearer light. As he did he could make out the lower halves of numerals. It was either 1936 or 1956.

"I'm betting on '36, myself." He managed a tight smile.

Leon Sandenny, hunched over a sliver of metal murmured, "*Mehr Licht.*"

"*Macht doch den zweiten Fensterladen auch auf,*" James said promptly. He remembered Yngvessen's fondness for the truncated version of Goethe's last words, and his anger at having the full quotation rendered, in quite acceptable German, by a poor Indian boy not yet in his teens. Then he realized. "What did you say?" he demanded.

"Look," Sandenny offered the scrap of metal to James. "That's what it says."

James let out a whoop of pure joy. "The watch fob. We've found the watch fob."

"So what?" Grey said. "It could have been planted. It might be Berenet's, if this is Berenet."

James scowled. "It might have been planted," he allowed. "But why? It's been in the ground quite a while. If it is a plant, who planted it; Yellow Sky? No, I'll bet this is a souvenir of Nils Christian Yngvessen." He leaned on the table, bright intensity lighting his face. "This could almost make up for the book."

Grey put a restraining arm on James's shoulder. "If the tests prove you wrong, Jamie . . ." He didn't finish. He, too, wanted the guilty party to be Yngvessen. "It's not a lot."

"It's enough. He'll have to answer one hell of a lot of questions about this." He looked over his shoulder at his assistant. "How soon can you have this ready, Leon?"

"About an hour?"

"Good. Choffe will be here by then. Grey," he turned impulsively to the Captain. "Suppose Choffe finds out that Yngvessen did this. What will he do then?"

Grey answered drily, "He'll ruin Yngvessen."

James drummed his fingers on the table, smiling.

At this Grey was genuinely alarmed. "You can't accuse him, Jamie, not with so little proof. Especially in your position. If it turns out you're wrong it will look like a put-up job from the first. Yngvessen will pounce all over you. He'll destroy you. He can do it, too."

There was mockery in James's eyes. "I'm not going to accuse anybody. I am simply going to tell those nice gentlemen of the press what we found while digging in our own graveyard. They might not respect me as an anthropologist, but you said yourself they respect me as a la crosse player. They'll pay attention for that reason alone. I'll remind them that we do not allow digging within twenty feet of our burial mounds, and that whoever buried that man knew it. Then I'll have Leon produce these little displays, and put a few words in about the probable identity of the skeleton . . ."

Grey relented. "It's Berenet. He had the fracture and the pin."

"Oh, we've got enough of a jaw to send along for dentals. That should take care of any doubting Thomases. Lincoln McCloud has taken some very interesting photographs, on Charlie's advice. And we've sent Henry off to meet Yellow Sky at the gates. So long as he is going to harangue the press we might as well get a statement from him. Without him, we'd never have found Berenet. I never thought I'd be happy for John's mischief, but I am now. I'll give him full credit for the find, if he likes. Publicly."

"But you can't be sure."

James smiled serenely. "That watch fob was a thing Yngvessen was very proud of. All the time he was here he boasted of it. It was a graduation remembrance from his family."

Grey nodded. "All right, Doctor, why did he kill Berenet?" Then, as he said it, he thought he knew the answer. "Berenet was writing a book, wasn't he? About the tribe."

James's smile deepened. "And Berenet didn't want Yngvessen's book published. He said Yngvessen was wrong. Talk about academic rivalry. Poor Berenet worked on that book of his for years. Grandfather said it was dreadful, but his history was right."

"There's the rest of it," Leon Sandenny said from the sink. "All we need is the bits around the edges and we've got it." He passed it over to James. "There you are, Doctor. 'Uppsala' and the date is 1936."

As his smile broke into a grin, "Great. Thanks," he said to Leon. "Well, Grey, care to wager what year Yngvessen graduated?" He put the missing sliver into the fob. "Aren't those nice reporters due here about now? It would be a crime to keep them waiting." He straightened up. "Coming, Grey?"

"You don't have a case yet."

"Oh, I'll leave it to you and Charlie to do that for me. There's certainly enough evidence to warrant a preliminary investigation."

"So you dump a case like this in my lap without so much as a by-your-leave?" He glanced at the watch fob and heaved a sigh of resignation. "Right. Lead on, James."

"Oh, no." Dr. Raven Feathers paused in the door. "After you, Liam."

They went out together.

Ray Russell, the original executive editor and now a contributing editor of *Playboy*, is perhaps best known for his Gothic studies in horror and madness such as his acclaimed *Sardonicus*. In this story he approaches another, if no less devouring madness: Bibliomania. And not merely bibliomania, but practicing, *organized* bibliomania. For those of you who do not already know, groups such as the Raven Society do exist, as this editor, a practicing member of what are herein called "the Sherlock Holmes nuts" can attest. The story is unusual in its blend of the classic puzzle with some trenchant comment on the so-called generation gap.

To save some readers unnecessary effort, the lamentably low valuation of Poe stories in original periodical appearance is correct; a sad commentary on the assessed worth of a work of literature in its first form. Take my unbound *Strands* of *The Hound of the Baskervilles* for example . . .

Quoth the Raven
RAY RUSSELL

Pushing a pound of hair out of his eyes, Corey Blake read the letter to his girl, Jennifer. They were between classes at the time, lolling at leggy length on the stretch of green outside the Humanities Building. The letter was on stiff, costly paper that crackled when he unfolded it. "Listen to this, Jen," he said, and read aloud:
"*My dear Mr. Blake—*"
"What is he, British or something?" interrupted Jen.
"No, just an old square." He started again:
"*My dear Mr. Blake:*
Your late father was a friend of mine. (That's a crock, Dad couldn't stand him.) *It has been brought to my attention that you are now the owner of a certain item that once belonged to him: a copy of Graham's Magazine, Volume 20, Number 5, May 1842, which is famous for including the first printing of Edgar Allan Poe's 'The Masque of the Red Death.' I am prepared to offer you $1,000 for it, in tax-free cash, which may strike you as excessive (and, indeed, it is considerably more than the item is worth on the open market), but I am a man in comfortable circumstances, and I assure you I can pay that sum, provided you meet certain conditions . . .*"

"A thousand dollars," said Jen. "You could finish school. Do you really have that magazine?"

Corey nodded. "It's in a safety deposit box, sealed in a transparent plastic envelope to keep it from falling apart. The damn thing is like a hundred and thirty years old. Just about the only thing Dad left me." He looked down at the letter again. "Where was I?" He resumed reading:

"*. . . provided you meet certain conditions. They are these: At 8:00 P.M., on January 19th, the anniversary of the birth of Edgar Allan Poe, you will present yourself at The Raven Society, of which I am a member. You will bring the copy of Graham's Magazine. There, in the presence of the officers and members of the Society, you will answer three questions I will put to you relating to the works of Poe. If you answer all three correctly, I will present you with the amount stipulated above and will take possession of the magazine. If you incorrectly answer even one question, you will forfeit both the magazine and the money. If you accept these conditions, you may signify simply by being present at the stated place, at the stated time.*

I remain,
Very truly yours,
ALGERNON DEWITT

"That's wild!" cried Jen. "What is this Raven Society?"

"A bunch of Poe nuts. My dad belonged. It's like that club the Sherlock Holmes nuts have, the Baker Street Irregulars."

"This DeWitt—is he for real?"

"Oh, he's loaded, all right. Bought most of my dad's Poe collection when Dad was dying and our money ran out. Paid him peanuts. But Dad held on to that one thing. And now DeWitt wants it."

"Hey!" she suddenly squealed. "January 19th! That's tonight!"

Corey nodded. "I got the letter a month ago. That's why I've been cutting so many classes—I've been boning up on the writings of Poe. Lucky I'm such a quick study—ask me something!"

"You're taking this guy up on his crazy offer?"

"I sure as hell am."

"But you might lose and not get a penny! Why don't you just sell it to a dealer?"

Corey shook his head. "DeWitt is right. His offer *is* better than what I could get on the open market. A *lot* better. I checked. Want to guess how much that issue is going for in rare book stores?"

"How would I know? I've heard you can get like a hundred dollars or something for old *Superman* comic books, so an 1842 magazine with the first printing of a Poe story . . . sounds like DeWitt is trying to get off cheap."

Corey said, "Ten bucks."

"What?"

"You can pick up a mint copy of that issue for about ten or twelve bucks. It's just not that scarce."

"Then why is DeWitt offering—my God—a hundred times what it's worth?"

"He's a nut. I guess he has his reasons. Anyway, I'm going there." He rose from the grass and brushed off the seat of his pants. "You want to meet me there tonight?"

"Can't we go together?"

"I've got too much to do. More Poe cramming. And I have to make it to the bank before it closes and get the magazine out of the deep-freeze. Here's the address on the envelope—see you there at eight."

The president of The Raven Society, a Mr. Simpson, greeted them when they arrived. He was a gentle, white-haired man who pumped Corey's hand and warmly said, "I knew your father. A wonderful man, wonderful. Please step into the library and meet the others . . ."

The library was what one might have expected: paneled walls, deep leather chairs, a fine antique sideboard gleaming with decanters and glasses, the pleasant masculine aromas of pipe tobacco and leather (as well as a less agreeable, faintly acrid undertone that Corey's nostrils recognized but his mind could not identify); and, of course, bookcases packed with the complete works of Poe, a fine oil portrait of the author, and (Nice touch, thought Corey) a pallid bust of Pallas, just above the chamber door.

Corey and Jen were introduced to the vice-president, the secretary, the treasurer, several assorted members, and, finally, to Algernon DeWitt.

He was a large, bald, bloated man (Buddha on an off day, thought Jen). His proffered hand, when Corey took it, felt like a rubber glove. "My dear boy," he said. "You don't remember, but we met once before."

"I remember," said Corey. "I was five years old. I kicked you in the shins."

DeWitt laughed. "Total recall, how charming. Yes, you took instant exception to me, but I bear no grudge. Ah, and this is your lady fair . . ." His eyes brightened with lust as he examined Jen, but blazed with feral fire when he spied the plastic-protected object Corey held under his arm. "Is that it?" he asked, licking his lips.

"That's it," said Corey, placing the magazine casually on a mahogany table. "Open it up and check the merchandise, if you want."

DeWitt said, "That will hardly be necessary. Your father was well known to us. There can be no question of it being anything but genuine."

Simpson asked the young people if they wanted anything to drink. Both declined.

"Then shall we begin?" said DeWitt, with impatience.

"Sure," said Corey. Everyone sat down, the leather chairs swallowing them.

"First question," said DeWitt, champing at the bit.

"One moment, Algernon," said Simpson. "Mr. Blake . . . Corey . . . may I call you that? . . . are you absolutely certain you want to play this little game?"

"Yes, sir."

"It's your business, of course, and Mr. DeWitt's offer is generous —I might even say outrageous in its generosity—*if* you win. But if you lose . . . well, I realize the magazine isn't worth much today, but you're a very young man, and perhaps the going price in ten or twenty or thirty years . . ."

"Come, come, Simpson," snapped DeWitt. "The boy knows what he's getting into."

"Let's hope so," Simpson said with a sigh. "I'm not sure that *I* do." His dislike of DeWitt was poorly masked. "The agreement, as I understand it, calls for three questions relating to the writings of Poe. The *writings*. Not the life. I emphasize that. No notes, no referring to books, no prompting from the sidelines. Everything from memory. Are you ready, Mr. Blake?"

"If Mr. DeWitt is."

"I'm ready," said DeWitt.

"Then proceed," said Simpson, settling back in his chair.

DeWitt leaned forward, looked Corey straight in the eye, and smiled icily. "First question," he said. "What is the name of William Legrand's friend in *The Gold Bug*—the one who helps Legrand and Jupiter dig up the buried treasure?"

Corey shut his eyes in concentration. He massaged the bridge of his nose. He chewed his lower lip. After about thirty seconds, he looked up at DeWitt.

"I don't know," said Corey.

DeWitt's eyebrows rose.

"And neither do you," Corey added. "He's the first-person narrator. Poe never bothered to give him a name."

"Very good!" said Simpson.

"Yes . . ." DeWitt admitted. "You've done your homework, young man. All right, then, second question. You're familiar with *The Cask of Amontillado*? Simply tell us the motto on Fortunato's coat of arms—in Latin, please."

Corey smiled. "I know what you want me to say, Mr. DeWitt. You want me to say *Nemo me impune lacessit*. But that's Montresor's motto. Fortunato's motto is never mentioned."

"Correct!" crowed Simpson. Turning to DeWitt, he said, "Watch your step—this young chap is more than you bargained for, I think!"

"Perhaps, perhaps," muttered DeWitt, rising from his chair. "I confess I thought I'd trip him up on that second question. Perhaps I might be allowed to have a brandy while I formulate something a bit more difficult than I had previously planned?"

Simpson shrugged. "Unless Mr. Blake objects?"

"No, no," said Corey. "But maybe Mr. DeWitt would be interested in a counteroffer?"

"Counteroffer?" echoed DeWitt, stopping halfway to the brandy decanter.

"Just a little switch," Corey explained. "Instead of you asking me a third question, I ask *you* a question. If you answer correctly, you get the magazine free. If you don't, I get the $1,000—but the magazine becomes the property of The Raven Society and you get *nothing*. Nothing at all. How about it, Mr. DeWitt? Are you chicken?"

DeWitt took a large silk handkerchief from his pocket and slowly blotted his damp brow.

Simpson said, "Well? Do you accept this amendment?"

DeWitt frowned. Then he smiled. "I am intimately familiar with everything Poe wrote. Every story, every poem, every essay, every book review. Even his juvenilia. Even his uncompleted play. I know whole passages by heart. Yes. I accept." He sat down again.

A murmur of anticipation went around the room. Jen squeezed Corey's hand, and whispered, "Honey, are you sure?"

Corey gripped her hand tightly in silent response. He turned to DeWitt, and said, "I'm going to recite a few lines of verse, and I want you to tell me which work of Poe's they relate to."

DeWitt's smile was a smirk of pity and superiority.

Simpson, with concern, said, "Mr. Blake, are you aware that Mr. DeWitt is an internationally known authority on Poe? He was considered second only to your father, and since his death, he's recognized all over the world as the foremost scholar in the field . . ."

"Shut up, Simpson," snarled DeWitt. "The young fool got himself into this. Now let's see him get himself out. Go on, Blake, let's hear this verse."

Corey cleared his throat and recited, in measured tones:

> *From Winter into Spring the Year has passed*
> *As calm and noiseless as the snow and dew—*

DeWitt's eyes narrowed. "One of his trashy youthful poems, perhaps . . ."

"Want me to go on for a few more lines?" asked Corey, obligingly, and did so:

> *The pearls and diamonds which adorn his robes*
> *Melt in the morning, when the solar beam*
> *Touches the foliage like a glittering wand.*
> *Blue is the sky above—*

"Rubbish!" cried DeWitt. "Doggerel! This is a shabby trick!"

Corey said, "What work of Poe's do the lines relate to? And 'relate to' is the operative phrase, isn't it? It's your phrase, Mr. DeWitt, you used it in your letter." Corey pulled the rumpled letter from his pocket and read from it: "'. . . *you will answer three questions I will put to you relating to the works of Poe.*'" Corey handed the letter to Simpson, and turned again to DeWitt. "Well?"

DeWitt bellowed, "Poe never wrote that tripe!"

"I never said he did. But that tripe definitely *relates to* a work by Poe. A famous work. Which one?"

DeWitt grew purple. "This is absurd!"

Simpson said, "I'm afraid you'll have to answer, Algernon."

"I won't answer!"

"You mean you can't," said Corey. "You give up."

DeWitt erupted with wordless sounds.

"*Do* you give up, Algernon?" Simpson asked gently.

DeWitt hauled his great bulk out of the chair and stomped over to the sideboard. He sloshed brandy into a goblet, and swallowed it in a single gulp. He was breathing heavily.

Simpson repeated his question: "Do you give up?"

"*Yes, damn it!*" shouted DeWitt. "But that young smart aleck better have a legitimate answer! If he doesn't, the magazine and the money are *mine!*"

Everyone in the room turned to Corey.

Corey said, "Those are the opening lines of a poem called *Spring's Advent*, by someone named Park Benjamin. The poem was used as a filler in that issue of *Graham's Magazine*. Page 259, the bottom half. Immediately following the Poe story. Okay?"

The plastic covering of the old magazine was delicately, reverently opened by Simpson, and the periodical extracted. With loving care, Simpson's fingers turned the desiccated leaves to Page 259. "Yes," he said, "here it is. The end of the Poe story—'And Darkness and Decay and the Red Death held illimitable dominion over all.'—

and then the Benjamin poem. I assume, Mr. Blake, you studied this edition rather thoroughly?"

With a shrug, Corey said, "This morning after I picked it up at the bank. I wanted to see what I'd be losing, if I lost. Then I sealed it up again. But I didn't lose, did I?"

"It's a delicate point," said Simpson. "Some might agree with you about 'Relating to' being the operative phrase. It could be argued that if Mr. DeWitt had meant the contest confined strictly to the Poe texts, he should have said so. 'Relating to' could be interpreted to embrace circumstances or conditions surrounding the original publication of the works. And this poem *is* very closely related to the story, of course—less than an inch away . . ."

Simpson reflectively stroked his jaw and continued: "But I don't know. Although I'm retired now, I was a pretty good attorney when I was younger, and I'm afraid that this business of 'Relating to' is rather hair-splitting, a merely verbal . . . what would you call it nowadays, cop-out? I would have to say that the story and the poem, although related to each other in one sense, are not related in any meaningful way. And the old Webster definition of a magazine as a 'miscellany' of various separate stories, articles, poems, and so on, would support that, I think."

"So the boy loses!" crowed DeWitt.

"Let us say he does not win," said Simpson.

"The same thing!"

"Not necessarily. I am forced to a Solomonic decision. Mr. Blake does not receive the thousand dollars—but neither do you receive the magazine, Algernon—"

"*What?*"

"No, I'm afraid not . . ."

"*You old fool!*" bellowed DeWitt. "*Give it to me! It's mine!*" He lunged toward the magazine, but Simpson snatched it out of his reach.

"Get control of yourself," Simpson said with distaste. "You're getting the best of the bargain. The boy is losing a thousand dollars he sorely needs, whereas you . . . well, I can only think that you suffer from a neurotic obsession to own the entire collection of our late member—under the delusion, perhaps, that you would then be his equal in the field. It's an expensive neurosis. A few dollars can buy you a copy of *Graham's* identical to this."

"Not quite identical," said Corey, with a smile. "This particular copy had an extra ingredient in it—an ingredient I found and removed when I opened the plastic envelope this morning. That's why Mr. DeWitt didn't want the envelope opened here."

An ugly animal sound erupted from DeWitt's throat as he suddenly sprang at Corey, flailing at him in a blind and mindless rage.

"Hold him!" shouted Simpson, and it took several members to pull back the mountain of blubber, to pin down his windmilling arms, to force him, purple-faced with frustration, into a chair, where he sat, breathing heavily and sweating right through his clothes.

After a moment, Simpson turned his attention to Corey again. "An ingredient, you said?"

"A letter," replied Corey, "in longhand, just inside the back cover. All scratched out and worked over, as if the writer had really worked to get it just right. Kind of a poetic letter from a guy to his girl, a proposal of marriage. I guess it was never mailed, but the girl did marry him, in November of the same year this issue was published, 1842. That's why my dad held onto the magazine to the bitter end, I suppose, and that's what Mr. DeWitt really wanted for his thousand dollars. It would have been cheap at the price. It's a letter to Mary Todd, from Abe Lincoln. The magazine probably belonged to him originally. He was quite a fan of Poe's, I understand."

Taking Jen's hand, Corey led her to the door, where he stopped for a moment under the pallid bust of Pallas and turned to DeWitt. "I remember why I kicked you in the shins," he said. "You smelled bad. You still do. Come on, Jen, let's go."

In his novel series about industrial spy Kane Jackson, William Arden draws not only on his long experience in business and industry, but on an innate optimism often masked by his unsentimental approach to the realism of a harsh world. "I write about the darkness in men," he says, "because I believe it doesn't have to be dark."

The same values hold true in the exotic locale of this story. The central figure is considered by many to be a "savage"; but this may mean only an adherence to a different, and perhaps more realistic, system of ethics.

The Savage
WILLIAM ARDEN

The East African Airways jet circled Nairobi once before touching down at Embakasi airport. The city shone in the sun and high plateau air. I saw the acres of green, the red roofs, the new multi-storied buildings, the industrial area to the east and the modern city square with the tall tower of the City Hall.

It was a far different city from the Nairobi I had first seen during World War Two.

Then, the city at the edge of the Kikuyu Escarpment was an outpost of empire of some hundred thousand people, rough and untamed. Now, it was the capital of a new country, a modern metropolis of three hundred thousand, with new and civilized ways. Yet beneath the urban polish, there was still the outpost at the edge of a savage land, and I was not returning to Kenya on any vacation. The trophies I was after this time were two New York animals named Carra.

Because Phil and Vincenzo Carra seemed to have chosen East Africa to hide in, I was making the nine-mile drive in from Embakasi to the city—a job handed to me because of that first visit in the Army and the three vacation safaris I had made since, and because I knew Frank Norman.

I asked for Norman first when I sat in the office of Colonel A. E. H. Davis at the Ministry of Defense. The colonel was an ice-eyed Britisher, thick and stocky. He examined my credentials with a gimlet eye.

"Detective Sergeant Joseph Marx," Davis read. "All in order, it seems."

"Is Frank Norman here?"

"No, up in the Northern Rift. You know Norman, eh?"

"From the war and three safaris."

Davis nodded. "Difficult fellow, Norman, but probably right, in this case. District Inspector up there, Parsons, agrees with Norman. Touchy affair, this."

"You haven't picked up the Carras?"

Colonel Davis frowned out a window at the glittering city. "Norman isn't sure they are *your* Carras. Norman doesn't want to take us in unless he's sure."

"You want my positive identification?"

"That's part of it. Mostly, we want you people in on any capture. Matter of responsibility." Davis gave me his iceberg eyes. "Our new government is careful about police authority. Your Carras—if it is them—are close to the border. If they skip across into the Sudan or Ethiopia it could be sticky, these days. In the old days, we'd simply have hopped over the border and grabbed them. Highhanded perhaps, but we got the job done and no nonsense." Davis sighed. "Would your Carras know about the border problems?"

"Maybe," I said. "They're smart. When they were indicted on the drug charges, they grabbed their cash and ran. Norman's report is our first trace of them since Rome, over a year ago."

"How much cash are they carrying?"

"We figure half a million is what they started with."

"That much? Wonder why they picked our bush to hide in? Dismal life up there, I'd think. For men like that."

"We may not be the only ones looking for them. Some of their associates don't seem to like it that they skipped."

"I see. Well, you better get cracking, then. A plane will take you as far as Lokitaung on Lake Rudolf. Norman and Parsons will meet you there. Give my best to Norman. We never see the stubborn brute down here. Won't leave his damned wasteland, the bloody savage." . . .

An hour later, I was in the air heading northwest. The pilot was a young Luo, reserved and all business, and I had plenty of time to think. As I looked down at the wide, dusty floor of the Great Rift Valley, I thought about Frank Norman.

The colonel was right: Frank Norman was a savage. I mean that in the best, oldest sense: a simple man—physical, direct, proud and fierce. He had spent his life in the bush, desert and mountains. First as a soldier, then as a hunter, trader and safari leader. His truth was the truth of the body—of strength, courage and aggressiveness. Frank was a bull in an open field, pawing the ground and contemptuous of the cunning cape work and concealed sword of the civilized world.

He wasn't a big man, but he had the shoulders of a buffalo, and muscles like the dry rocks of his dusty wasteland. When I had first met him, in our Army days, he had been as tough and as slender as one of the Masai warriors he admired. The last time I had safaried with him, he had put on weight and filled out in the belly.

"Soft and slack, that's what I'm getting," Frank had said. "It's a slack, twisted world. Even the Masai are turning in their loincloths and lion manes for trousers. A Masai in pants! Clowns! White men's jackals!"

It's a cliché that men like Frank Norman marry a quiet mouse of a woman with an implacable desire for conformity and a neat, suburban house. Like most clichés, it's rarely true. Angie Norman was tall, beautiful, easy-going, as savagely physical as Frank himself. She loved Frank and she lived as he lived. They had two sons.

"My boys will grow up free, Joe," he said a moment later. "I can't leave them much, but I can leave them a clean way of life and a place to live it in."

"Africa, Frank?" I asked him. "No. Your Africa is over, a thing of the past like yourself. They're not you, your boys, and their Africa won't be your Africa."

Frank only smiled, a kind of faraway dream in his eyes. "Wrong, Joe. They'll be just like me, and I'll leave them my Africa. There's a valley, never mind where, but it's pure and unspoiled. I own it—bought it for a song years ago. No one wanted it, and no one will get it now. There's a small tribe in it that live as they always did—hunt lions—all of it. Spears, no guns. Water—all of it. That's what I leave my boys."

Frank Norman was there in the dust and hot sun under the big African sky. A tall man in police uniform stood with him. They came toward me and I saw that Frank had trimmed down again.

I saw his eyes, and above his smile, the eyes were not bright. They were like empty tunnels into nowhere.

I had seen that look before, in the eyes of men who had been too long on the front line in a bloody war.

Then he blinked, his eyes became normal and he gripped my hand. "Damn me, it's been too bloody long, Joe!"

"A lot too long," I said.

"Ready for a sticky game?"

"I'll try not to fall over my feet."

"You damn well won't, you know. I'm not having my record sullied by the likes of a New York bloodhound!" He grinned, then nodded at the tall man with him who was standing back, silent and official. "This civil-servant type is Inspector Parsons. Parsons, meet Joe Marx, a Yankee sleuth we've got to wet-nurse."

"Pleasure, Mr. Marx," Parsons said.

"Glad to meet you, Inspector," I said.

We drove to the district police compound in Frank's remote village. Inspector Parsons' office looked as if it hadn't changed in a hundred years—ancient roll-top desk, rattan furniture, kudu heads, revolving ceiling fan.

"Tell me about your Carras," Frank said.

I told him about the rise of the Carras from the slums of East New York to millions from heroin, gambling, loan-sharking and every other dirty racket.

"They were middle-rank hoods, not too bright, and they made some mistakes. We have a good case, so they skipped out."

"Which one limps?" Frank asked.

"Phil," I said. "He can't bend his left knee."

Frank nodded. "Which one was a sailor?"

"The older, fatter one, Vincenzo."

"A sailor has a special walk that shows in his tracks," Frank explained. "You see, Joe, they've changed their appearance. The fat one has a beard, and the taller one is blond. They can't change their tracks." Frank produced a small ring. "One of my trackers found this out there."

It was a pearl and ruby pinky ring. It had an inscription inside in Sicilian: *To my brother—C.G.* I had seen others like it.

"It's a token of appreciation from a big racket boss. Both Phil and Vincenzo were supposed to have gotten one."

"Then that's it," Frank said.

"Do we start right now?"

"Tomorrow," Parsons said.

Angie greeted us on the steps of the veranda that surrounded the house Frank had built when he had married her. It was far out in the bush, twenty miles from any neighbors—and they were Masai.

"I'm glad they sent you, Joe," Angie said.

Angie served up a fine dinner. Afterward she went to bed. Frank and I drank alone.

"They won't get away," Frank said.

I remembered his eyes. "Is something wrong, Frank?"

He laughed, but not happily. "Shows, does it? I'm slowing up, Joe, I guess. Maybe it's time to retire to that valley of mine."

Then he slapped my leg. "Turn in, Joe. We'll get them for you, but it's going to be rough work, believe me."

Frank was right. The two days in the truck were hard enough. There were no roads, the truck broke down and we had to work on it in the killing sun. It was terrible, broken country, and with all our twisting, took hours to cover ten miles.

The third day, Frank, Parsons, myself and Frank's two Wanderobo gun bearers left the truck and began to walk. It was hell.

"The truck can't get where they are," Frank explained, "and they'd hear the motor at twenty miles."

Parsons said, "An old half-breed Kikuyu, Jake Musingi, made a fortune and built a house out here. That's where they are."

"Just the two of them there?" I asked.

"Apparently." Parsons said.

We climbed, slid, fell, bled, gasped for water and cooked under that fiery sun. Nothing moved in the desolate land, not even vultures.

It was just after dawn that we lay on the rim of the small, hidden rift and looked down on the fine, white house concealed under an overhang of the hill. Nothing moved. There was no cover near the house, and the windows were set with iron bars.

"Damn it," I whispered, "it's a fort."

"Old Musingi believed in self-defense," Parsons said.

"Tell me about them again," said Frank. "Are they clever tricky, or just thugs?"

"Clever," I said. "Not bright, but shrewd."

"Then I can get them," Frank said. "Parsons will stay here and keep the house covered. Joe, you work around and down to that ledge over to the right. That way, you can cover the side door. It's the only other door out."

"What are you going to do?"

"Go and visit them," Frank said.

I worked my way around to the small ledge that was some fifty yards away from the house. I could see nothing of Parsons up on the rim. I waited, and then I saw Frank and one bearer come walking casually into the small rift from its open end. He walked bold as you please.

I held my breath. Frank was carrying his rifle easily in his left hand. He got closer and closer to the house. I heard a safety snick off somewhere and metal strike metal. Someone inside the house had a rifle out between the bars of a window.

He was less than twenty feet away. "Haloo, in there" he called pleasantly.

The door opened and a man stepped out with his right hand in the pocket of his khaki bush jacket. A tallish, blond man with a stiff left knee. Phil Carra!

Phil advanced carefully toward Frank. "You looking for anyone, mister?"

"Anyone I can find," Frank said. "I'm afraid I'm almost out of water."

"The water's over there in the well house," Phil Carra said.

Frank knew that Vincenzo was covering him from the house, but he didn't hesitate. One minute, Phil Carra was standing with his hand in his pocket, and Frank was turning for the water, and the next minute, Phil was sprawled on his back from a savage punch in the face, and Frank and his bearer were down in the dirt.

A shot exploded from the house.

I was running toward the house.

Parsons shot at the window of the house from the rim.

I saw Frank roll, come up and hurl himself through the open door. I reached the house and heard two shots inside. I ran for the front door. Frank was coming out.

"Frank, you—" I started.

He jumped at me. I fell backwards. He knocked me over with a sweep of his rifle, and fired in almost the same instant. As I lay on the ground, I saw Vincenzo Carra fall with a rifle still in his hand. Vincenzo lay cursing through his new beard, and holding his bloody shoulder.

Phil Carra rose shakily to his knees with his pistol out. Frank moved swiftly and kicked the pistol from Phil's hand.

Inspector Parsons and the second bearer came down the rim into the rift as Frank Norman grinned at his two prisoners.

We found the Carra's money in a suitcase in the house. It was no longer a half a million dollars, but it was a good bundle. Frank located their Land Rover hidden under camouflage outside the rift, and the trip back to our truck was easier. Two days later, when we finally pulled into the police compound, I sure was one happy detective.

It was early evening, and we locked the Carras up in the single cell Parsons had with a twenty-four-hour guard on them. Their money went into the storeroom of the inspector's office—at their insistence.

"That's our dough, Marx," Vincenzo snarled as the doctor patched him up.

"Maybe so, maybe not. And it's dirty, anyway," I said.

"Money don't talk about who owns it, Joe boy," Phil said.

Angie came into town to pick up Frank. She was excited, keyed up. Gerd Booher and John McGee, neighboring ranchers, were in town, and they dragged Frank and Angie off to the only saloon for a celebration drink. I was dusty as the hills, but Parsons and I had our reports to write if I was to take the Carras back to Nairobi in the morning.

"We'll work at my residence," the inspector offered. "That way, I can furnish something to cut the dust."

We went to work in his home study with tall gin slings close at hand. The international aspects of the matter made a lot of work. There were fifty forms to be completed, most of them in triplicate.

Darkness came, and with it that vast sense of brooding that was the African night up in the empty bush country. We drank four gin slings each and smoked too many cigarettes. Paper work has never been my thing, and Parsons was even slower.

The single shot hammered the night like a physical blow in our ears.

"What in God's name?" Parsons cried, even as he was up and reaching for his pistol on his way to the door.

I didn't say anything, but I was right behind him with my pistol out.

We ran toward the cluster of buildings that made up the tiny village. In the police compound I saw her. "There!"

Parsons bent over her. It was Angie Norman. She lay on the hard, dusty ground of the compound, blood on her bush jacket. Parsons worked over her swiftly, skillfully. He looked up at me.

"Left shoulder. A scratch, but she's out."

"The Carras," I said. "Check them!"

Parsons snapped orders to his men. Two of them ran to check the Carras.

Frank Norman came running up then. His face went pale when he saw Angie on the ground. Parsons calmed him and the two of them bent over the now moaning Angie as she began to come out of it.

I went into Parsons' office. A window in the rear was smashed open. The door of the storeroom hung with its lock broken. I went into the storeroom. The money was gone, all of it. I went back out where Angie was now sitting up. Frank gave her a cigarette and she smoked. Gerd Booher and John McGee came up.

"What happened?" McGee said.

"Angie? You okay?" Booher asked.

Angie Norman nodded, smoked and looked around in the night at all of us. "I came out for some air. I was coming to see if Joe and the inspector were ready to join us for a drink. I walked past the compound and heard a noise in the office. I started to look in when I saw this shadow—a man, I think. He shot at me. No warning. I was hit, but I heard him running away. I got a glimpse, nothing more. A man in a city suit. That's all I remember."

I said, "The money's gone."

The doctor arrived, with some Masai women, and they took care of Angie. Parsons' men reported the Carras safe in their cell, and Frank went to find his 'Derobo gun bearers. He returned with one of them, and went all over the compound. Parsons and I searched the office, but there was nothing to see except the broken door and smashed window.

We went around to the rear of Parsons' office. Frank and his tracker were studying the ground near the smashed window. The tracker was pointing to the ground, pointing out into the night, talking rapidly.

Frank said, "He says it was one man, small. The track is a city shoe. The trail leads off toward the north."

I looked toward the north. A small man in city clothes. Maybe a friend of the Carras? Or one of the syndicate who had come all this way, as I had, to find them—and the money? The arm of the brotherhood was long.

"Maybe it was someone from the gang after the money," I said.

"A third man?" Frank said. "Someone out there at Musingi with them we missed?"

"Well," McGee said, "do we stand here, or go after him?"

"Let's get moving," Booher said.

"No," Frank said. "Not in the dark. A city man won't get far out here. Get some sleep, we'll go in the morning."

We went at dawn. Frank had rounded up his second gun bearer and the two led us. They tracked swift and sure, their faces grim and impassive. A half a day, north and west, in that hard, trackless land. It was the same hot, killing trek. And then it ended.

The two 'Derobo stood like thin statues at the edge of a rocky ridge. Frank joined them. The lead 'Derobo talked, pointed to the rocky ground.

Frank said, "He says the trail fades out. Rocks and wind."

Parsons came up and spoke to the bearer. Parsons seemed annoyed. The 'Derobo spoke briefly, swept his long, thin arm in a wide circle to take in all of that desolate land, and gave a brief shrug. Frank was standing apart now, his face blank, but a certain look in his eyes I couldn't place.

Parsons said, "How the devil could a city man leave no trail in a place like this?"

Frank shrugged as I watched them all. He said, "It happens, Inspector. Luck. We'll make sure."

He spoke to his bearers. They turned without a word and began to trot back and forth in a wide, tireless circle as Frank and the rest of us watched. It went on for more than an hour, the native trackers out of sight at times. Then they came back and shook their heads.

"No sign," Frank said.

"We'll fan out all across the country," Parsons said.

"All right, but if my trackers can't find the trail, no one can," Frank said.

But we fanned out. For two days, we combed that vast country that looked like the wild land of Arizona for mile after endless mile —only harder, dryer, more terrible. At the end of the second day, we regrouped. We had found nothing.

"He'll be in the Sudan by now," Gerd Booher said.

"Or Nairobi and New York," I said.

Parsons said, "We'll send out an alarm. It's all we can do now."

Frank Norman said nothing. He only squatted in the dirt, listening to us, watching his trackers with that odd look in his eyes. The 'Derobo could have been trees for all they showed.

We went back, and Parsons sent out his alarm and made his report. Nairobi was in a fit at the loss of that money, but they were helpless. If Frank and his men couldn't find the thief, no one could.

I waited around a few days. I wasn't sure why then, but I had something gnawing in my mind. A suspicion. I didn't like my suspicion, but I waited, anyway.

New York got anxious, they wanted the Carras—money or no money. Phil and Vincenzo howled about their lost money, but I ignored them.

After three more days, I knew I had to leave and take the Carras back. My uneasy suspicion still chewed at me, but there was little I could do on no more than a hunch.

Then Frank vanished at dawn on the third day. To give it one more try, he told Parsons. He took both his trackers.

I went to Parsons and got one tracker—a Kikuyu. We went off after Frank. He had a two-hour start and the Kikuyu was a good tracker, but he didn't know this country the way Frank and his Wanderobo did. I didn't have much hope and I wasn't even sure exactly what I thought I was after.

All I had was my hunch. A hunch based on the odd look in Frank Norman's eyes; on the losing of a city man's trail by two expert trackers and Frank himself; on a robbery of almost half a million dollars witnessed only by Angie Norman; on a close shot that had only grazed Angie while Frank was drinking in a bar.

I don't know if I really expected to track Frank Norman down in his own land. I know now that I could never have found Frank, not even with the Kikuyu tracker, if he hadn't let me find him.

We had been out six hours when they appeared. The three of them: the two 'Derobo above me on a ridge with their spears, and Frank behind me with his rifle.

"What do you want, Joe?" Frank said.

His voice was quiet, but his eyes were still strange. He had me covered and the two trackers were close above, alert and ready with their spears.

"I don't know for sure, Frank," I said. "Why did you come out here again? The trail is lost. Or is it?"

"You think it isn't lost?" Frank said softly.

"I think there's something not so right about that robbery by a small city man in city clothes. No one else ever saw him."

Frank watched me in that hellish sun for a full minute. It seemed like an eternity. Then he lowered his rifle, motioned with his head for me to follow him.

Frank and I went alone behind a ridge. Frank sat on a rock.

"You faked that robbery, Frank," I said. "There isn't any city man. One of your men, the one you didn't find that night, took the money and hid it out here. You, or the tracker, winged Angie to make it look good. You and Angie faked it together, for the money. You and your men led us on a wild-goose chase."

Frank said nothing for a time. Then he looked off into the wide, empty distance of that land he knew so well. "I'll tell you a story, Joe. There's this man, kind of a savage, I guess. He's lived all his life in a savage land. He can't live in civilization. He never made much money. He has a wife and two sons. All they have for the future is what he can make by his work."

Frank picked up a stone, traced patterns in the dust with the stone. "A year ago, this man went to a Capetown hospital. They told him he had a disease. Hodgkin's disease, Joe. A year to two years—a little more, maybe. No cure, fatal for sure. A year or so, and then his wife and two sons have nothing. He has nothing to leave them. His wife wants to go home, back to civilization. He's finished, blocked, can do nothing."

Frank looked up at me. "Then two human hyenas appear with half a million dollars. Dirty money that belongs to no one. The man's wife loves him, but she has two sons with no future at all anywhere when he dies. A half a million dollars buys a lot of future for two boys who have no future. There it is, waiting to be taken. It's too much to resist, Joe, too much."

I waited, but that was all Frank said. My mind was in chaos. I'm a cop and Frank was telling about a robbery. But I'm also a man and Frank was telling me he was dying. Frank was saying he was already a dead man even while he still walked and breathed. Frank, who had saved my life at the risk of the few months he had left. He had saved me, risking his few months, and knowing that I was the one man who might spoil his robbery scheme.

I said, "For nickels and dimes. You, too, Frank? Another dirty grab in a dirty, scheming world? Tough Frank Norman?"

He looked straight at me. "I guess even I had to wake up, join the pack, be like everyone else."

That odd look was still in his eyes and he held his rifle. I didn't think he would shoot me, but I wasn't sure. Civilization had caught up with Frank Norman.

"Will you kill me, Frank? And the Kikuyu, too?"

He thought about it calmly. "I don't know, Joe. Maybe, if I had to. But I don't have to. You owe me something, you have no proof, and no one will know."

I owed him, yes—and what could I prove? I'd never find the money. No one would, not in Frank's own country.

"I know," I said. "I know and you know. You'll have to live all your last days with what you did."

With that, I turned my back and walked away. My back crawled all the way to the Kikuyu, and all the way until we were out of sight of Frank and his two Wanderobo high on a ridge against that blazing, cloudless sky. But I knew he wouldn't shoot. He didn't have to. I had no proof. I could never tell.

In the village, I picked up the Carras and headed for Nairobi and home. I felt sick. Frank Norman down in the slime of greed with everyone else. The chips down and he crawled for nickels and dimes, too. A proud savage in the dirt.

I thought that, yes—and I should have known better.

Parsons found me in my office down in Centre Street less than six months later. He looked tired, and he carried a large suitcase.

"Frank's dead," Parsons said. "Two weeks ago. In the bush."

"I'm sorry," I said. I was still bitter. No cop likes to hide a crime, not even for a friend who saved his life.

"He told me to give you this," Parsons said, putting the suitcase on my desk. "He said you'd know how to explain it."

He opened the suitcase. It was money, of course. Almost a half a million dollars. I just looked at it. The Carras' money all there, sent back by Frank Norman.

Parsons said, "It was Angie, not Frank. He told me just before he died. Angie and the two 'Derobo worked out the scheme. Frank was never in it, but he figured it out when the trackers lost the trail. Angie stole the money for her sons, for the future in England after Frank was gone. He had nothing to leave her."

I didn't say anything. I remembered Frank's eyes. Yes, Angie had stolen the money and Frank had guessed and covered for her.

"He couldn't turn her in, admit what she'd done," Parsons said. "No more than a lion can turn on its mate. He couldn't take the money from her; it was for his family. He had to work it out his own way, man to man. Put himself on the line. Do it alone, hurt no one else."

"How then?" I said. "The money is here. If he didn't take the money from her, where did it come from?"

"From his blood, Marx. From his own soul. A savage heart," Parsons said. "You remember that valley of Frank's? The hidden valley he owned? The place where he was going to live out his life his own way, defy the modern world, and then leave it to his sons to carry on apart from the dirt of civilization?"

"Yes," I said.

"It has uranium in it, that valley," Parsons said. "Frank always knew it had uranium, knew it was worth a fortune. It was part of his triumph over civilization to know that no one would ever mine that uranium, spoil his wilderness. That valley was to remain pure, savage, untouched by greed."

"He sold it," I said. "He sold his valley, his last dream."

Parsons nodded. "So that Angie could keep her money. He paid for her crime his own way."

Parsons left not long after, to go back to his wilderness. I told my superiors that Frank had found the money in the bush. The Carras got their money back—not that it will do them much good in the prison where they'll be for a long, long time.

But it did Frank Norman good. I should have known that Frank would be himself to the end, a proud savage. Out in the open, telling the world what he was, daring the world to try to stop him from going his own savage way.

Suzanne Blanc was born in Springfield, Massachusetts, and traveled in such appropriate mystery-story locales as Mexico and Japan before settling in Oregon, where she is a writer and mystery reviewer for the *Portland Oregonian*.

Her writing career had a major advance when, during her college days at Smith, her English instructor recommended her work to Mary Ellen Chase. The first of her four novels, *The Green Stone*, did not begin, in her mind, specifically as a mystery novel; it was, however, a fine enough example of the *genre* to win the Mystery Writers of America Edgar for best first novel.

In this example of her unfortunately few short stories we meet Larry and Vi Simmonds, who may be just like a couple next door to you. But for your sake, we certainly hope not.

An Inside Straight
SUZANNE BLANC

Throughout the day Larry Simmonds had waited resolutely for evening to come. As soon as the sun had set, however, he began to waver. It turned bitterly cold and the chill wind that swept in from the gorge and whistled around the house seemed to undermine the firmness of his intention. Nevertheless, immediately after dinner, he shrugged into his heavy coat, checked to make certain that the gun was in his pocket and casually started for the back door.

Vi glanced up from the kitchen sink with mild surprise. Her face, flushed and shiny from the steam of the dishes, looked as scrubbed and wholesome as it had on the day they were married.

"Where are you headed for, Larry?" she asked with impersonal curiosity.

Knowing that she was neither as guileless nor wholesome as she appeared, it was hard for him to look at her. "Just out to get some anti-freeze," he lied glibly. "I won't be long."

Equally as smooth she returned the lie. "I might not be here when you get back. I promised Rosalie I'd help her shorten a dress."

Larry's vacillating intention hardened. He saw Marty frown over the schoolbooks that were spread across the kitchen table, heard the boy mutter, "Doesn't anyone in this family ever stay home any more?" And Larry knew he had no alternative. He had to kill Rod Mercer.

"I'll be back soon, son," he said. "Say hello to Rosalie for me," he added pleasantly to Vi . . . Then he was out in the chill night air.

He drove rapidly through silent streets. Windows glowed in the subdivision around him; flurries of dead leaves swirled in the beams of his headlights. There was very little traffic in the suburbs, less when he reached the downtown area. Most of the shops were already closed, a row of show windows silvered by the street lamps.

He followed Main into the empty cavern of the financial district. Here, as if the electricity had been disconnected, the office buildings were totally dark. As he passed the Equitable Insurance and Trust, he wondered, with unexpected alarm, whether he was too late, whether the weekly sales meeting had ended early, whether Rod had left. But the luck that had swept any casual wanderer from the streets was intact. Rod's car still crouched on the ebony pool of the parking lot.

Larry hid his own car in the shadows behind it, climbed into Rod's convertible, put the gun on his lap and waited. Cold seeped in from the night outside, numbing his face, his gloved hands. Mechanically he started to flex his fingers, over and again, so that they wouldn't stiffen, so that he would be able to pull the trigger.

From the recesses of the convertible the night seemed deceptively bright. The black skeletal arms of the maples along the curb were silhouetted against a spangled sky. Halfway down the block the Slipper's neon sign glittered in a vivid, flashing arc of light.

On and off it flashed, like the memories of last summer when Vi first started at Equitable. Then she used to ask him to meet her after work for a drink. Sarah, Rosalie, and a few of the salesmen would crowd with them around one of the tiny tables and talk shop. The salesmen were always attentive to Vi, especially Peter Erskine and Carleton Dodge, whose correspondence she handled, and, occasionally, when she exchanged a private joke with Peter or batted her large blue eyes at one of Martin's extravagant compliments, Larry would have an agonized moment of jealousy. But he looked back at those moments almost nostalgically now, as part of the time when everything had been all right—before Rod Mercer came to Equitable.

That was in the fall, and very quickly everything changed. For a while Vi still stopped for a drink at the Slipper and asked Larry to meet her there, but less often. Little by little she seemed to slip into a social round that excluded him . . . the women's bowling league . . . a weekly card party at Sarah's . . . sewing lessons for Rosalie . . . baby-sitting for Ellie, Rod's wife.

There had never been any bowling or card parties, of course. Very early in the game Vi's activities had assumed a measurable pattern. It was always after midnight when she came home, and she was usually a little drunk, but because he needed her desperately, in the beginning Larry closed his eyes. He pretended not to hear when she stumbled up the stairs, pretended to be asleep when she climbed into bed and afterwards he would believe her when she trotted out the hackneyed lies. He had to believe her; it was impossible for him to picture a future without her.

But underneath he was sick with fear. The deliberate blindness couldn't completely conceal the shadowy figure of another man, Pete's, he thought, at first, then Carleton's, until he really started thinking about it and settled on Rod. Vi was always talking about him and once, in the only outburst of jealousy he ever permitted himself, Larry accused her of being in love with him.

"In love with Rod?" Vi had laughed until tears brightened her eyes. "You're out of your gourd! He's a darling. I adore him, but he drinks too much. Ellie's welcome to him. I wouldn't have a man like that on a silver platter with an apple in his mouth."

Then she had kissed Larry and he felt better and trusted her again, but not for long. The fear that she was seeing Rod returned, and though he advised himself to leave well enough alone, he was driven by a spasmodic compulsion to check up on her.

Twice he called Rod's house when Vi had said she would be babysitting there. Both times Ellie had answered the phone with an anxious, "Hello, Rod?" After the second call Larry's self-deception was at an end.

The Slipper's sign flashed and faded as his hope had flashed and faded during that painful period of enforced awakening. One evening when Vi was out, sure that his suspicions were justified, he made a wild resolution and dug out the Army .45 packed in the attic. Having found it, he decided that he must be wrong and buried it again. Later he returned for it and put it in the pocket of the old winter coat where Vi wouldn't accidentally find it. By then the periods of hope had yielded to the despair that led to waiting here on this cold Monday night.

Although the rest of the murder had been recklessly planned, the time had been carefully selected. On Mondays sales meetings were held and Vi never left the house until after eight. But it was long past eight. Larry was beginning to fear that he had miscalculated. The building was dark. The sales session must be over. Rod could have stopped for a drink, but surely by now he should be on his way to meet Vi.

A new and terrible thought occurred to Larry. Perhaps they would meet indiscreetly at the Slipper and return to the car together. What would he do then? A sick uneasiness clouded his decision. It was pointless to kill Rod if it meant also losing Vi.

It was a decision he didn't have to face. The flow of his luck remained unchanged. Vi didn't meet Rod at the Slipper. Alone, shortly before nine, Rod returned to the car. Weaving slightly he crossed the black patch of the parking lot, climbed into the convertible, snapped on the dash lights and stared at Larry with a foolish, varnished smile. He had had just enough to drink to be more pleased than surprised to find someone waiting for him.

Afterwards Larry never really knew whether Mercer had recognized him. Rod gave a muffled exclamation of alarm when the gun went off. His pudgy, handsome face crumbled into a mask of reproachful amazement. His mouth fell open and he slumped slowly over the wheel.

With Rod's death the elastic band of tension, stretched too far, finally snapped. Larry sat inertly staring at the body. He expected to hear footsteps pounding toward him, but there were no footsteps, only a prolonged, congealed silence. Nothing stirred on the deserted street. He realized, suddenly, that no one had heard the shot and he began to believe that he had not only eliminated his rival but would get away with it. Leaving Rod's body slumped over the wheel, he hurried to his own car.

He was cautious now, overly cautious. He pulled out of the parking lot without turning on his lights, hesitated before driving on into the empty night. When he was almost home he remembered the anti-freeze, but he didn't stop to buy any. With each moment he had grown increasingly confident that luck was with him, that he'd actually made it, drawn to an inside straight.

For some illogical reason he expected to find Vi in the living room with Marty, but the boy was watching TV alone. Immediately Larry realized that Vi couldn't know yet that Rod was dead. She was sipping a drink somewhere, watching the clock, wondering why her lover was late.

"Mom's gone over to Rosalie's," Marty told him unnecessarily. "She said not to wait up."

"I won't. I'm beat. As a matter of fact I'm heading for bed. Don't you stay up too late, son. And don't forget to leave the porch light on for your mother."

He climbed to the bedroom, not expecting to sleep, just intending to stretch out while he listened for Vi. She would tell him an elaborate fiction about Rosalie's dress and he would pretend to believe her. Then she would crawl into bed beside him and he would hold her in his arms and everything would be as it used to be. But the watchful nights, the restless anxieties had taken their toll. Exhaustion blanketed his legs, his arms, pressed against his eyelids, pushing him into a deep, dreamless sleep.

The morning light streaming through the window aroused him. He awakened refreshed. Relief, as at the passing of a nightmare, colored the pattern of his thoughts. In the instant of awakening, he didn't remember killing Rod Mercer, merely luxuriated in an unaccustomed peace. When at last he recalled what had happened, it was without regret. Rod might have been a stranger who had died in a distant, disconnected dimension of time and space. Larry considered only the future and only in terms of Vi, grateful that he had found the courage to win her back.

The bedroom was empty, the door open. The aroma of coffee and bacon drifted up the stairs. He dressed quickly and hurried to the kitchen where she was serving Marty breakfast. She was obviously upset. The unnatural stiffness of her movements betrayed her. When he leaned over to kiss her he tasted the salty dampness of her cheeks and knew that she had been crying.

"What's the matter, Hon," he asked her gently, "something happen to upset you?"

She nodded. "Yes. Rod Mercer's dead. Someone shot him. Pete called to tell me before I could read it in the paper."

"That's terrible," Larry said. "Do the police have any idea who did it?"

"I don't know," she answered pouring his coffee. "Poor Ellie. Pete's over there with her now. He said he'd call back. I can't imagine who'd want to kill Rod. Everyone was so fond of him."

Larry carried his coffee to the table, sat down beside Marty and picked up the paper. But he didn't read it. He was watching Vi. She came over and joined them. He could smell the fragrance of her perfume, see the tear stains on her cheeks. Perversely sorry for her, he wanted to reach out and comfort her. He took a first, tentative step to end their estrangement.

"I've got an idea," he suggested. "Why doesn't Marty come downtown after school? I'll pick you both up. We'll go out for dinner and take in a movie."

Vi glanced at him warily as though the suggestion had caught her off guard, the secretive, nervous expression that had become so familiar gathering in her eyes.

Marty didn't notice. "Hey, that would be neat," he said. "Can we, Mom?"

But Larry already knew the answer; Vi was smiling her gentlest smile.

"I'd love to, darling." Her voice was smooth, apologetic as always when she lied. "I would if I could, but it's Tuesday. Sarah's expecting me." In the living room the phone started to ring and she jumped up at the sound. "You know we always play cards on Tuesday." Without a backward glance she moved toward the phone. "It must be Pete," she said.

Behind her beads of sweat were popping out on Larry's forehead. "That's right. I forgot. We'll have to make it another time. This is your mother's card night," he said automatically. He nodded and picked up his coffee cup, her words echoing in his mind.

It must be Pete, he thought.

The Alternate Universe concept, while most common in science fiction, has been used by such writers as Winston Churchill and MacKinlay Kantor to allow conjectures upon what would have occurred if pivotal events had been altered or reversed.

To outline the history of the Anglo-French empire: King Richard I of England survived his 1199 wound by a crossbow bolt by twenty years, outliving Prince John and passing the title to his nephew, Arthur of Brittany. King Arthur, by his wisdom and benevolence, coupled with military brilliance, retained and expanded his empire to include by the twentieth century the British Isles, France, and both continents of the New World. In the late thirteenth century, a cloistered monk perfected the elements and laws of Magic, which supplanted the vague and undeveloped field of the physical sciences as the guiding force of progress.

But the reader should be warned, or unwarned. Randall Garrett, a writer of distinctly Elizabethan mien in some respects, is a sinisterly fair plotter. In the Darcy stories, which include besides the adjacent work three novelettes and the novel *Too Many Magicians*, there is always, within the trapping of Empire and Sorcery, an impeccably fair set of evidence. *Discaveat lector!*

A Stretch of the Imagination
A Lord Darcy Story
RANDALL GARRETT

1

Late afternoon is not a usual time for suicide, but in Lord Arlen's case, it appeared that his death could hardly be attributable to any other cause.

Lord Arlen was the owner and head of one of the most important publishing houses in Normandy, Mayard House. Its editorial offices occupied the whole of a rather large building located in the heart of the Old City, not too far from the Cathedral of St. Ouen. On the day of the Vigil of the Feast of St. Edward the Confessor, Thursday, October 12, 1972, Lord Arlen was in his private office, sound asleep. He was accustomed to taking a nap at that time, and staff were well aware of it, so they moved quietly and spoke in low tones and only when necessary. No one had gone in or out of his office for nearly an hour.

At five minutes past four, three members of staff—Damoselle Barbara, and Goodmen Wober and Andray—heard an odd thump and further strange noises through the thick door of the private office. They all hesitated and looked at each other. They felt that something was wrong, but not one of them quite dared to open that door, fearing Lord Arlen's temper.

Within thirty seconds, Sir Stefan Imbry came charging into the room. "What's happened?" he barked. "I was in the library. Heard a noise. Chair falling, I think. Now it sounds as though my lord is being sick at his stomach." He didn't pause as he spoke, but went straight to the door of the inner office. The staff members felt a momentary sense of relief; only Chief Editor Sir Stefan would dare break in on Lord Arlen.

He flung open the door and stopped suddenly. "Good God!" he said in a strangled voice. Then, to staff, "Quickly! Help me!"

Lord Arlen was hanging by his neck from a rope that had been thrown over a massive wooden beam. He was still twitching. Below his feet was an overturned chair.

He was still just barely alive when they took him down, but his larynx had been crushed, and he died before medical aid or a Healer could be summoned.

2

Lord Darcy, Chief Criminal Investigator for His Royal Highness, Richard, Duke of Normandy, looked down at the small and rather pitiful body that lay on the office couch. Lord Arlen had been a short man—five-four—and weighed nine stone. In death, he no longer showed the driving, fanatical, and—at times—almost hysterical energy that had made him one of the most feared and respected men in his field. Now he looked like a boy in his teens.

Dr. Pateley, the Chirurgeon, had finished his examination of the body and looked up at Lord Darcy. "Master Sean and I can give you more accurate information after the autopsy, my lord, but I'd say he's been dead between half an hour and forty-five minutes." He smoothed his gray hair and adjusted his pince-nez glasses. "That fits in with the time your office was notified, my lord."

"Indeed it does," murmured Lord Darcy. Tall, lean, and handsome, he spoke Anglo-French with a definite English accent. "Master Sean? How goes it?"

Master Sean O Lochlainn, Chief Forensic Sorcerer to His Highness, was busy with a small golden wand which had a curious spiral pattern inscribed upon its gleaming surface. It is not wise to interrupt a magician while he is working, but Lord Darcy sensed that the tubby little Irish sorcerer had finished his work and was merely musing.

He was right. Master Sean turned, a half smile on his round face. "Well, me lord, I haven't had time for a complete analysis, but the facts stand out very clearly." He twirled the wand in his fingers. "There was no one else in the room at the time he died, me lord, and hadn't been for an hour. Time of death was fourteen minutes after four, give or take a minute. The time of the psychic shock of the hanging itself was five after. No evil influence in the room; no sign of Black Magic."

"Thank you, my good Sean," Lord Darcy said, his eyes focused upon the overhead beam. "As always, your evidence is invaluable."

His lordship turned to the fourth man in the room, Master-at-Arms Gwiliam de Lisles, a large, beefy, tough-looking man with huge black mustaches and the mind of a keen investigator.

"Master Gwiliam," Lord Darcy said, "would you have one of your men fetch me a ladder that can reach that beam?" He gestured upward.

"Immediately, my lord."

Two uniformed Men-at-Arms were given instructions, and the ladder was brought. Lord Darcy, with a powerful magnifying lens in his hand, climbed up the ladder to the heavy beam, ten feet above the floor, two and a half feet below the ceiling.

The rope which had hanged Lord Arlen was still in place, and Lord Darcy examined the beam and the rope itself very carefully.

Master Sean, staring upward with his blue Irish eyes, said: "May I ask what it is you might be looking for, me lord?"

"As you see," Lord Darcy said, still scrutinizing the wood, "the rope goes up over the beam, here, and is held firmly at the far end, tied to the pipe that runs just below the window behind the desk. It might be possible that Lord Arlen was strangled, the rope put about his neck, and hauled up to the position in which he was found. In that case, the friction of the rope against the wood would displace the fibers of both in an upward and backward direction. But—" He sighed and began climbing back down the ladder. "But no. The evidence is that he actually did drop from the end of that rope and was hanged."

"Would there have been time, my lord," Master Gwiliam asked, "to have hauled him up like that?"

"Possibly not, my dear Master Gwiliam, but every bit of evidence must be checked. If the fibers had showed friction the other direction, we might have been forced to recheck the timing."

"Thank you, my lord," said the plainclothes Master-at-Arms.

Lord Darcy went over to check the other end of the rope.

There was only one window in the office. Lord Arlen had liked dimness and quiet in his office, and one window was enough for him. It was directly behind his desk, and opened into a three-foot-wide air shaft that let in hardly any light, even at high noon. For illumination, his lordship had depended upon the usual gaslights, even in the daytime. They were all alight, but Lord Darcy, being his usual suspicious self, had sniffed the air for any signs of raw gas. There was none. Gas had nothing to do with the problem.

The window itself was of the usual double-hung type. To provide air flow, the upper lite was open about three inches. It was a high, narrow window, and the top of the casing was nine feet above the floor. The bottom pane was open about eight inches, and the end of the rope ran through it to tie to an exterior pipe about six inches from the bottom of the sill. It slanted up to the beam near the ceiling, and dropped to its fatal end.

A careful examination showed that the window had not been opened any farther than it was now; the whole apparatus had been varnished at least twice, and the varnish in the joints and cracks had almost sealed the window lites in place. That window hadn't been opened fully for years.

"Eight inches at the bottom and three inches at the top," Lord Darcy said thoughtfully. "Hardly enough room for a man to crawl through. And, aside from the door, there are no other ways in or out of this room." He looked at Master Sean. "None?"

"None, me lord," said the round little Irish sorcerer. "Master Gwiliam and meself have checked that over thoroughly. There's no hidden passages, no secret panels. Nothing of the like." He paused a moment, then said: "But there's no gloom."

Lord Darcy's gray eyes narrowed. "No gloom, Master Sean? Pray elucidate."

"Well, me lord, in a suicide's room, there is always a sense of gloom, of deep depression, impermeating the walls. The kind of mental state a man has to be in to do away with himself nearly always leaves that kind of psychic impression. But there's no trace of that here."

"Indeed?" His lordship made a mental note. His gray eyes surveyed the room once more. "Very well. Cast a preservative spell over the body, Master Sean; I shall go out and get information from the witnesses."

"As you say, me lord," said Master Sean.

Lord Darcy headed for the library. "Come with me, Master Gwiliam," he said as he opened the door. The big Master-at-Arms followed.

3

In the library, five people were waiting, guarded by two husky Men-at-Arms wearing the black-and-silver uniforms of Keepers of the King's Peace. Three of the five were staff: the brown-haired, dark-eyed Damoselle Barbara; the round-faced, balding Goodman Wober; the lanky, nearsighted Goodman Andray. The fourth was Chief Editor Sir Stefan Imbry, a powerful, six-foot-four giant of a man. The fifth—a bull-like brute with a hard, handsome face—was one that Lord Darcy did not know.

Sir Stefan came to his feet. "My lord, may I ask why we are being held here? I have a dinner engagement, and these others wish to go home. Why should His Royal Highness the Duke send your lordship to investigate such a routine business, anyway?"

"It's the law," said Lord Darcy, "as you, Sir Stefan, should well know. When a member of the aristocracy dies by violence—whether intentional, accidental, or self-inflicted—it is mandatory that I enter the case. As for why you are being held here: I am an Officer of the King's Justice."

Sir Stefan paled a trifle.

Not out of fear, but out of profound respect. His Majesty, John IV, by the Grace of God, King and Emperor of England, France, Scotland, Ireland, New England and New France, King of the Romans and Emperor of the Holy Roman Empire, Defender of the Faith, was the latest of the long line of Plantagenet kings who had ruled the Anglo-French Empire since the time of Henry II. King John had all the strength, ability, and wisdom that was typical of the oldest ruling family in Europe. He was descended from King Arthur the Great, grandson of Henry II and nephew to Richard the Lion-Hearted, who, after surviving a wound from a crossbow bolt in 1199, had been a great solidifying force for the Empire until his death in 1219. John IV was a direct descendant of Richard the Great, who had reformed and strengthened the Empire in the latter half of the fifteenth century.

The reminder that Lord Darcy was a Royal Officer cooled even Sir Stefan Imbry's ire.

"Of course, my lord," he said in a controlled voice. "I was merely asking for information."

"And that is all I am doing, Sir Stefan," Lord Darcy said gently. "I am collecting information." He gestured. "My duty."

"Certainly, certainly," Imbry said hurriedly, and rather abashedly.

"No offense intended." Imbry was used to giving orders around Mayard House, but he knew when to defer to a superior.

"And none taken," Lord Darcy said. "Now, as to information, who is this gentleman?" He indicated the fifth member of the waiting group, the heavily muscled, hard-faced, handsome man with the dark, curly hair.

Sir Stefan Imbry made the formal introduction as the man in question stood up. "My Lord Darcy, may I present Goodman Ernesto Norman, one of our finest authors. Goodman Ernesto, Lord Darcy, Chief Investigator for His Royal Highness."

Ernesto looked at Lord Darcy with smoldering brown eyes and gave a medium bow. "An honor, your lordship."

"The honor is mine," said Lord Darcy. "I have read several of your books. One day, if you are of a mind, I should like to discuss them with you."

"A pleasure, your lordship," Goodman Ernesto said as he sat down. But there was an undertone of surliness in his voice.

Lord Darcy looked about the huge room. It was richly appointed and spacious; the walls beneath an eighteen-foot ceiling were lined with well-filled bookcases ten feet high. Above the bookcases, the walls were decorated with swords, battleaxes, maces, and shields of various designs. Several helms sat upright on the top of the bookcases. Flanking the door were two suits of sixteenth-century armor, each holding in one gauntlet a fifteen-foot cavalry lance. The window draperies were heavy dark green velvet; the gas lamps were intricately shaped and gold plated.

The pause to survey the room was filled with silence. Lord Darcy had firmly established his authority.

He looked at Sir Stefan. "I know that you have gone through this several times already, but I must ask you to repeat it again—" He glanced briefly at the other four. "—all of you."

Master-at-Arms Gwiliam, standing near the door, unobtrusively took out his notebook to record the entire conversation in shorthand.

Sir Stefan Imbry looked grim and said: "I don't see the reason for such fuss over a suicide, my lord, but it seems—"

"*It was* not *suicide!*" Damoselle Barbara's voice seemed to snap through the air.

Sir Stefan jerked his head around and looked at her angrily, but before he could speak, Lord Darcy said: "Let her speak, Sir Stefan!" Then, more softly: "Upon what do you base that statement, Damoselle?"

There were tears in her eyes, and she looked extraordinarily beautiful as she said, in a soft voice: "No material evidence. Nothing concrete that I could prove. But—as is well known—I have been My Lord Arlen's mistress for over a year. I know him. He would never have killed himself."

"I see," Lord Darcy said. "Do you have the Talent, Damoselle?"

"To a slight degree," she said calmly. "I have been tested for it. My Talent is above normal, but not markedly so."

"I understand," Lord Darcy said. "Then you have no evidence to give except your knowledge of his late lordship and your intuition?"

"None, my lord," she said in a subdued voice.

"Very well. I thank you, Damoselle Barbara. And now, Sir Stefan, if you will continue with your recitation."

Sir Stefan had calmed down, but Lord Darcy noticed that Ernesto Norman had given the Damoselle Barbara a suppressed glare of hatred.

Jealousy, Lord Darcy thought. *Hard jealousy. A stupid reaction. The man needs a Healer.*

Sir Stefan, looming tall and strong, began his story for the third time.

"At approximately half-past two . . ."

4

At approximately half-past two, Lord Arlen had come in from having luncheon at the Mayson du Shah and ignored a spiteful look from the Damoselle Barbara. She had been brought up in the north of England by rather straitlaced parents and did not understand that it was perfectly permissible for a gentleman to go to the Mayson du Shah for nothing but luncheon. She was used to the more staid English gentlemen's clubs of York or Carlisle.

"Where's Sir Stefan?" he snapped at Goodman Andray.

"Not come back from lunch yet, my lord," Andray said.

"Any other business waiting?"

"Goodman Ernesto is waiting for you, my lord. In the library."

"Ernesto Norman? He can wait. I'll let you know. Send Sir Stefan in as soon as he comes back."

Lord Arlen had stalked into his office.

At half-past two, he had bellowed sharply: "Barbara!"

She had, according to her testimony, said "Yes, my lord," and rushed into the inner office. He had, she said, been seated behind his desk. It was an impressive desk, some seven feet long by three feet wide. Behind it, Lord Arlen seemed impressively tall as he sat in his chair—for the very simple reason that his chair was elevated an extra six inches, and he had a six-inch high footstool hidden beneath the desk. Anyone who sat in the guest chair, unless he was exceedingly tall, had to look up at Lord Arlen.

The Damoselle Barbara had, she said, gone into the office and stood at attention, as was proper, and said: "You called, my lord?"

Without looking up from the manuscript he was reading, he said, "Yes, my love, I did. Send in Ernesto."

"Yes, my lord." And she had gone to fetch the waiting author.

Goodman Ernesto Norman had been waiting in the library. Notified by the Damoselle Barbara that Lord Arlen would see him, he had strode angrily out, down the hall, and around to his lordship's office, and had walked in without knocking, slamming the door behind him.

Norman's testimony was: "I was ready to strangle the little jerk, my lord. Or slap him silly. Whichever was the handiest. I'd just read the galley proofs of my latest novel, A *Knight of the Armies*. The beak-faced little name-of-a-dog had *butchered* it! I told him I wouldn't have it published that way. He told me that he'd bought the rights and I had nothing to say about it. We exchanged words, I lost the argument, and I walked out."

The staff admitted that they had heard sharp voices, but none of them had heard any of the words.

Goodman Ernesto had slammed out of the inner office at fifteen minutes of three.

Sir Stefan Imbry had walked into the outer office as Norman had stormed out of the inner. The two ignored each other as Norman went on out.

"What the devil's eating him?" Sir Stefan had asked.

"Don't know, Sir Stefan," Goodman Wober had said. "His lordship asked you to report immediately you came in, sir."

Sir Stefan's testimony was that he had gone immediately into the office, where Lord Arlen was drinking caffe—which had been brought to him by Goodman Andray a few minutes before.

"It was just a short business conference, my lord," Sir Stefan said. "I was given instructions to the format of three books we will be publishing. Entirely routine stuff, but if you want the details, my lord . . ."

"Later, perhaps. Pray continue."

"I left his office at a minute or two after three. He always naps from three to four. I went to the Art Department to check on some book illustrations, then came in here to the library to do some research, checking some of the points in a book on magic we're publishing in the spring."

"A scholarly work?" Lord Darcy asked.

"It is. *Psychologistics* by Sir Thomas Leseaux, Th.D."

"Ah! An excellent man. Master Sean will be eager to obtain a copy."

Sir Stefan nodded. "The firm will be happy to supply him with two copies. Perhaps—" His eyes brightened. "Perhaps Master Sean would consent to review it for the Rouen *Times?*"

"He might, if you approached him properly," Lord Darcy murmured. Then, more briskly: "You were here in the library, then, sir, when Lord Arlen was hanged?"

"I was, my lord."

"May I ask, then, how it was that you were apprised of the fact?" Lord Darcy was fairly certain that he knew the answer to the question, but he wanted to hear Sir Stefan's answer. "You were in the outer office, apparently, within seconds after the—ah—unfortunate incident. How did you know of it?"

"I heard the noise, my lord," said Sir Stefan. He pointed toward a window on the north, shrouded with green velvet. As he pointed, he rose to his feet. "That window, my lord, opens directly to the air shaft."

He went over and moved the curtains aside. "As you see."

The air shaft outside the window was three feet wide. A yard away was the window of Lord Arlen's office. The window itself was partially open at top and bottom, as his lordship had noted previously. So was the library window. Lord Darcy tested it. Unlike the window in Lord Arlen's office, the lites slid up and down easily; they had not been varnished over.

"Master Sean?" Lord Darcy called in a normal conversational tone.

The Irish sorcerer's round face appeared from between the closed curtains on the other side. "Aye, me lord?"

"All going well?"

"Quite well, me lord."

"Very good. Carry on."

Lord Darcy drew the curtains to, turned, and faced the others in the flickering gaslight. "Very well, Sir Stefan; that explains that. One more question."

"Yes, my lord?"

"Why was it that when you rushed in to Lord Arlen's office and found him hanging—you did not cut him down? A simple flick of a pocketknife would have released the strangling tension of the rope around his throat, would it not? Instead, you *untied the knot*. Why?"

It was the Damoselle Barbara who answered. "You didn't know, my lord?"

Lord Darcy had expected that all eyes would have gone to Sir Stefan; instead, they had come to him. He recovered quickly.

"Elucidate, Damoselle," he said calmly.

"Lord Arlen was deathly afraid of sharp instruments," the girl said. "It was an obsession with him. He never went to the Art Department, for instance, because of the razor-sharp instruments they use for making paste-ups, and that sort of thing."

Lord Darcy's eyes narrowed. "He was, I believe, smooth-shaven?"

"Smooth, yes" she answered calmly. "Shaven, no. His barber used a depilatory wax which pulled the hairs out by the roots. It was painful, but he preferred it to being approached by a razor. He would not permit anyone near him to even carry a knife. We all obeyed."

"Not even a letter opener?" Lord Darcy asked.

"Not even a letter opener," she said. She gestured toward the walls above the bookcases that lined the room. "Look at those ancient weapons. Not one of them has an edge or a sharp point. Does that answer your question about Sir Stefan's cutting down My Lord Arlen?"

"Quite adequately, Damoselle," said Lord Darcy with a slight bow.

Great God! he thought. *They all seem a little mad, and their late employer was the maddest of them all.*

5

Seven o'clock. Nearly three hours had passed since Lord Arlen had died. Outside, the sky was dark and clouded, and the air held an autumn chill. Inside, in Lord Arlen's office, the gas lamps and the fireplace gave the room a summery warmth. The body of Lord Arlen, covered by a blanket and a preservative spell, rested silently.

Sean O Lochlainn, Master Sorcerer, stood in the soft gaslight and eyed the end of the fatal rope. Behind him, respectfully silent, stood Lord Darcy, Dr. Pateley, and Master-at-Arms Gwiliam. It is not wise to disturb a magician at work.

After a moment, Master Sean bent over, opened his large, symbol-decorated carpetbag, and took out several items, including a silver-tipped ebon wand.

"There's no difficulty here, my lord," Master Sean said. "The psychic shock of sudden death has charged the hemp quite strongly." Master Sean liked to lecture, and when he assumed his pedagogical manner, his brogue faded to paleness. "The Law of Relevance is involved here; scientifically speaking, we have here a psychic force field which, given the proper impetus, will tend to return to its former state."

Then his wand moved in intricate curves, and his lips formed certain ritual syllables.

Gently, gracefully, the rope began to move. As if an unseen hand were guiding it, the hempen twist made itself into a loop. Quickly, smoothly, it tied itself. For half a second, it hung in the air, an almost perfect circle. Then, suddenly, it drooped limply.

"There you are, my lord," said Master Sean with a gesture.

Lord Darcy walked over and looked at the looped and knotted rope without touching it. "Interesting. A simple slip knot, not a hangsman's knot." Without looking up, he added: "Master Gwiliam, may I borrow your measuring tape?"

The burly Master-at-Arms unclipped his tape measure from his belt and handed it to his lordship.

Lord Darcy measured the distance from the floor to the noose. Then he measured the overturned chair from the leg to the seat. Then, with all due reverence, he measured the corpse from heel to neck.

Finally, he said: "Dr. Pateley, you are the lightest of us, I think. What is your weight?"

"Ten stone, my lord," said the chirurgeon. "Perhaps a pound or two under."

"You'll do, Doctor. Grab hold of that rope and put your weight on it."

Dr. Pateley blinked. "My lord?"

"Take hold of the rope above the noose and lift your feet off the floor. That's it." He measured again. "Less than a quarter of an inch of stretch. That's negligible. You may let go now, Doctor. Thank you."

Lord Darcy handed Master-at-Arms Gwiliam his tape measure back.

Lord Darcy tilted his head back and looked up at the overhead beam which held the rope. "A singularly foolish thing to do," he said, almost to himself.

"That's true, my lord," said Master Gwiliam. "I've always considered suicide to be a very foolish act. Besides, as someone once said, 'It's so *per*manent.'"

"I am not speaking of suicide, but of murder, my good Master-at-Arms. And it is equally permanent."

"Murder, me lord?" Master Sean O Lochlainn raised his eyebrows. "Well, if you say so. It's glad I am that I am not in the detective business."

"But you are, my dear Sean," Lord Darcy said with some surprise.

Master Sean grinned and shook his round Irish head. "No, me lord. I am a sorcerer. I'm a technician who digs up facts that ordinary observation wouldn't discover. But all the clues in the world don't help a man if he can't put them together to form a coherent whole. And that is your touch of the Talent, my lord."

"*I?*" Lord Darcy looked even more surprised. "I have no Talent, Sean. I'm no thaumaturge."

"Now, come, me lord. You have that touch of the Talent that all the really great detectives of history have had—the ability to leap from an unwarranted assumption to a foregone conclusion without covering the distance between the two. You then know where to look for the clues that will justify your conclusion. You knew it was murder two hours ago, and you knew who did it."

"Well, of course! Those two points were obvious from the start. The question was not 'Who did it?' but 'How was it done?'" His lordship smiled broadly. "And now, naturally, the answer to that last question is plain as a pikestaff!"

"How are you so certain it was murder, my lord?" asked Master Gwiliam.

"For one thing, the measurements we have just made show that the late Lord Arlen's feet were seventeen inches off the ground when he was hanged. The seat of the chair is but eighteen inches from the floor. If—I say *if*—he had put up that noose and then kicked the chair away, he would have dropped one inch. He would have been strangled, surely, no question of that. But you have seen the cruel marks of that deeply imbedded rope in the throat of his late lordship, and you have heard Dr. Pateley testify that the larynx was crushed. By the bye, Doctor, was the neck broken?"

"No, my lord," said the chirurgeon. "Badly dislocated—stretched, as it were—but not broken."

"He was a light man," Lord Darcy continued. "Nine stone. A drop of one inch could not have done all that damage." He looked at Master Sean. "Therefore, you see, it didn't happen that way. All that was necessary was to use one's imagination to see how it *might* have happened, and then check the evidence to see if it *did* happen that way. The final step is to check the evidence to make sure it could not have happened any other way. Having done that, we shall be ready to make our arrest."

6

Fifteen minutes later, Lord Darcy, Master Sean, and Master Gwiliam entered the library, where four Men-at-Arms held the five suspects under guard. Master Sean, his symbol-decorated carpetbag in hand, stopped at the door, flanked by the pair of standing suits of armor with their fifteen-foot spears.

Sir Stefan Imbry, who had been reading a book, let it drop to the floor and stood up. "How much longer has this got to go on, Lord Darcy?" he asked angrily.

"Only a few minutes, Sir Stefan. We have nearly completed our investigation." All the eyes in the room, except for Master Sean's, were on his lordship.

Sir Stefan sighed. "Good. I'm glad it's over with, my lord. There will have to be a Coroner's Inquest, of course. I do hope the jury will be kind enough to bring in a verdict of 'Suicide while of unsound mind.'"

"I do not," said Lord Darcy. "It is my fond belief that they will decide that it was an act of premeditated murder and that they pray the Court of the King's High Justice to try Sir Stefan Imbry for the crime."

Sir Stefan paled. "Are you mad?"

"Only at times. And this is not one of them."

The Damoselle Barbara gasped and said: "But Sir Stefan was nowhere near the office at the time!"

"Oh, but he was, Damoselle. He was here, in this room, alone, scarcely a dozen feet from where Lord Arlen was hanged. The whole procedure was quite simple. He went into Lord Arlen's office and slipped a drug into Lord Arlen's caffe. It is one of the more powerful, quick acting drugs. Within a few minutes, his lordship was unconscious. He affixed the rope to the pipe outside the window, threw the other end over the beam, and tied that end around Lord Arlen's neck in a slip knot."

"But the little snot wasn't hanged till an hour later," Goodman Ernesto Norman interrupted.

"True. Let me finish. Sir Stefan then put the unfortunate Lord Arlen's unconscious body *up on that beam.*"

"Just a minute, your lordship," Goodman Ernesto interrupted again. "I have no love for Sir Stefan particularly, but, tall as he is, he couldn't have lifted Lord Arlen ten feet in the air, even if he stood on the chair. And there was no ladder in the office."

"An acute observation, Goodman Ernesto. But you failed to take into account the fact that there was another chair in the room. Lord Arlen's desk chair is a full twenty-four inches high, as opposed to the normal eighteen."

"An extra six inches?" Ernesto Norman shook his head. "Still wouldn't have done it. He'd need at least another six—" He stopped suddenly. His eyes widened. "The footstool!"

"Exactly," Lord Darcy said. "Put that on top of the chair, and you have your needed six inches. I could almost do it myself, and Sir Stefan is taller than I. And nine stone is no great load for a strong man to lift."

"Even supposing I had done all that," said Sir Stefan through ashen lips, but with a controlled voice, "what am I supposed to have done next?"

"Why, my dear fellow, you left the office—after replacing the desk chair and footstool behind the desk. And after quietly putting the guest chair on its side. Then you went out and did what you told us you did, knowing that no one would disturb Lord Arlen after three o'clock."

"But we heard the chair fall at four!" the Damoselle Barbara said in a hushed voice.

"No. By your own testimony, you heard a thump. But it was Sir Stefan's statement that he heard the chair fall that influenced your thinking. The thump you heard was the sound of the beam when the shock of Lord Arlen's body, dropping nearly four feet, slammed that rope against the wood."

The Damoselle Barbara closed her eyes and shuddered. The other two members of staff just sat silently and stared.

"You waited for an hour, Sir Stefan. Then, at four o'clock, you—" Lord Darcy stopped as he got a signal from Master Sean. "Yes, Master Sean?"

"This one, me lord. Definite." He jerked a thumb toward the suit of armor standing to the left of the door.

"That completes the investigation," Lord Darcy said with a hard smile. "You, Sir Stefan, took that fifteen-foot spear, which—like every other weapon in here—has no edge or point, and used it to push Lord Arlen's body off the beam. Then you put the spear back in the gauntlet of the empty armor and went running to the office. You knew it would take some time to untie the knot, and you knew that by that time Arlen would be dead.

"But the whole thing was incredibly stupid. You were up against a dilemma. The problem was the length of the rope. If he dropped too far, his neck would break, and that would be inconsistent with an eighteen-inch chair. But if he only dropped far enough to strangle himself, his feet would have been higher off the floor than the seat of the chair. So you tried a middle road. But the stupid thing was that you did not see that the physical evidence could not, in any case, be reconciled."

Lord Darcy turned to Master Gwiliam. "Master-at-Arms Gwiliam de Lisle, I, as an Officer of the King's Justice, request that you, as an Officer of the King's Peace, arrest this man upon suspicion of murder."

As the Men-at-Arms took the broken Sir Stefan off, the shocked Damoselle Barbara said: "But *why*, my lord? Why did he do it?"

"I checked at the Records Office on Lord Arlen's will before I came here," Lord Darcy told her. "He left half his interest in the firm to you, and half to Sir Stefan. He wanted control. Now you will get it all."

The Damoselle Barbara began to cry.

But Lord Darcy noticed that Goodman Ernesto Norman had a half smile on his face, as though he were thinking, *Now I can get my novel published the way I wrote it.*

Lord Darcy sighed. "Come, Master Sean. We have an appointment for dinner, and the hour grows late."

One could scarcely have better training for writing espionage novels than did former New Yorker Mike Kurland: a military career combining Army Intelligence service in Germany and, after hours, the directing of plays for Special Services. This may account for the fact that he is best known as a science fiction writer.

His espionage (and mystery) works, however, make up in originality for their lack in number. His novels about the American-based firm of professional military technical advisers, Weapons Analysis and Research (WAR), Inc., led to the third of the series, *Plague of Spies*, being nominated for best original paperback novel for the year 1970 by Mystery Writers of America. Which does not fully account for his story in this book being science fiction.

In actuality this story is not science fiction, it is merely set in a possible not-too-distant future. The main precept is the linear development of three concepts which are well-known even today; valid concepts, logical concepts, perhaps even worthy concepts. It is the story of a criminal, an enemy of his society. It cannot be soon forgotten.

A Matter of Taste
MICHAEL KURLAND

The envelope, square, old-fashioned, of stiff paper the color of rare beef, was placed on Margil's desk with the afternoon mail. He separated it from the duns, demands, requests, supplications, in-office memoranda and such, and caressed it and sniffed at it before slitting it open with a suitably sharpened knife. It crackled roughly and exuded a faint wood-acid odor, which increased as he withdrew the thick, glossy card.

Three words, neatly scripted, undated and unsigned:

MEET AT THREE

Margil felt the delicious thrill of the conspirator creeping up his backbone, effusing and blanketing the needlepoint chill of fear at the back of his neck. He would *not* look around to see whether anyone else in the office was watching him. Why should they take any interest in his mail? He stuck the card back into the envelope and flicked it into the waste chute. Gone now. One advantage of living in this garbage-conscious age: refuse didn't stay around long enough to become evidence. Meet at three. Subtle. Like thumbing your nose at a peace officer. *Meat* at three. Chops. Perhaps a roast. Drumsticks.

Curious to discover that a hamburger isn't made of ham. He wondered whether anyone else in the office knew that.

He felt an almost uncontrollable urge to swivel his chair around and yell, "Hey, pap eaters! Protein-enriched sea-cereal slobs! I eat *meat!* Slices of once-living flesh—*meat!*" Then lean back and watch the ripple of wide eyes and open mouths. There'd be a couple of loud sniggers, then some uptight female would tell him to stop talking dirty.

The idea of eating animal flesh revolted all good-thinking people, and the practice was a felony. Gizzard, hock, rib, tripe, steak; these were the dirty words of this generation. Human organs were just barely mentionable: heart, lungs, kidney, liver, pancreas; all the spare parts in the hospital body banks.

How then does one start as disgusting and antisocial a habit as meat-eating? What causes this indecent craving that sets one apart from society and can only be sated by the criminal devouring of the flesh of animals?

"*I don't know how to begin, Doctor. I'm afraid I'll disgust you.*"

"*Relax, Mr. Margil. You must learn to trust me. Tell me about it. Remember, it's your own guilt and fears that make this secret of yours seem disgusting. I like to think that nothing Human is alien to me.*"

The first time Margil ever seriously thought about meat-eating was at college. The Sarcophile Society met in secret to discuss the joys of forbidden flesh. It was very sophomoric, and they never did manage to get hold of any real meat. Soy protein steaks were ceremoniously grilled over improvised braziers. The windows were kept closed for fear of the smoke being seen, and staying in the room after the first half hour was a test of endurance. The Society was about as daring and antisocial as any of its members cared to get. A secret release valve for the pressures of an overcrowded society.

"*Is it some sort of sexual problem, Mr. Margil? Just relax and tell me all about it.*"

Sex? Mores were more repressive than they had been at the close of the century, as society found a new equilibrium and the world population stabilised at slightly under eight billion. Margil supposed that most mental problems were still sex-based, and most psychiatrists were still basically voyeurs. But Margil's problems, or at least his psychological ones, were not sexual.

He had been out of college for some years, and had just about forgotten about the Sarcophile Society, when he realized one day that he'd developed a taste for canned cat food. He was reading the label while he ate what was left in the can after feeding his aging tom.

There it was, in very small print: "*20% animal protein from certified surplus sources.*" He stared at the phrase for some time, reading it over and over until it had lost all meaning. Then he threw up in the sink.

He disposed of the can and the spoon, and refused to think any more about it. Six months later, three weeks after his tom died, he found himself in the supermarket buying canned cat food. He rushed home and was ill for two days, and didn't go back to work for a week. But he kept buying cat food.

"*There's no need to try and shock me, Mr. Margil. I assure you it's a usual fantasy. Let's get back to the real problem. Tell me more about your sex life.*"

Sometimes the seriousness of what he was doing would be brought home to Margil in a dramatic way. One evening on the Telly news:

> "In Cleveland today an illegal Carnivore Butcher Shop was raided by peace officers after what was believed to be several months of clandestine operation. Four persons, three of them confessed carnivores, were apprehended and a fifth was shot while trying to escape and declared legally dead by an intern accompanying the peacemen."
>
> (Here the announcer lifted his head and stared straight into Margil's eyes.) "Peace officers are now rounding up what they say is a nationwide ring of customers of this Cleveland butcher."

It was shortly after this that Margil discovered the magazines. Privately printed and distributed to the below-the-counter area of several downtown newsstands. Nothing *really* illegal about reading them. Immoral maybe. Plain paper covers with the printed disclaimer: *THIS MAGAZINE NOT TO BE SOLD TO MINORS.* Color pictures of roast beeves. Articles on the preparation of lamb chops and meat loaves. Famous meat dishes of the past. Classified ads.

> $10 for four issues. CARNIBAL
> a magazine of the flesh. Sold
> only through the mail. Box Mt.

Carnibal was the next plateau. Photographs of people (with their faces obscured or barred out) masticating meat. Articles on butchering and slaughter. Color reproductions of famous classical paintings of feasts. Margil cut these out, mounted them and hung them inside a closet which he always kept locked. He built a small bookcase for the floor of the closet to house his growing magazine collection. He would prop one of the pictures in front of his plate to stare at while he ate his cat food.

This almost satisfied him. It was reassuring to know that there were enough people interested in the same thing to support a magazine as well done and expensive as *Carnibal*. He gradually felt less as though there were something wrong with him and more a member of an unjustly persecuted minority. It was all well and good, as an editorial in the magazine pointed out, that there was insufficient animal protein available to feed the world's population. This was no reason to make the consumption of such excess protein an immoral and criminal act. Milk cows *did* die. Surplus bulls *were* slaughtered. This was an open secret. What happened to the meat? It was sold as cat food.

Margil gradually began to feel superior. He even began to detect a curious translucency in those around him. It was as though he were the only substantial person, and the others were becoming shadows. Occasionally he worried about this. It could be a sign of mental unbalance. He decided to seek professional help.

"Every day for dinner? You're not having me on? You really do? I'm sorry, Mr. Margil, but there's nothing I can do for you. If you like, I can recommend a colleague of mine, a fine abnormal psychologist. Well, that's what we call it; no need to get insulted."

What had made him think he needed help? These people were unable to understand him anyhow. He was alive and vital, no shadow could ever understand. It wasn't his problem, it was theirs. They were slowly fading away and didn't even know it.

Carnibal also carried classified ads. Some were for paintings and photographs. Some were for pen pals: "Correspond with one who understands and shares your hidden needs."

Some were more obscure and exciting:

> PRIVATE CLUB. Meet with others like yourself. Meet your secret desire. Meet often. Secrecy guaranteed. Must meet our requirements. Personal interview arranged. Write Box 666, this Mag.

"Thank you for your time, Mr. Margil. We'll let you know."

And then, a month of catfood dinners later: "We had to check your references, very discreetly, you understand. It's for your protection as well as our own. The government disapproves of our, hem, gustatory habits.

"You will receive a card in the mail about once every two weeks. There will be a number in the message that corresponds to an ad-

A MATTER OF TASTE 193

dress on this list. Memorize the list, then burn it. Ignore the rest of the message, just arrive at the address at seven-thirty. We'll look forward to seeing you, Mr. Margil. Remember, Man is naturally a carnivore."

The first card came two weeks later. The second three weeks after that. This was the third.

He stayed late at work that evening, clearing up trivia and sharpening pencils until long after everyone else had left. Then he went into the pay shower and dialed a hot needle spray, standing under it with his eyes closed until he felt that the last bit of grime and vegetable accumulation of the past two weeks had been washed away. A ritual cleansing, perhaps, before partaking of the sacrifice. He dressed carefully.

It was within a minute of seven-thirty when Margil arrived at the doorway of address number three. He knocked, and nothing happened; but he had the uncomfortable feeling he was being watched. Then a panel in the door opened, and he *was* being watched. After another interval the panel closed and the door opened. The man behind it was garbed in the costume of a gentleman of the nineteenth century, or a butler of the twentieth. He waved Margil on down the velvet-walled corridor.

A small port opened in the locked door at the far end, and a well-scrubbed, carefully manicured hand thrust out. "Your card, sir," a voice demanded. Margil handed over his Comprehensive Credit Card. After a few seconds, and a brief sound of rustling paper, the inner door opened. "Very good, sir. The card will be returned to your table. This will appear on your monthly statement as the purchase of several shirts at one of the better department stores."

The dining room faded into dusk on all sides, being large and lit in the manner of dining rooms. Margil was led down a well-carpeted aisle, past the twists and walls and screens that gave privacy to each of the tables, and to his own seat in a corner near a pair of double doors that, he assumed, opened onto the kitchen.

His table, like all the others in the room, was a single. Carnivation was a private vice. Margil settled gratefully in his chair and leaned back, letting his senses glide smoothly among the muted tones of sound and color. The table, the thick carpets, the walls, the drapes, the subdued lighting, the gliding waiters, the almost inaudible music, all meshed together into a dreamlike composite of wish-fulfilling satisfaction. Slowly, Margil relaxed.

"Your menu, sir," a waiter said, handing him a sealed, stiff envelope, bowing, and retreating. Margil slit the envelope open with practiced nonchalance, removed his Comprehensive Credit Card with two fingers, and then pulled out the menu card.

POTTED BEEF

it said,

please return this card

Margil put the card halfway back in the envelope and placed it on the corner of the table. A few moments later the waiter came and took it away, leaving in its place a bowl of onion soup. Real beef and chicken stock onion soup. Margil spooned the soup slowly into his mouth, savoring the aroma, the delicate flavor and texture. A feeling of pleasure akin, in Margil's mind, to religious ecstasy washed over him. The eating of flesh, he reflected while spooning the last of the soup, was important to the ritual of many religions. The flesh was often replaced, in these bloodless days, by a biscuit, but the symbolism remained.

The next course was a salad. Greens, reds, whites, and crumbled bacon, with a sharp dressing. Then a small glass of white wine to clear the head and palate for the main course.

The waiter whisked away the salad dish and replaced it with a large platter covered by a glistening hemisphere of German silver. Bowing to Margil, he retreated without removing the cover.

For a minute Margil stared, hands folded in his lap, at the platter. He watched the steam condense on the cover, smelled the hot beefy aroma, and listened to the muted clang of metal on china as his fellow diners removed the lids from their platters.

Then, napkin wrapped around his hand, he lifted the hot, German silver dome and placed it aside. There it was: three thick slices, covered with a rich gravy and flanked by braised new potatoes and fresh green beans. All of it organic. Nothing preprocessed, preprepared, paste, or plastic; it was all real food.

Margil picked up his fork and steak knife (think—a knife peculiarly created for the carving of meat) and cut a small piece of potted beef. He closed his eyes and masticated slowly, allowing the flavor time to fully activate the salivary and enzymic reactions. He took a second bite.

There was a sudden rapid series of crashing sounds from the other side of the room. One of the waiters skidded by Margil and slammed through the double doors to the kitchen.

"Hold!" An electronically augmented voice bellowed. "We are Peace Officers, and everyone in this room is under arrest. You will be informed of your rights. Stay where you are!"

Margil could see the first figures in light-blue uniforms shoulder their way through the entrance door. *Prison!* he thought. And then came the full realization: *everyone will know!* He stuffed one of the pieces of beef in his mouth and, bent almost double, scurried toward the double doors.

"*Halt!*"

Margil didn't pause to see if the command was directed at him. He raced the few remaining steps and pushed at the swinging doors.

"You have been warned!"

One shot, neatly aimed, and the target fell half out, and therefore half in, the swinging doors, which closed around him. The feathered dart struck high in the right shoulder, where it joins the neck, and drilled its way in, releasing the prescribed load of alkaloids through its side-vented hypotip.

Margil twitched as he lay on the floor, his muscles tensing and relaxing to drug-confused orders of his central nervous system. He could see and hear, but he could not move. He could reason and comprehend, but he could not respond or request. A half-chewed piece of meat lay on the floor next to his nose.

"*That's all of 'em, Captain. Whew! Smell that? Disgusting.*"

"*What about the one you shot?*"

There was a shoe by Margil's right eye. He stared at it. His left eye wouldn't focus.

"*Here. Perfect shoulder shot. Where's that intern?*"

"*Coming.*"

The shoe moved from Margil's view, and was replaced by a white trouser leg. Margil's vision blurred, and he realized he was crying.

"*Male, Caucasian, mid-thirties, brown hair . . .*" Margil's right eyelid was pulled back, and a pinpoint light shone in the pupil. "*. . . brown eyes, normal drug reaction.*"

"*I know all that, Doc, can you certify?*"

"*I'm recording. Yes, I can certify. For the record, with standard weapons the wound would have been mortal. You'll get your bonus.*"

"*Thanks. This cannibal's parts are certainly more useful to society than he was.*"

Margil heard the words and refused to understand. He couldn't stop crying.

"*Body certified for parts bank and subject declared legally dead.*" Something stung Margil's arm. "*We'll take him from here.*"

Sheila Lynds's background resembles a woman's version of the standard logger-salesman-stevedore-soldier of fortune author's sketch: stewardess, French Tourist Office representative, public relations director, management consultant, and currently a free-lance writer/editor working primarily for The Naval Civil Engineering Laboratory at Port Hueneme. She is also, however, the wife of a young writer who has, under a variety of names, authored a large number of outstanding mystery and suspense novels and short stories.

Her own ability at fiction is well indicated by this unusual espionage story, exhibiting as it does a fine knowledge of both technical methods and human psychology.

The Sleeper
SHEILA LYNDS

Joel Huber knew instantly that the innocent-seeming envelope in his wife's hand was the letter he had been waiting for.

Grace carried it in when she returned from her daily morning safari to school with their oldest boy, Tommy. She glanced curiously at the simple engraved return address.

Huber knew that there was nothing about the address to give it away, and fought down the urge to reach for it at once. To move, take the letter too fast.

"New York," Grace said. "Some publishing company. It must be a new company after you, Joel. I don't remember you ever writing anything for this company."

"Then I'm sure I didn't," Huber said. "Probably some scientific publisher asking me to buy someone else's book."

He made his voice remain calm, neutral. He continued to read his newspaper and sip his coffee, but with a small and polite smile to his wife to show that he was paying attention to the problem of a piece of junk mail.

"I suppose so," Grace said.

She placed the letter on the kitchen table.

Huber did not look at it. A man could not be too careful.

Grace turned her attention to the sink and the dishes. Her back to Huber, she said, "Tommy needs shoes again, Joel. I'm afraid both the girls need dresses, too."

Huber slid the letter into his suit coat pocket.

"Then buy them, my dear," he said.

"I know you don't like to spend money," Grace said. "Not on small necessities anyway."

"I simply like to have money in the bank, Grace," Huber said.

She smiled. "You're a good provider, Joel."

"I try to be. We're not rich, but I like my work."

"I know you do," Grace said.

Huber finished his coffee and folded his paper. He was anxious to get to the office. He would not risk opening the letter, even in his study. He kissed Grace and left the house.

As he walked from the modest ranch-style house he had bought ten years ago, he began to plan. He congratulated himself on how well he had prepared for the moment. The two vacation trips had given him a valid passport; there would be no trouble.

He waited in the cool morning sunlight in front of his house. It was Paul Thatcher's week to drive to town. That was good. Unlike most other mornings, he did not feel annoyed that Thatcher was late as usual. The letter was in his pocket, and now he was above small annoyances.

Huber greeted the sleepy-eyed bachelor with a cheery wave, and climbed into the front seat beside Thatcher. His boss, Ed Ross, and old Kandinsky sat in the rear as usual.

"Fine morning, eh, Ed?" Huber said to his boss.

"Joel is always happy," Thatcher said.

"That's because he doesn't want more than he can have," old Kandinsky said. "Show me a man with big schemes, and I'll show you trouble."

"Guilty, officer!" Thatcher said.

Kandinsky was chief of security at Huber's plant. He had been very useful to Huber in his slow preparations for the day when the time would come—for today!

"You look tired, Paul," Huber said to Thatcher as they drove. "What was it last night? Poker? A woman? A party?"

"As a matter of fact, Joel, it was scheming. Kandinsky is right. I was scheming with a friend to get rich quick."

"I like to know about a man," old Kandinsky said. "It's my job to know."

Huber glanced at Kandinsky. Did the old man know something? But Kandinsky couldn't know anything. There was nothing to know. Not yet. And Huber saw that Kandinsky was smiling. It was only one of the security chief's poor jokes.

Thatcher dropped the three of them at the plant gate. The bachelor drove on toward his office some miles away, and Huber, Ross and

Kandinsky checked through the heavy security at the gate of their plant.

Huber and Ross walked across the open parking lot to the design section building and entered through the electronic scanners that exposed any metal a man was carrying—including the trace of metallic pigment used in the ink for all the top secret drawings and plans.

"Good morning, George," Ed Ross said to the guard who operated the scanner.

"Morning, Mr. Ross, Mr. Huber," George said as he watched his scanner dial. "You're all clean this morning."

"No bombs today," Ed Ross said.

They all laughed, and Huber and Ross went on into the plant.

The corridors of the design section were quiet, air-conditioned and sound-proofed. They seemed like the corridors of any normal office building.

Huber knew better. To anyone else, the heavy security at the gate, the electrified and alarm-wired twelve-foot cyclone fence, the specially coded badges that completely identified each man, and the electronic scanners at the doors of each building, were a complete security system.

Huber knew that this was only the surface. He had helped design the security of the plant, and he was proud of the hidden results. He could always actually feel the secret devices that watched them all as they moved along the corridors. The X-ray units that took pictures at points where men were forced to stand for a moment and wait for doors to be opened from the inside had been his own particular idea.

The special devices that detected any film a man might be carrying had been Kandinsky's design, and a very sophisticated idea. Kandinsky knew his job. Ed Ross, with some help from Huber, had suggested the machines that read a man's badge at unexpected points to be sure that no unauthorized personnel had somehow reached inside the plant.

There were even machines that could tell if a badge were worn by the right man, or if it had been removed and was being worn by an imposter.

Huber took considerable satisfaction in his share of the work that had gone into making it impossible to bring anything dangerous into the plant, or take anything secret out of it. It had been part of his training, and he was proud of his training.

He reached his desk in the large design office, one of the supervisors' desks close to the private office of Ed Ross. He sat down and waited quietly until Ross had gone on into his private office, and until he could see Ross deeply immersed in reading the report of yesterday's work. Then, alone, he opened the letter.

The letter offered to sell him a book on electronic design at a large discount because of his professional status in America's design technology. It seemed simple and innocent. It was neither simple nor innocent.

Huber, unseen, took a piece of cardboard from his desk drawer, and placed it over the letter. There was a small hole in the piece of cardboard. Through the hole one word of the innocent letter could be read: *Now*.

For one brief instant Huber's hand shook. But it was not fear that trembled his hands, it was excitement. It was the release of an incredible tension he had never really known was in him all these years. *Now*. The purpose of his entire life to this point was about to be fulfilled. The time had come.

It was impossible to steal from this plant. But that was what Joel Huber was now going to do.

Joel Huber was a spy.

Joel Huber was a trained and professional spy, but one who had never stolen a word, had never spied on anything or anyone until now. For twenty years he had been a professional spy without working one day at his profession.

Huber was a special kind of spy—a *sleeper*.

Now, as he looked at the single word, *Now*, he saw his whole life in an instant.

His childhood in an Eastern European country when his name had not been Huber. His youth at the special school. The moment, fifteen years ago, when he had become Joel Huber. The real Joel Huber had been an orphan with no real home, no family, no public record such as fingerprints on file, and who had made the error of going alone on a European vacation during troubled times. An unknown man who was now quite dead.

He had looked enough like Huber to become, with a surgeon's help, his twin. He had become Joel Huber. Disguised as Huber, he went to America, went to college, took a special degree in electronics design, married Grace, because a man with a good job and normal habits was usually married in America, and had taken the good job in the electronics plant where he still worked.

Ten years in the same plant; three children; the normal house life and promotions; and he *was* Joel Huber. There was no one who knew who he really was; no one who could now. To himself he was Joel Huber—family man; normal American; reliable and simple. The only faint hint of difference was the fact that, despite offers, he had stayed at the same job.

A man above suspicion because he had done nothing to arouse suspicion. More, he had actually shown concern for plant security. A nice touch that, and he smiled as he thought of how he had used his special training to come up with good suggestions for security. While, of course, becoming thoroughly familiar with the security system.

Ten years without action, without any known contact with his true country. A *sleeper*. A spy who does not spy but only waits for the one moment when he will be needed. The moment that had now come.

Each year or so Huber had sent a simple letter to a post office box in New York. A letter that reported, in code, what his plant was working on, and what he might have access to in other plants. Each letter had received no answer. Until now.

His last letter had reported that he was working on a new self-contained missile defense system. The system that would be incorporated into all American missiles to defend against anti-missile attack. Anyone who knew this system could learn how to destroy any American missile in the air.

His country wanted to know the system. This was the project important enough for him to act at last. Huber was ready. He was no longer a sleeper.

He slipped the letter into his desk as his fellow workers began to arrive. They greeted him warmly, and he greeted them. After all, they were his friends and associates of ten years.

"Always the early bird, eh, Joel?" Marcus Dieter said.

Dieter was a former German engineer, a designer of gyro systems. A man of middle age, Dieter had been in Germany during the last war. Huber had been careful with Dieter. The German had had military training, and was accustomed to being suspicious.

"In an orphanage you learn to get up early. Now it's a habit," he said with a smile to Dieter. It was the same answer he had given a hundred times to the same question from Dieter. The German was a man of habit, too.

"Joel is no night owl," young Ujcic said.

Vic Ujcic was the newest member of the team in the guidance system design room. A bachelor and a good designer. Perhaps too good a designer for a man so young. And a bachelor whose comings and goings were unpredictable. Huber had watched Ujcic closely ever since the young man had joined the staff. A new man could always be a counter-agent. So far, Ujcic had shown no suspicion or evidence of being anything more than he was supposed to be.

"With a wife and three kids, who can be a night owl?" Huber said with a laugh. "Besides, my wife is so worn out with her Great Books, and her bridge club, and the PTA, and her Red Cross work she just collapses at night. You bachelors think marriage is one long orgy. Let me tell you different."

"Amen!"

"Yeh, yeh!"

The married men all echoed Huber's sentiments. Everyone laughed like the good ten-year companions they were.

"You should all be as steady as Joel," Ed Ross said.

The boss called that from his office, and grinned at his staff. The chatter went on quietly and pleasantly. Design work was not the kind of work where men could plunge right in like checking laundry bills. A man had to shift his gears slowly from home and private matters to the demanding brain-work.

Coffee came, and with it the easy talk continued to flow. It was the morning ritual of men who had worked together for years. They were old friends. They played golf together. With their wives they visited each other regularly. A typical office staff in a typical technical company. A little dull, perhaps.

Only Joel Huber knew that one of them was not typical, and not dull.

The talk subsided, the coffee was finished, and they went to work. Each man went to the vault for his work. Each man brought back his work and bent in silence and concentration over his desk. Each man thought only of his work. Except Joel Huber.

Huber worked with the others, but his mind was on a different work. It was Monday, and the job would be done on Friday. He had a week to restudy and firm the plans of ten years. A week to prepare in his mind while his body went about his normal routine.

That night, Monday, he watched television with Grace as he always did on Monday. They ate potato chips, drank beer, and Grace talked.

"I bought the dresses for the girls," Grace said. "The best this town has. You seem distracted, Joel."

"Dresses, good," Huber said. "I like a small town."

Huber thought: the plans for the missile-defense system were in many sections. They were worked on in the Top Secret Section, and no one man worked on more than a part. The complete plans were locked in the vault in the office of the Chief Design Engineer. Huber had no connection to them. But he would get them.

On Friday, and by Monday next he would be back where he had started fifteen years ago. The theft would be detected, of course, possibly even on Monday, but that was expected. The plans would give his country knowledge it did not have, in one-tenth the time it would take to develop them themselves, and expose and slow-down the Americans for a year or so. Such was the limited goal of modern espionage.

Fifteen years of waiting, one day of action, and a small advantage to his homeland. Then the *sleeper* would be of no more value. That was the advantage of a *sleeper*; there was no need to cover his tracks beyond a few days.

On Tuesday Huber went to his chess club with Dieter and Ed Ross. He won three out of four games, and drew the fourth. He played as well as he always did. On his way home he went to the bus depot and waited in the men's room, as arranged once ten years ago, for the envelope to be given to him over the partition by the man who came through on a bus and stayed in town ten minutes. In the envelope were all his tickets and the route he would take Friday night.

The only regret Huber had was his family. They must be left behind. Perhaps he could bring them over later, if they wanted to come. Grace was a patriotic woman. He would miss the children, yes, but he would leave them provided for, and a man had his work.

On Wednesday he remained at home with the children while Grace went to her regular Great Books lecture. When the children were in bed he packed his attache case and one suitcase. He had his cover story, a meeting with his New York publisher. He had already arranged this, and he had gone on such sudden trips before.

"I have to see Adams in New York on Saturday," he told Grace when she came home from the lecture and her coffee with the girls. "I'm sorry."

"Try to get a bigger advance this time," Grace said.

Thursday night Paul Thatcher and his sister came to play bridge at Huber's house. Huber won all four rubbers. Grace bid the guests good night. Huber was in bed before she came up. Earlier that day he had rented the car and parked it in the special place not far from the plant.

Friday morning he waited for Thatcher as usual. He carried the special attache case with the thin secret compartment lined with special lead sheets. Ed Ross was not with Thatcher, but Kandinsky noted the new attache case.

"Planning to take work home, Huber?" the chief of security said.

"I have to finish a job," Huber said. "I'm not sure if I'll stay late, or bring it home, or both."

"All work and no play," Thatcher said. "You're a strange man, Joel."

Alert, Huber glanced at Thatcher. But the bachelor seemed innocent enough.

"Don't stray out of your section," Kandinsky said. "My men are nervous."

Huber was sure it was another of Kandinsky's poor jokes. But it did not hurt to be careful. He would keep alert tonight.

At the plant he passed through all the security without trouble, the lead failing to be detected in his brief case.

As he worked the rest of the day he became nervous. That was only to be expected. Fifteen years ago he had been trained to expect nervousness. He had waited a long time. To keep his mind busy he took careful note of all his fellow workers, especially Dieter and Ujcic. Both men had made a point of being friendly to Huber over the years.

By five o'clock they were all gone except Ed Ross. Huber worked calmly. Ross came to see what he was doing. For one instant Huber almost panicked.

The work he was doing was not really vital. It was not actually necessary that he work late on it.

Had he made a blunder after all these years?

"That's not urgent, Joel," Ross said. "No need for overtime."

Huber thought fast. "The guidance job next week is urgent, Ed. I thought I'd clear the decks."

Ross considered, smiled. "Right as usual."

"I may take some home though. Over the weekend," Huber said.

"I'll tell them at the gate. Give me the document numbers."

Then Ross was gone and the office was empty. Ross would recall the conversation on Monday, but it would be too late then. Time, that was the tool of the sleeper. Time and trust. There was no way to steal the plans undiscovered. But a sleeper, trusted and working inside, would gain, perhaps, two days before discovery. A normal spy might not have those vital days.

Huber opened his bottom desk drawer and removed the false bottom. He took a miniature camera from the drawer. A camera he had brought in piece-by-piece inside other metal objects.

He also took a small, powerful flood lamp, and three keys. Finally, he took out a thin screw-driver-like tool made of specially strong metal—he had made it himself in the plant shop.

It had taken the ten years to slowly prepare these few tools.

He left his desk and walked with the tools to the men's room. Inside he climbed on a sink, removed the air-conditioning duct cover with his tool, and climbed into the duct. He crawled along the duct to the sixth register. He opened this and dropped down.

He stood in a small office. He used the first of his three keys to open the door between this office and the Top Secret Design Room. He crossed the dark Top Secret Room and used his second key to enter a locked storeroom. Inside the storeroom he locked the door behind him and looked up at the ceiling.

The storeroom was connected by an old ventilation duct to the closet in the office of the Chief Design Engineer. It was the major flaw Huber had discovered five years ago and prepared to use. Now he removed the duct cover, climbed up, crawled the few feet along the duct, and dropped down into the closet.

He carefully opened the closet door and peered out.

The office was empty. He reached the vault in a few quick and silent steps.

It was a large, walk-in vault, air-conditioned and designed for keeping a large number of valuable papers. It was not burglar-proofed or connected to an alarm, since it was in constant use and the company relied on plant security—plus some special measures with the documents themselves.

It opened with keys, not a combination. Each man who used the vault had a key, and the chief design engineer had another. Both keys were needed to open the vault. Huber's third special key was a copy of the chief design engineer's key. He now used it, and his own key, to open the vault.

Inside the vault he located the plans he wanted. He did not worry about fingerprints. The plans themselves were treated with a chemical that would react to the intensity of light needed to take good micro-film copies of them. When he did not appear, it would not take them long to find what he had stolen. It would not take them long to find that the plans had been stolen even if he did return, which is why he would not return.

He photographed the complete plans for the missile-defense, returned the plans, locked the vault, and made his return trip by the same route. He developed the film in the dark room.

In his own office he placed the tiny roll of film inside the lead-lined container. He placed his own work in the attache case. He returned all his tools to the secret compartment in his desk drawer. Then he left the office.

As he walked along the corridors he could sense the devices studying him. He had the proper badge. The X-ray films would show the drawings he was taking home. The film detector should be defeated by the lead-lined compartment.

At the door he heard the scanner react to the metal ink on his drawings. He smiled at George the guard.

"Caught," he said.

"Red-handed, Mr. Huber," George said.

The guard took his attache case, opened it, and inspected the drawings. They were all assigned to Huber, and Ross had left word. George did not inspect the attache case closely.

"Don't work too hard tonight," George said.

Huber smiled. He walked out of the building and across the parking lot to the gate. The guard on the gate was waiting for him. It was routine for George at the door of the building to call the gate, in case anyone tried to sneak around inside the plant grounds.

The guard on the gate inspected his attache case, checked his badge, and took the badge. Huber passed through. He walked to the bus stop as he had done a hundred times in the ten years when he worked late. The bus came and he got aboard.

The bus turned the corner and Huber got off at the next stop. He walked to where his hired car was hidden. He drove to the bus depot. There he placed the tiny roll of film in a coin-locker. He took the key and walked out and back toward the bus stop. He left his hired car in the parking lot of the bus depot. No one would notice it for days.

He stopped at an empty lot on his way to the bus stop, looked around, and dropped the key into a hole he had dug there days ago. Then he went on and caught the bus home—a bus no more than one later than he should have been on.

He left the bus at his corner and walked slowly up the curving tract street in the last twilight of the summer night. In a way he felt a little sad. It was the last time he would walk this street. After ten years he had come to like it. But a man had his duty in this world.

In a few days he would be walking the streets of his native country—after fifteen years. He felt both sad and excited. He would go home a hero, a success. Still, he had not even spoken the language in fifteen years, and it would be strange at first.

He turned up his walk—and came alert.

Huber blinked. There was something strange. For a moment he almost panicked again. Then he got a grip on himself. Nothing could be wrong. Even if they had accidentally discovered that the plans had been tampered with, there was no reason to suspect him. Not until he failed to return on Monday.

But . . . and then Huber almost laughed. What was wrong was

simply the silence of his house. His car was in the garage as it should have been, but there was no noise. The children were not at home. He opened the door and went in. He heard Grace in the kitchen. He called his normal nightly greeting.

"I'm home, dear."

"You're late," Grace called back.

"Sorry, work," he said.

He went into his study and put away the special attache case. He brought out his other attache case, an exact copy without the hidden features. Then he went upstairs and got his single suitcase, and brought it down, and put it neatly at the front door beside the attache case. He went into the kitchen.

"I have to get the nine o'clock bus to the city."

"Do you have time for dinner?"

"Of course," he said. "The nine o'clock bus will catch the night jet for New York."

He did not add that the night jet for New York would enable him to catch the morning jet for Paris, and that the morning jet for Paris would meet the jet for Berlin. Once in Berlin he would simply walk across into the Eastern Sector. He had all the proper papers.

"Then sit down, dear. I'm just ready," Grace said. "I know how you hate to rush."

Huber sat down with a smile to his wife. "Where are the children?"

He asked casually. It was unusual for the children not to be home at this hour.

"The girls wanted to stay at their friend Miriam's for dinner," Grace said. "Tommy asked to go to the Boy Scouts early, so I let him go. Did you want them, Joel?"

"No," he said quickly.

He would have liked to have seen the children once more, but perhaps it was for the best. He had always been most worried about leaving the children, about his strength to leave them. Of course, he hoped that they would decide, in the end, to join him in his own country. At least the children. After all, they were his children. He was a patriot of his true country. They should be proud of him someday.

By an effort of concentration, he put the children out of his mind and ate his dinner as if this were a day like any other day. He did not look at the clock once, but he was acutely aware of the time. He could feel himself growing nervous now that it was almost over. He knew that that was natural. He had been warned about the last-minute nerves often enough in the special school so long ago. Once on the jet he did not think that he could be stopped, and—

The ring of the telephone dried the thought in his mind.

Huber froze, became stone.

Grace stood up. "That'll be Lucy, dear. I asked her to call about the next lecture. We may take a field trip. You finish your coffee."

Huber felt the tension drain slowly. He listened to the distant voice of his wife in the living room. There was a giggle. He smiled. She had been a good wife. In a way, he realized, he had come to like American women better than the women of his own country. Except for their telephone habits. He smiled again, listened.

Then he frowned at himself. There was a danger to being too sure, too casual. More spies had failed from a fear of making a change in plan than from making the change. They could not have found out yet. It was not possible. The plans would not be checked until Monday. Still . . .

Huber finished his coffee, to be ready the instant Grace returned. Anticipation of trouble was the mark of a good agent. He would leave now, at once. He would take no chances. Instead of the bus he would hire a car and drive to the city. He could make some excuse to Grace, have her drive him to the bus station, and then take a car.

Yes, the sooner he was on the jet the better. Perhaps he could get a cancellation on an earlier flight. From New York he could try to take a jet to some other city than Paris, just in case.

Grace returned. Huber wiped his mouth, smiled, began to tell her of his change of plan.

Then he saw her eyes.

They were strange eyes. Eyes that looked down at him where he sat at the table in the seat he had been in at dinner for ten years, and seemed to be seeing a man they had never seen. There was anger in the eyes, and a certain triumph.

"Grace?" Huber said. His voice, the sound of his voice, was a question.

She blinked. "Did you know that you talk in your sleep, Joel? Not often. I mean a few times? Once or twice?"

"Talk in my sleep?" Huber said, echoed.

"I think it only happens under strong emotion," Grace said as if thinking about it. "The first time I heard you was the night I brought Tommy home from the hospital. We'd only been married just over a year, I remember. I loved you very much. I was so proud of my brilliant husband."

"Talked?" Huber said. "In my sleep?"

He felt like a stupid parrot, repeating meaningless phrases. But there was nothing else he could think of to say at the instant. It did not matter. Grace seemed lost in her own distant thoughts.

Grace's eyes watched the distance. "You never used your brilliance, did you? You preferred to stay in this town, in that steady job at the plant. I sometimes wondered why. I mean, most men would have taken some of those other offers. They would have advanced your career. Or what was supposed to be your career. I'm surprised the company never wondered."

"Wondered?" Huber said. "What did I say? When I talked in my sleep, Grace! What did I say?"

Grace shook her head. "I don't know, dear. I mean, I never knew exactly what you said. Not the words."

Huber felt a wave of relief. "Well then, I—"

"Not the words," Grace went on. "They were foreign, you know? I mean, you talked in some strange language. Some Eastern European language, Slavic. You know, Russian, or Polish, or Bulgarian, or something like that. That was awfully strange, you know?"

Huber's stomach dropped somewhere far below the floor. He tried to speak, but no words would come out.

Grace frowned. "It was very strange. I mean, how did Joel Huber know such a language? You're not even of Slavic descent, Joel. You're not supposed to be, are you?"

"Grace," Huber said, "listen to me. I—"

"No, Joel," Grace said. "Don't try. It's much too late. You talked more than once. I began to wonder. I made a very close check into Joel Huber's background. He couldn't have known that language. Then there was that trip to Europe. Then there were those letters you wrote, to that New York box number. You never got an answer, did you? Not until Monday. I saw how excited you were by that letter on Monday. I knew it was the time."

Huber was sweating now. "Grace, listen! I'll tell you . . ."

She did not hear. "Ten years, Joel. All the time you were someone else. All that time you planned to leave us! Before you married me you planned to leave me. It could have been twenty years, I suppose, or a year! I was nothing! I was just *cover*. The children were just *cover!* We didn't count at all. Your job was that important."

"Grace, you don't understand. I had my work. But I was going to send for you all when I got home. I—"

"Home?" Grace said. "This is my home, Joel. I'm an American, you know?"

"Grace, please . . ." Huber said desperately.

"At first I was stunned," she said. "I didn't believe it. Then I was angry, I was going to expose you and leave you. Nine years ago I was going to leave you. In a way I wish I had."

There was a silence. Huber felt the sweat dripping inside his shirt. But his mouth was as dry as a desert.

"At first?" he said. "Why didn't you leave me?"

Grace sighed. "They didn't want me to. They said it would be better if I waited until you—made your move. I never thought it would be nine years."

"They?" Huber said, and his voice was not a voice but a dry croak of sudden fear.

Before she could answer Huber heard the cars screech to a halt outside the house. Two or three cars that came up fast. Voices shouted. Huber started for the rear door.

"No, Joel," Grace said sharply. "Don't try. It's the FBI, and the police, too. They'll kill you if you try to run."

Huber stopped. Looked at her. "That phone call."

"They've been watching you, dear. They saw everything you did. They've been watching you for almost eight years. Ever since I went to them and told them about you talking in your sleep. The call told me they had found all you did tonight."

"Eight years?" Huber said, stared at his wife.

"Yes, Joel. You see, I had a job to do too, didn't I? This is my country, Joel, and—" She stopped, smiled. "By the way, dear, what is your name? I feel silly calling you Joel now."

Huber only stared. Moments later they were all around him. They took him away to the city. They had the film. They locked him up.

Back in the small house where she had lived ten years with Joel Huber, Grace Huber sat alone. An hour after they had taken Huber away, there was a knock on the door and Paul Thatcher walked into the living room. He looked down at Grace.

"We owe you our thanks, Mrs. Huber," Thatcher said. "Thanks to you we were ready for him."

"Yes," she said. "You had a long wait."

"It was worth it, Mrs. Huber," Thatcher said. "If we had picked him up eight years ago they would only have sent someone we didn't know. This way we lulled them into false security for eight years, and stopped him cold when he finally moved. It's a small victory, but every victory helps."

"The FBI has a hard job," Grace said. "You must have grown tired of it, too."

"I do my job," FBI man Thatcher said.

Grace nodded. "Yes. You did your job, and Joel did his job." And she looked up at Thatcher. "And I did my job, too, didn't I?"

"No counter-agent could have done it except you, Mrs. Huber," he said.

Grace Huber nodded slowly again. "A counter-agent. I suppose that's what I was. Imagine."

Suddenly the house seemed very lonely.

Among the numerous anti-heroes of modern fiction, one perhaps most deserving of the name is Augustus Mandrell. Mr. Mandrell is a commission agent. His most spectacular commissions are murders (or, as Mandrell would phrase it, "indetectable assassinations"), but he will accept almost any assignment admitting to two conditions: that a fee will be charged commensurate with the excellence of the service rendered, and that that fee shall be paid. Perhaps the one flaw in the career of Augustus Mandrell as so far recorded is that, for an international operative, his environment seemed rather strictly limited; one wished to know of how he might interreact with some of the other greats of history.

Therefore, when this editor chanced upon one passage in the second volume of Mandrell's memoirs, *Rather a Vicious Gentleman*, he was both intrigued and delighted. It read:

> The problem of the tell-tale hand has forced me on occasion to the extreme of manufacturing false hands. (*The Dr. Sherrock Commission* and *The Maltese Falcon Commission* come to mind.)

Had then Augustus Mandrell been involved in *the* Maltese Falcon Affair?

I contacted Mandrell's literary agent, Frank McAuliffe, a highly companionable California author whose cover identity is that of a civilian officer for the U. S. Navy, and who had won an MWA Edgar for recording Mandrell's exploits. He contacted Mandrell (it is rumored that they correspond by coded messages in the "Agricultural Implements—Wanted" column of the *Ventura County Star-Free Press*) and obtained permission to recount Mandrell's history of the incident.

It should be made clear that, although this account may be appreciated as it is, a recent familiarity with Dashiell Hammett's record will enhance it measurably. Mystery connoisseurs will detect other factors of interest; but they will find, oddly, no reference to false hands. This phenomenon has become known as the "Second Stain Paradox."

The Maltese Falcon Commission
FRANK MC AULIFFE

The first time I laid eyes on Samuel Spade he was drunk in a two-year-old Checker cab in the parking lot outside a nightclub called the Dancers. The parking lot attendant had just waved the cab in from the street and Spade was having trouble getting into the rear seat. His left foot was still outside the cab.

There was a girl beside Spade. Her hair was a lovely shade of dark red. She was quite impatient with her drunken companion. So was the tough-looking attendant. The cab driver pretended nothing unusual was going on. He sat solidly behind his wheel and hoped nobody noticed he already had the meter running.

A low-swung foreign speedster with no top drifted into the parking lot. Its owner strolled off to the bar entrance of the nightclub without a glance at the dilemma surrounding the Checker.

The attendant said, "Look, buster, I've got to put a car away." He let the door of the cab swing open. Mr. Spade slid off the seat and on to the parking lot blacktop.

Ahh, well. I walked over to Spade who was sitting up and shaking his head. The redhead was bent over next to him chatting fiercely in his ear. I got Spade under the arms and lifted him to his feet.

"May I assist you in getting the gentleman into the taxi?" I said to the redhead.

"I'm terribly sorry," she said distantly, "but I'm late for an appointment." She slid smoothly into the cab showing a nice hunk of bluestockinged leg, and told the driver:

"Get going." One passenger or two made no difference to the meter. The cab rolled off.

"So you got stuck with him," the parking lot attendant said as he returned. He sounded interested but only, I fear, because we were blocking his income producing property. I asked him to bring my car around and fumbled out my ticket while both of us held up Spade. By the time my vehicle arrived Mr. Spade had tripled his weight and grown to the height of a eucalyptus tree. My gratitude to the attendant for his assistance in depositing Mr. Spade in my car was of such proportions that I violated a long-standing principle of mine. I gave the attendant a gratuity; not that the lad appeared overly impressed by my generosity. He was still staring at the ten-cent piece as I drove off.

I took Mr. Spade to a small house I was living in on Lorre Drive. The walk up the steps to the house aroused him a bit. When I had him in the large chair he said he could handle a cup of coffee. He drank it silently, his eyes over the rim of the cup taking apart the room and my face.

"Where is this place?" he said roughly as he finished the coffee.

"My home. On Lorre off Cook. Do you know the area?"

"And what might the name be?" he said ignoring my question.

"Mandrell. Augustus Mandrell. We met in the parking lot of the Dancers. How much do you remember?"

"Got any more coffee, Gus?"

After the second cup of coffee the gentleman pulled out a bag of loose tobacco and a packet of brown cigarette papers. The bag bore the legend: Bull Durham.

"What happened to the dame I was with?" he growled, as he rolled a cigarette.

"She drove off. She appeared to be somewhat disillusioned."

He smiled, his lips pulling back to reveal the edges of his lower teeth.

"She wants her men always up on their hind legs ready to protect her. Me drunk wasn't her shining knight."

"She looked to be of Irish stock," I commented. "Their women tend toward romantic illusions."

"Brigid O'Shaughnessy sounds Irish enough," Spade said. "If that's her real name. She's pulled three names on me in the two days I've known her. When she hit my office yesterday she was Miss Wonderly. Claimed a guy named Floyd Thursby had lured her baby sister here to San Francisco and wanted us to trail him."

"Is that your business?" I asked, being polite. "Chasing after people?"

He extracted a card from his pocket and flipped it across the coffee table to me. It read SPADE & ARCHER Private Investigations.

"Archer is my partner," he said. "Or was until last night. He took one look at Miss Wonderly and jumped at the job of tailing this guy Thursby for her. What he got for his trouble was a .38 slug in his heart in a alley off Bush Street."

"Ah yes, I thought the names were familiar," I said. "Today's newspaper. The man your partner was trailing, this Thursby, was also shot?"

Spade nodded. "Pumped full of .45 slugs in the back not long after Archer got it. The cops think I killed Thursby to square up for him killing my partner. I might have if I'd had the chance. Miles Archer wasn't too bright—God, tailing a guy he knows carries a gun and letting himself get caught up a dark alley with his overcoat buttoned and his gun on his hip. He wasn't bright but he was still my partner."

"The lady could shed no light on the affair?"

"Naw, she fixed it for Thursby to pick her up at her hotel, the St. Mark, so Archer could get a fix on him. After dinner with Thursby she left him. This morning she calls up and says she's switched hotels. She's registered at the Coronet under the name Miss Leblanc. When I got over there the name was suddenly Brigid O'Shaughnessy. Tomorrow it might be Little Orphan Annie."

Ahh, one answer I sought was now mine: Miss O'Shaughnessy is at the Coronet.

"The story about the abducted younger sister was somewhat inaccurate then?" I asked.

Spade snorted. "She admitted this morning she and Thursby were partners in some game or other. They'd just bounced in from Hong Kong last week. I couldn't get any details out of her, other than she was scared silly by Thursby's death. I promised to help her. But I told her she gets my help only as long as she knows what the hell she's doing; where she fits in the game."

"She refused to enlarge on her plight?"

"I know more about it now. A little guy named Joel Cairo strolled into the office this afternoon. Smelled like a lollipop and as queer as your Uncle Matilda. He offered me $5,000 to find what he called a 'black figure of a bird.' He'd come to me because he saw the newspaper about Thursby and my partner. So that put him in the game. The son of a bitch had guts. He pulled a gun and wanted to search my office. I took it away from him and put him to sleep for a while. When he came around he gave me a retainer and I gave him back his gun. I'll be damned if the little fairy didn't point it at me again and tell me he still intended to search the office. I told him 'go to it.'"

Spade's chuckle had a healthy male sound to it.

"Then this shadow latched on to me after Cairo left the office," Spade continued. "A young punk in a long overcoat. I led him over to the Belvedere, Cairo's hotel, finally caught up with Cairo at the Geary Theatre and pointed the kid out to the queer. Cairo swore on his 'word of honor' he'd never seen the kid before."

My information was correct then: Mr. Joel Cairo was in residence at the Belvedere Hotel.

Spade continued: "I ducked the kid and went over to the Coronet for another chat with Brigid. I mentioned casually that I'd met Joel Cairo. She nearly dropped her hairdo. I really laid into her, telling her to spill the story or get out of my life. She finally said she'd tell me but only after she talked to Cairo. I set up a meeting at my apartment earlier tonight. Cairo came in all in a sweat. He'd seen the kid in the overcoat again outside my place. After calming him down he and Brigid had an 'old home week' chat. Once when they didn't think I was watching Cairo whispered asking who had killed Thursby. My talkative girl friend drew a 'G' in the air with her finger. Cairo finally left with a couple of cops who dropped by to accuse me of killing my partner because I wanted his wife."

"You lead a rather complex life."

"You think that's complex? I'm pretty sure it was Archer's damn' wife who sigged the cops on me. Anyway Cairo took off from my apartment with the cops and I tried again to get Brigid to open up.

She'd told me and Cairo that she has this bird they're all looking for and I wanted to hear more about it. She gave me the: 'It's late, I have to go' business. I said maybe the kid in the overcoat was still outside. That scared her. She asked me to look. The kid wasn't there but I said he was. We sat down to coffee and sandwiches and I squeezed some information out of her.

"It seems Brigid, Cairo, and Thursby stole the bird from a Russian named Kemidov in Constantinople. Thursby and Brigid thought Cairo was going to double cross them so they took off for Hong Kong with the bird, and from there to San Francisco. Brigid then got the impression Thursby was going to dump her. That's when she came to Spade and Archer, the reliable, efficient, bulletproof detective firm. The rest is in the newspapers."

"The young lady did say she has the bird?"

"She said she can get it within a week, maybe less. She knows where Thursby hid it."

Ahhh.

"For so pretty a young lady she has rather violent friends," I commented. "You say both Mr. Cairo and Mr. Thursby carried firearms?"

"I told her the same thing. She said she needed the protection of violent men. This Thursby is evidently a gunslinger from way back. Brigid claims Thursby was once the bodyguard of an American gambler who had to leave the States, probably with a big wad of somebody else's dough in his suitcase. It seems the gambler disappeared while under Thursby's tender care. I don't know much about the gambler."

I do chance to know his name, Mr. Spade. It is or was Dixie Monahan.

"I had no idea the detective business was so fascinating," I said. "International thieves, murders, mysterious treasure." I shook my head at the wonder of it all.

"It doesn't look so fascinating when you're looking at it through a hangover," Spade said.

"That's right," I exclaimed, trying in my own amateurish way to keep up with the plot, "you were at your apartment with Miss O'Shaughnessy. How did you end up at the Dancers?"

"She wanted me to take her home, get her past the kid. On the way I stopped us off for a couple of drinks. Then a couple of more. She didn't loosen up a bit; nice careful drinker Brigid is. I'm not."

He pushed on the arms of the chair and came to his feet, a big competent chap with yellowish eyes.

"Most intriguing, the whole affair," I said as we walked to the front door. "Is there any chance the lady has the bird at her hotel? The Belvedere, did you say?"

"No, that's where Joel Cairo is." He paused and ran the supposition through his experience factor. He shook his head. "If she had it I think she'd have run with it by now. She was supposed to get $7,500 from Thursby for helping him take it from the Russian Kemidov. Now she's willing to take $5,000 from Joel Cairo. I think her problem is she doesn't know where to peddle the thing. She doesn't even know why it's worth so much sweat. She saw it once and says it's just the statue of a bird about a foot tall. Just a black enamel bird."

Ah but, Mr. Spade, beneath that enamel . . .

I had called a taxi, it was waiting. Spade thanked me for my assistance.

"It was nothing," I said. "Traditional San Francisco hospitality."

"You from the city? You sound English."

"I'm with an English firm. Mandrell Limited. We're in import-export. Well, primarily export."

"Yeah? What do you export?"

"Oh, perishables mostly. Not very exciting."

"Sometimes I wish I was in something less exciting. Thanks again. Drop around to the office. I'll buy you a drink and tell you how this black bird business ended up."

"I certainly may." I had debated whether or not to tell him the rest. When he stopped on the porch and glanced up and down the street with a mien of proper defiance I decided he probably should know.

"Incidentally," I said, "just before Miss O'Shaughnessy left the parking lot she took something from your pocket."

"Yeah; cab fare, she said."

"I believe it was your key ring."

He patted his pocket and swore. "Thanks," he snapped, and ran to the taxi.

* * *

After Spade left I withdrew from the door and switched off the light behind me. Then I stood by the front window. Presently a young man in a long overcoat walked out of the darkness and stopped in front of the house. First he stared after the receding taillight of Spade's taxi. Then he looked up at my front door for a moment. The pockets of his overcoat were heavily weighted. He turned abruptly to wave into the dark and jumped into a taxi that rolled to meet him with no headlights. Off they went in pursuit of Spade's taxi.

The lad's name, according to the last report I'd had from New York, was Wilmer Cook. He habitually carried two .45 automatics in his coat pockets, an indulgence in firepower that struck me as clearly excessive.

I am not one to quickly criticize a man regarding the inefficiency with which he practices his trade. But in Wilmer's case you must grant that he was apparently confusing quantity with quality; not to mention the abuse being delivered his frail physique by the pure weight of his arsenal.

An incident that occurred just the night before illustrates the point. I had posted myself outside Floyd Thursby's hotel, the Poe Park on Geary near Leavenworth. Thursby exited and caught a taxi immediately, before I could get to him. I followed him to the St. Mark in my rented vehicle. Presently he and Miss Brigid O'Shaughnessy came out of the St. Mark. I approached them from the rear, having business with both of them.

Abruptly I became aware that another person was as interested as I in the couple. I did not know this party but events indicate this must have been Miles Archer, Mr. Spade's partner. Obviously Mr. Archer was trailing Thursby and Miss O'Shaughnessy. Just as obviously Mr. Archer was wearing a gun on his hip.

I elected to drop back into my previous post of waiting outside Thursby's hotel.

An hour went by. Thursby returned. He was alone; no Brigid O'Shaughnessy, no Miles Archer. As a matter of fact, judging by the newspaper account of the following day, Thursby had just concluded the demise of Miles Archer in an alley off Bush Street.

Again I started toward Mr. Thursby to remind him of an old debt. Again I was interrupted!

Wilmer Cook and his long overcoat slid from a vehicle up the block and approached Thursby. The entryway to the Poe Park Hotel had suddenly become a ruddy military outpost. Not only did Wilmer bring to the scene his twin ballistic hostility, Thursby, I had been advised, was another fancier of the munitions trade and frequently carried a Luger under his arm in addition to an ancient Webley-Fosbery .38 in his side pocket. Between them they could conceivably have attacked and captured Chinatown just down the road.

I chose not to interrupt their discussion. They drove off together. It was not until sometime later that I found that Wilmer had taken Thursby to talk to a chap named Casper Gutman. Even if I had known this in front of the Poe Park I would not have joined them. I had no interest in the obese Mr. Gutman. He did not have the black bird.

Another patient wait down the block from Thursby's hotel. Then, patience is a service the customers of Mandrell Limited have come to expect. It is delivered to them. Except—except, sir!—when they request the firm to demonstrate patience while waiting for the final payment of the fee. We do not bill, or extend credit, or consult solicitors or collection agencies. We collect!

Ah well, this is hardly the place to emphasize the business policies of my firm.

Mr. Thursby eventually returned to the Poe Park. As he disembarked his taxi just outside the driveway—there was the usual late-evening snarl of traffic clogging the driveway—I noted that Wilmer Cook had returned to the hotel with Mr. Thursby. Possibly Thursby was unaware of his traveling companion for Wilmer used a separate taxi and made some effort to avoid being seen by Thursby, alighting across the street from the hotel entrance, for instance.

The young man in the long overcoat came past me with his hands in his pockets and his glittering eyes fixed on Thursby, who was engrossed in paying his taxi fare across the street. Wilmer paid little heed to me. I was after all as inoffensive a figure as one is likely to find on the streets of San Francisco. I was at the moment disguised as a crippled newspaper vendor.

Wilmer jerked his two .45 automatics from his pockets and glanced quickly at the traffic pattern in force on the street separating him from Thursby. It was obvious that the lad was about to launch a flagrantly primitive frontal assault on his target. (In the American culture have the expensive lessons in survival taught the Paleface by the Plains Indians not been passed along?)

I could have none of this. Mr. Floyd Thursby was too pivotal a character in the Maltese Falcon Commission to have him frightened into hiding again by the immature judgment of a gunsel. I had no doubt Thursby would become aware of Wilmer's charging infantry maneuver prior to Wilmer's completion of his attack. Thursby had "been around" as the Americans say. He would retaliate in kind and, of more vivid importance to my objectives, Thursby would also initiate an evasive action that could well take him out of my reach again.

I stepped into the gutter behind the young man and yanked his overcoat down over his arms, thus isolating his guns to an impotent, low-profile trajectory. I tore the .45s from Wilmer's small hands. Drawing the startled lad back on the sidewalk I pinned him against the side of an automobile and thrust the oily snout of one of his pistols into his open mouth.

"Keep your pants on, kid," I snarled in an imitation of your typical cinema gangster. "You're in the big league now."

Thursby had just completed paying his taxi bill. He turned and started walking up the driveway of his hotel.

I lined Wilmer's second cannon across the roof of the auto and shot Thursby four times in the back.

Rather a respectful display of marksmanship when you consider that each successive wedge of lead caused an instantaneous relocation of the basic target. Wilmer may or may not have been impressed. It was difficult to read the lad's face with the other pistol protruding therefrom. The police coroner upon examining the deceased very likely expressed some compliment to my efforts. Mr. Thursby was obviously impressed.

Thursby, I might mention, had done me a similar service several years prior in Egypt during the Aswan Dam Commission. To this day I still retain the incision deposited by his incivility in my back muscles.

I disarmed both pistols, thrust them into Wilmer's pockets, and growled, "Better get outta here, kid. Go to the fat man. You can tell him you killed Thursby if it makes you feel any better."

I galloped into the darkness, not even pausing in my flight to merchandise the few remaining newspapers I carried to those who spoke for them.

Yes: Mandrell Limited is in the export business. We export perishable goods over long distances. Provided, of course, the fee is commensurate with the excellence of the service.

So, as I said, I was somewhat skeptical of the effectiveness of Wilmer Cook's addiction to massive firepower. As it turned out, Samuel Spade eventually drew the same conclusion.

* * *

It was the next evening that I saw Spade again. About a block from the Alexandria Hotel I noticed a police car double parked and the two cops in it staring at something over by a shop window on the sidewalk. The something was Sam Spade, or what was left of him.

He was leaning against a storefront. He had to lean against something. His shirt was open at the neck and partly outside his jacket and partly not. There was a terrible purple bruise on his temple.

It was obvious the cops were about ready to drop the hook on him so I went over quickly and took his arm. I got him to the curb where there was a taxi stand. I yanked open a taxi door and tried to get Spade in. The cabbie growled, "He goes first," and jerked his thumb at the cab parked in front of him. The cabbie took a closer look at Spade and added: "If anybody goes."

"This is an emergency. My friend is sick."

"He could get sick somewheres else," the noble Samaritan said.

"Five dollars," I said, my notecase cringing. "And let's see that beautiful smile."

He shrugged and stuck the magazine he'd been reading behind the sun visor. Just then the police car eased up beside the cab and a gray-haired cop with sergeant's stripes got out.

I eased Spade upright in the seat and walked around the taxi to meet the policeman. "What's with the guy in the soiled laundry?" the cop said. "You know him?"

"Well enough to know he requires assistance. His name is Samuel Spade."

"Yeah? Maybe what he needs is a night in the drunk tank."

"Your arrest record cannot be that undernourished, officer. I will remove the gentleman from the streets."

"Let's see some I.D."

I gave him a Mandrell Limited Import-Export card. The cop ran his thumb over the raised lettering. The exercise in Braille reading spelled: expensive, money, responsible citizen; possibly: influential citizen. But he couldn't let it go at that. You don't get to be sergeant by buying the song the first time it's played.

The cop stuck his head in the window and said to Spade, "What's your friend's name, buddy?"

Spade blinked his yellowish eyes hard and dug through the gray mist into his filing cabinet. His lips pulled back in part of a grin and he said, "Gus Mandrell. Works for an English import-export firm. What's the beef?"

The cop pulled his head out of the window and looked at me while running his thumb along his chin. It is possible he was even thinking. There are, unfortunately, some of them who do.

"All right," he finally said, "I'll go along with it this time. But get him off my beat." He and his partner left.

I directed the cabbie to my apartment on Leavenworth. Spade was able to stand on the sidewalk by himself with just a little swaying. I held out the five dollars to the cabbie. He gave me a stiff look and shook his head. "Just what's on the meter, Jack, or an even buck if you feel like it. I've been down and out myself. In L.A. Nobody picked me up in no taxi either. That's one stony-hearted town." I gave him the dollar; with surprisingly little resentment, I found, over the fact that the meter read but sixty-five cents.

Spade required hardly any assistance as we made our way to the elevator and up. "This is a different place isn't it?" Spade asked looking around at the apartment.

"Yes. I was in the process of moving when we ran across each other last night. It was too quiet in the little house."

It was to be honest the sort of place a young man in a long overcoat might lurk about waiting for the occupant to return home.

"While there is some alcohol in your system," I said, "your condition appears to relate to the ingestion of something stronger."

"Knockout drops," he growled. "Remember I told you Joel Cairo and Brigid O'Shaughnessy were talking about some guy whose name begins with G? Well I met G today. Twice. His name is Casper Gutman, a big fat slob with a silver tongue."

"He too had read the newspaper story about—what was his name, Thursby?—and got in touch with you?" My vicarious interest in the affairs of "Spade and Archer" was obvious in my voice.

"Not quite," Spade said and started to roll one of his Bull Durhams. "You were right last night. My friend Miss O'Shaughnessy did snitch my keys. She was at my apartment when I got home. She said she just wanted to teach me a lesson in how to treat a lady. That's why she ran out on me at the Dancers. I taught her how I treat ladies who walk around my apartment in my pajamas. When she went to sleep I took her key and went over to the Coronet to search her room. It was clean."

I beg to differ, sir. When I entered Miss O'Shaughnessy's room this morning it was in considerable disrepair. It is comforting to know that it was you, Mr. Spade, who conducted the commendably thorough search. Even the residue in her lotion jars probed with a fork, by Gadfry.

Spade continued. "After breakfast at my place I took Brigid home to the Coronet and then stopped by the Belvedere to see how Joel Cairo was doing. In the lobby of the Belvedere I found the goddam kid with the overcoat. I had the hotel dick throw him out but before the kid left I tried the G business on him. I said: "Tell G you'll have to talk to me before you're through." And by God by the time I got back to the office there was a message from G. He'd called and said he'd call again. Also Brigid O'Shaughnessy was in the office, all upset because she'd found her room at the Coronet had been searched."

"And of course you didn't tell her it was yourself who had searched the room," I chortled.

Spade smiled and a satisfied light illuminated his yellowish eyes. "For three days they've all dummied up on me. I've had to pry every new piece of information out with my eyeteeth. I did it by keeping them off balance, keeping their own fears, their own distrust of each other working on them. They thought they could come to San Francisco and run me through their hoops. They wiped out my partner and had the cops measuring me for two murders: my partner and this Thursby character. But this is my town. I know how to operate here and when you come into my arena, mister, you'd better know what you're doing.

"Okay, G called me. That meant G and the kid were a team. Cairo and O'Shaughnessy are both afraid of the kid. That means afraid of G. And when I had the kid kicked out of the Belvedere he had two big guns in his coat pockets. Thursby was shot by big guns. I'm putting the pieces together and they know Samuel Spade is putting the pieces together. In the background I'm beginning to hear the flapping of a large black bird."

He grinned to himself; a man pleased by his own competence. It's a good sight to witness, particularly when fully justified as in this case.

"Mr. Gutman did call back, I presume?"

Spade nodded. "But first I sent Brigid O'Shaughnessy off to stay at Effie's place; Effie Perine my secretary. Brigid was still jumpy because her room had been searched. Then Gutman called and asked me to come over to his room at the Alexandria Hotel. Before I could leave the office who the hell pops in but Iva Archer, my partner's widow. And I was right. She's the one who sent the cops up to my place with the story I'd killed Miles because I wanted her. Also Miles's brother Phil Archer is in the act. He thinks I killed Miles. Goddam mess."

"Is Phil Archer in the detective business also?"

"No. There's another brother or cousin, Lew Archer, who's in the business down the coast someplace. I hear he's pretty bright. So I finally met G, Casper Gutman. The kid was at his hotel suite too. Name's Wilmer Cook. All Gutman really told me is the black bird is worth more than I can dream of. He asked if Brigid and Cairo had told me the story of the bird. I said no. Gutman began kicking around the idea that maybe Cairo and the girl don't know the story. That's when he decided Sam Spade didn't fit in the picture—unless I had the bird in my hip pocket. I did a little shouting and bottle smashing. I told him he'd damn well have to deal with me or he would be out of the picture. And I warned him to keep Wilmer away from me or I'd kill the son of a bitch. That part was serious. The kid gets my skin crawling."

"Mr. Gutman agreed with you?" I asked.

Spade grinned. "Hell no, that was just the opening session. The 'feeling each other out.' There's a first-class brain hidden in all that fat. I told him he had until 5:30 to declare himself in. Then I stormed out of his hotel suite. It was a pretty good act."

We both chuckled.

"You said you saw G twice, today, Mr. Spade," I said. "He was taken in by your act then?"

"Yeah. He sent the kid over to get me at 5:25. Meanwhile I had another problem. Brigid O'Shaughnessy had disappeared. I'd sent her off earlier to stay at my secretary's place. Brigid never showed up. Effie was really worried when I got back to the office after my first talk with Gutman. Effie thinks Brigid O'Shaughnessy is the cat's pajamas; a classic 'beautiful lady in distress.' So I went out to find Brigid. The hack driver I'd sent her with told me she had him drop her at the Ferry Building. First she had stopped the cab and bought a newspaper. I went to her place at the Coronet. Her clothes were there but no Brigid."

"Perhaps she saw something in the newspaper?" the amateur offered. "I have a copy of the *Chronicle* here."

"Naw, I already looked. Anyway it was the *Call* she bought."

His statement saved us a spot of embarrassment. I had no newspaper in the apartment.

"When I got back to my office building," Spade continued, "the kid was waiting downstairs for me. He's a sketch with his tough-guy mouth. But he's a spooky bastard. We went to see his boss Gutman and the fat man told me about the black bird, the Maltese Falcon."

According to Spade—as told to him by Gutman—the Maltese Falcon was a statue about as tall as your forearm constructed of solid gold and garnished with precious stones. It had been constructed about the year 1530 by a group of knights involved in one of the Crusades. These knights had been granted territorial rights in the Mediterranean area by Emperor Charles V of Spain. The lands granted the knights included the island of Malta. In payment the knights were to present to Charles each year one falcon as a gesture of their continued loyalty.

The knights were fabulously wealthy since they had taken full advantage of a basic tenet of war: To the winner belongs the spoils. Thus when payment of the first falcon was due, they sent Charles not a living breathing falcon but the gold bejeweled bird.

On the way to Spain the falcon fell to pirates who captured the galley in which the tribute was being transferred. The bird took up a nomad's life for the next four hundred years, first in the hands of one owner, then another; occasionally purchased, more frequently wrested away by the stronger pair of hands. A black enamel was added to the falcon at some time to shield its beauty in a base world.

About twenty years ago a Greek named Charilaos Konstantinides found the bird in Paris. He saw beneath the black enamel façade. The

Greek eventually told Casper Gutman about his secret treasure. Before Gutman could take action to obtain the falcon, the Greek's shop was looted and burned, the Greek killed, and the falcon stolen.

For the past seventeen years Gutman had been scouring the world looking for the Maltese Falcon. He found it in the possession of a Russian general named Kemidov who lived in Constantinople. At first Gutman tried to buy the falcon from Kemidov, realizing that the Russian did not know the true value of the object. The Russian would not sell.

Gutman sent his agents Joel Cairo, Brigid O'Shaughnessy, and Floyd Thursby to get the falcon from General Kemidov. Gutman remained in New York. The threesome stole the bird from the Russian and then the fun began. Brigid and Thursby ducked out on Cairo headed for Hong Kong and San Francisco with the bird. Gutman, when advised of the treachery, arrived in San Francisco from New York. Joel Cairo followed Brigid and Thursby from Constantinople.

"That's why they're all here in town," Spade concluded.

"Fascinating story," I gasped.

"Yeah, if it's true," Spade said sourly and rubbed the purple bruise on his temple. "I'm going to have Effie check out the business about the Maltese knights in the history books . . . Damn I'm getting groggy again."

"What happened to your head?"

"I'm not sure. I guess that son of a bitch Wilmer kicked me after the knockout drops had me down. Wilmer was a little upset," he grinned. "I took his guns away from him in the corridor just before we went into Gutman's suite."

The poor lad must be growing weary of the disarmament policies of San Francisco. First my humble self had demonstrated same outside Floyd Thursby's hotel. Then two days later Mr. Spade re-emphasized the procedure in the Alexandria Hotel. Ah well . . .

"But why did they administer the sedative?" I asked. "Why did Mr. Gutman tell you the falcon's history and then so abruptly end your meeting?"

"Because, Gus, he thought I had the goddam thing. We were going through the business of splitting up the loot . . ." He paused and shook his head, his voice had become guttural.

"We were counting the chickens . . ." His chin slipped off the heel of his hand that had been propping it. "Then it came out I didn't actually have the dingus. I told him not to worry I'd get it from Brigid. That's when he got his fat ass out of the chair to mix me another drink. My last drink . . . goddam room is tilting . . . The stuff put me out for about an hour. I practically crawled out of that son-of-a-bitching hotel. The fresh air hit me hard. That's when you and the cops came along. I . . . I . . ." He couldn't get the words out.

"Here you'd better lie down," I said, attempting to pull him to his feet. "You must still have some of the drug in you." I got him on his feet but he was incredibly unwieldy. Abruptly he collapsed to the floor. As he rolled still with his mouth against the carpet he muttered. "Two million bucks . . . He said two million . . ."

"I'll get a doctor," I cried and fled the apartment.

Once on the street I purchased a newspaper—yes, the *Call*—and hailed a taxi. "The Ferry Building, please," I told the driver.

I glanced through the newspaper quickly. On page 36 I finally found the item. In the lower left-hand corner was a list of the ships arriving in San Francisco that day. The eighth entry read: 8:25 A.M. —*La Paloma* from Hong Kong.

Miss O'Shaughnessy and Floyd Thursby had been in Hong Kong and had the Maltese Falcon with them at that time. They moved on to San Francisco. There had been no evidence thus far that the bird came with them.

The *La Paloma* from Hong Kong . . .

* * *

The *La Paloma* dedicated her life to hauling crated and baled cargo and a few low-income passengers between San Francisco and the Orient. On a good day she could make 8 knots. When I first saw her tied up at a pier a few blocks from the Ferry Building she rode low in the water since only a portion of her cargo had been hoisted from her holds by longshoremen since her arrival at 8:25 that morning. Most of the ship's crew was ashore in the bars along the Embarcadero by the time I reached the ship. A watchman who worked for Hammett and Chandler Shipping Company, the *La Paloma*'s owners, was stationed at the head of the splintered, creaking wooden gangway. As I clomped up the gangway a faint residue of the watchman's supper floated out to meet me. Muscatel or port was my guess.

"Goddam people," I cursed as I pulled a handkerchief to wipe my hands that had grasped the gangway railing. "Can't they at least keep my equipment clean? Who's aboard?" I demanded of the watchman.

"The captain, sir," said the properly impressed wino. "And some lads in the engine room."

"Which captain?" I snarled. "Do you think I keep track of every jackanapes on the payroll?"

"Captain Jacobi, sir. I can fetch him for you, sir."

"Yes, I want a private chat with Captain Jacobi about the condition of my ship."

"Well, he has a few guests, sir."

"Is Greenstreet with him?" I asked. "Big fat man, probably has his son Wilmer with him."

"Yes, sir, Mr. Greenstreet, if that be his name, is here, and his lad. And there's a young lady who's been here most the day and another little man who . . ." He paused.

"Who smells pretty and walks a bit ladylike, is that what you meant?" I chuckled then and clapped the old reprobate on the shoulder. I'm not above demonstrating a degree of informality with my employees. You have to know how to handle the working class if you're to be a success in the shipping business.

"Lead on, lead on," I said. He took me along the deck and up two levels using his flashlight to guide us. "Everybody in the captain's cabin?" I asked.

"Everybody except the lad—Wilmer did you say his name was? He's been off prowling around the ship for the past hour."

At the door to Jacobi's cabin I dismissed my watchman. I knocked and a voice I didn't recognize asked for my identity through the door.

"Message from H and C office, Captain," I said, referring to the ship's owners.

Jacobi opened the door. Great Scott, the man was a giant! At least seven feet tall. His shoulders were permanently slumped from a life of avoiding doorways, overhead piping, and the additional structural obstructions designed for normal men.

The players in the Maltese Falcon game were scattered about the room. Joel Cairo sat in a straight chair near the captain's desk resting his chin on the handle of his umbrella. Brigid O'Shaughnessy lay on her back on the captain's bunk, her thin forearm over her eyes, except for one quick glance at me as I entered. Casper Gutman sat at the round table in the center of the cabin, a bottle of Oriental wine in front of him, its contents diminished by only a few drinks.

Captain Jacobi had probably been sitting on the bunk at Brigid's feet for the only chair in the room built for the big man was being used by Gutman.

"Yes, what's the message?" Jacobi asked. He was frowning at the black shirt and silver tie I wore with my plaid suit. Possibly the officers of H and C Shipping tended to more conservative attire.

"Which one of you bumped off Floyd Thursby?" I demanded, glancing around at all of them.

Joel Cairo's eyes sprung wide. Brigid slowly lifted her arm from her eyes to stare at me with cornflower blue eyes. She had a remarkably lovely face. The framework of red hair could hardly be regarded as a deficit.

Mr. G continued to stare at me with the same intensity he had unleashed upon my entry. He took no intrusion lightly. You learn not to when your objective becomes a seventeen-year odyssey.

"Who killed that rotten son-of-a-bitch Thursby?" I said. "I want to shake his hand."

It was Casper Gutman who took over as master of our confined room. He would do so in any room by the sheer weight of his confidence, not to mention his considerable cubic displacement.

"Can you tell us who you are, sir?" Gutman said. "We may indeed find we have mutual friends."

"The name's Buzz Carpenter. Who killed Thursby?"

Slouched over Captain Jacobi moved over to sit on the bunk with Brigid, relinquishing the role of host.

"You are evidently absorbed with that inquiry, Mr. Carpenter," Gutman said. "Surely you can tell us a bit more? How you happened to know we were here, for instance?"

I leaned my back against the cabin door. "I ain't much for gabbing," I said.

"Splendid," Gutman said. "I distrust a man who talks too much. The spoken word delivers our innermost secrets. A man who unnecessarily strips himself of his armor leaves no shield for the hard times. Come, sir, come have a drink with me and we'll discuss Mr. Floyd Thursby. And your totally unexpected arrival."

As I walked over to sit at the table Gutman poured some of the Oriental wine into a water glass. I said, "When. That's enough."

"Ah better and better," Gutman said. "I have little regard for a man who does not monitor his drinking carefully. Alcohol is a sedative scattered over the earth by the more insecure of the gods to insure our docility. Don't you agree?"

"I don't know about that stuff," I said gruffly. "All I want to know is what Floyd Thursby did with my boss' two hundred grand."

"Ah, you do not represent yourself then, Mr. Carpenter?" Gutman said, his pink face lighting with increased interest. "You speak for your employer, someone to whom you are loyal. You are not the boss?"

I chuckled at the absurdity of his suggestion. "Me the boss! Holy mackerel, pal, I couldn't handle that job. I don't know how Mr. Bogart keeps up with all the damn' details. You know: the slot machines, the bookies, the breweries, the cat ho . . ."—I glanced at Miss O'Shaughnessy—"the girls. All that stuff. I work for Mr. Bogart."

"Unquestioned loyalty," Gutman exclaimed. "I like that, sir, I like that. Indeed I do. I distrust a man who tells me he is out for himself and himself alone. This is a cold world and we cannot survive without the warmth of those close around us. Nor did Nature intend us to. Service to one's fellow man, is there a more noble ambition? Now, sir, as to how you chanced on our meeting here tonight?"

"I'm looking for the two hundred thousand bucks Floyd Thursby stole from Dixie Monahan that Monahan stole from Mr. Bogart," I said stubbornly.

Brigid O'Shaughnessy swung her legs off the bunk and sat up. She spoke to Gutman. "Floyd was a bodyguard for a man named Dixie Monahan at one time. According to the story, this Mr. Monahan fled from the United States and had to be protected from his old associates in the Chicago gambling business."

"You bet he had to be protected, lady," I fumed. "That rat Dixie ran out on Mr. Bogart with two hundred grand in his pocket. We was looking for him all over the world. And if we'da found him we'da blasted him."

Joel Cairo's soft little voice spoke up. "Dixie Monahan, didn't he take with him another item presumably of value to Mr. Bogart?"

I shifted uneasily in my chair and admitted, "Yeah, well Mrs. Bogart did go with Dixie too. But Mr. Bogart was well rid of that bitch Zerelda . . . ah . . . Begging your pardon, ma'am," I apologized to Brigid for my coarse language.

"I heard the story too," Captain Jacobi said from the bunk. The voice coming out of the seven-foot frame was deep and marked with the brusqueness of a man always on the defensive. "Thursby and Dixie Monahan were in Singapore when Monahan disappeared. All of a sudden Thursby was living in the swankiest hotels and out with the most expensive dames."

Brigid tossed the big captain a disapproving look that had something to do I believe with the competitive nature of females.

Gutman addressed me: "It would seem then, Mr. Carpenter—you say your Christian name is Buzz?"

"Yeah. You know: a carpenter, wood, cut it with a buzz saw? I'm Mr. Bogart's buzz saw."

"Ah yes. We can visualize what it is you cut for Mr. Bogart." Gutman glanced at the bulge under my jacket. "Your quest then is for the two hundred thousand dollars—that is a good deal of money, sir, and no doubt about it—" He glanced over at Joel Cairo, shifting his whole upper torso since the thickness of his neck made rotation of his head difficult. Joel and Gutman smiled at each other, two international financiers agreeing that two hundred thousand dollars was indeed a lot of money.

"You then are trying to find the money stolen from your employer Mr. Bogart by Mr. Dixie Monahan," Gutman continued. "Your assumption is that Mr. Thursby eliminated Mr. Monahan in Singapore and took the two hundred thousand."

"Mr. Bogart don't expect the whole two hundred grand back," I said. "Dixie Monahan liked to spend dough but we figure some of it was left and Thursby got it after killing Dixie."

Brigid spoke. "I knew Floyd Thursby. He didn't have two hundred dollars never mind two hundred thousand. I had to lend him money."

"And that's the truth Mr. Buzz Saw," Gutman said, his tone indicating he was growing a bit weary of me. "We all knew Mr. Thursby after a fashion. He was not what one would call a 'well heeled' citizen. I'm afraid he must have spent whatever moneys he received from Dixie Monahan's estate."

"Yeah I know he spent it," I said casually. "That's why I come to you folks. Thursby bought a black bird with the money. Mr. Bogart wants the black bird."

I believe the term is: one could have heard a pin drop.

The uproar was started by Joel Cairo. He screeched: "That is absurd! Unfounded! A lie, lie, lie . . ." Brigid's face flushed with her anger. "I got that bird!" she cried. "I put up with that greasy, pawing Russian! I have more claim." Cairo then turned on Brigid and fumed: "But who was it that broke into General Kemidov's house? Who risked twenty years in a Greek prison?" He was on his feet also, his umbrella in his hands like a baseball bat. Captain Jacobi slouched over to stand between Cairo and Brigid.

Gutman finally lost his patience also. He slammed his fat fist on the table three times knocking the bottle of wine and the drinking glasses to the floor. The debaters quieted and returned to their places.

"Now, sir," Gutman said to me, holding his hands together tightly in an attempt to slow the blood roaring through his body. "Now, Mr. Buzz Saw, this is one of the most preposterous stories I have ever heard. Mr. Thursby did not finance the removal of the black bird from General Kemidov's hands. I did. Mr. Thursby provided only transportation facilities for the other participants, Mr. Cairo and Miss O'Shaughnessy."

"You mean he drove the getaway car," I said smugly. "What's the matter, can't you say that straight out without the fancy words?" I grinned over to Brigid. "It's not how you say things that counts, it's how you do things. Right, baby?"

She smiled back weakly. This was my first look at Brigid O'Shaughnessy since the night I saw her in the parking lot of the

Dancers. Even after the weariness of eight or ten hours in Captain Jacobi's cabin she was still one hell of a good-looking dame, as the Yanks say.

Gutman was holding onto his aplomb but just barely. He said, "Mr. Buzz Saw, kindly convey our regrets to Mr. Bogart. Advise him that his money was dissipated by wastrels. Surely there will be consolation of sorts for him in the fact that Mr. Dixie Monahan and Mr. Thursby are both dead?"

I chuckled. "You sure don't know Mr. Bogart. He wants to see the black bird. He said to me: 'Buzzy you bring me that black bird. I'm gonna see a bird what cost me two hundred grand. I'm gonna maybe eat the son-a-ma-bich.' I gotta bring Mr. Bogart the bird, Mr. Gutsman."

"Ah, you know my name," Gutman said, ignoring the mispronunciation. "Where, Mr. Carpenter, have you obtained your information? Have you perchance spoken to Mr. Samuel Spade?"

From the edge of my eye I saw Brigid sit up straighter. "That's it, that's undoubtedly it," Joel Cairo said. "Mr. Spade is an unruly, undisciplined man. He must have sent the . . . the moose here."

"Shut up, Joe," Brigid snapped listlessly at Cairo.

"I used to know a Digger Spade out of Cincy," I said. "But he's at the bottom of the Ohio River, last I heard."

Gutman threw up his hands. "I must get out of this room," he said peevishly. "The very confines surround and compress a man's thoughts. Joel, get Wilmer. We're leaving."

Cairo went to the cabin door. He paused before exiting and said softly to Gutman: "It appears to me that Wilmer should be advised of our decision. Am I correct in assuming it is open season on certain . . . er . . . North American caribou?"

"Yes, yes," Gutman said absently. "Tell him I want to leave within ten minutes."

When Cairo left Gutman turned to Brigid and Captain Jacobi. "We are in agreement then? The terms we worked out this evening are satisfactory? You will bring the item with you to my hotel?"

Brigid nudged Jacobi with her elbow. The captain said, "Yeah, okay. We'll go to your hotel if that's where the money is."

"But we'll hold onto the package until we get there," Brigid said.

"Excellent," Gutman said and pushed on the table to get to his feet. "Let's drink to understanding. The world has so little of it, we—" He tried to reach over to the floor to pick up the bottle of wine. His girth would not permit it, as he must have known. He also possibly had heard the light footstep in the passageway outside the cabin.

"Mr. Buzz Saw," Gutman said to me, indicating the bottle on the floor, "would you be so kind?"

"Sure, pal," I stood and walked to his side of the table. "You should look into that weight problem. I know a guy—"

As I bent over for the bottle, Gutman yelled, "Wilmer!" At the same moment Gutman slashed his heavy forearm down at my neck.

The kid in the long overcoat burst through the flung-open door with both .45s at the ready.

Unhappily for their intentions Mr. Buzz Saw Carpenter was familiar with the term "open season" as applied to hunting. One even suspects that the chap may have been able to associate the terms "moose" and "caribou."

Anyway, as Gutman cried out, Mr. Carpenter flung himself across the floor, rolled on his back once and came to his feet at precisely the point where the cabin door swung through its opening arc and struck the wall. Thus he was actually out of Wilmer's line of sight —hidden by the opening door—as the lad charged in. This placed Mr. Carpenter slightly behind the boy.

Gutman, meanwhile, finding no resistance to the downward slash of his arm, fell to his knees and nearly over on his face.

I kicked both of Wilmer's forearms upward and slammed him on the head with the wine bottle. One of the pistols went off sending a bullet high into the bulkhead above Brigid's head.

I picked up the guns and disarmed them. I was gratified to see that the lad had installed fresh clips and bullets in the weapons since our last meeting outside Floyd Thursby's hotel. A craftsman should never ignore the maintenance of his tools.

"Anybody know the kid?" I asked casually, looking around at all of them with innocent eyes. "You're getting a lot of traffic in here, buddy," I commented to Captain Jacobi. "Wadda you got, signs out in the street or something?"

Joel Cairo was attempting to help Gutman to his feet. Gutman shook off the assisting hands and climbed up using the heavy table to obtain the necessary leverage. Joel went over and knelt next to the unconscious boy.

Gutman, breathing heavily, said, "Remind me sometime to compliment Mr. Bogart on the excellence of his employees. You show a nice timing, Mr. Carpenter, indeed you do. Well, sir, you have the advantage. What do you suggest?"

"You said you wanted to go into town, to your hotel. Suits me. Let's all go up and talk about the black bird."

"Splendid, sir, splendid," Gutman said. "You and I can do business, indeed we can."

"Perhaps Mr. Carpenter would rather do business with someone else," Brigid said. Her eyes on mine were pleading. "There are some of us involved in this adventure against our will, Mr. Carpenter. Forced by circumstances to bow to—"

"That's enough of that, Miss O'Shaughnessy!" Gutman roared.

The girl flinched and stepped backward and away from Captain Jacobi, putting her a bit closer to myself. She was biting her lip and might have been on the verge of crying. I walked over toward her.

"I trust in your judgment, Mr. Carpenter," Gutman said, mopping his face with his handkerchief. "You have proven worthy of such trust. As I said, you and I can do business together."

"Okay," I said shrugging. "I don't know what's going on but I got no beef as long as I get the bird for Mr. Bogart." I was standing next to Brigid, waiting for her to choose sides. Her thin hand crept into mine, hidden from the others in the room by the fold of her skirt. I squeezed the maximum amount of communication into her fingers. She squeezed back. I was attempting to say "Trust me." What was she answering?

"Hey," I said, "I got a car parked outside the dock. I can take some of you with me." I turned my face to Brigid's. "C'mon, cheer up, little lady," I said chucking her under the chin. While my voice was casual, my eyes on hers were hard and probing. I winked very seriously. She and Captain Jacobi were the only ones who could see my face. I left her then.

"I'll bring my car into the yard," I said to Gutman as I went to the door. "Want I should get you a cab?"

"Yes that will be fine, Mr. Buzz Saw. I must insist we all travel together in the interest of good business practices. Some of us will follow your car to my hotel."

"Okay. By the time you bring the kid around, I'll be back."

I departed. The watchman was not at the gangway when I left. I moved swiftly. Two vehicles would be able to handle the load of passengers. There would be seven of us: 1. Myself, 2. Casper Gutman, 3. Miss O'Shaughnessy, 4. Joel Cairo, 5. Wilmer Cook, 6. Captain Jacobi, and 7. —the Maltese Falcon.

The black bird had been the one participant missing in the cabin. He must have been aboard. No other conclusion made sense. But Gutman had not been able to force Brigid and Jacobi to bring it forth, else why was Wilmer prowling the ship?

I could make no move until I saw the damn' bird.

*   *   *

I directed the chauffeur through the gate and on to the pier where the *La Paloma* was docked. The taxi followed us. Obtaining the proper transportation had taken a bit longer than I'd anticipated.

My passengers were coming along the main deck toward the gangway.

I met them halfway between the parked vehicles and the foot of the gangway. Wilmer, still a bit groggy, was being assisted by Joel Cairo who held a wet cloth on the boy's head.

But my eyes noted that medical detail only in passing. They slashed among the group for the seventh passenger.

Ahhh, there you are! Clutched against Captain Jacobi's chest was a brown parcel tied with string, a bit larger than an American football.

As I took Brigid's arm, Gutman said peevishly, "How far away was your car, Mr. Carpenter? It seems ages . . . Well, you're here now and that's what matters, is it not?"

I led Brigid to my chauffeured auto. Jacobi followed us. Gutman said, "All right, Cairo, the boy and I will follow in the taxi. The Alexandria Hotel. We'll be right behind you all the way. Indeed we will." He assisted Cairo in getting the boy to the cab.

Brigid froze for a second looking at my chauffeured vehicle. She exclaimed, "Why that's a funeral hearse!"

"C'mon, we have to move fast," I told her and dragged her to the front seat passenger door. Jacobi came behind us with his precious bundle.

"In you go," I told Brigid urgently. "Go into the back. Go on straight through and out the back door. Hurry, goddammit, before they pull up next to us."

The hearse was parked facing the front gate, as was the taxi. But the rear end of the hearse was hidden from the view of those in the taxi by a stack of orange crates. The passengers in the cab could see us enter the hearse but once we moved past the front seat they could not see us.

"Move, move," I urged Brigid and pushed against her backside. "C'mon, Jacobi, you'd better crawl."

Brigid exclaimed, "There are people sitting back here!"

"They won't bother you. Go right on by. Hurry!"

Brigid sucked her breath. "They're . . . they're dead people!"

"Goddammit, do you think I had time to conduct auditions? They'll look real enough through the rear window. It's the best I could do. That's it, climb out."

As we scooted out the back door one could hear Gutman passing instructions to the driver of the taxi. ". . . and if you lose that black car, I'll have your license. What is taking them so—"

My chauffeur heard me click the back door of his gloomy conveyance closed. He immediately eased the big car out. The headlights of the taxi caught the rear of the hearse illuminating the interior where the silhouettes of three figures, one with long hair, were to be seen.

As the taxi took after the other vehicle, Joel Cairo's soft voice could be heard. "Look at that, Mr. Gutman," he giggled. "A funeral car. These American gangsters, they are absolutely absurd."

Gutman's chuckle trailed back to us as the taxi followed the hearse out the gate.

"They may get the chauffeur to talk," I commented, "but I doubt if the passengers will."

"Oh, Mr. Carpenter, how can I thank you," Brigid cried and threw herself against me. "Those men had taken complete advantage of me." Her face tilted up and she pulled my head down. Even in the dark behind the orange crates I could feel the heat from the maid's eyes.

At approximately the same moment Captain Jacobi struck my head with whatever it was he used, possibly the Maltese Falcon.

I was unconscious for about thirty minutes. I staggered from the pier, my mind a jungle of curses. A taxi took me to Brigid's room at the Coronet. Her wardrobe was there but not Delilah. Joel Cairo was not in his room at the Belvedere. No one was home at Gutman's. I even tried Sam Spade's place. Empty. Presumably Mr. Spade was still asleep on the floor of my apartment.

It was now daylight.

I returned to the *La Paloma*. The possibility that Brigid and Captain Jacobi had never left the rust-stained hulk should have occurred to me sooner. The ship, however, represented a rat warren of hiding places. It could take days to search all the holds. I set the old tub afire and waited on the pier to intercept Brigid and Jacobi should they exit.

A half-dozen crew men deserted the burning ship but they were all of normal height and none had long red hair. I waited until the fire department started towing the ship out of the harbor past the incoming ferry from Berkeley.

Damn her! I had underestimated her self-confidence. She had the bird and only that lummox Captain Jacobi to help her. I had been certain she would need the strong arm of Mr. Buzz Saw Carpenter. Where was she taking the bird? She had been willing to accept $5,000 for it from Joel Cairo. Where had she found a higher bidder?

I returned to my apartment. Spade was gone. A note on the table said: *Thanks for the coffee. Now I owe you two drinks.*

I called Spade's office. A young lady told me he wasn't in. Good.

I put on a different suit and a different face and went to the office of Samuel Spade. The lettering on the door was new. A bright-eyed, sunburned girl asked me the introductory questions. She was Effie Perine, Spade's secretary. Again she told me Spade wasn't in but she expected him shortly. I said I'd wait.

I took a chair off to the side where I could see her profile. After a minute or so she became sufficiently conscious of my staring that she turned and asked, "Is there anything I can get you? A magazine or something?"

"Would you mind bending forward just a bit?" I said. "Get your face in the brighter light?" I held up my hands to form a square with my fingers and stared at her through the square.

Effie looked properly puzzled.

"Oh, I'm sorry," I said. "It's just that I'm struck by the bone structure. You've heard the term photogenic? People who photograph well?" She nodded. "It all has to do with bone structure. We have some of the most gifted actors and actresses from Broadway under contract and can't use a damn' one of them. On film their facial expressions do not register properly."

"You're from Hollywood?" Her eyes opened several fractions.

I smiled my modest smile. "Would you mind walking across the room just once please? Nothing exaggerated now. Just your normal walk. The public is up to here with blondes who know how to wiggle."

She complied but with all the typical embarrassment of a person under abnormal scrutiny.

"That's very nice," I murmured, obviously absorbed in some thought. "Wholesome. Girl-next-door. College campus. Very nice. Darryl Zannuck was saying just the other day . . ." My voice trailed off. I shifted so I could look out the window, give myself time to think.

Effie remained standing for a while. Then I heard her move back to her desk.

I turned a minute later and stared at her again. A very red flush rose up her neck and face.

"Well, something to look into sometime," I said dismissing from my mind an idea I'd had for the moment. "Tell me, Miss Perine, this must be a fascinating business. A dozen good movie plots must pass through that door each week, eh? We're shooting one now here in San Francisco about international smugglers. Got some great footage this morning of a ship burning in the harbor. If Tom and Ralph got the angles they claim they did we'll change the plot to throw in a fire aboard ship."

"I saw that ship," Effie exclaimed. "It was awful." Her diction had improved noticeably.

"The international thief movie is a hot item right now," I said.

"I don't suppose Mr. Spade ever gets involved in that sort of thing does he? Pretty much domestic cases I would imagine?"

"Not always," she said eagerly. "Why just the other day . . ."

She paused. I sat looking properly attentive. "Yes?" I prompted.

"Oh, we do get some strange cases. But you'll have to ask Mr. Spade about them."

Obviously we needed stronger motivation. Spade had told me of Effie's empathy for Brigid O'Shaughnessy.

"The thing we always need most in these movies is expert counsel. You know, someone who has actually been in it and can give those little bits of expert information that really lend the movie authenticity. If I could lay my hands on a man—or a woman for that matter—who knows the problems of moving illegally from country to country, the difficulty of establishing meeting places in strange cities, a person like that would be worth a fortune to my studio. Heck, we might even put them in the movie. If they were photogenic."

There, my dear, do you chance to know of such a person? And has she been in contact with your office today?

The door opened and Sam Spade walked in. Ah well . . . The bruise on his temple had become more purple but the yellowish eyes were as intelligent as ever.

Effie told him I'd been waiting. Spade waved me into his office. As I passed through the door Effie handed Spade a slip of paper. Before following me in Spade asked his secretary: "Any news on that other matter?"

"No, sir."

Spade started to close the door then he thought of something else. "Effie, look up a company called Mandrell Limited. Import-export. See what you can find on the boss, Augustus Mandrell."

As Spade walked to his desk he glanced at the slip of paper. He said, "You're in the motion picture business, Mr. . . ."

"Gordon. Solomon Gordon. To my friends: Sol. Down on Market Street there's a motion picture theatre? The Astor? A place where my children are being robbed of their college education. That's a business?"

"You own the theatre, Mr. Gordon? Who's robbing you?"

"Who isn't? The girl with the tickets, she sleeps with the doorman. Who cares? Her mother didn't tell her right. But my money they should use for hotel rooms? The candy butcher, he has to feed all the needy families from Nob Hill for free?"

"You want me to look into it? It will cost you fifty dollars."

"Fifty dollars! And I thought all the thieves were in my theatre."

The money left my notecase with understandable reluctance. It was an investment in shielding from Mr. Spade the fact that his office had been invaded by an unknown party in the Maltese Falcon affair. I didn't want him distracted. I didn't want him looking over his shoulder for a "shadow" constructed along the general specifications of Augustus Mandrell.

Spade left his office about fifteen minutes later. I was waiting across the street and followed him to the pier where the *La Paloma* had been tied up. He questioned various people for an hour and took a taxi back to his office. I had just settled down to a cup of coffee in the cafeteria across the street when Spade came bursting out of his building again. His urgency led me to assume some startling communication had taken place. A call from dear Brigid hopefully.

I followed him to the Belvedere. From across the lobby I watched his conversation with the hotel detective, reading their lips as best I could. It appeared that Joel Cairo had checked out of the hotel, just how long previous I couldn't quite make out (the hotel dick, in addition to a frail grasp on the elements of precise diction, was chewing gum).

After searching Cairo's room Spade returned to his office. Dusk was upon the city by this time. The night people of San Francisco were edging out onto the streets, pulling their thin, wine-bottle-stretched overcoats about their undernourished bodies like the webbed wings of bats. The sun, their enemy, had left his post. The streets were free and built of comfortable shadowed doorways.

One such night crawler stumbled out of the alley next to Spade's building. He had evidently started with his bottle much too early. He staggered and nearly fell but caught the grillwork on a window and pulled himself upright.

My God, he was seven feet tall!

I jerked open the trunk of my rented auto and grabbed up the gift package that had lain there for three days. When I caught up with him Captain Jacobi was already inside Spade's building, in the lobby next to the night watchman waiting for the elevator.

Even judging by the minimal evidence of our short acquaintance it was obvious the captain was not in the best of health. But I had little attention for his person. He passed my one most demanding requirement with flying colors.

He was carrying a paper parcel tied with string.

So was I, for that matter.

The exchange took place on Spade's floor when, in exiting the elevator in front of Jacobi, I tripped causing the giant to fall over me into the dark corridor with a good deal of flailing and some healthy seafaring expressions. For a moment I thought he had injured himself, for he was slow in rising. I assisted him up with multiple apologies and passed to him a package. Not the one he had dropped, of course. He proceeded on his way to Spade's office.

In the elevator I noticed the smear of blood on Jacobi's package. I did not learn until later that Captain Jacobi had been carrying five lead bullets in his body during our encounter.

These seafaring people and their obsession with ballast . . .

* * *

The door of suite 14C was answered by the hotel guest himself, not one of his staff. "Ah, Mr. Mandrell, I was beginning to worry. I presume that is it?" He indicated the blood-stained parcel I carried.

"Yes, General, this is your Maltese Falcon. Home to roost."

General Kemidov spoke English rather poorly so we conversed in Russian. "Help yourself to some brandy," he said as he undid the strings on the package.

"And how is Miss O'Shaughnessy?" Kemidov asked. "She was such a delight. Slender, so very slender." The general was not very slender. Quite the opposite.

"What . . . what is this you have brought me, Mr. Mandrell?" he asked very calmly. He was staring at the statue of a black bird about the height of a riding boot. The wrapping paper and shredded excelsior that had enclosed the bird were carefully folded in his hands.

I looked at the falcon. Then I stared at the general.

"That's not my Maltese Falcon," he hissed, the impact of his disappointment beginning to erode his patience. "This is not the item for which I am paying the firm of Mandrell Limited so outrageous a fee."

"How do I know it's not the real falcon?" I asked.

"You do not trust me? Here—" He snatched up the bird with two hands and heaved it into my arms. "Take it with you. It is worth perhaps five American dollars. Bah!"

I called the desk and asked if Mr. Casper Gutman was in. They told me he had just returned but was in the process of checking out. I hung up before they could ring his suite two floors below.

"I'm going down to see Gutman," I told Kemidov. "And don't close out your American checking account just yet. I will find your damned bird."

"I will go with you. I want to see the look on his fat face when we show him this . . . this book end."

We used the stairs. I didn't knock at suite 12C, just barged in. Gutman was hanging a huge suit in a steamer trunk. He turned a startled, dangerous face to our entry, but when he recognized Kemidov he smiled. "Ah, General, how good to see you again. You must excuse my haste. I have a train to catch. And who are you, sir? Not that any friend of General Kemidov's isn't a guest in my home; not at all." I was not wearing my Buzz Saw Carpenter disguise.

"This is Mr. Mandrell," Kemidov said. "He has something to show you."

"Mandrell, I believe I've heard that—"

I brought the black bird out from behind my back and set it on the coffee table. Gutman's stare froze on it. Then his eyes squeezed closed a bit as he looked closer.

"May I ask where you obtained this, sir?" Gutman asked quietly.

"It's the bird Brigid O'Shaughnessy and Captain Jacobi had on the *La Paloma*," I said.

Gutman looked at the figure and without turning his head shouted, "Cairo!"

Joel Cairo came out of a bedroom with his hand in his side pocket. "So nice to see you again, General," he said in an embarrassed voice to Kemidov, the man from whom Joel had helped steal the Maltese Falcon. Then his eyes went to the statue.

"What do you think, Mr. Cairo?" Gutman asked.

Cairo picked up the bird. After looking at it a second he hissed, "Mama Tanaka's."

"Yes," Gutman agreed. "Mama Tanaka's Foundry on Bell Alley in Hong Kong. Where a traveler can have his gold bars coated with lead to avoid prolonged discussions with customs officials."

"Even for Mama Tanaka, this is an incredibly poor piece of workmanship," Cairo said, still rubbing the bird.

"Miss O'Shaughnessy must have rushed her," Gutman said. "So that's the item we've been running all over San Francisco for?" He chuckled a bit, then laughed with a great blubber shaking laugh.

That's how I'll always remember Casper Gutman, enjoying his last laugh. In the middle of it Wilmer Cook slid past the corridor door and shot poor Casper dead.

"You were going to let Spade give me to the police!" Wilmer screamed as he fired a small-caliber pistol again and again. "You were going to let me die in a gas chamber."

It would appear that the camaraderie in force between Gutman and the boy had deteriorated dramatically. I wondered what had happened to the lad's normal arsenal, the two cannons.

The boy was still shooting when the black statue I threw hit him in the head and knocked him unconscious.

Joel Cairo was frozen staring from Gutman to the boy. I grabbed his shirt front and shook him.

"Where is Brigid O'Shaughnessy?" I repeated several times.

Finally his eyes focused and he stammered vaguely, "I guess she's still at Mr. Spade's apartment. That's where we left them less than an hour ago."

I took General Kemidov's arm and pushed him toward the corridor. Passing Wilmer I picked up the ownerless black bird. The general and I had just pressed the elevator button when the doors of one elevator opened and a hoard of San Francisco police poured forth. "What's the number?" one called out. A man in a business suit answered, "Spade said 12C." The general and I looked on like startled bystanders, which indeed we were.

I left General Kemidov after again advising him to be prepared to pay Mandrell Limited for delivery of the real Maltese Falcon to his hand.

* * *

It was to be a day of frustrations evidently. Ten minutes after leaving Kemidov I was talking to another gentleman who had a peripheral interest in the Maltese Falcon. We were in the back room of a close-mouthed bar on Powell Street. The gentleman's name was Dixie Monahan. Yes, the same chap who had run off with Mr. Bogart's $200,000 and his wife Zerelda, taking along Floyd Thursby as bodyguard or a third for gin or something.

Mr. Monahan was a Mandrell Limited client. He had commissioned the firm to supervise the demise of Floyd Thursby, which, as you'll recall, I attended to with one of Wilmer Cook's cannons as Mr. Thursby returned to his hotel after reportedly killing Miles Archer in the alley off Bush Street.

Now, Mr. Monahan was a somewhat unique customer. He was dissatisfied with the service rendered by the firm. An assumption made by Mr. Monahan and myself had proven invalid. We had thought that Floyd Thursby's death would cause Mr. Bogart and his associates to discontinue their search for Dixie Monahan. Documents indicating that Thursby had killed his boss, Monahan, had been placed in Thursby's hotel room to be found following Thursby's death.

"Bogart and his boys haven't fallen for it," Monahan told me. "They smell a rat. Joe the Jeweler and another torpedo are still here in town looking for me."

"What motivates their skepticism?" I asked. "The police obviously believe Thursby killed you in Singapore, that the body found on the waterfront was yours."

Monahan shrugged. "The cops don't have two hundred thou invested. Remember when I hired you in Hong Kong our agreement was bump Thursby but also get Bogart off my back. I don't pay until Bogart is convinced I'm dead."

"There is no need to remind me of the terms of our contract, sir," I said, a bit testy I'm afraid. First the damn' Falcon from a Hong Kong foundry. Now this.

I assured Mr. Monahan that within a week Mr. Bogart would cease to count Monahan among the living.

I did not feel required to advise Dixie Monahan that not only were Mr. Bogart's "torpedoes" (chaps in rather the same profession as myself, as I understand the term) in San Francisco, Mr. Bogart was also. In fact I spoke to Bogart on the phone not ten minutes after leaving Monahan.

"Did you find the party I sent you looking for?" Bogart asked.
"Yes."
"Boy, whoever made up that thing about revenge being sweet sure knew his apples. That baby is going to burn. When can I make the pick up?"
"I'll call you tonight."

* * *

Sam Spade, highball in hand, opened his apartment door and stood there looking at me. His stare wasn't unfriendly but it did appear he had not been counting the minutes until my arrival.

After a few seconds of silence he said, "Okay, Gus, come on in and let's talk." While he mixed me a drink he said, "That's a funny import-export business you run. Mandrell Limited. After you followed me around most of yesterday afternoon I figured I'd better check. A guy I know who used to work for Scotland Yard gave me the 'form' as he called it. You're a high-class Murder Incorporated."

"Not really," I explained. "As I understand their mode of operation they appear to have developed only that talent required for folding the remains of insolvent bookmakers into the trunks of deserted automobiles. There is hardly a comparison."

"Okay, who are you after? Me?"

"Obviously not you, Mr. Spade. There have been several opportunities. Also I doubt that we would be sitting here on such a friendly basis if you thought that even remotely possible."

"You never know," he said. "There might be a kicker in that drink I just gave you."

I stared at the glass in my hand and said, "It has passed my taste and aroma test. It is precisely what the label says it is: 6 years of age, 86.8 U. S. proof, blended at the distiller's plant in Ontario, Canada."

"I wish I'd had that kind of a nose when Casper Gutman handed me that drink the other night."

"Are you aware that Mr. Gutman is presently deceased?"

"Yeah. I had a bunch of cops here a little while ago. They told me. I guess little Wilmer got over excited because Gutman was going to let the kid take the fall for my partner's murder and Thursby's murder and the killing of a sea captain named Jacobi. It all happened here in my apartment last night. They were all here: Gutman, Wilmer, Joel Cairo, and Brigid O'Shaughnessy. Everybody who's anybody in the Maltese Falcon business."

Not quite, Mr. Spade. You were missing General Kemidov, Dixie Monahan, and Mr. Bogart.

"You see, Gus, I'd finally gotten my hands on the bird," Spade said. "They ran me ragged and elected me Mr. Dummy in their game but I ended up with the Maltese Falcon. They had to deal with me. The deal was simple. Gutman would give me ten thousand and I'd give him the bird. Gutman said 'fine.' Then I told him the rest: they also had to give me a 'fall guy.' Somebody the cops could hang the murders on. Gutman balked but finally saw it my way. We decided little Wilmer was our fall guy. What the hell, he'd killed Floyd Thursby anyway and a sea captain named Jacobi."

"That's the second time you've mentioned this gentleman Jacobi," I said. "I don't recall his being in the affair?"

"Are you getting cute with me, Gus? You know a hell of a lot about the Maltese Falcon. You followed me to the pier where the *La Paloma* burned. You hung around while I talked to people. I'd be disappointed if you didn't do some snooping on your own. You should have come up with the name Jacobi easy enough."

"Excuse my subterfuge," I said sincerely. "One becomes so accustomed to dealing with incompetents I occasionally forget . . . Yes, I'm aware a seven-foot sea captain named Jacobi brought the falcon to San Francisco on the *La Paloma* for Miss O'Shaughnessy and Floyd Thursby."

"Yeah, he did. And Gutman and Cairo found it out before I did. They had a big meeting on the boat night before last: Gutman, Cairo, the kid, Captain Jacobi, and Le O'Shaughnessy."

"That must have been just after Mr. Gutman fed you the knockout drops," I remarked. "Did he mention what happened at the meeting?"

Spade shook his head. "He didn't enlarge and I didn't ask him. The people I talked to at the pier didn't know anything except a gun went off at one point and the ship caught fire the next morning. When they were all here this morning Gutman said they had reached an agreement aboard the ship. Jacobi and Brigid were to go to Gutman's hotel with Gutman and the rest and turn over the bird for a price. Somehow Brigid and the captain and the bird gave Gutman the slip on the way to the hotel. The fat man spent all day yesterday beating the San Francisco bushes looking for them. Wilmer finally found Jacobi and Brigid hiding out in an apartment. Jacobi tried to beat it down the fire escape with the falcon. Wilmer caught him in the alley and pumped enough lead into him to sink the *La Paloma*. But a guy as big as Jacobi takes some killing. He got past Wilmer."

"The lad's marksmanship is possibly not of the quality one could desire."

"No, he's a pretty good shooter. The cops tell me he put four slugs from a .45 into Thursby's back from across a street. That's pretty good shooting in my home town."

Ahhh; so there were some discriminating ordnance critics within the San Francisco policing establishment after all.

"The kid ended up killing Jacobi," Spade continued. "But first the tough son of a bitch staggered to my office and gave me the falcon. So Gutman and crew trooped up here last night and waited for me to come home. It was quite a show. I had to take two guns away from the kid and one from Joel Cairo. The thing went on all night because we had to wait until this morning for me to get the bird out of the place I'd checked it."

"So you finally beat them at their own game?"

Spade grinned. "Naw, the guy who won was this Russian general in Constantinople; Kemidov. The bird was a phony. Kemidov put one over on the bunch of them."

"I'm afraid that is inaccurate," I said. "The falcon Miss O'Shaughnessey, Floyd Thursby, and Mr. Cairo stole from General Kemidov was the real Maltese Falcon. Incidentally what did you do with the statue?"

"Gave it to the cops as evidence along with all the guns. I told them I'd like it back someday."

"I'll be back in a minute," I said getting out of my chair. I went to the street and took the black bird from the trunk of my car. When I showed it to Spade he said, "Christ, even I might have guessed this one is a phony. Where did it come from?"

I explained that he was looking at the bird Captain Jacobi had brought from Hong Kong. His yellowish eyes got a bit hard when I told him I had switched falcons with Jacobi in the dark corridor down from Spade's office.

"If you think Casper Gutman was surprised when your falcon

turned out to be counterfeit," I said, "you can imagine General Kemidov's disappointment when he saw this."

"Where did the bird you gave Jacobi come from?"

"General Kemidov had it made in Constantinople. The Turkish craftsmen are evidently more qualified than the Chinese Miss O'Shaughnessy employed to make this."

"Where the hell is the real falcon?"

"I had thought to ask Miss O'Shaughnessy. She must have it secreted somewhere."

"I don't know where she'd have it," Spade said. "I've been through her stuff a couple of times. And if you want to ask her anything you'll have to do it through steel bars. The cops took her out of here less than an hour ago."

I was startled; nay: dumfounded. I had to have access to the maid.

"You didn't assist her in eluding the police?"

"Assist her hell. I turned her in. It was pretty goddam tough—she and I have been getting along—but I turned her over to the cops."

He grinned at my astonishment and said, "You see, Gus, when somebody bumps off your partner, even a partner as half ass as Miles Archer, you've got to do something about it. In my business you do."

"You believe Miss O'Shaughnessy killed your partner? I thought Floyd Thursby . . ."

"Everybody thought Thursby did it. That's what sweet Brigid was counting on; Thursby taking the fall for Archer's murder. Exit Thursby; meaning he wouldn't be around to collect any of the dough she got for the bird. She even used Thursby's gun, which she borrowed or lifted from him. In fact things were really looking great for her when Thursby was gunned down in front of his hotel by little Wilmer."

(The charitable reader, I feel certain, will forgive Mr. Spade his ignorance of the actual facts surrounding the demise of Floyd Thursby.)

"Did the young lady admit the killing?"

"Yeah, once she realized I knew the facts. She's the only one who could have gotten Miles up that alley. Miles was dumb but he'd never have followed Thursby into a dark alley. Not without his gun in his hand. But he'd have gone up there with Brigid if she smiled that little old sweet smile and worked him over with her blue eyes. She got him up against a fence and pumped one into his heart. That's our Brigid."

He rolled one of his Bull Durhams. His big hands trembled with some thought that would come to him on many nights in a cold bed.

After a while he said, "You working for General Kemidov, Gus?"

"He has engaged the firm to restore his property."

"That's going to be tough. She isn't likely to tell anybody where it's hidden now that she's on ice. The damn' thing is probably still in Hong Kong."

"We don't think so. A good deal of research was conducted in Hong Kong by myself and some others; including Joel Cairo, who was trying to catch up with Thursby and the girl. The real Maltese Falcon is here in the United States someplace. My best estimate is it came over on the *La Paloma* with the fake bird Miss O'Shaughnessy had made in Shanghai."

"Then it's probably a melted pool of gold by now down in some corner of the ship."

"I think not. There are other possibilities."

"Well, go down to the lock up and ask her. Who knows, maybe she's dying to tell somebody."

I did precisely that, a few days later.

* * *

Miss O'Shaughnessy did not tell me where she had hidden the Maltese Falcon but she did perform a different service I requested. She confessed to the proper authorities that she and Floyd Thursby had killed Dixie Monahan in Singapore six months previous. She said she did it in order to obtain the money Dixie had stolen from Mr. Bogart of the Chicago gambling Bogarts.

By this time the newspapers had discovered Brigid O'Shaughnessy. She was, as it turns out, exceedingly photogenic. Her eyes, with their touching appeal for male assistance, their little-waif-lost-in-the-snowstorm configuration, came off the front page like a stab in the heart.

"I'll tell you," Dixie Monahan said, looking up at me from his copy of the *Call*, "she even has me believing she killed me. Great coverage. Great. I've already gotten the word that Bogart has run a line through my name. He's finally convinced I'm dead. In fact he's getting ready to throw a party. He and all his boys are getting together." He laughed. "You know where they're throwing it? Right here in San Fran! They're coming in by the carload from Chicago. But I'll be long gone before they arrive."

I completed my count of the money Mr. Monahan had presented to me and reported that the sum was correct. We were in his house in Oakland.

"Sure it's a square count. I ain't no welcher. Even that dough I took from Bogart was coming to me. He muscled me out of a couple of spots on the North Side I controlled once. How the hell did you get the dame to confess to this?" He slapped the newspaper.

"She is a reasonable girl. Her position is rather confining for so lively a creature. I was able to offer her some solace."

"Anyway you did it is jake with me." He stood. "Well thanks for the job, Mr. Mandrell. I gotta be packing."

I didn't move. He stared at me, a tall compact man with a holster and pistol strapped under his arm. He was at the moment coatless.

"Since your travel is sure to be hurried," I said, "why encumber yourself with unnecessary luggage?"

"I don't get you."

"I want the black bird, Mr. Monahan. General Kemidov is in the city and is also anxious to depart. He has requested that I bring him his property. I am aware that the statue is not here with you in your house. I took the liberty of searching early this morning. Where is it?"

"So the bitch told you," he said through his teeth. "She figures she's in the clink and she doesn't want me cashing in on the falcon."

"No, sir, she did not tell me. Whatever your association is with the young lady she has remained loyal. You see, you are a man on the run, your friends from Chicago are conducting a rather diligent search for you. Yet you managed to slip into San Francisco without alerting them, and without alerting the Immigration officials I'll wager. It occurred to me that if the Maltese Falcon could arrive secretly aboard the *La Paloma* why not a passenger?"

He grinned. "Plus I had to keep an eye on Jacobi. I didn't want him jumping ship with the bird at Honolulu."

"Why did you bother with the false falcon?" I asked. "You had the real one, what was the other for?"

"Oh, she had the idea we could use it to throw people off the track. That little creep Joel Cairo nearly caught up with us in Hong Kong and there were some other people nosing around. Then while she and Thursby were waiting here in San Fran for the *La Paloma* she pulled that dumb stunt to try and get rid of Thursby; that business with the detective trailing them."

"Didn't she know you had commissioned Mandrell Limited to take care of Mr. Thursby?"

"Yeah, but she didn't like your price. She figured to save us a little money by getting Thursby sent to the gas chamber. Then, Christ, as soon as Thursby's name hit the papers we had everybody swarming into town: Gutman and his gunsel, Cairo, this guy Sam Spade. I even heard a rumor General Kemidov was here; which you tell me now he is. She was trapped and evidently asked this guy Spade for help. Guys help her a lot." He grinned.

"Were you aboard the *La Paloma* when they had their meeting there?"

"I had just gotten off to go bury the bird. When I came back there was the whole gang. I couldn't let any of them see me. Gutman in particular because he would have gotten word to Bogart. I waited for them to leave. Some joker named Buzz Saw Carpenter who claimed to be Bogart's torpedo showed up with this hearse with God damn dead people in it and helped her and Captain Jacobi give Gutman the slip. I stepped out and worked over Mr. Buzz Saw with my sap and we cleared out."

Ah, so I owe that headache to you, Mr. Monahan.

"We went to an apartment I'd rented and I left her and Jacobi and the fake bird and was out trying to line up a car when Gutman evidently found them again. I'd told her we shoulda come out here to the house but she said 'no' she didn't want Jacobi to know about this place. Anyway they're trapped in the apartment with Gutman at the door so she turned the baby blues on Jacobi—we had to get rid of him anyway—and the big jerk went down the fire escape with the fake bird. Of course he thought he had the real one. According to the paper Gutman's torpedo Wilmer met Jacobi in the alley and shot him up but Jacobi somehow got the bird over to this guy Spade before he died."

"You do lead a complex life, Mr. Monahan."

"I guess you did too, Mr. Mandrell. Up until tonight." He removed the pistol from its holster with a swift smooth movement.

"I was going to let you go," he said. "I mean even though you know I'm alive but you pushed too hard on this bird business. I need that falcon. The money I gave you is nearly the last of what I took from Bogart. And now that baby is in jail, I don't got to split with her. On your feet, jerk. They won't find you until they come around to collect next month's rent."

I stood up and started to remove my jacket. "You were probably too absorbed to notice," I said, "but when you removed your pistol from its sheath just now you broke a small thread. The fact that the thread was still in place means you have not inspected the weapon today. Careless, sir, careless. I placed that thread there last night."

He pulled the trigger and we both listened to the clicking of the hammer which contained no firing pin. The gentleman then attempted to lacerate my skull with his pistol. My retaliation was possibly a bit more severe than his incivility warranted but then my head still ached a bit in the area where his blackjack had bitten it two nights previous. He was unconscious before he hit the floor.

Now, where to look for the Maltese Falcon?

Miss O'Shaughnessy had not wanted Jacobi to know about the

house in Oakland. Her reluctance, I felt, was related to keeping Jacobi ignorant of the black bird's roost. Dixie Monahan had said he left the *La Paloma* to ". . . bury the bird . . ." Could he have meant that literally?

And, by George, that's where it was; in the backyard under a newly planted bush. General Kemidov was somewhat offended by the particles of soil adhering to his treasure but he paid his bill in full which is what counts with Mandrell Limited.

Mr. Bogart was anxious to complete his transaction with the firm also. We discussed the matter in the rear seat of his bulletproof Packard limousine.

"Come on, come on," he snarled at me, "when do I get my hands on my party?" He was a wide beefy chap with the deep chest of a man with strength to burn.

"I want my hands squeezing around that neck," Mr. Bogart continued, "while my blood is still boiling."

"Tomorrow at three o'clock," I told him. "Here's the map showing the route the vehicle will take. Personally I would recommend the 1400 block. Enjoy your revenge."

* * *

As I mentioned, the news media was delighted with Brigid O'Shaughnessy. She received a bit better than normal coverage when first arrested and charged with the murder of Miles Archer of Spade and Archer. When she confessed to an involvement in the murder of Dixie Monahan in Singapore the news chaps really went after her with elbows and knees and, most of all: cameras. She was: Bloody Brigid, Bullet Brigid, the Sex Queen Sadist, the Red Headed Hatchet Girl, the Continental Cat Killer (spelled Ciller by the newspaper favoring this title). You can therefore visualize the uproar when she escaped from prison.

It happened at three in the afternoon while she was being whisked by police car from the District Attorney's office back to the Women's Detention Center on Sutter. A hoard of touring cars, moving with split-second timing, sealed off the 1400 block trapping the police car in the middle. The men who poured from the touring cars shot up everything in the street, except people, with their machine guns. Brigid was taken from the badly frightened police guards and hustled off to a car waiting in the alley.

Only one person got a very close look at the car that carried the girl away, a Negro bus boy who was sneaking a cigarette in the alley.

"It was a black car," the eyewitness reported. "One of them big Packard dudes, man. They throws that gal in there where there's this big gorilla sitting like a general waiting for the end of the war. And then, man, the car's pulling out and this big old boy he grabs the chick by the red hair and stares at her like as mean as you'll ever see. And then boy he just starts kissing her to beat the band. And he's crying and she's crying and he's just smothering her with kisses."

Ah well, it was rather in keeping with their relationship. The young woman was after all his wife.

* * *

As Sam Spade said while he and I were sitting in Victor's reading the newspaper: "Zerelda Bogart has returned home and all is forgiven. That poor sap."

Spade grabbed up his gimlet and gulped it down. "C'mon, Gus," he said. "Let's go and do some serious drinking." He started for the door.

I remained on my bar stool. Spade walked out of Victor's and went away. That was the last time I ever saw him.

AFTERWORD

Mr. McAuliffe adds the following comments:

"Like many others, I feel that the writers who have most influenced the mystery field in the past fifty years are Dashiell Hammett and Raymond Chandler.

"Hammett, in such works as the 1930 *The Maltese Falcon*, took murder, in Chandler's words, 'out of the Venetian vase and put it back in the alley where it belongs.' Chandler, in books like the 1954 *The Long Goodbye*, polished the rough edges with the fine emery of characterization and smooth dialogue.

"'The Maltese Falcon Commission' is an experiment involving these ingredients:

1. Mr. Hammett's Private Eye, Sam Spade, and his colorful *Maltese Falcon* associates: Casper Gutman, the fat man; Joel Cairo, the fairy; Wilmer, the gunsel; Brigid O'Shaughnessy, the maid in distress; and, of course, the black bird.

2. Private Eye Philip Marlowe's meeting with the very polite, haunted Terry Lennox, from the opening of Mr. Chandler's *The Long Goodbye*.

3. A new, exotic ingredient unknown to either Mr. Hammett or Mr. Chandler: Augustus Mandrell.

"Mix well in a tributary vessel and serve."